Acknowledgements

Once again I thank the expert professionals whose advice and guidance has made this a better book than ever an author could produce by himself: my editors Julia Wisdom and Anne O'Brien, and my agent Antony Topping.

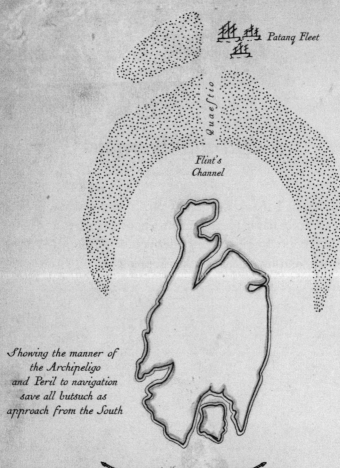

Patanq Fleet

Quaeſtio

Flint's
Channel

Showing the manner of
the Archipeligo
and Peril to navigation
save all butsuch as
approach from the South

A True Repreſentation of

~ *Flint's Island* ~

Conſolidating The previous Drafts of Mr. J Silver, Maſter Mariner &
Mr W Bones, Quartermaſter and Diſplaying all entrenchments & Perils

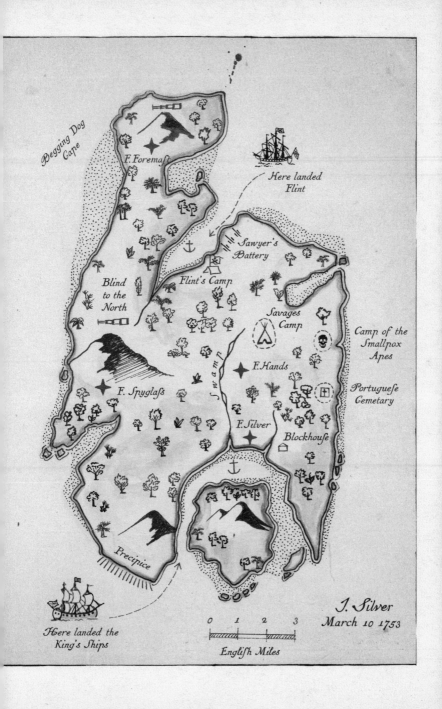

Legging Dog Cape

F. Foremast

Here landed
Flint

Sawyer's
Battery

Flint's Camp

Savages
Camp

Blind
to the
North

Camp of the
Smallpox
Apes

F. Hands

Portuguese
Cemetery

F. Spyglass

F. Silver

Blockhouse

Precipice

Here landed the
King's Ships

0   1   2   3

English Miles

J. Silver
March 10 1753

Chapter 1

*T*he corpse lay in a lake of blood that drenched its pious black coat, its lank white hair, and the clerical bands that descended from its comprehensively slit throat where bone gleamed from the bottom of a tremendous slash. The mutilating fury of repeated knife strokes had rendered the face unrecognisable, such that the victim's identity was given only by his clothes and the wide-gaping mouth full of long brown teeth that were one reason – though not the only one – that he'd so seldom smiled in life.

"Good God!" said Captain Peter Garland. "Cover him up, and get the women out of here!" He looked to Mr Bains, the house steward, and then to the two menservants, and finally to the herd of maids and cooks peering in horror through the chapel door. But none of them moved.

"Pah!" said the captain, and set about doing the job himself. A sea-service officer in his thirties, Garland had

1

faced shot and shell, and this wasn't the first time he'd dealt with dead men and the pieces of them. He stepped up to the altar, laid aside the wooden cross, ripped the white altar cloth from its moorings and draped it across the body of his late brother-in-law, taking care that, whatever else showed, the face was covered.

"So!" said Captain Garland, looking away from the corpse to the bloodstains on the whitewashed walls. "What happened?"

Mr Bains was trying his best, but he was an elderly man, long in the reverend's service, who – along with the rest of the congregation – had thought him the font of all wisdom. And now here was the reverend dead and murdered in his own chapel! Bains stood weeping and wringing his hands with his entire world overturned, the women wailing at the sight of him and the two male servants snivelling besides.

"Brace up, man!" cried Captain Garland. "Brace up all of you, dammit."

"Yes, sir," said Bains. "Sorry, sir. We didn't know if you would come."

"What?" said Garland, "D'you think *that* man –" he pointed at the corpse "– could keep me from my sister? My Rebecca – her that was a mother to me when our own ma died?"

"God bless you, sir," said Bains.

"God bless you," said the rest.

"So! Where is she? And m'nephew?"

"Upstairs, sir. In the parlour."

They were halfway up the stairs when three blows sounded on the front door knocker, and everyone jumped. Again nobody moved so Garland went down and opened the door himself. Outside was a carriage and pair that he'd not even

2

heard arrive, what with his mind so full of other things. A coachman stood in the doorway in his caped cloak and livery hat, wrapped in scarf and mittens against the cold.

"Ah!" said Garland, peering out into the miserable grey November where the coach body swayed as a fat gentleman in boots and greatcoat was helped down by one of his footmen. "Sir Charles!" he said, and ran forward to shake his friend's hand.

"Captain Garland!" said the other. "Came as soon as I got your note." He was a middle-aged, heavily overweight man, who moved slowly and breathed with difficulty, except when standing still or sitting down. "T'aint my jurisdiction, this," he cautioned, "and the proper authorities will need to be informed." He peered at Garland, "You do know that, don't you?"

"Yes-yes-yes! But you must have experience of such cases."

"What cases?"

"Damned if I know, Sir Charles. It was only chance that I happened to be in London and Bains knew where to find me. I sent for you the moment I heard . . ." He looked around. "I've not set foot in this house in years!"

"Have you not?" said the other, and Garland saw that all eyes were on him.

"Now then!" he cried, clasping his hands behind his back. "Silence and pay heed! This gentleman is Sir Charles Wainwright, Police Magistrate at Bow Street, who is here to take this matter in hand." He looked at his friend. "Sir Charles . . . ?" he said.

Sir Charles took charge. Getting the basic facts from Captain Garland, he directed a number of sharp questions at the reverend's servants, then stumped into the chapel –

respectfully doffing his hat as he did so – and poked the cloth off the corpse with his walking stick.

"Bless my soul!" he said. "Not the sweetest sight, is he?"

"No," agreed Garland.

Sir Charles looked round the chapel, noting its severe simplicity, disdain of decoration, and rows of plain wooden chairs.

"What denomination worships here?" he asked. "Quaker? Moravian?"

"Presbyterian," said Garland. "A branch, at any rate: 'Church of the Revelationary Evangelists'. Or at least that's what they were calling themselves when last I was here."

"Aye," said Wainwright, nodding, "these dissenters are morbidly fissiparous."

"They're what?"

"Dividing: always dividing. That's what you get for denying the authority of the bishops!"

"Hmm," said Garland. "Well, he was very strong in his beliefs, my brother-in-law. It's why I was turned out of his house – for I used to be one of them, d'you see?" He shrugged. "But I was in love with the service, and wanted to be like my shipmates and say chaplain's prayers."

Sir Charles turned from the hideous corpse, looked the chapel up and down, and sniffed.

"Place stinks of soap and polish. Never seen anywhere so clean in all my life, I do declare!"

"Huh!" said Garland. "That's the reverend! Detested dirt of all kinds. Every stick and pot scrubbed, and the servants made to bathe daily in a wash-house out the back."

"*What?*" said Sir Charles, incredulous. "*Every day?* It's a wonder they didn't leave him."

"Not they! Not once *he'd* got his hooks into 'em. Terrified, they were."

"Of him?"

"Him and his good friend the Devil!"

"What about the family? How did he treat them?"

For a moment Captain Garland seemed lost for words. He was a plain man bred up to a hard service where a loud voice satisfied all needs of communication . . . but that wouldn't do now.

"There's only his wife – m'sister Rebecca – and her son," he said. "And Rebecca . . . well, she was a *woman,* and to him all women were damned as *pedlars* of lust, while children were damned as *fruits* of lust . . ." He bowed his head in memory. "He used to say to them . . . he used to say to m'poor sister and her boy – and I heard this m'self, mind – he used to say . . ." Captain Garland stood silent as he tried to bring himself to repeat the words. Finally he shook his head, and rubbed the back of his hand across his eyes.

He looked at Sir Charles. "He weren't very nice to them. Can we leave it at that?"

"Bless my soul!" said Sir Charles, for Garland had shed tears. "Come along, Captain. Enough of this – let's see the widow."

The stairs to the first floor were a fearful obstacle to Sir Charles, and it was a long, slow climb, but finally – led by the miserable Bains – he and Garland entered the front parlour: another fiercely scrubbed room, almost bare of furnishings, where they found the reverend's wife and son, sitting waiting in a pair of Windsor armchairs.

"Good day, ma'am," said Sir Charles, advancing towards her, then stopping short as he saw the blood spattered over her clothes. The woman sat unmoved. She was a tired creature: wrinkled and prematurely old, with wispy hair and sad eyes.

"Ma'am?" repeated Sir Charles. But she never even blinked.

"Rebecca?" said Garland in a hushed voice, shocked at the sight of her. "It's me, m'dear. Little Peter that sat on your knee . . ." Odd as the words were from a grown man, they stirred the woman and she looked up at them.

"I did it," she said. "And it may not be denied, for 'Every man's work shall be made manifest' – First Corinthians, chapter three, verse thirteen! And I am not ashamed: 'I have fought a good fight. I have finished my course. I have kept the faith' – Second Timothy, four: seven! And if I have sinned, then, 'Charity shall cover the multitude of sins' – First Peter, four: eight!"

"Sir Charles," whispered Garland, "she's raving! She's come adrift and cast loose her moorings." But he whispered too loud.

"No!" said Rebecca sharply. "It is my husband who was mad! Thus I killed him because he had gone too far. 'Behold! Now is the accepted time' – Second Corinthians, six: eight!"

Sir Charles sighed and turned to the boy sitting alongside her.

"Now then, my lad –"

"He must have seen it, sir," said Bains, who was hovering at the door. "He was in the chapel with her, sir. They went in together."

"Yes, yes!" said Sir Charles, waving the servant away. He turned back to the boy. "My lad, I am a magistrate and I must ask you what has gone on here?"

"I don't know, sir."

"Then why is your mother covered in blood?"

6

"I don't know, sir."

Sir Charles asked more questions, but learned nothing. Finally he took Garland aside.

"He's a good boy. Credit to his mother, poor soul. He'll not betray her, while she, poor soul, has lost her mind. I've seen the like before: husband a bully, wife stands it twenty years, then one day takes a knife and stabs him fifty times!"

"Aye," said Garland, nodding, "that'd be the way of it – and the swine deserved it, too! 'Tis only a pity she did it in front of the lad."

"Indeed," said Sir Charles, "But I know a doctor who'll say what's needed to keep her from the hangman and safe in a private madhouse." Sir Charles glanced at the boy. "What about him, though? Shall you take him?"

"That I shall!" said Garland. "I've no other family, aside from the sea-service, so I shall enter him as a gentleman volunteer, first-class, and it shall be my pleasure to help him up the ladder!" He turned to his nephew and managed a smile: "Now then, young Joseph," he said, "come along o' your uncle Peter and you shall be a king's officer one day, and maybe even a captain. How'd you like the sound of *Captain Flint?*"

Chapter 2

"Remember," said Long John, "a round turn and two half-hitches! Keep it simple. Don't go trying to work a Turk's head, nor a cable-splice!"

Ratty Richards, ship's boy, grinned. "Aye-aye, Cap'n!" he said. Skinny, tired, and dripping wet, he was the only one of the seventy-one men and three boys on the island who could dive in six fathoms of water and still do a few seconds' work at the bottom.

"You sure, lad?" said Long John. "You've already had a good whack. You don't have to go again if you don't want to . . ."

"I'm ready, Cap'n!"

"Ah, you're a smart lad, you are. I knew it the moment I set eyes on you. So here's your sinker and in you go."

Splash! Ratty Richards rolled over the gunwale of the skiff into the cool water, one hand pinching his nose and the other clasping the heavy boulder that would take him down. As he sank, the safety line round his waist and the heavy rope looped through it paid out from their coils while Long John, Israel Hands, Sarney Sawyer and George Merry leaned over the side to see him go down.

"Bugger me!" said Israel Hands. "Is this goin' to work, John? I've lost count how many times he's been down." He sighed heavily. "Don't want to drown the lad."

"Oh?" said Long John. "Weren't it yourself as pleaded for the Spanish nine?" He jerked a thumb at the sea bed. "For myself, I'd not've tried to raise a twenty-six-hundredweight gun with this –" He looked at the two boats, joined by a pair of spars, floating with barely a yard between them. Long John and Sawyer were in the skiff, with Hands and Merry in the jolly-boat; Ratty Richards's rope fed into a heavy block suspended from the spars and then to an iron wind-lass that had been firmly bolted to the midships thwart of the jolly-boat. The block-and-tackles were sound, but the boats were too small. Unfortunately, they were the only boats on the island.

"He's down, Cap'n!" cried Sarney Sawyer, looking below. "And he's workin' on her. Go on Ratty, my son!"

"Go on, Ratty!" they all cried, peering through the clear water pierced to the bottom by the hot morning sun, showing every movement the boy made.

Down in the booming depths, the weight of water crushed Ratty's chest as if a horse were rolling on him, and he strained to remember his orders. Water bubbled from his mouth as he grabbed one of the gun's dolphins. The Spanish founders had followed obsolete style in adding these elegant decorations, but they were ideal for work such as this. The plunging sea-beasts, cast integral with the barrel, formed loops of iron perfect for lifting the gun. Ratty tugged the

9

rope from the line round his waist then slid it through one dolphin and into the next.

So far, each attempt had failed. Now, lungs pounding, he struggled to secure the rope. In a ship, he could tie a knot without thinking; it was bred into him, instinctive. But not down here.

He threaded the rope through the second dolphin . . . *a round turn* . . . Ratty passed the rope around itself . . . *and two half hitches* . . . he tied the first hitch . . . torture and suffocation . . . he fumbled for the second hitch. He lost the rope. He fumbled again and again . . . blindness and agony . . . fear of death . . . Ratty kicked his bent legs almightily against the gun, launching himself like a soaring lark . . . up, up, up, frothing and bursting and spouting breath and blood and stretching for the blessings of light and air.

"Uhhhhhhhhhhhhhhhh!" he thrashed and splashed and breathed water and choked and broke surface.

"Gotcher me lad!" cried Long John, hauling him into the skiff and dumping him between the thwarts.

"Urgh! Uch! Yuch!" Ratty's guts vomited seawater and his eyes stared wide, not quite believing he wasn't dead.

"Did you do it lad?" said Long John, looming over him. "Did you make fast and secure?"

"Dunno," said Ratty.

"Bugger!" said Israel Hands.

"Clap a hitch there, Mr Gunner!" said Long John, and laid a hand on Ratty's shoulder. "This man's done his best, and no man can't do no more!" He stabbed a finger. "Or p'raps you'd like to heave off your britches and take a dive yourself?"

"Not I," said Israel Hands. "Ah, you're right, John! Bloody

gun's too big. What we needs is a proper longboat, and a good big 'un."

"The which we ain't got," said Long John.

"Aye, but the gun did have dolphins," said Israel Hands wistfully. "And Flint left us this, or we'd never have tried." He patted the powerful iron windlass that sat beside him. "I wonder what he wanted with it?"

"Nothing good," said Long John. "And I'll have less jaw and more work, if you please, Mr Hands, else we'll never recover your blasted nine-pounder!"

Silver sighed. They were marooned on the island, with Flint's treasure buried who-knows-where, and Flint liable to return at any moment with a shipload of men hell-bent on skinning, gutting and roasting every one of them. Since they couldn't build a vessel to carry all hands before Flint returned, and none could be left to face him, their aim was to defend the island. But how? Long John worried worse than anyone, being in command, for he'd been duly elected captain by all hands . . . excepting only Mr Billy Bones, who was still loyal to Flint, and who couldn't now be harmed because he was the only man capable of navigation and would be indispensable if ever they *did* get off the island.

And so the old guilt came pressing down upon Long John for his total inability to master the art of navigation . . .

Israel Hands saw the look on his face.

"Easy John," he said. "We follow where you lead. We all . . ."

"Cap'n!" cried Sarney Sawyer, hauling on the rope. "*He done it!* The little bugger done it!"

"What's that, Mr Bosun?" Silver was so deep in thoughts of Flint that he'd forgotten the Spanish gun.

"He made fast the line, Cap'n!" Sawyer grinned. "Double grog for Mr Richards, and no mistake!"

"Did I do it?" said Ratty, "I thought I didn't."

"Well, you did, lad," said Silver, "and well done indeed, for it was you alone as was down there! So it's all hands to the windlass!"

In fact, there being only two cranking handles and little room for manoeuvre, it fell to George Merry and Israel Hands to man the windlass. As the two of them groaned under the strain and the pauls of the windlass clattered merrily, Long John, Sawyer and Ratty Richards peered intently at the black shape of the gun, half-buried in sand, still in the wreckage of its carriage.

With Merry and Hands heaving on the rope like a pair of tooth-pullers on a molar, the windlass began to slow, the rattling giving way to a groaning of the rope, until suddenly the gun gave a mighty tremble. Then:

"Whoa!" they all cried as the nine-pounder lurched almost free of its carriage, hanging on by one half-shattered capsquare. Having cleared the swirling, sand-clouded bottom, it now hung, swaying to and fro on the rope, rocking the boats alarmingly.

"'Vast hauling!" roared Long John. "All hands stand fast!"

Nobody moved. They hung on, white-faced, until the gun finished its turning and the boats stopped plunging. It was fearfully easy to overturn boats and swimming was rare among seamen; of those aboard, Ratty was the only one who could swim. If the boats sank it would be death for all but him.

"Right then, lads," said Long John, when the boats had steadied, "handsomely now, and up she comes. *Give way!*"

Hands and Merry cranked the handles round, but much

more slowly now. The rope grew taut as an iron bar as the gun rose from the sea bed. Straining and groaning, the two men laboured and the gun moved inch by painful inch... and then stuck.

"Stap me, John!" gasped Israel Hands. "Can't do it." He and Merry were soaked with sweat and their arms trembled with the effort.

"Lay a hand there, Mr Bosun!" said Long John, and he and Sawyer clambered awkwardly from skiff to jolly-boat, cramming themselves alongside Hands and Merry. With the strength of four men behind it, the windlass began to turn again. Until:

"Ahhhh!" The gun broke suddenly free and spun viciously on the rope. Both vessels wallowed violently; Silver and Sawyer were sent tumbling as the jolly-boat rolled gunwale under and began to sink, while the joining spars lifted the skiff out of the water entirely.

"We're goin'!" screamed George Merry.

"Cut the line!" yelled Silver, struggling to dislodge Sawyer, who had landed across his one leg, stunned senseless by the fall. Hands and Merry, cramped against the windlass, pulled their knives, but Merry's was knocked from his hand as the boat lurched, while Hands was held fast by the iron handle jammed into his chest and could only hack feebly with his left hand, barely able to reach the rope.

"God save us!" screamed Israel Hands. "She's lost!"

"Gimme a cutlass!" yelled Silver, for he'd left his own weapon in the skiff. Ratty scrambled to pick it up and made to throw it – scabbard, baldric and all – across to his captain.

"No!" cried Silver. "Draw the bugger!"

"Here, Cap'n!" said Ratty, passing the blade, hilt-first.

"Ah!" said Silver and sat up, grabbing the gunwale to steady

13

himself. With the boats going over, over, over . . . he swung with all his might . . . and thump! The rope snapped like a gunshot, the jolly-boat rolled, the skiff hit the water, spray flew in all directions and Silver, Israel Hands and George Merry wallowed in the saved but half-sunk boat as flotsam, jetsam and the bailing bucket washed around their knees.

"Ohhh!" said Sarney Sawyer, roused by the wetting.

For a while four men and a boy sat gasping and glad to be alive.

"That's enough!" said Silver, finally. "We've got the four-pounders out of *Lion* and we'll have to make do with them. Let's get ship-shape and pull for the shore. And *that* bugger –" he jabbed a thumb at the lost nine-pounder – "stays where it is!"

Soon they were pulling past the burned-out wreck of *Lion* herself, beached in the shallows of the southern anchorage. Once she'd been a beautiful ship, but all that was left of her now was the bow and fo'c'sle, clean and bright and untouched by the fire that had destroyed her. Aft of the mainmast, she was black, hideous and chopped-off short.

"Huh," thought Silver, "'tain't only me what has a stump!"

He stared miserably at the wreck where it lay canted over: masts and shrouds at a mad angle, and yards dug into the shallow, sandy bottom. It felt indecent, gazing upon the insides of the ship with everything on view instead of planked over. These days she was more of a shipyard than a ship; her decks rang to the thump and buzz of tools as a swarm of men, led by Black Dog, the carpenter, carried out Long John's orders to salvage everything useful: guns, rigging, timbers and stores.

"Cap'n Silver!" cried Black Dog, as they pulled level. "A word, Cap'n."

"Easy all," said Silver. "Stand by to go alongside." The

awkward double-boat nudged up against the wreck until Silver sat almost eye-to-eye with Black Dog, a tallow-faced creature who never darkened in the sun, and who'd lost two fingers of his left hand to Silver's parrot, back in the days when it was Flint's. He was working, bare-legged with slops rolled up, on the waterlogged lower deck, and he touched his brow in salute.

"Cap'n," he said, "see what we found!" Then he yelled back over his shoulder, "Haul that box aft!"

A rumble and bumping followed as a man came backwards, dragging a large sea-chest. It was like any other seaman's chest, except that the initial "B" had been burned into the top with a hot iron, and the corners were somewhat smashed and broken by rough usage.

"What's this?" said Silver.

"Why, it's Billy Bones's!" said Israel Hands.

"That's right, Mr Gunner," said Black Dog. "You and me had the ballasting of the old ship, and we came to know every man's sea-chest what had one."

"That we did, Mr Carpenter," said Israel Hands. "But it ain't right that a sod like Billy-boy should get his precious goods back when better men than him has lost their all," he scowled. "And him the bastard what started the fire in the first place! I say we open her up and divvy her out!"

"Belay that!" said Silver. "How many times must I tell you swabs that we needs Billy Bones plump and fair and on our side?"

"Easy, Cap'n," said Israel Hands. "We knows it, but we don't have to like it."

"Like it or not," said Long John, "just you heave that chest into this boat, and back to Billy Bones it goes. I needs a word with the swab and this'll make it all the easier."

* * *

15

Later, Long John led Billy Bones away from the palm tree to which he'd been tethered to the camp of tents set up on the shores of the southern anchorage, which was Silver's headquarters. Cap'n Flint, the parrot – who hated boats and had waited ashore – was back on his shoulder. Silver moved at ease over the soft sand, thanks to the wide wooden disc secured around the end of his crutch to stop it sinking. He was fast as any ordinary man, and faster than Mr Billy Bones, who plodded deep and slow, puffing and blowing as he went.

Billy Bones was a big heavy man, broad-chested, with thick arms and massive fists. He was a pugilist of note, the terror of the lower deck, and had once been a sea-service officer: one of the old school, with mahogany skin, a tarred pigtail and pitch-black fingernails. But the service had lost him to Flint. For Billy Bones was Flint's through and through. That was why he'd set fire to *Lion* and why now – even though Silver was the only man in the world who Billy Bones feared, and Silver was armed and he was not – Billy's arms were secured with manacles and two men walked behind him with muskets aimed into his back.

"Now then, Billy-my-chicken," said Long John, drawing to a stop. Even leaning on his crutch he was taller than Bones, just as he was taller than most men. He took off his hat, wiped the sweat from his brow with a handkerchief, and stared into Billy Bones's eyes, until Bones flinched. "Huh!" said Silver, and Billy Bones bit his lip and looked sideways at Silver's big, fair face. Silver wasn't a handsome man like Flint, but he had the same overpowering presence, and he made Billy Bones nervous.

"See that sun, Billy-boy?" said Silver. Bones looked up at the blazing sun, climbing to its full height in the deep blue

16

sky. "Precious close to noon, and it'll soon be too hot to fart, let alone talk, so I want this over quick."

"What?" said Bones, eyes widening in dread. "What d'ye mean?" He glanced back at the two men with muskets.

"No, no, no!" said Silver. "Not *that*, you blockhead. If I'd wanted you dead, I'd have hung you. There's plenty of men wanting to haul you off your feet, and only myself stopping 'em."

"Well what then?" said Bones, still mortally afraid.

"Just look," said Silver. Bones looked. He saw the sands shimmering with heat, and the salvage crew wading ashore from the wreck, all work having stopped, while men fresh from other duties were getting themselves into the shade of the neat rows of tents where all would soon be sleeping until the midday heat was past.

"Look at what?" said Bones, deeply puzzled. Long John sighed.

"Billy-boy," he said, "you never were the pick of the litter when it came to brains! I meant you to see the works what's going forward." Bones blinked, still fearful, not knowing where this was leading. Silver looked at the coarse, thick face with its deep-furrowed brow, and sighed that such a creature could wield a quadrant while he could not.

"Billy," he said, "did you ever know me to lie?"

"No," said Bones after intense pondering.

"Did you ever know me to break a promise?"

"No," said Bones, with surly reluctance.

"Heaven be praised! Then here's a promise: If you come and sit with me in the shade of them trees –" Long John pointed at the line of drooping palms that edged the vast curve of the sandy shore "– and if you promise to listen fairly and act the gentleman . . . why! I'll send these two

17

away," he nodded at the guards, "and I'll send for some grog and a bite to eat. But if you try to run, Billy-boy, or if you raise your hand . . . I promise to shoot you square in the belly and dance the hornpipe while you wriggle. Is that fair, now?"

"Aye," said Bones, for it was much what he would have done in Silver's place, especially the shooting in the belly. So they found a comfortable place to sit, and took a mug or two, and some fruit and biscuit, and Long John brought all his eloquence to bear on Billy Bones.

"Billy," he said, "Flint's been gone a week. My guess is he'll head for Charlestown to take on more men and arms, and he'll come straight back, at which time I want to be ready. He'll have greater numbers, but we've got plenty of powder and shot and small arms, and most of the four-pounders saved out of *Lion*, besides which Israel Hands says there's the wreck of a big ship up in the north anchorage, with nine-pounders that we could use, though they're too heavy to move very far."

"Aye," said Bones, "that'd be the *Elizabeth*. I sailed aboard of her with Israel and . . ." He dropped his eyes.

"And Flint," said Silver. "Never mind, Billy-boy, for it comes to this: You know the lie of this island: latitude, longitude and all. I want you to tell me how soon Flint'll be back, so's I can be warned."

"And why should I help you?" said Bones.

"First, 'cos I saved your neck from a stretching – which it still might get, if you ain't careful – and second because we've found your old sea-chest, with all your goods aboard, and none shall touch it but you."

"Oh . . ." said Billy Bones, for a seaman's chest held all that was dear to him. "Thank you," he mumbled, and thought vastly better of Long John. But Silver's next words stung him.

"Good! Now listen while I tell you how that swab Flint has betrayed you."

"Never!" said Bones fiercely, making as if to stand.

"*Billy!*" said Silver. "*Don't!*" And he laid a hand on his pistol butt.

"You daresn't!" said Bones, but he sat down again.

"Billy," said Silver, gently, "Flint left you, and ain't never coming back except to kill you, along of all the rest of us."

"Huh!" sneered Bones. "You just want that black tart – Selena. You can't stand that Flint's aboard of her, fuckin' her cross-eyed!"

"Ugh!" This time the pistol was out and cocked and deep denting Billy Bones's cheek. Silver was white and he leaned over Bones like a vampire over its prey.

"Don't you *ever* say that again, you lard-arsed, shit-head, land-lubber! Just listen to me, Billy, for there's things about this island that ain't right and I need you to explain 'em, and I need you to make ready for Flint – 'cos if you won't help, then we're all dead men . . . but *you* the first of all of us! So what course shall you steer, Billy-boy?"

Chapter 3

*T*he Bishop of Barbados refused.

"There can be no wedding!" he said. "I am well aware that Mr Bentham – who is a damned pirate – enters into so-called *marriages* every time he visits this island, choosing as his bride any trollop that takes his fancy, and whom he might have had for sixpence, and whom afterwards he abandons!"

"Quite so!" said his chaplain, standing beside him in nervous defiance of the crowd of garishly dressed, heavily armed men who were crammed into the bishop's study.

"I'm sorry, Your Grace," declared Brendan O'Byrne, who commanded the intruders. He was frighteningly ugly and the gallows were groaning for him, but he'd been raised to give respect to a bishop. "I'm afraid you mayn't say *no*, for I'm first mate to Captain Bentham, and Captain Bentham is resolved upon marriage. So, will you look at this now?"

He produced a little pocket-pistol, all blued and gleaming.

Then, showing its slim barrel to His Grace, he explained what he was going to do with it, and had his men remove the chaplain's drawers and breeches, and bend the chaplain over a table, to demonstrate precisely how it would be done.

Five minutes later, His Grace was stepping out under a burning sun, sweating in mitre and chasuble, with crosier in hand. His chaplain followed bearing a King James Bible and a Book of Common Prayer while attempting to keep the hem of the bishop's robes clear of the mud and dog-shite of Queen Mary Street, main thoroughfare of Williamstown.

Beside the bishop marched O'Byrne, arms crossed and a pistol in each fist, while two dozen of his men capered on every side, taking refreshment from bottles. No matter how the bishop looked with his quick, clever eyes, there was no way out but forward, and he made the best of it by smiling to the cheering populace who'd turned out for Danny Bentham's latest wedding.

"Bah!" said the bishop in exasperation as O'Byrne turned him left into Harbour Street, in sight of the dockyard and the Custom House with its Union Flag, and a small group of the island's foremost citizens: those who by blind-eye and bribery allowed outright piracy to flourish when it was stamped out in every other place but this.

"Cap'n!" roared O'Byrne, seeing Danny Bentham among them. He waved his hat in the air. "Give a cheer, you men!"

"Huzzah!" they cried.

"Huzzah!" cried the mob, and everyone dashed forward, the bishop and his chaplain bundling up robes, dropping and retrieving sacred books, and managing by sweat-soaked miracles of footwork to avoid falling over completely. Finally, bedraggled and gasping, they arrived at the Custom House, where a wizened man in a red coat stepped forward to greet them.

"My lord!" said Sir Wyndham Godfrey, the governor, doffing his hat and bowing in his ceremonial uniform as colonel of the island's militia. The bishop caught his breath, took the thin hand, and nodded curtly. The governor had once been an honest man who fought corruption, but now he was a figure of pathos: disease and the tropical climate having taken their toll.

Standing next to him was Captain Danny Bentham, with his bride-to-be. He was a huge man, six foot five inches tall, muscular and upright, with blue eyes, a heavy chin and a thick neck. He wore a gold-laced blue coat, a feathered hat, gleaming top-boots, and a Spanish rapier hung at his side. Sir Wyndham introduced this thieving, murdering rapist as if he were a nobleman.

"It is my pleasure, Your Grace, to present Captain Daniel Bentham, a worthy master mariner and owner of two fine vessels."

"Milord," said Bentham, taking the bishop's hand. "Gaw' bless you for agreein' so kindly to do the honours!" The voice was soft but the handshake crunched like pincers. The bishop winced as he looked up into the tall man's eyes, and was surprised at Bentham's youth, for the big chin was as smooth as a boy's.

"And this is my little Catalina, milord." A small, plump tart was pushed forward in a cheap dress, a lace cap, and half-naked breasts. She was a mulatta: dark-skinned, pretty and with big eyes, the sort that Danny Bentham liked. He gazed upon her with urgent lust, hoisted her off her feet, and kissed her deep and hungry, with loud groans of pleasure.

His men cheered uproariously and fired pistols in the air,

while Sir Wyndham and his followers simpered, and the bishop wished his post abolished and himself back in England, albeit as the lowest curate in the land.

"My little Catalina," said Bentham, putting her down and wiping the slobber from his lips. "Fresh from the Brazils, milord, and speaks only Portugee, of which I has a few words meself. So she don't know all our ways." For some reason this provoked laughter from Bentham's men, but he swiftly went among them and restored order with his fists and shining boots.

The rest of it passed in horror for the bishop, as a procession set out from the Custom House, led by the garrison band and a company of grenadiers. Next came the bishop and the Happy Couple, followed by the governor and prominent citizens, then the populace in general, with slaves, dogs and hogs to the rear.

The destination was Miss Cooper's whorehouse, a large, stone-built mansion to the windward side of Williamstown, all laid out for a huge banquet.

But first there was the wedding ceremony, which took place in Miss Cooper's salon: a splendid chamber, but it was Sodom and Gomorrah combined, so far as the bishop was concerned. He looked despairingly at Captain Bentham standing before him doting over his Catalina, while behind them the room was packed stinking full and sweltering hot with coarse and leering persons, mostly drunk and none of them quiet, with the governor and his entourage long gone.

"Ahem!" said the bishop. "Dearly beloved, we are gathered here this day in the sight of God and this congregation . . ."

Eventually they let the bishop go, shoving him out the front door, his chaplain close behind. There, Mr O'Byrne capped insult upon injury by presenting each clergyman with a gratuity of fifty Spanish dollars in a purse tied up with ribbon.

Bang went the door, and they were free. For an instant the bishop stood trembling and close to tears. Then he snarled, "Give me that!" And, snatching the chaplain's purse, he hurled it, together with his own, straight back into the house through one of Miss Cooper's windows. If he'd hoped the gesture to be accompanied by the smashing of glass, he was disappointed; all was thrown open for the cool night air. "Bah!" he cried. "A lost labour and an affront to God!"

"What is, Your Grace?" said the chaplain.

"This!" said the bishop, spreading his arms to encompass the entire island.

Inside, roaring and swaying in unison, the men of the company were helping Cap'n Bentham upstairs for his wedding night, bellowing obscene advice. The women, meanwhile, were assisting the new Mrs Bentham out of her clothes, before tucking her into the house's best bed.

"Ah!" said Bentham at last, leaning his back against the locked door, and "Huh!" as from outside there came the rumble and thunder of Mr O'Byrne removing all those who would have pressed their ears to the wood for further entertainment.

"Now, my little Catalina!" said Bentham.

"Oh, *senhor*!" she said, and the blood pumped into his loins at the sight of her, sat small and helpless against the pillows, with a linen sheet pulled protectively under her chin. Miss Cooper's girls had expertly combed out her hair and spread it around her shoulders, while Catalina herself had been a virgin recently enough to remember a maiden's modesty, and to deliver a representation of it sufficiently convincing for Danny Bentham.

"*Senhor*," she pleaded, "*seja delicado . . .*"

"Be gentle?" said Bentham. "I'll show you gentle, my girl!" and he swept off clothes, boots, belt and sword, to stand magnificently naked before his bride, legs spread wide and hands on hips.

"*Oh!*" said Catalina, sitting up straighter and staring in wonderment, for Danny Bentham's body was something to see: slim-waisted, smooth and muscular, with long legs, strong arms, and gleaming skin. Catalina thought it a sight to please any bride – apart from the undoubted *presence* of a fine pair of breasts and the undoubted *absence* of anything between the legs that stood to attention, or even dangled at ease. In fact there was simply nothing. (Indeed there was doubly nothing, since to explain his smooth chin, Cap'n Bentham called daily for razor, soap and water, and having nothing else to shave, shaved what he had.)

"Hmm . . ." said Catalina, who understood a lot more than these stupid English thought, and who'd never for a moment believed she'd got a *permanent* husband: one that would last longer than the dollars she'd been paid. But she had thought she'd got a handsome husband and had been looking forward to the wedding night.

Que piedade, she thought; *what a pity*. But Captain Bentham thought otherwise. There was not the slightest equivocation in "his" mind as he leapt on to the bed, throwing sheets aside and seizing his wriggling, naked bride with absolute conviction, abandoned passion, and remarkable technique, for Danny Bentham liked women, and only women, and had learned how to please them.

Outside, Mr O'Byrne was at his station, lounging in a

chair backed against the door with a bottle of rum for company, still keeping dirty-minded eavesdroppers from their sport.

"Uh! Uh! Uh!" came Bentham's voice, muffled through the door.

"Go to it, me hearty!" said O'Byrne, and drank a toast.

"Oh! Oh! Oh!" came the other voice.

"Give her one for me, by Christ, Cap'n!"

"*Oh! Oh! Oh!*"

"Go on, my galloping boy!"

"*Ohhhhhhhhhhhh!*"

Chapter 4

"*N*o!" said Selena, "I won't go below. I want to see."

"Damn it, girl, do as you're bid," said Flint while beside them, at the tiller, Tom Allardyce the bosun worked hard not to notice the argument, focusing instead on the ship they were chasing.

"She's Dutch, Cap'n!" he said. "Round stern and bilander-rigged, and she's hard up in a clinch with no knife to cut the seizing!"

Flint snapped out his glass and looked. Allardyce was right – he must have marvellous eyes: it was a Dutchman, heavily storm-damaged, and plodding along helpless. So much the better! He turned to Selena. "Go below, girl!" he muttered. "Don't play the little madam with me!" Then he raised his voice cheerfully to the men standing to the guns and ready at the sails: "There's our dockyard, lads!" he cried. "Our planking and rum, and our pickles and pork!"

27

The men cheered. *Walrus* had taken a battering in the fight against *Lion*; heavy shot into her hull had spoiled stores, sprung leaks, wrecked her windlass, and blown away her binnacle and compasses. Desperately short of provisions and fit only for a short voyage, *Walrus* remained sound aloft. Now, charging onward under foresails and gaffs, mainsail and topsails, she was going like a mail-coach on a turnpike.

"Go below!" said Flint. "There's danger . . . and things unfit for you to see."

"No!" she said. "Not this time. I won't be shut up below!"

Flint's eyes showed white all round. Nobody said *no* when Flint said *yes*. In agitation he reached up to his shoulder to pet the parrot that was his friend and darling . . . and which was no longer there because he'd lost it to Silver. Just as he'd got Selena, Silver had got the parrot

"Huh!" he said, snatching down his hand before anyone should see. "You shall do as you are bid!" And he grabbed Selena, pulling her close and breathing the scent of her. He breathed it deep and felt her warmth and looked into her eyes. This was a new game. He knew it. She knew it. He'd been playing it ever since the island: finding excuses to brush past her, to touch her, and even – on one occasion – attempting to slide a hand inside her shirt to touch her naked skin.

Yes. A shining dawn was breaking for Joe Flint. Thanks to Selena, his lifelong, shameful incapacity seemed to be on the mend, and the dormant contents of his breeches were stirring. Conversely, Selena felt that for her the sun was going down. Flint was master aboard *Walrus* and would take whatever he wanted the instant he became capable of taking it.

"Flint!" she said sharply. "Look!" Flint turned and saw every eye was on himself and the lovely black girl in her boots, shirt and breeches, with two pistols stuffed in her belt. It'd been Flint's joke to rig her out like this, but by God Almighty didn't it just suit her! And now the swine were ogling and nudging one another for the fun of seeing a shapely seventeen-year-old defying him on his own quarterdeck.

Flint measured choices: he could wrestle her bodily through a hatchway – proving to all hands that she was beyond his command; he could order someone else to do it – allowing another man to handle her . . . or . . .

He came to a swift decision. "So be it, my chick!" he cried, slapping her backside merrily, as if it were the biggest joke in the world to have a woman on deck as the ship went into action. Turning to his men, he smiled his glittering smile . . . and it worked! For Flint was a man to admire: handsome, charismatic and splendid.

"A-hah!" roared the crew, united in shared pride of their magnificent captain . . . even if he was a mad bastard that popped out men's eyes like pickled onions when the mood was upon him.

"So, my dear," Flint said to Selena, smiling and smiling, "do try to keep your limbs clear of flying shot, and let's see how much you relish what you now shall see!" He dropped his voice: *"Because you won't like it, not one little bit, that I do most solemnly promise you!"*

The chase was short, for the wretched bilander was as slow as *Walrus* was fast. As soon as he came within cannon shot, Flint broke out the skull and swords – his personal variation of the black flag – and on the upward roll discharged a thundering load of chain-shot into the Dutchman's rigging: some ten pounds of iron apiece from each of *Walrus*'s seven broadside guns. It was more to terrorise than to disable, for the bilander was already in ruins aloft: jury-rigged on the stump of her foremast, most of her bowsprit gone and the big

29

crossjack yard on her mainmast fished with a spar where it had sprung.

The Dutchman shuddered under *Walrus*'s fire and those aboard were blinded in the smoke. She was a little ship, no more than sixty feet in the hull and a hundred tons burden, with an old-fashioned rig and shallow draught to suit the Netherlands' waters. Against the heavily armed, sharp-keeled *Walrus* she was already lost. But she raised the red, white and blue of her native land and fought like a tiger.

One after another, the four one-pounder swivels that were all she had for a broadside blasted their charges, hurling dozens of pistol-balls across *Walrus*'s decks, prompting roars of rage as men were struck down or staggered back under the impact of shot, even as they stood ready to hurl grappling lines.

"Bastards!" cried *Walrus*'s men.

"Give 'em another!" cried Flint. "Grape and round-shot!" And it was a race between his gunners and the Dutchman's as to who would fire next. The Dutchman won, and got off just one more volley of canister, killing a few more of Flint's men before *Walrus*'s main battery, thundering fire and smoke, comprehensively smashed in the Dutchman's bulwarks, blasting half her men into offal, and sending her swivel guns tumbling into the air as iron wreckage.

"Stand by, boarders!" cried Flint. "Put us alongside of her, Mr Allardyce!"

"Aye-aye, sir!"

The two vessels rose and fell, rubbing paint and splinters off one another as the grappling lines bound them together.

"Boarders away!" cried Flint, leading the scramble up on to *Walrus*'s bulwark. He leapt aboard the Dutchman followed by nearly sixty men, all of them armed to the teeth, fighting mad and seeking vengeance for their dead and wounded mates.

A mere handful of the Dutchman's crew remained alive amongst the wreckage of broken timbers, shards of iron, smashed gratings and hanging sails that encumbered the narrow, smoke-clouded deck. It was hard enough to walk the deck, let alone fight on it. But fight they did, with pike, pistol and cutlass, led by a man in a grey coat boasting a big voice.

"*Christiaan Hugens!*" he cried, calling on the name of his ship.

"*Christiaan Hugens!*" cried the others, and then it was hand-to-hand.

Slick! And a man shoving a blade at Flint found the steel parried and himself spouting blood from a cut throat. Thump! And another man, pulling the trigger with his pistol aimed right at Flint's chest, found Flint gone and a cutlass cleaving his own skull. But that was all the fighting Joe Flint had to do that day. Six men cannot fight sixty. Not for long, however brave they may be. Soon all was quiet except the sounds of the sea and the groaning, creaking of ships' timbers.

A thick, squat man came lumbering through the wreckage. He was Alan Morton, Flint's quartermaster, and he saluted Flint with his best man-o'-warsman salute: hand touching hat and foot stamping the deck.

"Cap'n," he said, "there's just three o' the buggers left alive, and a dozen o' dead-'uns, mostly killed by our gunfire afore ever we stepped aboard." He pointed to the three prisoners, waiting by the mainmast. "There they are, Cap'n. Shall we slit 'em and gut 'em?"

"Good heavens, no!" said Flint, jolly as ever after a fight.

"Not at all, Mr Morton – I have other plans for them." He smiled and most cordially took a handful of Morton's shirt front to wipe the blood off his cutlass. "Just make the gentlemen fast and we'll see to them later. But now we have work to do."

Flint sighed inwardly. It was on such occasions that he missed Billy Bones, who'd once been his first mate, and whose heavy fists had driven men to their duties without Flint having to do the tiresome work of punching heads and kicking behinds. Flint sighed wistfully. Bones did so wonderfully have the knack of terrifying the men, combined with just the perfect quantity of initiative: enough to fill in the outline of his orders without ever daring to question them.

"Huh!" Flint peered at Morton, now shuffling his feet and looking puzzled under his captain's gaze. The low-browed, stupid clod was the best fist-fighter on the lower deck – which was why he held his rating – but like the rest he was infected with the equality of those blasted "articles" which were Silver's legacy to *Walrus*; Silver who, believing himself a "gentleman of fortune" had drawn up a list of articles like those of Captain England, Captain Roberts and all the other pirates who wouldn't admit what they were.

The thought that Morton believed Flint was captain by consent and could be deposed at will made Flint laugh out loud. Morton, basking in the sunshine of Flint's merriment, grinned back at him.

"So," said Flint, "here is what we must do, Mr Morton . . ."

"Aye-aye, sir!" said Morton, saluting and stamping again. At least he was keen.

The rest of the day passed in work: intense and heavy work, as everything useful was stripped out of *Christiaan Hugens,* which proved to be an expedition ship, fitted out by Utrecht University and sent to study celestial navigation in the West Indies, in the hope of advancing Dutch trade. Flint gleaned that from the papers in her master's cabin. He had no Dutch, but many seafaring and astronomical words were similar to the English equivalents, and he filled in the rest by intelligent guesswork.

This was one of the rare occasions when Flint was happy to take a prize which carried no rich or valuable cargo: no silks or spices, no bullion nor pieces of eight – the fine Spanish dollars that the whole world used as currency. No, this time his most pressing need was ordinary ships' stores. He especially valued the excellent compasses, charts and navigational instruments.

Flint's men also took sheet lead, nails and carpenter's tools to repair the shot-holes *Lion* had blown through *Walrus*'s hull, along with some spars and planking, a windlass and a fine new kedge anchor that was better than *Walrus*'s own.

They took particular delight in seizing *Christiaan Hugens*'s entire stock of foodstuffs: salt beef, salt pork and biscuit, together with more exotic victuals: ham, cheeses, tongue, tea, coffee, gin, brandy and wine, for the ship was only two weeks out of Port Royal, Jamaica, and was bursting with fresh provisions. There was even a coop full of chickens on the fo'c'sle; these hardy fowl survived the battle only to have their necks pulled by Flint's cook, to provide fresh meat for the gluttony and drinking that always followed the taking of a prize.

Later, with a fiddler playing and all hands half drunk and full of good food, and the blazing hulk of the Dutch ship lost under the horizon, Flint stood before the tiller, with Selena, Allardyce and Morton beside him, to address the

33

crew. Mr Cowdray, the ship's surgeon, who had been busy with the wounded below, now joined them on deck. Like the rest, he was in his best clothes for the occasion. He nodded to Selena, who smiled.

For Selena, this was a cruel time. John Silver was stranded on Flint's island where she might never see him again, while Flint's stunted desires for women were changing and growing. She desperately needed a friend, and – aboard this ship – Mr Cowdray was the only honest man.

"Well," he said, "have you seen a battle?"

"Yes."

"And what did you think of it?"

"I've seen worse." It was true. She had.

"Hmm." Cowdray frowned. "Be careful. There might be more."

"What?"

"Brothers and fellow gentlemen of fortune!" cried Flint, in a great and happy voice. Cheers followed, with raised bottles and hearty toasts. "Thank you, brothers!" said Flint. "Look at our ship! Go on, my lads, look at her!" That puzzled them. They stared around almost nervously. "Soon she'll be good as new," said Flint. "Re-fitted, re-provisioned, leaks plugged and rigging spliced. We've all the tackles and all the gear . . . *and her luck shall be re-made!*"

That was clever. They all knew Flint's treasure had been left behind on the island and that, until she was stabbed in the back by Billy Bones, *Lion* had had the better of them. Nobody dared say it who sailed under Flint, but they all feared their luck was broken. Now they cheered and cheered and cheered.

"Brothers!" cried Flint, raising a silver tankard. "Here's to old friends and new luck!"

34

"Old friends and new luck!" they roared.

"Fifteen men on the dead man's chest..." began Flint, lifting up his fine, ringing voice and the fiddler following him.

"Yo-ho-ho, and a bottle of rum!" roared the crew.

"Drink and the devil had done for the rest!"

"Yo-ho-ho, and a bottle of rum!"

When he chose to be, Flint was irresistibly charming and now he worked his magic, with verse after verse of his favourite, hideous song, each more grim than the last, but always seeming funny when Flint sang it; he passed from man to man, pulling noses, clapping shoulders, poking ribs, and all the while dancing to the beat of his own song. Even Selena and Cowdray laughed, who both should have known better. As for the crew, they worshipped and adored their captain in that happy moment.

But Cowdray was right. There was worse to come.

"Now, shipmates!" cried Flint when the song was done, and he beamed at the close-packed ring of red faces, leering as the tropical sun went down. "Now, my jolly boys..." And Flint changed the entire mood with a solemn expression and hands raised to heaven. "Lads, let us remember those of our brothers foully slain in today's action. Those slain against all the laws of war, when we had offered honourable surrender!"

"Aye!" they roared.

"What's he saying?" said Selena to Cowdray. "That's nonsense."

"I think you might wish to go below, my dear," said Cowdray.

"Why?"

Cowdray looked away. "*Experto credite!*" he said. "Trust one who knows."

Selena paused. She looked at Cowdray. He was a scholar who loved Latin, and had the habit of spouting it when swayed by strong emotion, be it happiness, fear . . . or shame.

"What do you mean?" she said.

"Just go below."

"I see you recognise the villainy we endured today!" cried Flint. "And since we still have, under hatches, three of the guilty ones . . ." A deep and animal growl drowned out his words. "Silence between decks!" cried Flint, and instantly they obeyed.

"Since we have three of them, I have made preparations in the name of justice." He grinned wickedly. "Justice – and your amusement. So, clear the decks, and hold your patience!" He nodded to Allardyce and Morton, who had their orders and immediately stepped up to the lee rail.

There was an intense buzz of conversation among the hands as Allardyce and Morton took a two-fathom plank (fresh from *Christiaan Hugens*) and shoved it over the lee rail so that half its length stuck out over the side, while the rest remained inboard, nailed firmly to the top of a heavy barrel. When this was done, they went below and brought up one of the prisoners. Barefoot, wearing only a pair of calico slops and with his hands tied behind him, the man was already shaking with fright, and he flinched pitifully as *Walrus*'s crew bayed like the mob at the Roman games. Finally, Allardyce and Morton heaved him bodily up on to the plank, where he stood swaying and shaking and gazing about in terror.

"What is this?" whispered Selena to Cowdray.

"I don't know. This is new." He turned to face her. "But I am going below now, and I think you should too."

"No . . ."

"Selena, please follow me."

"Can't we stop him?"

"Flint? Never! But I beg you, on my knees, not to see this."

Selena, horrified and fascinated, remained where she was.

Cowdray sighed and shook his head. "On your own head be it!" he said, and vanished down the quarterdeck hatchway.

"Brothers!" cried Flint. "Those who know me will recall some of my merry games – Flint's games!"

"Aye!" they roared, nodding at one another in glee. There was one that they knew all too well, played atop an overturned tub with a belaying pin, where all the player had to do was move faster than Flint to avoid getting his fingers broken. They laughed and laughed, even those whose fingertips had been smashed. Indeed, some now displayed their scars with pride, and laughed louder than all the rest.

"But this is a new game," said Flint, lowering his voice like a conspirator. "And this the first time it's been tried. So watch me, shipmates. Watch and learn!"

With that, Flint picked up a boarding pike and began to sing his song again:

"Fifteen men on the dead man's chest . . ." He cocked an ear to the audience.

"Yo-ho-ho, and a bottle of rum!" they cried, and burst into laughter as – on the word *rum* – Flint pricked the victim's side with the sharp point of the pike.

"Aaah!" cried the man.

"Drink and the devil had done for the rest . . ."

"Yo-ho-ho, and a bottle of rum!"

Flint jabbed again, sharp on cue, and blood flowed. Selena, sobbing, finally took Cowdray's advice and ran below.

"Aaah!" cried the victim.

And so it went on. Since the plank led out over the side, even the dullest spectator knew how the game must end, and any fool could simply have driven someone off its end with prods of a pike. But Flint was an artist. He worked to music and to rhythm, constantly leading his man to the end of the plank, then allowing him to stagger to safety, only to drive him back again or push him to one side, then to the other, with a dozen wounds oozing blood and the poor devil deranged with horror and begging in his own language for mercy.

The special horror of it was any man's innate fear of falling, especially from a wobbling plank run out over the ocean, so the victim collaborated in the entertainment, even torturing himself by fighting to keep his footing, leaning against the sharp point that was driving him into the sea in a desperate attempt to resist the final plunge, hands-bound, into the hungry waters below. And Flint's evil genius – his unique gift – was to make this funny.

Finally, when Flint judged the time was ripe, he paused proceedings for conversation with the victim.

"My dear fellow," he said, "King Richard of England was ransomed with one hundred thousand marks. What will your nation pay for you?"

This brought howls of laughter from the crew, and desperate pleas – understood by nobody – from the victim.

"What will you give me then for your life?" said Flint, snarling and vicious now, rousing the blood lust of his crew. "Nothing?" said Flint. "Then take this . . ." Slowly and deliberately he pushed the steel pike-head into the man's flesh, forcing him agonisingly backward, resisting all the way and spattering blood and sweat, shaking his head and grinding his teeth.

"Goodbye!" said Flint, and pushed him off the edge with a final thrust.

The crew shrieked in delight and *Walrus* rolled heavily as they rushed to the side to see him drown.

The game wasn't over yet, though. It was time for the second Dutch prisoner to be brought up, the man in the grey coat who'd led the fight by *Christiaan Hugens*'s people. He was fit and muscular with sandy hair, a beard and moustache, and high, slanted cheekbones that made him look more Slav than Hollander. He struggled cunningly as he was dragged forward, being particularly nasty in the way he kicked: cracking sharply into shins and stamping a heel sideways into one man's kneecap such that he limped ever after. But finally he was heaved up on the plank and menaced by blades so he couldn't jump off.

The game proceeded as before; the crew, deeper in drink by this time, were bellowing Flint's song, while their captain danced and spun and switched hands on the pike-staff, all the while jabbing and jabbing and jabbing. As before, it ended with the prisoner, dripping blood, at the end of the plank with the pike's tip in his guts and Flint demanding a ransom. The only difference was that this man spoke English. He spoke it well enough to curse Flint – which Flint played upon with cruel skill to make the game even more entertaining. His men were near paralysed with laughter and begging for him to stop.

"King Richard of England was ransomed with one hundred thousand marks . . ." said Flint.

"You go fuck your mother!" cried the man.

"Sadly she is deceased so I cannot," said Flint. "But what will your nation pay to ransom you?"

"Damn you to hell!"

"Where else? But how much?"

39

"Bastard!"

"Perhaps," said Flint. "But *how much*?"

Finally, judging his moment, Flint turned nasty, spitting out his words in anger.

"I say, for the last time, what will you give me for your life?" He twisted the pikehead into flesh.

"Argh!" gasped the man on the plank.

"Nothing?" said Flint. "You have nothing for me? Then over you go!" And he readied the pike for a long, slow thrust.

"Longitude!" cried the man.

"What?" said Flint, lowering the pike.

"I give you longitude. I find it at sea."

"Nonsense," said Flint, "that's impossible!"

"No! I do it by lunar observation."

Flint blinked, and his heart began to thump as he realised what quality of man he was about to push into the sea: a man who offered longitude in the face of death. Flint thought of every year's crop of shipwrecks and the thousands drowned, the rich cargoes lost through ignorance of a ship's true position. Fine navigator that he was, he was limited like all others to working by latitude. If he could find longitude at sea, it would give him the most colossal advantage over the rest of seafaring mankind . . . It was an undreamed of prize. It was magnificent. It was priceless. Flint made another quick decision, this time an easy and obvious one.

"Take him down!" he said. "You! Allardyce and Morton! Take him down and free his hands."

The crew didn't like it. *They* didn't know longitude from a loblolly boy. They wanted their fun, and they bellowed in anger at being deprived of it. Allardyce and Morton worked fast. They hauled the man off the plank and dragged him aft, followed by Flint.

40

"Get him below, quick!" said Flint.

"No!" said the man. "I am Cornelius Van Oosterhout. I am a Christian and I do not move from here."

"What?" said Flint. "Are you mad? Get down to my cabin this instant, before they turn ugly." He looked at the crew, muttering and scowling.

"You want longitude, yes?" said Van Oosterhout.

"Yes," said Flint. He wanted it like all the jewels of Arabia.

"Then you save the man below. He is from my crew. If you put him there –" he looked at the plank "– I tell you nothing. I jump in the sea. You don't need to push!"

"Poppycock!" said Flint, sneering. "Do as I say, or I shall put you back on the plank, and you'll sing any tune I choose!"

"No," said Van Oosterhout firmly. "One day I stand before God. I am responsible. You save two, or you save none. It is your choice."

Chapter 5

*D*rums beating, colours flying and bayonets fixed, the eight hundred men of the Craven County Regiment of Militia marched splendidly into the tented camp established on the southern bank of the Ashley River where it opened into Charlestown harbour, less than a quarter of a mile from the town itself and close enough that their fifes and drums could be heard from the city walls. The officers were in British scarlet, with gorgettes and soldierly cocked hats, while the ranks wore whatever was practical for campaigning in the field. But every man shouldered a Brown Bess musket and carried sixty rounds of ball cartridge in his pouch, and stepped out to the beat of the drum.

They advanced in two columns, and between them – escorted, guarded and enclosed – came the Patanq nation: first the warriors, then the old men, then the women and children burdened with all the nation's goods. The marching militia – in columns of three – just covered the three hundred and four warriors, leaving the tail of old men, and women

42

and children stringing along behind. Nobody worried about them.

The formation was received with drum-rolls and dipped colours by the remaining five militia regiments of the Royal Colony of South Carolina, paraded in arms, and which – together with the Craven County Regiment – numbered close on six thousand men, not to mention the three troops of horse militia that trotted outside the marching columns, with spurs and broadswords jingling, and who were over one hundred strong in their own right.

Mounted, uniformed, and with flashing swords drawn in salute, the colonels of the five regiments stood before their men, with Colonel Douglas Harper of the Charlestown Regiment – who was the senior – in the middle and a horse length to the fore, an aide on either side of him.

They sheathed swords and Colonel Harper spoke to the young officer to his right, who on other days was his eldest son Tom.

"Fine sight, Lieutenant!"

"Indeed, sir!"

"What a day for the Colony!"

"Aye! Damned Indians."

"Hmm," said Colonel Harper, and pondered, for he'd been a great man in the Charlestown fur trade, and had grown rich by it, and every fur he ever sold was trapped and brought in by the Indians. Still . . . he looked back at the walls of Charlestown, which weren't there to protect against the French and Spanish only, but against Indians too. And today the Colony was taking the wonderful opportunity to rid itself of the entire Patanq nation, all fifteen hundred of them, in their moccasins and blankets. These days they weren't the most numerous of the Indian nations, but they *were* Indians and times were changing, and better they should live *anywhere* other than South Carolina, and preferably in the moon if only they could be got there. So thought Colonel Harper.

"Pa?" said Lieutenant Harper.

"*Colonel!*" corrected Harper.

"Sorry, Pa . . . Colonel."

"Well?"

"Why's there so many of us? All the regiments? There's more of us than there is of them, even counting the women and little 'uns!" Harper frowned.

"Don't you ever listen? Haven't I told you about them savages?" Colonel Harper was fifty-five years old and had been more things than a trader. He'd fought the Patanq in his time, and shuddered at the thought of it. Especially the recollection of going to battle against them in the woods. "Listen, boy, if there's enough of us here today to put the idea of fighting clean out of their heathen heads, then there's not one man too many! So shut up and face your front."

Colonel Harper looked at the Indians, raising dust as they tramped in, bedraggled from their long march. In fact Tom was right in a way; there were not more than a few hundred warriors in all. But you never knew with the Patanq. They moved like ghosts, you wouldn't hear them coming, and you'd only realise they'd cut your throat when your shirt front turned red.

He turned in the saddle and raised his voice:

"Three hearty rousing cheers for the Craven County men. Hip-Hip-Hip . . ."

Thundering cheers bellowed out as the mustered regiments raised their caps on their bayonets and gave three tremendous huzzahs. In response to the cheers, bells clanged and pealed from the town.

"Colonel?" said a voice from his left: Lieutenant David Harper, his second eldest, and by far the brightest son. "Is that the Dreamer?" He pointed to the head of the Patanq column.

"Aye," said Colonel Harper, pleased that one son had paid attention, "that's him, their famous medicine man. And that's Dark Hand, the war *sachem,* or chief, at his side." Harper looked at them as they came past. He knew Dreamer very well. Him and all the Patanq leaders. Now he drew steel to salute them. And the sachems raised their right hands formally to acknowledge him. For they knew him, too.

There were a dozen of them, leading their nation in procession with Dreamer and Dark Hand. Dreamer was a small, shrivelled man, marked by long illness. He looked a miserable creature beside Dark Hand, but he was the soul of the Patanq nation, and a formidable negotiator – as Harper knew all too well, having attended the lengthy council sessions that had brought the Patanq here today, granted safe passage and a fleet of six ships to carry them off, along with the gold they'd accumulated through years of fur trading and bringing in scalps for the bounty.

The thought of scalps made Harper glance nervously at the warriors, fearful creatures that they were . . . tall men every one: lithe and muscular, upright, hook-nosed, black-eyed and stone-faced. They wore bright-coloured trade blankets round their shoulders and carried long guns in their arms. Their heads were shaven except for dangling, befeathered queues, their cheeks were tattooed in geometric lines and they wore silver nose-rings and elaborate, beaded jewellery.

At last the Patanq came within sight of the harbour, and the ships anchored under the guns of Fort Johnson, with the launches and longboats beached and ready on the shore. And a chatter arose, first from the sachems, and then from the warriors. Harper shook his head in wonder. This was an unheard of vulgarity for the Patanq, who habitually endured the shocks of life in silence. But the chattering was nothing to the shrill cries of the women and children, to whom the ships and the boats and the endless rolling waters were magical wonders.

They surged forward, led by the matriarchs who even the warriors must treat with respect. They shouted and yelled and urged the children forward, elbowing aside the Craven County Militia, who grinned indulgently and opened ranks to let them through. After all, who were they to stand in the way of Indians about to board ship and sail away for ever? So the militiamen grinned, the young girls shrieked, the children laughed, and the watching regiments cheered in delight as the women and children of the Patanq nation ran headlong down to the shore.

The sachems and warriors maintained their dignity, keeping a steady pace and manly bearing. But Harper saw that some of them were in doubt and arguing noisily.

Oh no! he thought, and a tingle of fright shot up his spine. *Don't let them baulk at the last moment. Please no. Not after all this ...*

"Colonel," said his second-eldest, "what's going on, sir? Some of their chiefs are stopping."

"No they're not," said the colonel. "They're just puzzled. Most of them have never seen the sea before, nor ships neither. They're surprised, that's all."

He wanted it to be true, but it wasn't. As the arguments

grew, the sachems came to a halt, and nervous conversations began among the colonels behind Harper, and among the troops too. Up and down the lines of infantry, men stopped cheering and began fingering their muskets and wondering if they might have to use them. Harper took a deep breath. He couldn't let all this come to nothing.

"You two follow me," he said to his sons, "the rest of you stand fast!" He was digging in his spurs and riding forward, wondering what he'd have to say, what he'd have to offer them, when he saw Dreamer raise his hands and lift up his voice to address the sachems in the Patanq tongue. "Whoa!" said Harper to his horse, and patted her neck. His heart thumped as Dreamer spoke, and spoke... and then the sachems were following behind the medicine man like lambs, down towards the shore and the boats and the laughing women.

The fearful moment had passed.

Dreamer turned to face Harper and lifted his hand. Harper raised his hat and bowed, and rode back to his place at the head of the colonels, heart thumping and head dizzy with relief.

At dusk there was a formal council. Dreamer and his sachems sat down with Colonel Harper, the other colonels and the leaders of the city of Charlestown. To the white men it was long, incomprehensible and tedious. But it was necessary. It was part of the passing away of the Patanq nation from its homeland.

Next day the Patanq embarked. And it took all day to get them out and aboard the six ships, for there were serious matters of precedence to be considered, and families and clans to be kept together. There were long discussions, led by Dreamer, and the sachems, while Colonel Harper and the rest of the South Carolinians did no more than stand by and watch.

But some of the white men – while they were glad the Indians were going – were puzzled as to the reason.

"Why are they doing this, Colonel?" said his second-eldest, as they sat on their horses and looked on.

"They have their reasons, Lieutenant."

"Where are they going?"

"North! At least, that's what they told me."

"But *why* are they going? They've been fighting us on and off since white men came here. Why should they give up their lands and pay in gold to be taken into ships and carried away?"

Harper sighed.

"Boy, you've asked me that a hundred times these past months, and I just don't know."

"But this has been planned for over a year, and you've spent weeks among them. Didn't you ever ask?"

"'Course I did, but they'd never tell me."

"Not anything? Not at all?"

Harper paused and gazed out across the harbour, where busy boats slid across the water like insects with flashing limbs, and the decks of the six ships swarmed with excited Indians. Only a couple of dozen Patanq remained ashore, climbing into two big boats with oarsmen ready, helmsmen at the tillers . . . and Dreamer looking on, determined to see all his people safely away before he stepped into a boat himself.

"I don't know the truth of it, boy," said Harper, "but it's all to do with *him*."

Chapter 6

*B*illy Bones was pumping ship among the trees, only his broad back visible as he turned away for privacy, fumbling with the falls of his breeches and aiming at the roots of a big palm. Grunting in relief, he let loose a stream like that of a brewer's dray horse.

"Can you trust him, Cap'n?" said Israel Hands, a hundred yards off, preparing to help launch the jolly-boat. It was rigged for sail, with provisions for a week, two men standing by as crew, and Long John ready seated in the stern-sheets. Silver shrugged his shoulders.

"We got to trust him, shipmate. There ain't no other way."

"Then let me come along o' you."

"Can't do that, matey. There's too much to do and too few to do it. I want you out with your party, along o' Sarney Sawyer and Black Dog and their crews. I want this island mapped and charted, and not an inch that we don't know the bearings of."

49

"But, John, it might be half a year or more before we sees Flint again."

"Not him, Israel!" Silver thumped the gunwale. "Not him, my cocker! He'll flog all hands to their duties, and whistle up the Devil if need be." He shook his head. "No, he'll be back before you can blink, and we has to be ready."

"Then take the pistols off Billy-boy. At least do that," said Israel Hands.

"No," said Silver, "them are to show we trust him."

"But we *don't*."

"Israel!" said Silver, taking hold of his arm. "Yes, we do, and I'll tell you for why . . ." He nodded in Bones's direction. "I saw the look on the bugger's face when he opened his sea-chest and saw the cargo untouched. He piped his eye like a babby."

"Looks as though he's done," said Israel Hands, for Bones was now busy shaking off the last drops. Heaving everything back into place, he turned towards the boat, making fast his britches as he stumped across the sand, head down, lips pursed.

In addition to restoring Bones's pistols and cutlass, Silver had issued him with a blue coat and tricorne to signify that he was, once more, an officer and jolly companion. Now he gazed upon these icons of resurrection.

If a thing's worth doing . . . he thought. But even then he knew that Billy would turn traitor the instant he caught sight of Flint.

"Come aboard, Mr Bones," said Silver with a smile.

"Aye-aye, Cap'n," said Billy Bones, touching his hat with utmost respect. The broad nose occupying the centre of his rough, heavy face was a constant reminder of the need to show respect to Silver, for it was Silver who'd flattened it in past days aboard *Walrus*. Billy's piggish eyes blinked nervously as – seaman born and bred – he gave a hand to shoving the jolly-boat out till she floated, before leaping aboard with the others.

The two seamen immediately took up their oars in the rocking boat, set them in the rowlocks, feathered, and looked to Silver for orders.

"Give way!" said Silver, and the boat shot forward, clear of the shore. "Take the tiller, Mr Bones, and set a course for Foremast Hill." He looked at the oarsmen. "We'll set sail, just so soon as she's clear o' the inlet. Wind's fair from the west."

"Aye-aye, Cap'n."

Out they went, pulling through the land-locked waters where – surrounded by hills and jungle, and shielded by the mass of a craggy islet that was the island's companion – the winds blew feeble and erratic. As soon as they cleared the narrows and came about, with the heights of Haulbowline Head on the starboard beam, the fifteen-foot boat began to lift and plunge, and all aboard her felt their spirits lift as the fresh salt smell, the wind and spray and the wheeling gulls blew away the foetid heat of the enclosed anchorage.

"Make sail, lads," said Silver, and in came the oars, and up went a gaff and headsail, to fill in the steady westerly blow, driving them onward. The speed was exhilarating. Too small for deep sea work, and dangerously stretched even for a coastal cruise, the jolly-boat – chosen for the job because she was all they had – was rising to the occasion magnificently.

"Fine sport, there!" said Silver, pointing to the honking, trumpeting sealions that frolicked – fat, black and slippery

– among the breakers pounding the rocks off Haulbowline Head.

"Fine for them, Cap'n," said Billy Bones, with a broken-toothed grin, "but not for us." It was the first time Silver had seen him smile. "And there's the Cape of the Woods to clear, half a league ahead, so I'll steer a point to windward, to give us sea-room."

"Well and good, Mr Bones," said Silver approvingly. "I see you knows your island."

"Aye, Cap'n, 'deed I do. When I was here under . . ." His words died.

"Tell the truth and shame the Devil, Mr Bones!" said Silver. The two seaman were looking on with round eyes. "When you was here under *Cap'n Flint* . . ."

Billy Bones swallowed, studied the sea rather than Silver, and went on, "When I was here . . . before . . . we . . . that is *he* . . . charted her from north to south and east to west, and all the seas around."

"So he knows the island well?"

"Every blessed inch."

"And the seas to the north? Does he know what lies there?"

Bones bit his lip and mumbled. If ever a man wore his thoughts on his face it was Billy Bones, and Silver knew he'd touched on something important. But he let it pass, and waited until they'd forged further out to sea, where more of the island's mysteries became visible over the line of cliffs.

"Mr Bones," he said, "d'you see Spy-glass Hill, there, fair on the starboard bow?" he pointed at the great hill – more of a small mountain – that rose above all else on the island: heavily wooded at its roots, but almost naked near the peak.

52

"Aye, Cap'n."

"And d'you see how it's flattened at the top?"

"Aye, Cap'n."

"And I s'pose you know why Flint – who gave it its name – called it *Spy-glass*?"

Billy Bones said nothing.

"He called it that, Mr Bones, because it's the finest lookout point on the island, except for one thing. D'you know what that is?"

"No, Cap'n . . . well . . . *yes,* Cap'n."

Ah, thought Silver, *so you're coming about, Mr Bones.*

"What is it, then?" he said.

"You can't see to the north," said Bones. "There's a spire of rock in the way, right at the top. *The Watchtower* he called it, but it was one of his jokes. It's smooth as a church steeple, and you can't climb it, and short of months of work by engineers with gunpowder, you can't get rid of it, nor get round it, nor cut a way to the top."

"Thank you, Mr Bones," said Silver. "So the Spy-glass is blind to the north."

"That she is, Cap'n."

"And can't be cured. Not without months of work, as you say." Silver paused. "So! How long have we got, Mr Bones? You're the navigator. You know Flint better than any man. Where's he gone? How long till he gets there? And how long till he comes back?"

There was a lengthy silence as Billy Bones considered his loyalties. Finally – Silver had been quite right – what brought Bones round was the thought of all his precious things, given back to him, safe and sound, in his old sea trunk.

"It'd be Savannah first, Cap'n, to get money out of Charley Neal, his agent."

"Aye," said Silver, who knew Charley Neal as well as Flint did.

"Then maybe to Charlestown, which is only a day's sail north, given fair winds. It's a big enough seaport for him to get more ships and men, and take on powder and shot and so forth."

"And then back to us here?"

"Aye."

"So how long till we see his blessed face?"

Billy Bones closed his eyes and did heavy sums in his head. He alone, of those on the island, knew exactly where it lay. Silver, Israel Hands, and one or two others could make a rough guess, but Billy Bones knew. After much pondering, he spoke.

"Best he could do is about three months, I'd reckon. But it could be much longer if there's hurricanes, or if he's becalmed, or if . . ."

"Or if there's fire, wreck or mutiny," added Silver, laying a hand on Billy Bones's shoulder. "I know, Mr Bones. Three months is what I'd have guessed myself, but thank you for your opinion, the which I value greatly."

After that, Silver sat quiet and studied the island as it sped past: cliffs and shingle, grey vegetation streaked with yellow sands, and an occasional mighty pine rising like the spire of Salisbury Cathedral. For some reason, Silver thought it a miserable sight. Bones was busy with his steering, but Silver saw the same solemn mood on the faces of the two seamen, and that weren't right! They had a fair wind, a lively boat and should have been merry. Seamen lived for the moment, mostly, and the present moment was jolly enough.

It was the island, he thought. It depressed him and he couldn't think why. He looked at its hills and plains and jungles. It was like Jamaica, with every landscape from Norway's to Africa's, yet perverse, for in the southern anchorage the noon-day heat would sizzle your eyeballs, but at night and in the morning it could be thick with chilly fog.

And then John Silver bowed his head as depression led to despair, because it led to Selena, the woman he loved, and that with a fierce intensity for her beauty and her dainty grace, and her sweet little face looking up at him as she said *John*. Flint had taken her. She was away with him to Savannah and Charlestown. Silver groaned. The last he'd heard, Flint couldn't do his duty where women were concerned, but you never knew with him. You never knew what he'd do next. He might be ramming and boarding her this minute!

"Shite and corruption!" cried Silver.

"What?" cried the others, looking around in alarm. "What is it, Cap'n?"

"Uh!" said Silver, snatched from his thoughts. "It's the leg," he lied, "the one as ain't there. It pains me sometimes."

"Ahhh," they said, and nodded.

"Happens sometimes," said Billy Bones. "Take a pull o' the rum, Cap'n."

After a few hours' steady sailing they arrived at a vast sandy beach near the north end of the island, which offered a good landing place for Foremast Hill: the shabby, northern relation of the mighty Spy-glass. They dragged the boat beyond high tide, and took a rest and a meal in the shade of the shore-line trees – mainly pines and live-oaks, with thick broom bushes between, a world as different as could be from the jungles of the southern anchorage, for a strong wind blew off the sea here, and it was cooler by far.

55

Later they trudged to the modest summit, no more than a few hundred feet, Silver as agile as any of them, hopping smartly along on the hard, stony ground, and merry again too. It was *work* that drove his pain away, not rum, and there was plenty of work to do.

"Here we are then, mates," he said cheerfully when they reached the top and paused to gaze at the splendid view around them – shimmering ocean, deep-blue dome of sky, rolling hills and forests – while insects chirped, birds sang, and the heavy breakers rumbled against the island's shores. "This is a good spot for a lookout," said Silver. "And I shall station men here with stores and a glass, even though it'll be a fair run to bring news to us . . ." Then he saw that Billy Bones wasn't paying attention. Bones was peering fixedly towards the northern inlet, the island's other anchorage, clearly visible below. He was staring at the wreck of a ship, a big three-master in a state of utter ruin.

"Mr Bones!" said Silver sharply. "Won't you join us?"

"Beg pardon, Cap'n," said Billy Bones, guilty as a schoolboy caught playing with himself.

"Oh," said Silver, "I see you're casting an eye over the old *Elizabeth*." Bones said nothing. "The ship what you and Flint took from King George?" Billy Bones flinched. His memories of that atrocious mutiny were shameful, for he'd been an honest man before Flint got hold of him.

As ever, Billy Bones's thoughts were plain on his face, and Silver smiled. "Never mind, Mr Bones, King George can only hang you once, and he'll do that anyway for your being a gentleman of fortune! So come along o' me and look to better days."

"Thank you, Cap'n," said Bones, touching his hat, and came as close as ever he did to changing masters.

"Now see here, Mr Bones," said Silver, producing a telescope from one of the deep pockets of his coat. "I've been up here before, and there's a thing I've brought you special to see."

"Aye-aye, Cap'n."

"Can you see, Mr Bones, to the south, to the east and to the west . . . there's clear blue ocean?"

"Aye, Cap'n."

"But look to the north, and look to a compass point east and west of north on either hand." Billy Bones looked. "D'you see the fog-banks there?"

"Aye," said Bones.

"And d'you see the broken water an' all?" Billy Bones peered hard. He swallowed, he fidgeted, he blinked. He said nothing. "Here –" said Silver, handing him the telescope. Bones drew it and took a brief look, and gave it back to Silver.

"It's an archipelago of rocks and islands, mostly half-sunk, and there's massive sandbanks like the Goodwins," he babbled nervously. "And there's always fog about, for a vast oceanic current of cold water wells up from below, and meets the warm wet air –" he waved a hand. "And the sands are all around, and there's more 'n we can see, an' no ship can't come safe to this island, but from the south . . ."

Bones stopped in mid-flow as he saw the expression on Silver's face.

"Why, you're a sharp 'un, Mr Bones," said Silver. "All that from one squint through the glass?" Silver laughed. "And *arky-pel-argo*? And *oshy-anic*? Shiver me timbers, but them's monstrous words for the likes of you!" He put his head on one side. "You knew all that already, didn't you, Mr Bones? You knew it 'cos Flint told you!" Billy Bones fell silent again. "Never mind, Mr Bones," said Silver. "I thank you for warning me, fair and square, that we must look to the south for Captain Flint, which should make our work all the easier. I'll keep a man up here, just to be sure, but the main danger comes from the south – don't it, Mr Bones?"

This was plain truth – at least, Silver thought so – but Bones just mumbled and looked at his boots.

"Huh!" said Silver, and shook his head.

There was no more work that day. It was late afternoon, and Silver wouldn't risk the island's coast in a jolly-boat except in full daylight. They made camp by the beach, lit a fire, and settled down for the night.

Just before Silver fell asleep – and into nightmares of parting from Selena – he thought how nervous Bones had been when talking about the rocks and sandbanks. Now what could have caused that? Obviously it was one of Flint's secrets; Bones must be frightened of giving something away. Was it that Flint wanted rival treasure-seekers wrecked on the sandbanks or lost in the fog? Silver didn't know. But he wondered just what Flint *had* told Billy Bones about his precious archipelago.

Chapter 7

*I*t was some days before Cornelius Van Oosterhout and Teunis Wouters became gentlemen of fortune, and even then only with Captain Flint's most grudging approval, for he hated all the nonsense – and equality – that went with it, and he insisted – with much truth – that there was heavy work to be done: replacing the smashed windlass, making proper repairs to the plugged shot-holes, and trimming the ship afresh, now that her hold was bulging with stores.

Much of this time, Captain Flint spent in discussion with Van Oosterhout in *Walrus*'s stern cabin, where Flint's big table, which all but spanned the cabin, was covered with charts, papers, navigational instruments and books of tables wherein numbers marched in ranks and columns, smart as Prussian guardsmen. They were books so boring as to suck the life out of most men. But not Flint. In him they excited all the lust of the Devil in pursuit of a soul.

"The tables are the key," said Van Oosterhout the first time they were brought out. "Are you a navigator, Captain? How good a landfall do you make?" And he twirled the ends of his moustaches, brushing them fiercely upward, all the while casting an appraising eye at Flint like a school-master quizzing a pupil.

"I can get to within ten to twenty miles of my destination," said Flint, "running down my latitude."

"Hoof!" said Van Oosterhout, puffing out his cheeks. "Good! Most men are wrong by scores of miles, maybe worse! Me – I get to within a few miles."

Flint met the Dutchman's challenging gaze with a frown. Either the man was a liar or the finest navigator God ever made.

"So," said Van Oosterhout, "we begin the explanation. Longitude is time, and time is longitude, yes?"

"Yes," said Flint. "And *on land* we find longitude from observation of the occultation of stars. But it needs a steady surface and repeated observations from the same site over many days. So it can't be done at sea."

"Oh, but it can, Captain," said Van Oosterhout. "Imagine, it is night; I take a quadrant. I measure the height of the moon. I measure the height of the chosen star. I measure the angle between the star and the moon. And so to the calculations . . ."

The first time Van Oosterhout determined *Walrus*'s longitude, Flint worked separately – using Van Oosterhout's tables and method – to see who should finish first. Flint worked swiftly but the task took hours, and when he was done, Van Oosterhout was waiting with a smile on his face. Eventually Flint smiled too. It was nothing that he couldn't learn in time, but he wasn't going to waste hours every day in tedious calculation.

So Van Oosterhout was rated as first mate; or, as Flint saw it, a navigating engine for heavy mathematical labour ... which happened to suit Van Oosterhout splendidly, for he relished the work and constantly sought to improve it by practice. But he had other skills too, as *Walrus*'s crew discovered when one of them, a carpenter's mate named Green, walked past the new first mate without a respectful touch of his hat and casually knocked Van Oosterhout aside.

Green was a big man who thought himself superior to mere Dutchmen, but Van Oosterhout reacted with lightning speed, flashing one hand across Green's face to draw attention, poking his eyes with two fingers of the other hand, deftly tripping him as he staggered blinded, and then stamping between his legs ... And all done so neat it was more like a dance than a fight.

"Ahhhhh!" said the fallen one, and "Ooof!" as Van Oosterhout stamped again and drove the breath from his belly. But Green was a hard man and now he was angry. He jumped up, only to find Van Oosterhout calmly waiting, poised like a pugilist but with hands open-palmed, not clenched. "Swab!" said Green, and went for the Dutchman hammer and tongs. At least he tried to, but couldn't get to grips. Instead he was repeatedly tripped and thrown, and kicked in painful places, until even his mates laughed at him. Finally, trembling and sweating with not a drop of fight left, Green thought it best to beg forgiveness and hobble away.

"It is called *silat*," said Van Oosterhout, when Flint asked about this peculiar manner of fisticuffs. "My father served the Verenigde Oostindische Compagnie. What you call 'Dutch East India Company'. Thus I was born in Batavia where the natives fight this way. It is a great art." He shrugged. "I know a little."

"I think you are modest, Mr Van Oosterhout," said Flint. "Perhaps."

After that, the hands remembered their manners where Van Oosterhout was concerned, and Flint realised that he'd got a proper first mate – not just an arithmetician.

Meanwhile repairs proceeded, until eventually the works were complete and *Walrus* was as well-found as if fresh from a royal dockyard. The crew, who'd been waiting for this moment, came to their captain in a body, seeking boldness in numbers as they faced him on his quarterdeck. Even so they were at the limit of their courage, standing with their hats in their hands, and grubby fingers to their brows.

The quartermaster, Morton, with a good tot of rum inside him, was their spokesman. Those behind egged him on, while poised for retreat should Flint turn nasty.

"A word, beggin'-yer-pardon, Cap'n, beggin'-yer-pleasure . . ."

"Oh?" said Flint, acting surprised, as if he hadn't seen this coming. "And what would that concern?" He blinked dangerously.

"All's got to be made shipshape according to articles, Cap'n."

"Aye!" said his mates, trembling.

"What has, my good man?" said Flint.

"*New brothers*, Cap'n. The old ship – why, she's runnin' slick as grease, an' the work's done, and . . ."

"Stop!" said Flint sharply, and forty men flinched as he raised his hand, but they relaxed when he smiled and continued: "The work is done when *I* say that it is done."

"Aye-aye, Cap'n, that it is, sir," said Morton, attempting to bend his squat body into a bow. But still he pressed on, insisting with desperate politeness that the two Dutchmen must sign articles and become brothers according to tradition.

Watching from the fo'c'sle, Selena and Cowdray saw the terror that Flint inspired, and the cruel wit that alternately made men shake with laughter and then with fear as he mocked and resisted their entreaties.

"He's mad," said Selena, "you know that, don't you?"

"Yes," said Cowdray, "I know that very well. *Piscem natare doces* – you're teaching a fish to swim."

"Then why do you stay with him? I'm a prisoner, but you're free."

Cowdray gave a grim laugh. "Free till the hangman catches me, you mean."

"But you can say you were forced."

"Perhaps."

"You're a surgeon – and a fine one. You saved Long John's life!"

"I'm glad of that."

"So why *do* you stay with him?"

Cowdray looked away, then at the crew as they roared at Flint's latest joke.

Flint was prancing about in his laced coat, plumed hat and bright sash: handsome and brilliant with shining eyes and teeth.

"He saved me," said Cowdray, "when I was ready to open my veins."

"How?" said Selena.

"In Charlestown, where we're going; I was fallen very low. I was pox-doctor and abortionist to the town."

Another roar of laughter from the crew. Cowdray looked miserable, and hesitated, and finally took the risk, and told the rest of his story, for all men wish sympathy from a beautiful woman.

"Selena, I'm a simple man. I know surgery, anatomy, and

craft. I learned by doing and not from books. And when I began developing theories that the physicians didn't like, I was laughed out of my post, and then from England – even though I was right." He shook his head. "They hated me for being right, and they sneered that I learned Latin to try to be like them. And I still use Latin, even now, which shows what a fool I am!" He smiled weakly, and glanced across at Flint. "But *him* . . . he needed a ship's surgeon. He could find none better, so he took me. And I can never cease to be grateful. For now I am a surgeon again, and a good one, as you say."

"Bring forth the postulants, Mr Morton!" cried Flint, conceding at last. "Bring forth the Book of Articles! Bring forth the black flag . . . and bring forth the fiddler and the rum!"

"AYYYYYE!" they roared.

Having plenty of time, and only two brothers to induct into the fellowship, Flint's crew, led by Allardyce and Morton, made a holiday of the affair and wallowed in the full ceremonial. Van Oosterhout and Wouters were stripped, blindfolded and subjected to a variety of horseplay, and to duckings in a big tub brought up from the hold for the purpose. But finally Allardyce called for silence and off-hats, and the two men, dripping wet and gleaming white in their nakedness, were brought before Flint, and before the Book of Articles which had been laid reverently on a table spread with the black flag.

Van Oosterhout was made to read the articles aloud, then the two Dutchmen signed their names beneath all the others – mainly crosses and similar scrawl – already in the book.

Afterwards, when Van Oosterhout was dressed, and before he could take too much of the rum now going round – and for which he definitely had the taste – Flint drew his first officer aside for another private conversation in his cabin.

"There's much for you to learn, Mr Mate," said Flint.

"Aye-aye, sir," said Van Oosterhout, grinning and red-faced.

The grinning stopped when Flint told the story of his island, explaining what had happened there, and what had been left behind, and how he intended to get it back . . . and just how large Van Oosterhout's share would be. A story which captured Van Oosterhout's profoundest and uttermost attention.

Naturally, the version of the story which Flint presented was one which reflected to John Silver's utter discredit, depicting him as a master of spite, greed, and treachery. And as always with Flint, it was amazing how few lies he needed to tell in order to give the exact opposite of the truth.

Finally he produced a map: *the* map, the map of the island. The only map in existence which showed everything of the island, including its true size, the extent of its surrounding archipelago, the location of the treasure . . . and the latitude and longitude.

"Ah!" said Van Oosterhout. "Was it you found the longitude?"

"Yes," said Flint. "An earlier map existed, but the latitude and longitude here –" he tapped a finger on his map "– were found by myself."

"I congratulate you, Captain," said Van Oosterhout.

"Thank you, Mr Mate, but I direct your attention to the archipelago, which I was the first to survey and to chart properly, and the details of which are known only to me."

"Wait, Captain," said Van Oosterhout, befuddled by drink and confused by conflicting emotions. This was the same murderous pirate who'd killed his friends and burned his ship, yet now he was treating him as an equal – even a favourite – and offering a share in a fortune. "Why do you show me these things? It is great confidence in me . . . why do you do this?"

Flint gazed at Van Oosterhout's solemn, gleaming face. The temptation to laugh sprang urgently within him and was instantly suppressed. Instead of laughing, just for once, Flint told the truth . . . or half of it, at least.

"The reason I confide in you, Mr Van Oosterhout, is because I stand in vital need of your skills. Thus I must have another navigating officer aboard, in case of any accident to myself."

Van Oosterhout nodded and Flint smiled, for he'd not mentioned the other reason for his trusting the Dutchman, which was Mr Van Oosterhout's sure and certain fate, the moment he was no longer needed. Meanwhile . . .

"Look *here* at the archipelago," said Flint. "Do you see? There is something here that will be of utmost use to us . . ."

Van Oosterhout looked, and listened carefully, and nodded in approval, and even made constructive suggestions of his own. In the days that followed, Flint found him to be an excellent officer, obedient, dutiful and competent. Soon all matters of navigation were delegated to the Dutchman, leaving Flint with two nasty festering splinters to trouble him.

First, Flint's vanity was wounded that any man should be his master as a navigator; second, he was deeply jealous when Van Oosterhout, like Cowdray, found natural companionship with Selena. This was a new emotion for Joe Flint; being incapable of physical love, he'd always been immune to jealousy. But Selena fascinated him, and was beginning to arouse the sort of passions any normal man felt for a woman. And this fierce resentment at Selena's friendships with other men was made all the worse because Flint could not admit his feelings to himself.

And there was more. Something heavy and dark that sat upon Flint's soul. These three – Selena, Cowdray and Van Oosterhout – whom Flint could not harm or remove, now constituted a faction that would constrain his behaviour. It was like the days when he'd sailed with Silver and was constantly looking over his shoulder to see if he approved . . . tainting his enjoyment of practices such as playing with prisoners. Flint sighed. The plank would not be appearing again for a while, and just when he'd discovered its possibilities!

By day, Flint bore these burdens manfully: there was much to do in driving the ship hard, watching constantly for another prize on the horizon – not to mention avoiding the ships of the various navies that infested these waters. These activities kept Flint merry all day, and *Walrus*'s people enjoyed a pleasant voyage to Savannah. But by night Flint groaned for the loss of the freedom he'd enjoyed on his island. At night, in his dreams, that part of the human mind which is animal, primeval and beyond conscious control, punished Joe Flint with memories of the most dreadful time in his entire life. The time when he had enjoyed no freedom at all, only bitter constraint . . . His childhood.

Chapter 8

Twelve-year-old Joseph Flint stood trembling as his father got up from his prayers. The Reverend Mordecai Flint rose like a great, black snake, turning to face the wife and son who had so inexcusably interrupted his devotions. Although no speck of dust was suffered to exist within the chapel, he brushed his knees with a clean white handkerchief, which was then painstakingly folded before being returned to his pocket. When this was done he positioned himself, back to the altar, looming over them in his pious black coat, ominously stroking the clerical bands at his neck.

The reverend was a man of tremendous intellect; dominant, charismatic and vastly learned in Holy Scripture. Years of profound study and introspection had resulted in an unshakeable conviction that he was damned for uncleanliness of spirit, and he had therefore made it his life's work to save those less wicked than himself – in particular, those he loved – in the

68

hope they might yet be shriven by repentance. It was his tragedy – and still more that of those around him – that not a drop of love did they see, only an ocean of chastisement and castigation. Thus Joseph Flint flinched as his father stared at him, and clutched at his mother's hand for comfort.

"Wretches!" said the reverend. "'Thou art weighed in the balances, and art found wanting.'" He cocked his head expectantly . . .

"Daniel, five: twenty-seven," said Joseph and his mother in unison. The reverend nodded and turned his eyes on his wife.

"So," he said, "you come again to me, even into God's house, with the matter that I have declared closed. I see it in your eyes! 'All is vanity and vexation of spirit!'"

"Ecclesiastes, one: fourteen," said Joseph's mother. Then: *"Mr Flint!"* she cried, that being the constant manner of her address to him, for he was not ordained but self-appointed, and well he knew it. She took a step forward, shaking off Joseph's hand. "Mr Flint," she said, and the colour drained from her face and her eyes began to blink. She screamed in his face, her body shaking with rage, *"You took our Joseph to the Turk!"* She seized Joseph's shoulder and thrust him forward. "See!" she cried. "Our boy stands before you even now, with the poison in his arm!"

Joseph sobbed as the awful weight of their emotions fell upon him. He clutched his bandaged arm and bowed his head, and believed that he was to blame.

"I'm sorry," he said, "I'm so sorry."

But his guilt was nothing compared with his father's. The reverend groaned as pain wrenched the depths of his belly. For he'd broken faith, even if in a noble cause. And worse than that . . . far, far worse . . . he'd been found out!

"Ah!" said Joseph's mother, seeing his reaction. "You hypocrite! You swore on the Bible! You said that you would not do it ... *and you did!*"

And so the parents screeched, and as the child looked on the hideous quarrel grew until words became blows and finally ... Joseph Flint watched as his mother drew the hidden knife. He stood, eyes wide, as she fell upon his father and cut his throat. He looked on as she sat upon the reverend's prostrate body and plunged the knife again and again into his face, paying back thirty years of mental cruelty with thirty seconds of demented revenge.

Chapter 9

One bell of the afternoon watch
2nd October 1752
Aboard Hercules
off Cape Castillo, Niña de Cuba

*S*ince Captain Bentham liked music, the ship's band of musicians was scraping and blowing fiercely even as the bosun's pipes saluted the coming-aboard of Captain Parry of *Sweet Anne*, and Captain Nichols of *Favourite*: these gentlemen, and their first mates, being summoned aboard the flagship for a council of war. The noise was terrific, and powder smoke swirled as the guns of the three ships added their voices to the din.

All was good fellowship and satisfaction, what with Captain Bentham having led his squadron safe and sound from Upper Barbados, making landfall exactly as he'd boasted and with fair winds and a swift passage besides.

Of the greasy mob that filled *Hercules*'s maindeck, only Brendan O'Byrne was frowning. He frowned because he hadn't the guile to hide his feelings, and he was scrutinising the new arrivals as they clambered over the rail, in their best

71

clothes and their best hats, and into the arms of Cap'n Bentham and his crew, to be welcomed as jolly companions.

Ugh! thought O'Byrne There it was: the *look*. He'd seen it on three faces. Not Cap'n Parry's, God bless him! Not him, for he knew Danny Bentham of old. But his first mate didn't, and Cap'n Nichols didn't, and nor *his* first mate neither. So they were staring at Cap'n Bentham in the way men did who met him for the first time.

So it was a puzzled, questioning look and one that tormented O'Byrne. Worse still, it filleted the backbone out of him, so instead of being fired with manly anger he was cast down and enfeebled.

The fact was that O'Byrne couldn't bear any insult to Cap'n Danny. Not when his feelings for the captain were so intense, and their precise nature — stemming as they did from his *own* nature — were a mystery even to himself. For while O'Byrne didn't normally care for women, any feelings towards men were ruthlessly denied . . . such that Cap'n Danny was a unique door through which desires might emerge that otherwise must be contained.

With a heavy sigh and a shrug, O'Byrne told himself that it was all part of the privilege of sailing under Cap'n Danny — like never mentioning the captain's latest wife once Williamstown was under the horizon.

Fortunately, Cap'n Danny himself was immune to such concerns. He *was* what he *was*, and he was used to it, though he swaggered a bit at first meetings, and took care to deepen his voice.

"Rum!" cried Bentham now. "And lay out the chart!" The crew cheered, and with much good humour kegs of spirits were brought up from below decks. A big empty cask was then up-ended by the landward quarterdeck rail to serve as a table, and as the shipmasters and their leading men gathered around it, all hands pressed forward, as befitted their status as equals under the articles they'd signed.

"So," said Bentham, one finger on the chart and one pointing towards land, three miles to the north. "That there's Isabel Bay, into which the River Ferdinand runs. The bay's a thousand yards wide at the mouth, between Cape Castille and Cape Aragon, with a great anchorage within, and Isabel Island sits between the two capes, like a sausage in a dog's jaws."

"So where's the fort?" said Captain Parry.

"And the dollars!" said Captain Nichols.

"See here —" said Bentham, studying the chart "— to the east of Isabel Island is sandbanks and shoals. The safe channel lies to the west, between the island and Cape Aragon, past the fort, which is down here at the southernmost tip of the island."

Nichols took off his hat and fanned himself against the heat.

"If we take the channel," he said, "we'll be under fire from the fort all the way in. An' it'll be eighteen-pounders at least, and maybe twenty-fours."

"It's twenty-four-pounders," said Bentham, "but we'll go in at sunset with the light in the gunners' eyes, and them having to split their fire between three ships, and ourselves firing back to hide us with smoke."

"Hmm . . ." they said.

"And," said Bentham, "the fort's got emplacements for thirty guns, but there's only a dozen pieces within the walls."

"Aye," said Parry, nodding, "that's often the way of it. No bugger'll pay for the full set! Not King George, King Louis, nor the King o' the Dagoes."

"A dozen twenty-four-pounders?" said Nichols. "That's still enough to sink the three of us, even with the sun in their eyes."

"Not if they're spread round the fort, so as to cover an attack from any side," said Bentham. "There's only five guns facing the channel, and the guns aren't exercised more than once in three months!"

"How d'you know that?" said Nichols.

"Same way as I know that an' more," said Bentham. "The fort's a slaving station – blacks is offloaded there from the middle passage, and paid for from a chest of dollars in the fort's strong room – an' there's never less than twenty thousand dollars in the chest!"

"Ahhh!" they said.

"But how'd you *know*?" said Nichols.

"Ask him –" Bentham winked confidentially at O'Byrne "– he's the boy for secrets!"

O'Byrne stepped forward, cheered by the merry recollection he was about to share.

"We know," he said, "'cos we took a Dago slaver in June. And when we'd done pluckin' 'em, we hung the crew by the ankles and I beat their bollocks with a belaying pin until they told us all they knew."

"*Oh! Oh! Oh!*" cried Danny Bentham, holding his crotch with both hands and staggering bandy-legged as if in agony. That drew a great laugh, for men followed where Bentham led. He had that gift. He cut a fine figure – and was respected for being big and dangerous; especially dangerous, for Bentham could turn nasty over a wrong word or a sour look, and then God help any man within reach of his long arm and his Spanish sword.

So they laughed, Nichols, Parry and the rest, and they

74

nudged one another and were impressed. And when Danny Bentham explained his plan for taking the fort, they cheered from the bottom of their hearts. Across the water, *Sweet Anne*'s, and *Favourite*'s people cheered along with them, for they caught the merry mood even if they didn't know what was afoot.

As the sun set, *Sweet Anne* and *Favourite* formed line astern on *Hercules*, and the three came up the Ferdinand River with the flaming sun to larboard and the guns of the fort booming and thudding ineffectually on their starboard beams. Just as Bentham had predicted, they came through unscathed, and in the great anchorage to the north of Isabel Island they found five slavers that duly lowered their colours, and cringed in fright, and begged only to be left alone.

At dawn the three ships, now double-anchored, hoisted out their longboats. Loaded with armed men, they pulled for the northern end of Isabel Island, each with a ship's captain at the helm: Bentham leading, followed by Parry, followed by Nichols.

"Give a song, you men!" cried Bentham, leading off with the first line:

"Farewell an' adieu to you fair Spanish ladies . . ."

"Farewell an' adieu for 'tis parted we'll be!" they sang.

"For we have our orders to sail home to Eng-er-land . . ."

"And t'will be a sad time till we shall see thee!"

And thus, with a great deal of noise, and much waving of blades and firing off of pistols, the three boats crossed the anchorage to their chosen destination, which was thickly wooded and the only part of their journey that was not under plain sight from the fort at the other end of the island.

In due course, the three longboats emerged from the cover of the trees, and only the oarsmen and helmsmen could be seen as the boats returned to their squadron, passing out of view behind the flagship. Then came more roaring and carousing and the boats emerged, dense-packed again, pulling strongly for the shore. As before, they returned with just oarsmen and helmsmen to take on yet another load of armed men. And so it continued, to and fro.

These activities were studied with interest by a group of gentlemen peering through telescopes on the northern ramparts of the fort. They wore the cocked hats of sea-service officers, and their blue coats and red vests marked them out as men of the Real Armada Española: the Spanish Royal Navy.

Their commander, Capitan de Navio Frederico Alberto Zorita, turned from his telescope to smile at his subordinates.

"And so they spoil a good plan!" he said.

Chapter 10

"*A*ll hands mustered and ready for to march, Mr Gunner!"
"Very good, Mr Joe," said Israel Hands, and did his best to look over the men as Long John would have done.

There were a dozen of them, paraded on the beach, with muskets, water canteens, and big hats constructed of sliced and plaited palm-leaves for protection against the sun. They stood grinning and yarning, some of them chewing tobacco, but they were cheerful and ready, and Israel walked up and down the line, making sure that each one had a good pair of shoes, and water in his canteen rather than rum, and that no lubber had primed his firelock without orders.

"You! And you!" cried Israel Hands, picking two of the nimblest. "You're the advance guard, which shall march ahead as lookouts." Then he picked the two biggest: "You two shall follow on behind, a-walloping and a-belting of them as won't keep up!" The men laughed.

"And the rest shall proceed in line astern of myself and

77

Mr Joe, and shall attend to my signals –" He put a bosun's call to his lips and blew a single sharp note. "Well?" he said.

"Forward!" they cried.

"And this?" he said, blowing a sharp double-note.

"'Vast heaving!" cried some.

"Belay!" cried others.

"Stop!" said Israel Hands. "That'n means *stop*!"

"Stop!" they said, nodding.

"And this?" A long trembling call.

"Enemy in sight!" they roared.

There were a few more simple signals: easily understood, and a credit to Israel Hands's capacity to innovate, since never before had he led men through a forest.

"Stand by!" cried Israel Hands.

"Huzzah!" cried the men.

"Forward!" cried Israel Hands.

In single file, they set off up the beach towards the palms, leaving the tented encampment almost empty. "Camp Silver" they were calling it now. A few men were still working on the wreck of *Lion*, while most of the others had already left – on Long John's orders – on expeditions led by Black Dog and Sarney Sawyer.

There was also a small guard of ten men left to defend the camp with a quartet of four-pounders charged with canister and mounted in their carriages on firing platforms of ships' timbers, the better to load and train in case of attack. These men were also responsible for Long John's parrot, who'd never go willingly into a boat – even with him – and awaited its master's return here, with its own perch and a supply of food and drink, and a bit of shade rigged over it.

The bird squawked at Israel Hands as he scrunched past, ankle deep in sand, bobbing its head in greeting.

"Ahoy there!" it cried, and Israel Hands grinned, knowing himself favoured, and he plodded on.

He smiled again as he looked at Mr Joe marching ahead, a heavy Jamaican cane-cutlass in his belt, ready to clear a path if need be. The lad was a slim, wiry black who'd grown up with such a quick temper that he failed to see the joke when an overseer, finding Joe bent over to cut cane, had merrily cracked his arse with a whip. Thus Joe replied with a cutlass slash that removed a diagonal quarter of the overseer's head, plus all hope of promotion for Joe in his career as a plantation slave, obliging him to seek advancement elsewhere.

Israel Hands grinned at the thought. Joe was quick and intelligent, and under Hands's instruction he was speedily learning his letters and his numbers, to the point that he was now rated gunner's mate, and addressed as *Mr* Joe by all hands, even Long John himself.

Joe had his little faults, of course. He could not stand to be teased, and he was dreadfully afraid of the dark, since as a child he'd been told by his mother that, if he didn't behave, at midnight the Jumba-Jumba man would come in his big black hat and fetch Joe away in a sack. Even at nineteen years of age, Joe was still looking out for him, but Israel Hands thought no worse of the lad for that, since all sailormen believed such things: Mr Hands himself – when alone – would never look over the side at night for fear of seeing Davy Jones, the hideous fiend that lay in wait for the souls of drowned men.

A day's marching, with stops for meals and the heat of noon, had taken Israel Hands's team clear of the palms and sweltering jungle that lined the island's southern shores. Steering by a small brass compass, they had moved steadily north into a terrain of sandy hills interspersed with small, open clearings surrounded by broadleaf trees: mainly live-oaks, but with an increasing number of pines, and all with dense foliage at their bases. With night falling, they set about making camp – and made their first discovery.

"Look, Mr Hands," said Joe. "You see them stumps there?"

"Aye, lad," said Israel Hands. The spot they'd chosen was a clearing that the forest was slowly reclaiming. About a dozen big trees, all pines, had been felled many years ago, leaving stumps which were now so heavily overgrown with moss and fungus, and so surrounded by undergrowth and young trees, that it was hard to spot them. But they were there if you looked; proof that men had been this way before.

"Looks like this island ain't so secret as some would believe!" said Israel Hands.

"Aye, Mr Hands," said Joe, peering into the darkness between the standing trees. "Now we get back with the others, eh? And we make the fire?"

"Aye," said Israel Hands, smiling, for the others were only a few steps away.

That night Joe had the horrors and no mistake. He woke constantly. He heard noises in the night. He got up and paced about, and repeatedly told the sentries to keep a sharp lookout.

"Yes, Mr Joe! No, Mr Joe!" they said, levelling their muskets at nothing, just to keep him quiet.

They all thought him a bloody fool, until early next morning when the expedition made its second discovery. As the sun came up, those on guard duty saw a figure peering at them from behind a tree: looking, but afraid to come forward.

"There he is, Mr Hands!" said one of the sentries. "It's a white man, not a savage. Miserable-looking sod, though." He cocked his musket. "Shall I take a pop?"

"No!" said Israel Hands, as the camp stirred and men gathered around him. "I think I know who that is!" He stepped forward and called out:

"Ahoy there! Come alongside! We're all friends here. Friends and jolly companions."

There was a stir of surprise as the bedraggled figure left the cover of his tree, and – with utmost nervousness – crept forward, hunched over in humble supplication, with fearful eyes staring out of a simple, pleasant face. He was bareheaded, bare-chested and barefoot, deeply sunburnt with a sprouting beard and hair like broken straw. All that he had in the world was a pair of breeches, an old belt, and a sailor's knife in a sheath. But the thing that drew gasps of surprise was the creature holding his hand like a child and scampering along beside him: a large and most beautiful monkey.

The ape was handsomely marked, with thick fur – mostly dark brown, apart from its creamy breast, arms and face – and a shock of black, upstanding hair on top of its head. It had the most appealing and intelligent face and came forward entirely without fear.

When the man thought he was close enough, he stopped, and began to speak in a self-pitying whine.

"I'm Ben Gunn, I am," he said, shaking off the monkey and clapping his hands together as if in prayer. "Poor Ben Gunn, what's lived alone for weeks with not a bite of Christian food, nor what's not spoke to a Christian soul."

"Step up, Ben Gunn!" said Israel Hands. "You know me, don't you?"

"That I do, Mr Hands," said Ben Gunn. "An' you knows

me, for I'm Ben Gunn what was blown clear o' the old *Walrus* in the battle, and what clung to a shattered timber and what floated ashore and what's lived on fruits and roots these past weeks and never a taste of pork nor cheese . . . especially cheese."

Ben Gunn was duly fed and watered, and the monkey became an instant favourite for its friendliness and cleverness. Jumping from man to man, it took the bits of fruit they offered, and looked its benefactors in the eye with the most charming expression.

"Bugger's almost human!"

"Ain't he a jolly little bleeder!"

"Look at the little face on him – he's laughing!"

"Chk-chk-chk!" said the monkey, climbing into Mr Joe's arms and reaching its small, inquisitive hand towards one of the pistols hooked to his belt.

"Belay!" said Joe, laughing. "Don't touch that, child, else you be blowin' me bollocks off me!" And the men laughed.

But always the creature ran back to Ben Gunn.

"Followed me, he did," said Ben Gunn, stroking its head. "There's a whole tribe of 'em in the trees, up that way –" he pointed vaguely into the forest. "Don't reckon they ain't never seen men before, and they's tame as pussy-cats . . . ain't you, matey?"

"Chk-chk-chk!" said the monkey.

The rest of Israel Hands's expedition was uneventful, except that it took nearly five days to reach the far north of the island and return to Camp Silver in the southern anchorage, not the two days they'd expected. Sarney Sawyer and Black Dog told the same tale on their return – the island was at least twice the size they'd supposed it to be, based on what Flint had told them.

There was just one further discovery to be made, which awaited Israel Hands on his return.

"Look, Mr Gunner," said one of those who'd been guarding the camp. He was holding out the remains of a small, broken egg. "Long John's parrot laid it. It's a *she*!"

"Well bugger me tight!" said Israel Hands. He looked at the big green bird, rocking on its perch nearby. "That'll tickle Long John when he gets back!" Hands halfway reached out to stroke the bird, but then recalled Black Dog's missing fingers and thought better of it.

"Bugger me tight!" said the parrot.

Silver's voyage round the island, taking bearings and soundings, took a week. The morning after the jolly-boat had finally grounded in the shallows of the southern anchorage, he called a council of his leading men in his tent – the biggest in the camp – where there was a table and some chairs saved out of *Lion*.

First on the agenda was the matter of Ben Gunn. With his monkey trailing along behind him, Gunn was brought before them. He stood outside the big tent, in the cool of the early morning, awaiting their judgement.

"Well, Ben Gunn," said Silver, "it appears you've been Flint's man. So, whose man are you now?"

Ben Gunn blinked in fright. He shuffled his bare feet in the sand, and looked up at the tall figure of John Silver in his blue coat. He marvelled at the sight of Captain Flint's parrot on Silver's shoulder, nuzzling his ear as once it had Flint's. Ben Gunn was further puzzled by the presence of Mr Billy Bones, standing alongside Israel Hands, Black Dog and Sarney Sawyer. The latter three, he knew to be Silver's men . . . But Billy Bones was Flint's to death and beyond . . . or so Ben Gunn believed.

"Mr Gunn's been living wild," said Israel Hands. "He's

more than half witless and he was frightened to come near us. He was starving when we found him, weren't you, Ben Gunn?"

"Aye," said Ben Gunn. "Mr Hands gave me some cheese!" He smiled. "He likes cheese, does poor Ben Gunn!" The smile died. "An' he don't like bein' hungry, an' he don't like bein' lonely, an' he stands ready now to sign articles and do his duty . . . if only he might have permission to come aboard." And with that he raised a dirty finger to his dirty brow, and held it there, mouth open, awaiting Silver's decision.

"Huh!" said Silver. "Come aboard, Ben Gunn! There's work to do, and a need for hands to do it. You shall sign articles, and be judged afresh." He pointed to a gang of men standing ready with their tools for the day's work clearing the final remains of *Lion*. "You join them there. At the double now!"

"Aye-aye, sir!" said Ben Gunn joyfully, and he skipped off at great speed before Silver should change his mind.

"Poor sod!" said Sarney Sawyer.

"He were a good man once, Mr Bosun," said Israel Hands. "He were a prime seaman, till he got flogged and it turned his mind."

"Flint's work?" said Sawyer.

"No," said Billy Bones stoutly, "Cap'n Springer's! That no-seaman swab as ran the *Elizabeth* aground. Ben Gunn was at the helm, and Springer flogged him for it, though it were Springer's fault, as all hands knew!"

"Aye," said Black Dog and Israel Hands.

"Flint warned him!" said Billy Bones. "Flint wanted a boat ahead taking soundings, but Springer wouldn't have it. Flint had the right of it all the while."

"Aye!" said the others, for it was true.

"Flint's a seaman and no mistake!" said Black Dog admiringly.

"Aye!" they said, nodding in united agreement.

"Split my sides!" cried Silver, who'd been listening in growing amazement and anger. "It sickens my heart to sail with you!" he glared at them. "Have you lubbers forgot what Flint did to Springer and the rest! And have you forgot who'll be back here in a month or two, a-cuttin of our precious throats if we don't look sharp!"

"Oh . . ." said Israel Hands and Black Dog, while Billy Bones blushed and studied his boots.

"Now batten your blasted hatches till you're spoke to," said Silver. "And come along o' me!"

He led the way to his tent and sat down, fuming, and daring any man to speak before he was allowed.

"Put your blasted chart there, Mr Bones," he said, "and find something to hold the bugger down!"

Billy Bones produced a big, rolled chart, which he laid flat on the table – and for want of anything better, pinned it down with his pistols.

"Now, see here," said Silver, as they all leaned over the map, "this is Mr Bones's map, drawn of its shores and with all included as you swabs has learned from marching up and down of it . . ." He waited till they'd had a good look, then produced another sheet, this time showing the planned location of four forts.

"And now here's my own plans, drawn by myself," he said, and calmed as he warmed to his subject. "What do you lubbers know of entrenchments and suchlike . . . ?"

Hours later, Sarney Sawyer and Israel Hands, sent about their duties, had a brief word while spades, picks and axes were handed out to their men.

"Was Long John ever a soldier?" said Sawyer.

"Not him!" said Hands. "Begotten in the galley and born in a boat."

"So where'd he get all that learning about forts?"

"Along o' Cap'n England. He were the one for forts, was England."

"And Long John served under him?"

"Aye, in the days when John had ten toes."

What Israel Hands didn't say was that England had a reputation for cracking forts. He cracked them like walnuts. But he'd no reputation for *building* them. Israel Hands shrugged. Perhaps it was the same thing in reverse. He hoped so, because forts were desperately dangerous things, especially for a sailorman.

Chapter 11

*C*apitan Zorita looked at the two *tenientes* and five young *guardia marinas* who were under his command in the task of stiffening the defences of Niña de Cuba against the coming world war. Zorita pointed at the longboats and their bustling crews, and he shook his head at the puzzled faces of his subordinates.

"Do you not see through it?" he said. "It's an old trick of the English pirates – Morgan and England used it on many occasions." There was a silence and all present tried to avoid his eye.

"So!" said Zorita, and shrugged. "Well, gentlemen, you must listen carefully, for the object of these . . . *activities*," he looked at the boats, "is to make us think that a major force has been landed for an assault upon the northern walls of the fort, compelling us to move our guns up here, leaving the other walls undefended."

"*Oh?*" they said, for they'd been duly deceived and would have done as he said.

"But," said Zorita, "they've overdone it. Let's say each of those boats holds thirty men, besides the crews. That's ninety per trip, yes?"

"Yes, Capitan!"

"And this is their fourth trip, making three hundred and sixty men landed."

"Yes, Capitan!"

"Which is a great number of men to land from ships of their modest size."

"Yes, Capitan!"

"But what they're actually doing is rowing ashore with the men sitting upright, and rowing back with them hidden in the bottom of the boats."

"Ahhhhhh!"

"And if they keep on doing it, then I'll be *certain* it's a ruse, for they'll be pretending to land more men than they could possibly have on board."

That night there was a great lighting of campfires and making of noise at the north end of the island, where those ashore – under Cap'n Bentham's orders – gave the fort to believe that a large storming party was bedding down for the night, ready for an assault next day. Meanwhile the same boats that had been busy all day crept quietly down the eastern side of Isabel island with muffled oars, making their way slowly across the shoals and sandbanks to land a large force of men on the beach facing the fort across a few hundred yards of still water.

Neither was it a quiet night in the fort, where Capitan Zorita ensured that guns were indeed moved and prepared, and the ready-use lockers filled with cartridges and shot, and the crews made sure of their duties.

At dawn, Bentham's northern shore party opened fire on

the fort with a six-pound gun, brought ashore for the purpose and emplaced on planking so the trucks of its sea-carriage shouldn't bog down in the soft ground.

Bang! went the gun, and its cannonball screamed through the air and . . . crunch! It buried itself harmlessly in the twenty-foot thickness of brick-faced earth ramparts that formed the outer defence of the fort's inner stone walls. It did no harm, and wasn't meant to. The gun was burning powder only to keep the fort's garrison focused on the northern wall. In that case, the six-pounder crew might have taken early warning from the fact that the fort didn't bother to reply to the insult . . .

Down at the southern tip of the island, Danny Bentham – followed as ever by Mr O'Byrne – waved a cutlass over his head, called for three cheers, and led the rush to the boats, which were swiftly launched and oars manned, and filled in deadly earnest with armed men – over two hundred of them – equipped with scaling ladders, ropes and grappling hooks.

"Now, my boys," cried Bentham, "pull your hearts out! Break your backs! It's Spanish dollars for all hands, and whores aplenty!"

Clank! Clank! Clank! The boats drove forward, crammed with yelling, cheering men, aiming for the south-east walls of the fort, which by Cap'n Bentham's matchless cunning would have empty emplacements, blind of guns.

Unfortunately they weren't the only boats setting forth with deadly intent, and four gunboats pulled clear of the small jetty that Bentham should have noticed as he came up Ferdinand channel. Each was nearly twice the length of a longboat, driven by fifteen pairs of oars and commanded by a guardia marina – a midshipman. And each mounted a twenty-four-pounder in the bow: a tremendous armament for so small a craft, and one that was capable of swift movement, to fire from any quarter, irrespective of wind and weather.

"Pull!" cried the guardia marinas, leaping with boys' excitement as the graceful oars beat and swayed, sending the gunboats forward like the triremes of Athens. Capitan Zorita watched from the walls of the fort. He nodded. He knew now that he'd guessed correctly, for his lookouts had heard the boats in the night, even with muffled oars. The pirates were making their real attack on the south-east. The demonstration before the northern walls was a sham . . . one which served Zorita well, since by placing so many men ashore the pirates would have left their ships half-manned, firmly anchored, and utterly vulnerable to what was bearing down upon them as fast as Zorita's oarsmen could pull.

"With me! With me!" cried Bentham as he leapt over the bow of his boat, splashing knee deep into tepid, flat water and charging up the beach towards the walls of the fort and the V-bottomed dry-ditch that encircled it. There came a huge cheer and a roar from those behind him, and Bentham's heart soared in delight at his own cleverness, for not a gun was in action in the walls ahead, and not a single snout of a firing piece was visible in the embrasures that faced him.

A rumble and battering of shoe leather, and screeches and cries from all hands brought the pirates to the brink of the ditch, and still no gunfire. Bentham was yelling at the men, shoving half a dozen of them into the ditch to form a human bridge, and leading the way over, boot heels grinding into arms and shoulders, standing on the narrow walkway under the wall, and unwinding the line and grapnel from his waist, and beginning to swing it, O'Byrne beside him, ugly face yelling in delight, and more and more men and ladders raising and figures scrambling up and over the wall . . .

And then the wrath of God beat down upon Bentham's men. The sound alone was enough to strike men bleeding and broken. The orange flame seared and sizzled. It scorched and burned and turned living bodies into blackened, red-glowing rags of meat.

An unseen heavy gun had fired from the inner angle of one of the fort's bastions, from an emplacement designed for just such a moment, and which enabled the gun to fire horizontally across the face of the wall. Capitan Zorita had prepared most carefully and made best use of the guns that he had. Thus the load was double canister: forty-eight pounds of musket balls, sewn up in canvas bags: some eight hundred projectiles blasted forth in a hideous cloud by gunners who instantly served their smoking gun, ramming home a second charge, and running out and firing again.

"Fire!" cried the senior guardia marina, and four heavy guns thundered and slid back up the ingenious slides designed to absorb their recoil. Even so the gunboats heaved backwards, but the oarsmen took the way off them and lined up the boats again, so their guns bore directly into the stern windows of the chosen ship: *Favourite* was its name, picked out in yellow paint just over the rudder.

The range was too close for a miss and the gunboats were placed so that they could fire into *Favourite* from a position where none of her guns, nor those of her consorts, could retaliate. That was why *Favourite* had been chosen. Like everything else in the Spanish attack, it was logical, skilful and effective.

"In your own time, now . . . fire at will!" cried the senior guardia marina, but he needn't have bothered. The gunners were fighting mad, delighted to punish a despicable enemy, and cheering at every ball they sent tearing from end to end of the damned-to-hell pirate ship with its black flag and its crew of heathen savages come to burn churches, rape maidens and to piss upon the holy banner of Spain.

Bentham was lucky. So was O'Byrne. So was Parry. By the caprice of war, they were untouched. Captain Nichols was not lucky. He was among the one hundred and sixty-three left dead or wounded. Or perhaps he *was* lucky, since he was killed outright, unlike the man next to him: still alive and sat stupefied with the side of his skull blown away and mashed brains running down his neck.

Captain Danny led the rout. He ran. All those who could came after him, to the total of twenty-eight fit men. They managed to launch a boat, and pulled away, closing their hearts to their shipmates that slithered after them on shattered limbs, begging not to be left behind. They didn't need to close their ears, for they were all deaf for days afterwards, thanks to the concussion of the single gun that had ruined their attack with just a few rounds fired at point-blank range into a packed and helpless target.

Hercules and *Sweet Anne* likewise cut their cables, abandoning *Favourite* to the enemy. And they too were lucky, for there was just enough wind in the anchorage for steerage way, and just enough hands aboard to man the guns. But even so they were comprehensively shamed, for once the gunboats had smashed *Favourite* into a wreck, and seen her heel over till her yards touched bottom in the shallow bay, they went after the pirates like hungry sharks, seeking to get under their sterns where no enemy gun could return fire, and the pirates all the while manoeuvring crabwise, constantly attempting and failing to deliver a broadside of grape into their agile enemies.

Only at the mouth of Isabel Bay, where the fresh wind gave advantage to the ships, did the gunboats back oars, but they had the satisfaction of one enemy sunk, dozens of prisoners taken for the hangman, and a goodly tonnage of shot sent thumping into the two ships that they'd driven off for the honour of His Catholic Majesty King Ferdinand VI.

Then, as the oarsmen headed for home with the guardia marinas standing at their tillers, heads held high, perhaps they were careless, perhaps they dwelt too much on the hero's welcome awaiting them ashore, else they should have seen the longboat creeping out from behind Isabel Island, and pulling desperately after the pirate ships. As soon as they were sure the gunboats weren't coming after them, this bedraggled crew raised a shirt on an oar and waved it to attract the attention of uncaring shipmates who were forging out to sea under all plain sail.

"Bastards!" said Bentham. "Can't they see us?"

"Swabs!" said O'Byrne. "Wouldn't trust a mother's son of 'em!"

"The sods are going to leave us!"

But they didn't, and Bentham and the rest were saved. They were saved by that last, pitiful companion of the desperate, the sentiment that remained in Pandora's box when all the world's evils escaped. For when those aboard *Hercules* saw the longboat, they found that they still cherished *hope*: the beloved hope that the storming party might have come away from the fort laden with Spanish dollars.

So *Hercules* backed her topsail, hove to, and took the long-boat aboard. Then all hands peered mightily into the bottom of her for any sign of treasure chests.

They found no treasure, only their captain and twenty-eight desperately shaken men, most of whom hadn't even the strength to go down to the spirit room to get drunk. They just called for rum and sat about looking dismal, some sobbing with self-pity, when their mates asked what had happened.

Only O'Byrne was anything like himself. He went round cussing and blinding, and punching the heads of all those he considered to have been safe aboard while better men died. But even that was only for show. They could tell. So it was a dangerous time for Danny Bentham and there was much muttering in corners as *Hercules* rolled onwards and left Niña de Cuba behind.

Facing mutiny, a more honest captain than Bentham would have told the truth and trusted his men, while a more sinister captain would have terrified them. But Bentham was only his modest self, and aside from a talent for skewering men with a rapier, his only real gift was to cut a dash. So he put on some good clothes, and told all hands what he was going to do next, by heaven, and he uttered great lies and swore fat promises. And what with O'Byrne and Parry and the other survivors wanting never to hear of Isabel Island again . . . he got away with it.

So, no black spots were made nor passed into Cap'n Danny's hands. But he knew that he was humiliated, and that one more failure would see him rising to the yardarm, his hands tied behind him.

Danny Bentham needed a success. He needed one badly.

Chapter 12

10 a.m., 12th November 1752
Half Moon Bastion, Bay Street
Charlestown, South Carolina

Captain Flint was surprised. He was surprised because Mr Meshod Pimenta had finally said something surprising.

So far this morning, Joe Flint, Charley Neal and Selena had toured – in succession – the Ashley Bastion, The Pallisades, Granville's Bastion, a bastion whose name Flint had forgotten, and had gazed upon a twelve-foot moat. All the while, Pimenta had refused to discuss business, lecturing instead on the enormous, concrete-faced earthworks and the great numbers of guns that made the walled city of Charlestown one of the most powerful fortifications in the entire British colonies. When he was not doing that, he was praising the city for its energy and resourcefulness in recovering from the hurricane, which – he said – had thrown it flat on its back in September.

Charley Neal had arranged the meeting and Flint was in his shore-going rig: plain hat and coat and no weapons – at least none visible. He'd insisted on having Selena in tow, dressed in some plain but respectable women's clothes he'd found for her, because he was jealous of Van Oosterhout and Cowdray and wouldn't leave her on the ship with them. He'd even acquired a nice respectable name for the occasion; in Charlestown he was Captain *Garland*, that being Uncle Peter's name, who'd first taken him to sea, and his mother's maiden name besides. Pimenta, though, knew exactly who he was.

To make matters worse, it was a horrible day: grey, cold, drizzling with rain, and the waters of the Cooper River flowing dark and dismal. Flint, unused to tolerating fools, was heavy with dull rage with Pimenta's endless prattle about the great world war that was coming, the war which according to him would be the conclusion of all previous colonial wars· King George's War, Queen Anne's War, and the rest.

Pimenta said this would be the final fight for the North American continent. He said the Catholic French would march down from Montreal with beating drums. He said the Catholic Spaniards would march up from Florida with banners flying. He said the heathen Indians would fall upon the loser with scalping knives.

Flint was bored. War between various combinations of Britain, France and Spain was the natural condition of the world he knew. He could imagine no other state of affairs. All he cared about was raising a loan so he could hire ships and men to re-take his island. But Pimenta spoke only of war ... until Neal and Selena hung back to look at one of the big rampart guns, which *she* then proceeded to explain to *him,* Selena now being knowledgeable about such things where he was not, to his considerable amusement and admiration.

Then Pimenta surprised Flint.

The short, fat young man, in his expensive, untidy clothes, stuck a finger under his hat, ran it through his curly black hair, scratched his head, and stopped talking. He stared at Selena, and sidled up to Flint, coming far closer than Flint liked. He took Flint's arm and whispered:

"Nice little nigger-bitch you got there. Have you thought of selling?"

"Nigger?" said Flint. "Where?" He saw only Selena.

"Her!" said Pimenta. "How much . . . to a friend?"

"*Selena?*" said Flint. "*Sell* Selena? As a *slave?*" At that moment Meshod Pimenta's life hung on a thread, for Flint was struck by a lightning bolt of emotion at this gross insult to the woman that he . . . the woman that he . . . that he . . . that he . . .

Pimenta survived only through Flint's inability to recognise, to define and to accept.

"Oooof!" said Pimenta, stepping back with hand to mouth. Flint was positively fizzing with anger, like a bomb with a lit fuse. In such a mood there were few men alive who could look Flint in the eye without being paralysed by terror, and Pimenta felt his legs quivering beneath him.

Fortunately for him, Neal had been listening. Charley Neal was sharper than Flint knew. He'd only been brought along from Savannah because Flint needed a bridge to the money-men, but Neal saved Flint's plans and his neck by darting forward, grabbing Flint's arm and linking it with Selena's. He then hustled them away together and took Pimenta aside for a lecture of his own.

In the unthinking instant, Flint threw his arms around Selena, turned his back on Pimenta, and trembled as he stroked her cheek, ignoring the amazement of those citizens of Charlestown who beheld a white man embracing a black woman. But their amazement was nothing beside Selena's, for she'd seen Pimenta's leering face and guessed what he wanted, and realised that Flint was *protecting* her. He who'd only ever shown a covetous lust that he couldn't even consummate! Now he was holding her with fierce passion, and physically placing himself between her and danger.

Flint was unusually quiet after that. He kept looking at Selena, and finding excuses to touch her, which was unwelcome in the extreme to Selena for fear of where this might lead. But she'd grown fast and far when it came to understanding Joe Flint – even exercising a degree of control over him – so while she gave no sign of favour at his attentions, she didn't flinch or pull away but waited to see what opportunities might present from this new behaviour.

Flint turned nasty again when they went to board the launch. Alan Morton, Flint's quartermaster, who was in charge of the boat, stood forward with his hat in his hands, ducking and bobbing and grovelling.

"Cap'n, sir," he said, "one o' the hands has run."

"*Run?*" said Flint. "What d'you mean, *run?*"

"Hopped ship, Cap'n, sir. Deserted, sir."

Flint looked into the boat. There should have been four hands sitting with oars vertical, awaiting orders. There were only three. And they were avoiding his eye.

"Who knows about this?" said Flint.

"It were Tommy Farrell, Cap'n, sir," said Morton. "Had his trug in the boat, Cap'n, sir, and legged it."

Flint scowled. He reached out and took Morton by the scruff of his shirt.

"Joe!" said Neal. "Don't. It'll draw attention."

"Will it, though?" said Flint, and squeezed Morton's throat. "Tommy Farrell, eh? What if he blabs?"

"Dammit, Joe," said Neal, "do you think half Charlestown don't know who you are? It don't make no difference what Farrell says!"

"Farrell?" said Flint, and let go of Morton's throat. "Well, he's no great loss! Farrell's one of the ship's 'white mice', that none of the rest will have at their mess-table." He smiled slowly at Morton, who dared to sigh with relief. "But it's *stopped grog* for you, my lad, till you learn to keep order among the hands." Morton shed tears, Flint boarded the boat, and Farrell was forgotten.

Later, as the launch pulled out to *Walrus* where she lay at anchor among the forest of masts in Charlestown harbour, Neal – so far as he dared – read the rule book to Flint concerning Meshod Pimenta. He was a brave man to do so, for Flint, Selena and he were huddled in the sternsheets under a tarpaulin at the time, and they were damp and miserable with cold.

"He's the biggest merchant in Charlestown, Joe," said Neal.

"He's a tight-fisted Hebrew," said Flint.

"And I'm a papist! *Cormac O'Neal,* I was christened."

"'Tain't the same. He's too mean to talk business!"

"Joe," said Neal, greatly daring, "in the first place it ain't easy to find men that wants to deal with you . . ." Flint's eyes blinked and Neal gulped in fright. "You've got a reputation, Joe, so you've got to offer a sweetener. Pimenta wouldn't talk business 'cos *you* wouldn't do what I said. You wouldn't tell him about the island."

"Nor will I!" said Flint, and fell silent. Charley Neal groaned in despair for the unravelling of all his diligent diplomacy.

"Charley," said Selena, "what about Bentham? In Savannah you said we might see him here."

"Danny boy?" said Neal. "Danny Bentham?" He sat up in the launch, peered among the dark hulls and spider-web rigging of the dozens of ships moored in the harbour. Neal had a sharp eye for ships, keen as a seaman's.

"There –" he said, pointing over the cold water "– the snow *Hercules*: three hundred tons, bearing ten six-pounders, two brass nines, and about thirty men. That's Danny's flag-ship. And alongside of it, there's his second vessel, the sloop *Sweet Anne*: Captain Lewis Parry, a hundred and eighty tons, bearing eight six-pounders, six four-pounders, and about twenty men."

"*Snow?*" said Selena. "Like in winter, in the north? How's that different from a sloop?" She was fast learning the arcane naming of ships, but this was a new one.

"Well, a sloop, you know," said Flint, "being a two-masted vessel, handy and fast, and usually of no great size." She nodded. "A *snow* is also two-masted, but strongly built, with an auxiliary mast stepped a few feet aft of the mainmast, on which the gaff is set."

"Hmm," said Selena, "but why does Captain Bentham have only fifty men, in two vessels? That's not many for a gentleman of fortune!"

Flint nodded in approval. "That's my little chick!" he said, and turned to Neal. "My lady is right. It's not many men."

"Ah," said Neal, "Danny's had some bad luck."

"What sort?" said Flint.

"This and that," said Neal. "But he's got two good ships. And, he's a man in need. So he'll meet you. But for God's sake, be sweet, Joe!"

"Isn't he a pirate?" said Selena, looking at the great number of guns on the walls and bastions of Charlestown, and the Union Jack that flew over them. "Why don't they sink him?"

"There's good reasons!" said Neal. "This isn't Savannah, where anything goes, but if a captain knows people, and he comes in nice and quiet, and brings letters of introduction . . ." Charley shrugged. "Just as we've got a letter from the Governor of Savannah, Danny –" he nodded at *Hercules* "– well, Danny's got one from Sir Wyndham Godfrey of Upper Barbados, who'd oblige Old Nick himself for the usual fee."

Flint studied Bentham's ships.

"Those two, with *Walrus,* would answer my purpose."

"Aye," said Neal, "but Danny won't do it for the love of you."

"I know," said Flint. "And it comes back to ready money. So how did you say farewell to Mr Pimenta?"

"Ahhhh . . ." said Neal. "Hmmm . . ."

"Well?"

"Now you'll appreciate, Joe, that you made it hard for me?"

"Perhaps."

"No, but you did. You scared the shite out of the poor man."

"Bear up and shake a reef, Charley! Get on with it."

"Well, I told him Miss Selena is your wife . . ."

"*What?*" said Flint.

"*Huh!*" said Selena.

"And I went so far as to say that there is a very great deal of money involved in your business, and all of it in ready coin or precious metal."

Flint scowled. One of the oarsmen – who'd seen that

expression before, and knew what might follow – missed his stroke and went over in a rumbling clatter of confusion. The boat swerved.

"Avast there, you no-seaman lubber!" cried the stopped-grog Morton, happy to take out his misery on another. "Do that again and I'll kick my boot heel-deep up your bastard arsehole!"

Clunk . . . Clunk . . . Clunk . . . the stroke resumed.

"Joe," said Neal, "I didn't mention the island, or John Silver, or anything. But if there isn't gold in this for Pimenta, then he won't touch us. He knows who you are and what you are." Neal raised a hand in defence. "Joe, don't give me that look! This is a very big man. You're only safe from the guns of Charlestown because he knows you. You and Danny Bentham both."

"Huh!" said Flint. "So what does this big man say to me?"

"He says you're invited to his house for dinner with some other gentlemen this afternoon at three," said Neal, and looked at Selena. "And *Mrs Garland* is invited to call upon Mrs Pimenta tomorrow, the which is an astonishing act of condescension towards a lady of colour and shows how much Pimenta is interested."

"Good!" said Flint.

"What shall I wear?" said Selena.

5 p.m., 12th November 1752
21 Broad Street
Charlestown, South Carolina

"To freedom, gentlemen!" said Meshod Pimenta, raising a glass when the meal was done and the port going round. The dining room was the biggest in Pimenta's splendid residence, a town-house equal to any in London and built on classic Palladian lines.

"Freedom!" they said, and drank to it.

There were eight men round the table, all in their finest embroidered coats, silk stockings, diamond-buckled shoes, and Flint was the most splendid of them all: gleaming, shining and charming. He was surprised to note that, while two of the guests were Sephardic Jews like Pimenta, the rest were gentiles – merchants from the top rank of Charlestown society – and all parties easy and comfortable together.

"I am three generations a Carolinian," said Pimenta. "My father and myself born here, and my grandfather – God rest him – came as an infant, loyal to no other land. Thus I pray for the time when the democracy of the Greeks reigns in Carolina and we shall rule ourselves as free men!"

"Enough!" said one of his friends, smiling. "No republicanism tonight, Pimenta. Spare us this day at least! Here's health to our sovereign, say I. Gentlemen . . . the king!"

"The king!" cried the self-same men and drained their glasses, Pimenta among them. But he wasn't done.

"Delacroix –" he said, turning to the young man who'd toasted the king, "– you're a modernist, so you must be a lover of freedom."

"What?" said Delacroix.

"Yes," said Pimenta, "your plantation is the biggest in the colony. You are the future!"

"Am I?" said Delacroix, who was not the brightest man present.

"Indeed," said Pimenta. "This colony was founded on the Indian trade –" he pointed to the magnificent ceiling above them, painted in celebration of colonial trade, depicting idealised noble savages exchanging skins and furs for knives and blankets – "but all that's past. The Indians are an obstacle now, not an opportunity. They can't be put to work; they love to fight, and they're dangerous!"

"Aye," said his friends.

"Which is why we were pleased to be rid of the Patanq," said Pimenta, warming to his subject. "We *need* to be rid of them, for the future – the modern way – is the importation of blacks to raise rice, cotton, sugar and tobacco. That will make the colony rich and will give us freedom!"

"Aye," they said.

"And what about the blacks?" said Flint.

"What about them?" said Pimenta.

"Shall they be free?"

"Sir!" Pimenta smiled. "Shall our cattle be free? And our horses?"

Everyone laughed, including Flint. He'd only asked for devilment.

Later, when Pimenta's friends were admiring his new billiard table – imported at great expense from England – Pimenta had a private word with Flint. Thanks to Charley Neal's intercession that morning, he'd overcome his fright at Flint's anger, and had managed to deceive himself that he was dealing with a normal man: a man of business like himself.

As before, he came too close and he grasped Flint's arm with patronising familiarity. Flint peered down at this arrogant little maggot, and hoped to get him – one day soon – at sea on board the *Walrus,* where a certain plank was patiently waiting for him.

"Captain," said Pimenta, "you must be a fine fellow, 'cos Mr Neal says so." And he whispered confidentially, "We do a deal of business, Charley and I, and Charley says there's money inside of you." He poked Flint. He actually poked his short, podgy, white finger into Captain Joseph Flint's belly! But Flint smiled. He never flinched, he never budged, he never moved. He simply smiled, and charmed Pimenta, who was completely deceived and sufficiently encouraged to develop his argument a little further.

"So, Captain," he said, "you're situated thus: you *need* money to *get* money. Yes?"

"Yes," said Flint. He spoke smoothly, easily, handsomely, as if he hadn't the least objection – not in all the world – to being cross-questioned by a greasy little goblin that needed slitting and gutting and salting.

"So," said Pimenta, "I have to know three things. First: how much have you got? Second: where is it? Third: how much is for me?"

"Ah," said Flint, and smiled and smiled. "Now we touch upon most confidential matters."

"But nothing you can't tell *me*," said Pimenta, edging so close that Flint could smell the wine on his breath. He nudged Flint and winked, "Trust me, Joe, as I trust you . . ."

Chapter 13

An hour before noon, 11th October 1752
The southern anchorage
The island

"*D*etail!" said Silver. "Detail is everything!"

"Aye," said the dozen men who would man Fort Silver, the biggest of the planned fortifications, the one most nearly complete, and the one which overlooked the southern anchorage. It was a forty-foot-square earthwork revetted with ships' timbers and cut with emplacements for two four-pounders in each wall.

"Come close, lads," said Silver, beckoning the hands to the guns that covered the beach. "See them tubs? You gun-captains pay heed! Once 'general quarters' is sounded, I want glowing matches in every tub, so's every piece is always ready to fire."

"Aye, Cap'n."

"Good – see that it's done." He picked out a man: "You there: Crooky Cruickshank –"

"Aye-aye, sir!"

"– what've I said about 'falling back', Crooky?"

The man gulped, uneasy at being singled out.

106

"You said men's more important than forts."

"And what might that mean?"

"It means we's to abandon ship and fall back if ordered."

"An' where should you fall back to?"

"To Fort Hands, inland."

"And what then should you do with your guns?"

"Spike 'em, Cap'n."

"How?"

"With this, Cap'n!"

Cruickshank reached down among the gun tackles and produced a long iron nail and a fist-sized rock.

"I knock the sod into the touch-hole and keep on pounding till it's squashed to buggery and can't be pulled out!"

"Aye," said Silver. The rock was Israel Hands's idea. There were nails for every gun, but not enough hammers. "You – Dick Douglas," he said, choosing another man, "when d'you fire round-shot, and when canister?"

The questioning went on until Silver was entirely sure that each member of the team knew not only his own duties but those of his mates.

"Well enough," he declared finally, and looked at the sun. "Time to go," he said, and led the way.

Israel Hands came out from Camp Silver to meet him. He drew Silver aside for a word.

"It's getting worse, John," said Israel Hands. He looked at the men walking ahead. "It's all right when *you've* got 'em, but as for the rest of us . . . we're losing discipline. Most of 'em wants to be looking for Flint's gold –"

"Flint's gold be buggered!" said Silver. "It's *our* blasted gold!"

"I know, I know, Cap'n – but that's what they's calling it, and they wants to be a-searching for it and a-digging it up! Ben Gunn run off this morning after Billy-boy kicked his arse. And if *he's* run, then others might follow."

Silver sighed, and wiped the sweat from his face with a grubby handkerchief.

"Ben Gunn's a poor, broken soul," he said.

"Aye. But it ain't just him. Nor ain't it just the gold neither. Some of 'em don't want to *fight* Flint when he comes, they wants to *join* him – anything to get aboard a ship again – and none of 'em likes digging trenches. They thinks they's gentlemen of fortune, not farmers. And they's splitting into gangs, Cap'n, and we can't do nothing if they won't pull together."

"It's this blasted island," said Silver, "there's something in the air! I'll talk to 'em, Israel. Has Black Dog done what I said?"

"Aye, Cap'n," said Israel Hands.

"Then we shall have to brace up, and hope I'm steering a true course."

He set off again, crutch thumping on the ground, parrot clenched to his shoulder, making for the camp, where all hands were mustered by the great heaps of timbers, spars and gear that were all that remained of their ship. The men looked surly and they were grumbling while the surf boomed dolefully in the background.

Silver found Billy Bones.

"What's this about Ben Gunn?" said Silver.

"Never laid a hand on the bugger!"

"That ain't what I heard."

"Well . . . might have made him jump a bit."

"Oh, Billy! Didn't I say to treat the hands gentle?"

"Hats off!" cried Sarney Sawyer, and blew a long call on his pipe. The men stood to a poor version of attention. Silver, Billy Bones and Israel Hands stood together, facing the men, and raised their own hats in salute.

"Stand easy, lads," said Silver, "and gather round." He hopped nimbly forward, stopping by a long spar laid out in front of all the rest, drilled with a line of holes and a pile of rods laid next to it. Alongside the spar, a six-foot pyramid of timbers stood covered with a tarpaulin.

Silver looked at the men, and was shocked to see how they clustered in groups, glaring at one another. He looked from man to man. Some he could rely on to the last, like Israel Hands. Others, like Billy Bones, would go over to Flint so soon as he beckoned. Most would trim their sails to the prevailing wind. All that he could understand. But beyond that, there was a festering, suspicious anger that had no good cause, that came from Devil-knows-where, and that had to be lanced like an abscess.

"Lads . . ." he said, and began to speak, drawing on all his natural powers of oratory, but telling them the truth. He told the truth because he couldn't abide to lie, not even when the truth was grim.

For the truth was that all their hard work digging ramparts and mounting guns couldn't make them rich, nor even get them off the island. It was only to save their lives, since Flint would return with overwhelming force, and could drive the defenders into their forts, raise the treasure, and sail away leaving them marooned. And as for Silver's men finding the treasure for themselves . . . what a fine thing that would be. It could be used to bargain with Flint for a ship, except there wasn't the time nor the manpower to dig up the whole blasted island to find what only Flint knew the bearings of!

"So," said Silver, "is there any man as knows a better way, or as chooses to step forward with a question?"

There was silence. Men shuffled and sniffed and looked at one another and scratched their heads. The surf boomed, the gulls called . . . and no man moved. Silver had drained the abscess. By telling the full, plain truth he'd left no room for suspicion. They were sombre and miserable now, but they weren't looking to knife one another.

Ah, thought Silver, *got you my buckos. Wormed, parcelled and stayed!*

Having brought them down, now he must lift them up.

"But before all else, lads," he said, "we must be a crew. We must be jolly companions together."

"Uh?" they said.

"So here's two things to help. First, our calendar –" he rapped the tip of his crutch against the spar. "Mr Carpenter!"

Black Dog stepped forward and began putting a rod into each hole. There were a hundred of them in one long line, each rod two feet high.

"This here's the clock that shall tell us when to expect Flint," said Silver. "Mr Bones and me reckon the fastest he can be back – in round figures – is a hundred days. So we shall take a peg out each day, for all hands to see how close we are to action stations."

"Hm," they said. It was plain, clear and simple, and focused their minds still further on the threat that faced them all, and on the need to face it united.

"Now this –" said Silver, coming to the tarpaulin cover and the pyramid. "Lads," he said, "the old ship is gone. *Lion* is burned, beached and buggered . . ." He paused as powerful emotions worked in the men. A seaman's ship was everything. Without her they weren't bold rovers nor gentlemen of fortune. They were maroons, they were land-lubbers, they were miserable, abandoned wretches. The men groaned.

Billy Bones and Israel Hands looked on in alarm. They'd never have dared remind the men of such things.

110

"But we saved something out of the wreck," said Silver, and nodded at Black Dog, who swept off the tarpaulin to reveal a finely crafted tripod of spars on a timber base, with *Lion*'s brass bell hung burnished and gleaming in splendour. "Lads, the bell is the heart and soul of a ship, as all true seamen know," he said. "And this here's the heart and soul of *our* ship, the which stands for all that she ever was, and all that she still is. From this day forward, it shall sound eight bells every day at noon." He reached down, and took the lanyard. "Give a cheer, lads – a cheer for *Lion*. The old ship may be gone, but she lives on in us. For we are her people! We are her Lions! Lions, one and all – *Lions for ever!*"

Clang-Clang! Clang-Clang! Clang-Clang! Clang-Clang!

Peering between the trees, with his monkey cuddled to his chest, Ben Gunn saw the cheering and tears and the pride, and the jolly companionship re-made, and he near as dammit ran back to join in. But he saw Billy Bones and remembered how Billy Bones had cuffed him and threatened him with a flogging . . . and poor Ben Gunn fell to sobbing and weeping, for he couldn't stand another dose of *that*.

Chk-chk-chk! The monkey, sensing his distress, clung to him with all its might. Ben Gunn hugged it and turned and fled: swiftly, silently, barely disturbing the leaves and bushes as he passed. At least he had a shirt now, and a hat . . . and a spade. He had a long-hafted spade, for he'd been working on the entrenchments and had kept hold of it.

He ran deep into the forest till he could hear nothing of Silver and his men, only the surf and the birds and the insects. When he was tired, he rested, and the monkey found fruit to eat, and later they found a stream for water . . . and time passed sweet and easy for Ben Gunn. Nights and days followed. He wandered. He found the monkey tribe again, and his own pet was welcomed back among chattering kindred that picked over its fur and climbed aboard Ben Gunn, and frolicked and skylarked and played.

Some days later – Ben Gunn kept no reckoning – he found yet another sign that men had been here before. He was on high ground, by the western shore of the island, where the trees grew sparse, and the sea glittered to the horizon. Here, he found a place with no trees at all, for they'd all been felled and the stumps dug up. There were lines of crosses: squat wooden crosses, hewn from ship's timbers. Most had fallen over, but a few stood more or less upright. At one end was the caved-in remains of a little house, also of heavy timber, but moss-covered and half-flattened with age.

"*Cetemary*," he said, mis-pronouncing the word, and he took off his hat. He looked around and felt at peace. To Ben Gunn, a cemetery was like a church. It was holy. It gave him the same pleasure as being in church with his mother – which he dimly remembered – but with the benefit of being out in the sunshine with the birds and the flowers.

He walked up and down the lines of graves, peering at the crosses, which seemed to have names carved into them. Ben Gunn couldn't read very well, not having attempted the feat for many years. But he wasn't illiterate either. It just took a lot of time for him to spell out the words and to understand them.

He pushed his way into the little house: just one room, ten foot by twenty, where the wind and the rain had penetrated for decades. There was a ruined bed with a body on it. A leathery skeleton under dust and leaves and filth, clad in rags, with some bits missing, and the rest twisted and broken . . . but on one narrow bone a bright green emerald twinkled in a golden ring – which was off that instant and on to Ben Gunn's finger, and Ben Gunn grinning and chuckling and merry.

He searched further. There was quite a lot more: a chest of writing materials – pens, ink-bottles, and a leather-bound notebook – together with what looked like a bible and a prayer book. He ignored these, as well as the remains of rosary beads, and a brass crucifix – he could tell it was brass by the taste – and there were some rusty tools. But there was a good dagger in a sheath, a few gold coins, and a pair of silver-mounted pistols, still un-rusted inside a tight-shut box that he prised open with his spade. They were of antique design with external mainsprings in the Spanish style. Useless as they were without powder or shot, Ben Gunn took these too.

That night he slept under the trees, but he came back next day, followed by some more of the monkeys, which joined in the fun of turning the ruined house inside out.

He found no more loot and was going away in disappointment when a thought occurred to him. Perhaps some of the dead had been buried with rings on their fingers?

It took little time to reach the first coffin, which was buried shallow, no more than three feet down. Ben Gunn scraped the earth clear with his spade and wondered how best to get inside . . . and then he wondered whether he really wanted to *see* what was inside . . . Hmmm . . . it couldn't be much worse than the dry bones in the house, could it? But the ground was dry here, and the wood of the coffin looked sound. There might be more meat inside the coffin than there'd been inside the house . . . Ben Gunn dithered.

Then the emerald spoke to him from his left hand, and he raised the spade and drove it into the middle of the coffin . . . which surrendered with a rotten crunch, letting

113

in the spade, and letting out such a stench as sent Ben Gunn staggering back, heaving and snorting and pawing at his face to rid himself of the contamination.

The monkeys didn't seem to mind it so much. They perched on the shattered lid, sniffing and chattering and endlessly grooming one another's fur. But that was the end of Ben Gunn's career as a resurrectionist. He went off and found a stream and soaked himself in it to get rid of the smell.

He didn't go back, except once to the house to check he'd missed nothing, this time taking the old notebook for curiosity, and later spending hours trying to pick the meaning out of it. After some effort he concluded that it was a diary, written by someone called de Setubal, who wrote not in English but some other language: Spanish, perhaps? And he could easily read the year dates that appeared at each entry, and which started at 1689.

Days passed. For a while it was a pleasant time for Ben Gunn. There was no Billy Bones to frighten him, and he had the monkeys for company . . . except that they weren't proper company, not being able to talk, and he began to get hungry too, through not having proper victuals. Worse still, the monkeys fell ill. They lay in their tree-nests trembling, and developed festering spots on the palms of their hands and the soles of their feet. Ben Gunn was dreadfully afraid then, in case they should die and leave him absolutely alone – for he hated being alone – but eventually they all got better, and resumed their playing, unharmed except for tiny grey scars where the spots had been.

Ben Gunn cuddled his favourite, caressed its little hand and noticed that the scars were just like those on his own cheeks . . . those left after his childhood survival from smallpox.

Chapter 14

*D*ark Hand and Dreamer stood at the rail of the ship, wrapped in their blankets. They looked at the other five ships of the fleet, and they looked out to the open sea beyond the harbour. They stood in silence and wondered what to do, for there was a great unease among the Patanq, and fifty warriors stood waiting their word.

It was not that the ship was bad or uncomfortable. There were two hundred and forty-nine Patanq aboard, and to a people accustomed to being crammed in a smoky long house, there was room enough. Nor was there the least threat from the ship's crew, who numbered only twenty-five and were not fierce men.

The problem was that the ships had not moved since the Patanq had come aboard.

"Do you think they truly wait for the wind?" said Dark Hand.

"Yes," said Dreamer. "They need the wind to fill the sails, and who can command the wind?"

"But the wind blows all the time."

"It blows the wrong way."

"The old women say the sailors can bring the *right* wind if they choose."

"Nonsense!"

"And the old women talk to the young women, and *they* talk to the warriors."

"Then let the warriors talk to me, and not mutter in corners!"

Dark Hand gathered his courage.

"Dreamer . . . I speak to you now for the warriors. They fear that a great mistake has been made. They believe we should never have given up the homeland."

Dreamer sighed. He closed his eyes. He looked back forty years . . .

He was eight years old, it was the Time of the Planting – the year's most joyous festival, with singing, dancing and feasting, and the young women of the Sisters of the Corn running from house to house, drenching everyone with water – supposedly to drive out things evil, but actually in fun.

It was night. The village slept behind its moat and heavy palisade: whole tree-trunks trimmed and set in place, with watch towers, fighting platforms and gates. Inside, there were four long houses, each a hundred paces long and twenty wide: timber-framed, bark-covered, round and smooth, highest in the middle, sloping towards each end, and cut with smoke-holes for the hearth-fires. In each house, many families slept on their benches, surrounded by kinfolk.

It was peaceful and quiet, until the Dreamer awoke and screamed. He saw the lights that flashed, and he howled and sobbed as the pain stabbed again and again. Around him the people awoke and grumbled and coughed and spat and scratched themselves, and asked what was the noise ... until they heard that the Dreamer was dreaming again. Then they fell quiet and listened, because already the child had a reputation.

The Dreamer's father and mother were young. They were inexperienced. But the grandmother was a powerful matriarch, and she summoned her even more powerful brother, Teller-of-Stories, leader of the False-Faces. This revered wise man got up in the middle of the night, donned his mask of office, and hurried to the Dreamer's bedside. It was dark in the long house, with more shadow than light from the fires, and people were clustered around the bed where the boy lay moaning and vomiting into the bowl his mother had put beside him.

"Ah," said Teller-of-Stories, seeing this great crowd all talking and pointing and looking over one another's shoulders in awe and in fear. And the old man nodded in satisfaction that so many were here to see his magic.

So he sat on the ground by the child, and he rocked to and fro, and he chanted a powerful poem, and shook a tortoise-shell rattle, and the people echoed the responses ... After a while, the child was comforted and ceased to howl. When he opened his eyes and saw the red mask, and recognised the noble figure sitting beside him, he smiled.

"Ahhhhhh," said the people, and they smiled too. And when dawn came, and the sun shone, the people entirely lost their fear of what the little Dreamer might have dreamed this time. But later, when Teller-of-Stories talked with Dreamer and heard what the child had seen, even Teller-of-Stories trembled. And then he thought deeply and summoned all his considerable knowledge and experience, and gave his explanation.

"The things you have seen are not of our nation," he said, "nor any nation of the Iroquois peoples. We have no 'Satan', we have no 'Hell' – this is nonsense from the priests of the white man! You have heard these things from them."

"No, Teller-of-Stories," said the child, "I saw them myself."

"It is not possible."

"It is. I saw Satan."

Teller-of-Stories sighed.

"There is no Satan. Listen now to the truth!" He closed his eyes and began to tell one of the Great Truths: "In the beginning, the daughter of Sky Woman had twins . . ." But then he looked at the child, and smiled. "You know this already. You tell it."

Dreamer nodded. Of course he knew. Everyone knew. He spoke:

"She had twins. One was called Upholder-of-Heaven, Sky-Grasper and Sapling. He was the right-handed twin who made all that is straight and beautiful in the world. The other was not born but cut his way out of his mother. He was called Warty-Skin, Ugly-Face and Stone-Blade. He was the left-handed twin, who made all that is crooked and ugly in the world."

"You see?" said Teller-of-Stories. "There is balance in the world. Beauty balances ugliness, but *goodness* and *badness* are the acts of men! There is no god of evil."

"There is," said Dreamer. "He is Satan. I have seen him."

Dreamer opened his eyes and returned to the present. The dream of Satan was only the first of many dreams. They had taught him much about the power of the white man. Now he turned to the warriors, who stood apart in the gathering dark, afraid to approach him.

"Come here, my brothers," he said. "Come close and we

shall sit down together." So they came and they sat. They sat in council as if around a fire, and Dreamer spoke.

"Who says that we should not have left the homeland?"

It was a long council. Every man spoke who wished to, and Dreamer listened to them all, not seeking to argue or interrupt.

"Now listen to me," he said when the last man was finished, and a proper silence had shown that his words had been considered.

"You say that we are strong? That we are one of the seven nations . . . the Mohawk, the Oneida, the Patanq, the Onondaga, the Cayuga, the Seneca and the Tuscarora?"

"Yes!" they said.

"And I say that if we were *seventy* nations the white man would still be stronger, because *he makes iron and we do not*." He looked at them. "Or perhaps I am wrong? Perhaps there is one here that can show me how to make a musket? And the powder and lead to feed it?"

They were impressed. But this was just the beginning. Dreamer had much more to say and it was fearfully convincing.

"So," he said, when he was done, "we are finished here. There is nothing for us in our homelands. Believe me, for I have seen it! Within our children's lifetime there will be no long houses, no nations, no confederacy. We shall be gone –" he shrugged "– except as mice, in the corners the white man does not want."

Silence.

"So we must move the nation," he said.

"Yes," they said.

"But *now*, you say, 'If we must move, then we should go by land.'"

119

"Yes," said some.

"And march through the lands of the other nations – when already the confederacy is failing, and trust is dying? No, brothers! They would not let us pass, and we are the smallest of all the nations and could not fight our way through."

Silence.

"So we must go by sea. We have bought ships with gold. It is the only way to save the nation. We shall go north to open lands where we shall make a new homeland. We shall survive! Listen, my brothers, while I tell you of the new lands we shall win . . ."

They smiled and made themselves comfortable, for Dreamer painted wonderful pictures with words.

It was dawn before the council ended. Dreamer had calmed the doubters: a great achievement, for his plan demanded unimaginable courage of a land-locked, forest people. And all this he did with the same arguments that he'd used before, and would doubtless have to use again, for it is commonplace that men must hear the truth many times before they will believe it.

Finally, with these great matters settled for the present, and with the sun rising out of the ocean, and the women bringing food and drink, Dreamer should have relaxed. But he couldn't because, as so often it did when the work was done, blindness struck the centre of his eyes, and the shimmering crescents flickered yellow, violet and black . . . and Dreamer knew that he would suffer.

And in the suffering there came another vision of Satan.

And Dreamer saw the Hell that, despite all his efforts, Satan was bringing to the Patanq nation.

Chapter 15

Two bells of the forenoon watch (c. 9 a.m. shore time)
13th November 1752
Aboard Walrus
Charlestown harbour

"*D*on't make me, Joe," said Selena. "Don't make me . . ."
Her intuition had told her to ask nicely. And it was
working: Flint was hesitating. She was wildly upset, bitterly
resenting being forced to do something she hated, and she
wanted to lose her temper, and scream and stamp. But she
didn't . . . just.

She looked at him, sitting on the seat that ran under the
stern windows of his cabin. He sighed and shifted and looked
back at her. There were just the two of them alone together,
and he was deeply worried, but he wasn't threatening.

He'd changed. On the island he'd been mad and dangerous.
But he wasn't like that now, especially after yesterday on the
ramparts. Now he was trying to square what *she* wanted
with what *he* wanted. And that was new.

Then, to her amazement, he got up and took her hand, and
looked straight into her eyes . . . and smiled. He'd never done

121

that before. To him, she'd never been more than a possession: an object of lust, like the paintings of naked flesh that gentlemen kept in their private rooms. He was incredibly handsome when he smiled, and – being dangerous – he was exciting too. Nobody seeing that smile would ever guess what he was really like. Selena wondered what *was* he really like?

But then he shook his head.

"I'm sorry, my chick," he said. "Pimenta's too important to insult. I need his help and you've got to go – and that's my last word in the matter."

Then there *was* stamping and shouting. Plenty of it, on both sides. But in the end, Selena found herself in *Walrus*'s launch, being rowed ashore by four hands, with Tom Allardyce in command, plucked of his cutlass and pistols and jammed into landsman's clothes. Selena may have been unhappy, but Allardyce was terrified.

"What if I'm seen, Cap'n?" he'd said. "Seen by them as knows me? I'd be took and hanged!" But it didn't take long to convince Mr Allardyce that the fury of those ashore was the least of his worries. Flint achieved this by gripping the reluctant sailor by the throat and explaining that he shouldn't fear a hanging, only what would happen to him should he disobey orders here and now. After that, Allardyce kept quiet, even when he was ordered to follow Miss Selena like a fart-catcher once they were ashore, and under no circumstances to go ahead or alongside of her, because today she weren't Miss Selena at all, but Mrs Garland.

The launch made fast to Middle Bridge, one of the big wharves that stood out on piles over the Cooper River. There were proper stairs up to its deck, where Selena and Allardyce were transported out of their misery by the heaving life of one of the New World's most prosperous towns.

Even the bridge itself had a market and shops, the city walls stretched out on either hand, and beyond that, fine brick buildings reared up in ranks, chimneys smoked, spires rose, flags waved, dogs barked, and there was an enormous bustle and jostle of people: old and young, black and white, rich and poor, master and servant, ladies in gowns and tradesmen in aprons, all stepping out before swinging inn-signs, painted shopfronts, paved sidewalks, bellowing hawkers and bright-striped barbers' poles.

Selena had never seen a city before, only the log cabins of Savannah, and even though Allardyce came from Bristol, it was years since he'd seen it, and both had been months at sea or on an island devoid of life. So Charlestown hit them like a punch in the face, except it was a joyful punch, if such a thing can be. It was exhilarating, fascinating, and totally, utterly absorbing.

They forgot their orders and strolled along – not quite hand-in-hand, but very much united in wonder – and were led deeply astray by the shops along the western side of Bay Street. Selena had only two eyes where a hundred were needed to drink in the wonders that lay behind the huge glass windows of the shops, and in the end it was Allardyce, only slightly less fascinated than her, who remembered what they were here for.

"Miss Selena . . . ma'am?" he said. "We'd best up-anchor and set sail, ma'am. To Mr Pimenta's house in Broad Street. Orders, ma'am." He touched his hat.

Selena rejoined reality. She looked at her clothes, which in fairness to Flint were the best he could get by sending her ashore with Charley Neal the previous afternoon. At least Neal was familiar with the town and its shops, for Selena wouldn't have known where to start. She'd never been shopping in her life. The result was the outfit she was wearing.

The gown wasn't cheap – it was made of embroidered silk – but it was green, which didn't suit her, and it was a poor fit. The lace cap was good, but she had no means of dressing her hair. The English redingote she wore against the cold was shabby and old, the shoes were ugly.

Selena was sunk in shame as Allardyce thundered on the iron door-knocker of Mr Meshod Pimenta's intimidating house. When the shiny door opened to reveal a black man-servant gleaming in livery, Allardyce – nervous and seeing gold lace – saluted deferentially and jerked his thumb at Selena.

"Mrs Garland come ashore, Cap'n," he said, "for to parlay with Mrs Pimenta."

Fortunately, Thomas – Mr Pimenta's butler – was used to receiving guests of all ranks and races, for Charlestown society was not that of London, and a far wider spectrum of humanity came through Mr Pimenta's front door than would ever have been welcome at the Court of St James's.

So Mr Allardyce was smoothly led off to the servants' hall by a lesser minion while Mrs Garland was relieved of her redingote and ushered up to the first floor by Thomas himself, and into Mrs Esther Pimenta's salon.

Two ladies were waiting, both young, both with hair in ringlets, both wearing large quantities of jewellery. They were olive-skinned, Hispanic, and had bright faces but no claims on beauty. One wore an elaborate brocaded dress in pink, the other an elaborate brocaded dress in blue. They were perched on French chairs with bright-gilded, filigree limbs, en suite with a gilded table supporting a Sèvres porcelain tea-service in blue, white and gold. The room was elaborately furnished in bright colours, and crammed with everything that glittered or twinkled or shone: cloisonné fish bowls abutted Canton enamelware, and the walls were hung with

Chinese wallpaper of unworldly exoticism and fierce brilliance.

Selena was not quite blinded, but it was close.

"Mrs Garland," said Pink Gown, rising, "I am Mrs Esther Pimenta, and this lady –" she indicated Blue Gown "– is my friend, Mrs Zafira Nuñez Cardoza." She took Selena's hand and presented her as if to a duchess. "Zafira, my dear," she said, "allow me to introduce Mrs Garland, wife of one of Mr Pimenta's most important new friends."

Even hideously embarrassed and wishing herself dead, Selena noted those words. Flint would be impressed.

Meanwhile Blue Gown was frowning. Blue Gown held strong views on blacks, and was present solely to oblige Pink Gown, who held identical views and was receiving a nigger-woman in her salon *only* because Mr Pimenta had first cajoled, then begged, and finally screamed in her face a dreadful secret never made know to her before: Meshod Pimenta had over-extended his credit and was in desperate need of Captain Flint's trove of gold and silver coin. Mrs Flint must therefore be received – and in this matter there was to be no denial – for Captain Flint must at all costs be indulged in the hope that he might be persuaded to become a little more open about how much he'd got and where he'd damn-well got it!

Pink Gown knew all this. Blue Gown didn't. She'd not been told.

"So," she said nastily, "who are your friends, Mrs Garland? Where do you come from?"

Selena thought of the master's special house, and the master on his back, half-naked, eyes bulging, and choked on his own vomit. She thought of Flint, peering at her through holes drilled in the cabin wall. She thought of Long John, probably gone from her life forever . . . and tried to invent a family history on the spot.

125

It wasn't very good. It wasn't very convincing. Blue Gown and Pink Gown sneered. More questions followed. Awkward questions, drawing evasive answers. When tea was served, even Selena's obvious familiarity with the etiquette of teacups didn't help. They sneered at that too.

Selena was sunk in despair and fighting the tears. She stared at the floor and hoped that they'd leave her alone. But they didn't. It just got worse.

Then the door burst open and a third lady rushed in, too fast for Thomas to announce her. This one had a silver-laced gown.

"Esther! Zafira!" she cried, then, "Oh!" as she caught sight of Selena and turned her delicate nose up. Silver Gown's views on the place of blacks in society were even stronger than those of Pink Gown or Blue Gown.

"Judith!" said Esther Pimenta, and took fright. This could irreparably damage her standing in Charlestown society. Mrs Judith Harrow was not exactly a friend; she was more of a rival.

"This is Mrs Garland," said Mrs Pimenta defensively, "the wife of a most important and prosperous merchant."

"Mrs Garland," said Mrs Harrow, nodding briefly. That done, she set about ignoring the insufferable presence of a black, for she had come with more satisfying sport in mind. Triumphantly she waved a newspaper at Esther Pimenta. "Look! Look!" she said. "The latest edition, just arrived, of *Le Mercure de France*! Only five weeks old! And it describes La Pompadour's latest gown!"

Esther Pimenta gritted her teeth. The entire world of fashion was led by France, and the entire world of French fashion was led by the beautiful thirty-one-year-old Madame de Pompadour, official mistress to King Louis XV. Wretched

126

outposts like London or Charlestown could only follow and adore, and Esther Pimenta had made it her business to be first with the news from Paris. Mrs Harrow was here to gloat.

Selena was forgotten as the three ladies fell upon the newspaper, brows furrowed, lips pursed, eyes peering as they fought to pull meaning out of the article in question.

"See! It *is* about La Pompadour – there's her name!"

"*Douilles de lacet* . . . what's that?"

"What's *that* word? That one there –"

Selena stared. They couldn't read French! She was amazed. She'd been raised as companion to Miss Eugenie Delacroix, the master's daughter, a society belle who had enjoyed the finest clothes – endless hours had been spent making alterations to her vast array of gowns – and whose education had encompassed the arts of elocution, etiquette, dancing, drawing . . . and a mastery of the French language. To which end a French governess had been on hand to ensure that the girls spoke with the accent of Versailles as they read aloud from the latest journals and books shipped in from Paris.

Selena's life had turned upside down since then. Rejected by Miss Eugenie, she'd seen things and done things these Charlestown ladies couldn't imagine. She'd grown fast in a hard world, and in that world she was more than a match for them, for all their status as married women – *white* women – with rich husbands. How ironic to discover that she was also their superior in *their* world.

"May I see?" she said. She had to say it several times before they noticed. Even then it was only with utmost bad grace that they handed her the newspaper.

"Hmm," she said, "*douilles de lacet* – lace sleeves '. . . Madame was enchanting in lace sleeves worn treble:

long and trailing at the wrist, but narrow at the bend of the elbow where they were gathered with ribbons of lace en suite. The effect brilliant, cascading . . .'"

Selena looked up and saw their faces. Round eyes, round mouths. It was hard not to laugh. She read on, unconsciously sitting up and straightening her back as she did so, and speaking in the clear, precise manner of her upbringing, not the lazy speech she'd fallen into in the company of seamen.

After that things happened by quick stages. First there was a discussion on La Pompadour's outfit, with Selena accepted first as an equal, then as leader, for these Charlestown ladies had few ideas of their own and were accustomed to being ruled by their dressmakers. Next, Esther Pimenta called for her collection of *moppets* – Parisian fashion dolls, not toys – of which she had a number, and which she loved dearly but did not properly understand. Selena duly explained them, showing how their tiny pleats, seams and cut, gave detailed guidance to the dressmaker. Finally they went into Mrs Pimenta's dressing room, where she kept her gowns, and Selena explained them, too. As she talked, a great truth was hammered into three thick heads: namely that Mrs Garland – be she black as the Devil's boot – was an outstandingly beautiful and clever woman: graceful, cultured and charming.

When Selena finally emerged from Mr Pimenta's house, it was in triumph, head high and servants grovelling, with Tom Allardyce gaping in her wake. And in due course . . .

Mrs Garland was invited back.

Mrs Garland became a friend.

Mrs Garland was introduced to Mrs Pimenta's entire circle.

She was loaned some of Mrs Pimenta's gowns.

And within a week, she had become the sensation of Charlestown.

Chapter 16

Dawn, 14th November 1752
Camp Silver
The island

"Sixty-seven days to go," said Israel Hands, looking at the log-calendar outside Silver's tent.

"Aye, Mr Gunner," said Silver. "An' it'll be sixty-six when the bell strikes noon and we take out today's peg. But remember, it ain't reckoned by the Astronomer Royal at Greenwich – it's only our best guess." And with that he hitched up his pack and started off along the path into the trees, with Billy Bones and two dozen hands following along behind.

There was a planked pathway now for heavily laden men to make their way off the sandy beach and on to the firm ground beyond, and there were well-hacked paths through the jungles, connecting the island's four forts: Fort Silver above the southern anchorage, Fort Foremast in the far north, Fort Hands by the swamps in the middle of the island, and Fort Spy-glass protecting the main lookout station.

Silver had elected to build four small forts rather than one big one because he didn't plan to hide behind walls but to strike Flint from behind and at night. With four forts, Silver's men would have the chance to move round the island secretly, knowing there was always safe shelter nearby once they'd struck their blow.

Under Silver's leadership, life on the island had settled into a steady pattern of heavy labour, with working teams – each under their rated leaders – completing the four forts, cutting the trees and bushes around them to give clear fields of fire, and now, with the main works complete, taking care that stores were equally distributed, signals agreed and the nimblest men and boys practised daily – and at night too – in running messages between the forts, finding the best and fastest routes, against the time when they *would* have to fight against overwhelming numbers, and fight as a team.

Today, leaving Israel Hands in command at Fort Silver, Long John himself was setting out with Billy Bones, Sarney Sawyer, two dozen men and two ship's boys, for the northern inlet, where the *Elizabeth* lay in ruins. Captain Springer, having grounded the vessel, had unloaded everything in the attempt to re-float her and fourteen brass nine-pounders now lay abandoned on the beach. Silver hoped to use these guns to fortify the island's other major anchorage, in case Flint should come in that way.

They had plenty of powder, saved from *Lion,* and there was still time to dig earthworks and mount the guns, which, being brass, ought to be weather-proof. But everything depended on the gun-carriages with their specialised iron fittings being sound after nearly three years lying on a tropical beach, and likewise that there was enough nine-pounder shot left un-rusted.

"Mr Bones," said Silver as he hopped steadily along the path through the palms, his parrot firmly anchored aboard his shoulder, "a word, if you please."

"Aye-aye, Cap'n," said Billy Bones, and came alongside.

"The shot, Mr Bones," said Silver, "you say you stacked it clear of the tide?"

"Aye-aye, sir. That we did. Right off the beach an' under the trees, lest it should rain."

"Weren't there no caves nor nothing?"

"No, Cap'n. Leastways, not nearby . . ." said Bones uneasily, as was habitual for him when thinking of Flint. "And . . . *him* . . . he took the best of the shot for *Betsy,* the new ship as we built out o' the wreck of the old 'un."

"But there was still shot left?"

"Aye, Cap'n. *Betsy* could only bear six guns, and *Elizabeth* had shot for twenty."

It took a long day for Silver and his men to reach the northern inlet. Skirting to the west of the marshes which occupied the middle of the island – a region thick with bulrushes, willows and outlandish swampy trees – they found a bit of open ground bordered by marshland on one side and thick forest on the other. It was hot, stinking and buzzing with mosquitoes, but at least they could step out without hacking a path . . . and there was an old friend waiting for them.

"Cap'n," said Billy Bones, as they trudged along, "look'ee there!"

"Bah!" said Silver, aching and raw from heavy exercise. "That bugger can please himself. I'm not stopping for him."

It was Ben Gunn. Crouched over, half hidden, fleet of foot and muttering to himself and the monkey that ran alongside him, he was keeping pace with the marching column.

"Prob'ly wants some cheese, I shouldn't wonder," said Bones, which was precious close to the truth. Ben Gunn couldn't stand loneliness, nor a diet of nuts and fruit.

Little by little, he closed the gap until finally he joined the column, ducking and bobbing and with a finger always to his brow, cringing before Long John and Billy Bones.

"All right, Mr Gunn," said Silver when they next stopped to rest. "Come aboard again, and take your share o' the load. But if you join this crew, you must work your passage. You *and* your soddin' monkey!" They all laughed at that, and the monkey chattered and larked and ran from man to man in the most affectionate way. And Ben Gunn was happy again.

The monkey became a great favourite. Though it always went back to Ben Gunn, it spent a little time with everyone, leaping into men's arms, climbing up their legs and curiously examining their clothes and gear. Silver alone was not touched by its little hands, for it steered clear of him – the parrot saw to that.

"Bugger off! Bugger off!" she screeched, flapping her wings and snapping her beak, sending the monkey running away in terror.

When they reached the northern inlet, they found the brass guns in fine condition and the shot stacked in pyramids, just as Billy Bones had left it; and while those on the top and the outside were rusted useless, there was plenty of good round shot within. Furthermore, most of the gun carriages were either sound or could be repaired.

This was a huge relief to Silver, and he immediately set Bones to work, surveying the inlet, and marking out new battery with sticks knocked into the ground.

That night, as they sat by their campfire with the grog going round, Long John stood up and addressed his men.

"Shipmates," he said, "this shuts the back door in Flint's face." He turned to Sarney Sawyer: "I'm leaving you in charge, Mr Bosun. Mr Bones and I shall be off tomorrow, back to Fort Silver, but I've drawn a plan for mounting a dozen o' them guns behind earthworks, and on good timber platforms, so's to bear on any ship as comes in to anchor. So –" he raised his mug "– here's to ourselves, and hold your luff . . ."

". . . plenty of prizes and plenty of duff!" they cheered.

Ben Gunn's monkey chattered and scampered round the camp. The men tickled it and offered it rum.

Next morning, Silver, Bones and two men set off, leaving Sarney Sawyer with twenty-two men, two boys, Ben Gunn and the monkey. Sawyer's crew worked busily and – as ordered by Long John – sent one of the boys each morning to run a report to Fort Silver and back. This could be done within a day, provided the lad carried only a water canteen – which was indispensable – and no other load.

But on the seventh day no runner came to Fort Silver.

At first, Long John didn't worry. Sarney Sawyer had plenty to do and there could be good reason for not sending his daily report. But no reports came the following day either, or any day thereafter.

It was just before noon on the eleventh day, as Silver was preparing to send a man north to find out what was going on, that Ben Gunn entered the camp.

Gunn was madder than ever: thin, wild-eyed and snivelling. He mumbled and sniffed and wrung his hands. There were sentries on watch, now, day and night, and one of these escorted him to Silver, who was seated in his big tent, re-rigged inside the fort.

"Won't speak to none but you, Cap'n," said the man, and

nudged Ben Gunn with his musket butt. "*Oi . . . you!* You won't talk to no bugger, will you?"

"No," said Ben Gunn. "None but John Silver."

"Well," said Silver, "you're here now, matey. So what've you got to say?"

"I killed him," said Ben Gunn, and the tears rolled down his face.

"What?" said Silver, sitting up sharp. "Killed who? What's happened to Sarney's crew?"

"I killed him, I did. Cut his little throat . . . as the quickest way, like."

And Ben Gunn broke into sobs and groans, and pulled a leather-bound book out of his shirt and put it on Silver's table. Then he wept some more, sighed and wiped the snot and snivel from his face.

"I didn't know, Cap'n," he said. "'Tweren't my fault. I didn't know till I saw this."

"What are you talking about?"

"*This*," said Ben Gunn, and opened the book at a place he'd marked with a twig. Silver saw a page of neat drawings of monkeys. And there was a sketch of a monkey's hand, heavily marked with little round scars.

"So what's this, Ben Gunn?" said Silver, deeply puzzled.

"It's like when I was a lad, Cap'n, and they was burying old Mrs Abercrombie, and they dug in the wrong place an' broke open a coffin of one old sod what'd died of it thirty year ago, and the stink came out, an they *all* got it: the grave-diggers, their famblies an' all, an' I got it too 'cos I smelled the stink, an' most on 'em died, but I didn't and I got these here –" he pointed a dirty finger at the marks in the middle of his cheeks.

"You had the smallpox, Ben Gunn?"

134

"That I did, Cap'n, an' I've told all, fair an' square." He laid a hand on the book. "An' there's a deal more in here, the which I ain't the scholar to read." Blinking and trembling, he raised a hand in salute. "An' now I've done my duty like a seaman, and begs leave to be excused and stood down from this watch."

"Aye," said Silver, "but what about Sarney Sawyer and his men?"

Gunn wouldn't say. He simply drew in on himself and muttered that it weren't his fault, not at all. Silver frowned. This was bad.

"Take him away," he said to the sentry. "Get some food and drink inside of him, then maybe he'll tell us what's happened."

"You leave him to me, Cap'n," said the man. "I'll get it out of him!"

"No," said Silver, "none o' that or I'll have the bollocks off you!"

"Aye-aye, Cap'n."

Ben Gunn was led off. Silver looked at the book. It was a diary, written in a good, round hand, in Portuguese – the language of his own father, who'd always used it at home. So Silver spoke Portuguese fluently. *Reading* it was more difficult. It was something he'd not done since childhood. But he persevered, and old skills returned . . . and soon he found that there was not one dull word in the entire book, which was the journal of Father Lucio de Setubal, a Jesuit priest, and sole survivor of an expedition that landed on the island in 1689 and which was ruined by mutiny and pestilence.

Chapter 17

Evening, 28th November 1752
The northern inlet
The island

"Now, lads," said Silver, "you must follow me, just as if we was goin' over the side to take a prize!"

"Aye!" they said: twenty men, every one a volunteer, and every one with a loaded musket and a belt full of pistols. They stood round the tall figure of Long John Silver in the thinning forest, in the fading light, with the waters of the inlet visible through the trees, and just a glimpse of the wreck of the *Elizabeth*.

"I've told you what has to be done, and why," he said. "So, are you with me?"

"Aye!" they said, but they said it half-hearted. Silver looked them over and wondered how far he could trust them. He wondered if they'd obey orders should it come to the last extreme. And could he even rely on himself?

"Maybe we won't have to do it, lads," he said. "But follow my lead." He turned to his two best men: Israel Hands and Billy Bones. "You, Mr Gunner, to one side, and you, Mr

Mate, to the other, and all hands to advance in line-abeam between you, so soon as we's on the sand."

"Aye-aye, Cap'n."

"With a will, lads!" said Silver, and led them out of the forest, and on to the beach, where they could see the glowing fires and huddled figures of the camp set up by Sarney Sawyer and his men, some two hundred yards off.

"Shoulder-to-shoulder, now," said Silver. "And no man fires before I gives the word. Come on, lads!"

They moved forward with Silver a few paces ahead, and Billy Bones and Israel Hands dressing the line as they went. It was an uncanny moment, for the enemy they faced wasn't mortal . . . and the light was going. The figures round the campfire stirred and murmured. But they didn't get up as they should have done. They didn't wave, and shout, and joke. They were a circle of grey faces, listless and slow, and not making enough noise to be heard even over the soft crunch of footsteps in the sand.

Then one of them did get up and swayed and staggered and moved towards the oncoming line of men.

"Cap'n!" said a boy's voice. "Cap'n, you've come!"

"Avast!" cried Silver, raising his hand. The marching line stopped and the steel barrels came up together. "Is that you, Ratty Richards?" said Silver. "Stay put, boy!"

But Ratty Richards kept coming, and round the campfire others were moving. They were hauling themselves up. They were leaning on each other. They were getting to their feet. In a second they'd be coming forward.

"We sent a runner, Cap'n," said Ratty, "but he never come back."

"Stay there, Ratty!" cried Silver as the boy slowed but kept walking.

137

"But, Cap'n . . ."

"Drop anchor, my son!" cried Silver fiercely. "Not another inch!"

Ratty Richards stopped. He was only ten yards away. Silver tried to make out his features. He tried his utmost. But in the near darkness he couldn't see Ratty's face . . . not properly. Still Silver raised a pistol and lined up the barrel on the centre of Ratty's chest. The pistol shook because Silver's hand was shaking.

"Make ready!" bawled Silver, and clack-clack-clack went the locks.

Ratty Richards gaped at the line of muskets, every one aimed at himself.

"But it's me, Cap'n," he said. "It's me!"

Silver groaned. It all depended on an old book. A book written by a poor devil tortured with loneliness. They'd all died of it, had the Portuguese. All those that went ashore. All but Father Lucio and three others who proved naturally immune. That was nine out of every ten who'd been touched by the monkeys. Then the galleon sailed so her crew shouldn't catch it, and never returned, leaving the old Jesuit to bury the other two as they fell to old age, and himself the last of all, in his little house by the graveyard, weeping and raving in his journal.

Weeping and raving . . . and one other thing.

He killed every monkey with scarred hands.

De Setubal had learned that there were two tribes of monkeys, which never met, for they detested each other. One tribe – the one his shipmates had found – had the smallpox, while the other did not. Over the years, he trapped and caught every infected monkey. He grew very cunning at this and he did the foul job with kindness, where he could. Thus he caressed those he caught: he calmed them and stroked them and fed them . . . then killed them at night, and buried them in secret, so the rest shouldn't see. It was his personal mission to save others from the pestilence, should ever anyone return to the island. But to him it was like killing children. It drove him mad in the end, and he died cursing God.

Silver shuddered at the thought of it, and peered over the trembling barrel and tried to decide if it was possible for the *same* pestilence to jump out of the ground after sixty years and infect the second monkey tribe, because he still couldn't get a good look at Ratty Richards's face, and he dared not move closer.

Ratty stood wondering and puzzled, looking as if he might step forward at any minute, and he was only a few paces off . . .

"Go on, Cap'n!" cried Billy Bones. "Drop the sod!"

"Aye!" said some.

"No!" said others.

"How do we know he's got it?"

"Looks all right to me!"

"Aye!"

And the line of muskets wavered, and wobbled . . . and came down. Ratty was the youngest of them all. They could see no harm in him. Not in Ratty Richards.

"Hallo, Ratty!" said a voice.

"Hallo, Ratty!" they cried. "Here we are, lad!"

"Stand off, Ratty," Silver pleaded. "Stay there, sonny, I'm beggin' you . . ."

But Ratty Richards blinked and stepped forward. And behind him the men round the campfire began slowly to walk towards their captain. Silver could see them. It wasn't just Ratty. They'd have a dozen in their arms in a minute or two.

Silver thought of Father Lucio who'd gone mad . . . who might have been wrong . . . who might have been mistaken . . .

But what if he'd been right?

"Hallo, Cap'n," said Ratty Richards, "I don't half feel buggered . . ."

BANG! Silver's pistol flashed and roared. It jumped in his hand and put a twenty-bore ball into Ratty Richards, eleven years old, who could work in six fathoms of water. By God's grace in an evil hour, the ball struck him instantly dead. The small body dropped like a stone and never moved.

"Bastard!" said a voice.

"Bloody bastard!" said another, and Silver's men muttered and started towards Ratty's body.

"NO!" cried Silver at the top of his voice, and hauled out another pistol. He was tortured with guilt for the thing he had done. It would be his burden and nightmare forever, and it would change him. "Not another step! You've seen me kill a child, here, so d'you think I'd think twice about shooting any of you?"

They growled and cursed but stood fast while Silver hopped as close as he dared to Ratty Richards's body, and finally got a good look at the pale face, staring up at the stars.

Ratty was heavily disfigured. It was worse than ordinary smallpox, and *that* was bad enough! The rash was continuous. Whole, thick sheets of skin were peeling off the face, and arms and neck, and every other inch of skin that Silver could see. Blood wept and crept out from the cracks between the dying skin, and red-raw flesh gaped naked and oozing where the skin had dropped off.

"Ugh!" said Silver, and leapt back. He'd been right. The old book was right. But in that dreadful moment it didn't make him feel any better. "Keep clear o' that!" he said, pointing at Ratty's body, but he needn't have bothered. They'd seen him jump. "Now, let's get this thing done," he said, and led them through the darkness. He led them to within hailing distance of the camp, but no closer.

On both sides, a lesson had been learned. Silver's men raised their muskets, and those by the campfire made no attempt to move.

"Where's Mr Sawyer?" cried Silver.

"Here, Cap'n," said a weak voice.

"He's bad, Cap'n," said another voice. "He can't get up."

"Then listen to me, shipmates," said Silver. "I've always told you the truth, good or bad, and this time it's bad." He paused, searching for words. "It's the smallpox, only worse. It's something brewed on this island. You got it off Ben Gunn's monkey, and anyone as comes nears you gets it too, 'cept only them what's had it before, like Mr Bones here. So we brought you all the supplies we could carry, and plenty o' rum, but you've to stay here and not move. I mean it, lads, I'll shoot any man as tries to come near the rest of us!"

There was a long silence. Then Sarney Sawyer spoke in the darkness.

"Are you leaving us to die, Cap'n?"

Silver looked away. He was deeply ashamed. And it didn't help that he could see no other way.

"Yes," he said finally. "It's that or lose all hands."

"Can't nothing be done, Cap'n?"

"No." Silver struggled for words. The best he could manage was: "But we did bring you the rum."

"Thanks, Cap'n."

"Sarney?"

"Aye-aye, Cap'n?"

"We'll be gone in the morning, but a few hands has

141

volunteered to keep watch. Some of them what's had the smallpox. They'll be keeping watch . . . understand?"

"Aye-aye, Cap'n," said Sarney Sawyer. "But me an' these poor lads here . . . we been low for days, Cap'n, heaving of our guts up, an' aching. So set your guards if you must, but we ain't going nowhere."

Nor did they. Of the twenty-four Silver had left behind at the northern inlet, all but one died within a week. The body of the runner – a ship's boy sent out for help – was found later, near the swampland where he'd fallen, too sick to move, and slowly died. Like all the rest, he was buried – at Silver's orders – in the old Portuguese graveyard, together with the skin and bones that had been Father Lucio.

If ever there was a tribute to John Silver's leadership, then it was that graveyard, since all the disgusting work of corpse-hauling and burial had to be done by the half-dozen hands who – like Ben Gunn and Billy Bones, but *not* Silver himself – were immune to smallpox, having had it and survived it, and this work they did because they trusted Silver, who'd told them it was the proper way to honour their fallen comrades, every bit as much as standing to attention with hats off as a man's body went over the side, beneath the flag, sewn in his hammock, to the sound of the bosun's call.

Now Silver had only forty-eight men to defend the island. Forty-nine, if he included Ben Gunn, who was anchored somewhere downwind of peculiar. Silver searched to the depths of his imagination for a plan, something that might suit. He remembered the words of the men whom he'd served under in the past, especially Captain England and Captain Mason. Good men and true. Gentlemen of fortune! He wondered what they'd have done, if placed as he was.

He wondered, but found no answer. So what was he to do?

Chapter 18

*T*he room was long and narrow: the basement of a ship chandler's warehouse. There were two rows of tables, the floor was spread with sawdust. Candles were needed even in daytime, and the clientele were sailormen: shipmasters, mates and bosuns. It was a place where deals were made and news exchanged. It was passing clean and smelled of tobacco, tar and beer.

"Where's Bentham?" said Flint, following Neal down the stairs into the room.

"Through there," said Neal, pointing to one side. "See the door?" Flint frowned, fearing a trap. "It's all right, Joe," said Neal, "there's other doors in there. T'ain't the only way out." Neal was nervous. He was taking a risk. He was telling Flint only as much as was needed to get him to this meeting. The rest Flint must find out for himself . . .

"Who are *they*?" said Flint. "We agreed one man each!"

Three big men in long coats and black hats were sitting outside the door, holding pint-pots. They looked like ship's officers.

"They're all right, Joe," said Neal. "One's Cap'n Parry of *Sweet Anne,* the other's Dan Parker, second mate aboard *Hercules* . . ." He smiled weakly. "They wanted to see the famous Captain Flint."

"Oh," said Flint. He shrugged. He didn't mind. There could be no false names here . . . and besides, he was flattered. "So who's the third – the ugly one?"

"Brendan O'Byrne," said Neal, "Bentham's first mate."

Flint nodded as Parry and Parker got up and left, touching their hats to Flint and gazing in awe as they passed.

"Mr O'Byrne," said Neal, "this is Captain Flint."

"Cap'n!" said O'Byrne. But like Billy Bones he worshipped one man only, and wasn't impressed. "Cap'n's in there," he said, looking at the door. It was a very thick wooden door and nothing could be heard beyond, until Flint opened it . . . then there were voices and laughter: women's laughter, and squeals . . .

Flint looked inside and turned on Neal with a face like doom. Neal shook.

"What game is this?" Flint demanded.

"Joe," said Neal, "Danny has his own ways, but he's a good 'un – trust me."

"What . . . damned . . . stupid . . . game . . . is this?"

"What d'you mean, Joe?" Neal's voice cracked in terror.

"Bentham! Don't you know what he is?"

"Of course," said Neal. "Didn't you know?"

Flint's expression answered. It took a desperate flood of words to persuade him to enter the side room, which surprised Neal, because he knew exactly what was in there along with

Danny Bentham, and he couldn't see why Flint didn't step forward at the double with a smile on his face.

The trouble was that there were some things even Charley Neal didn't know about Flint. When Flint bought Selena off Charley, and herself a little darling, it had seemed to him proof that Flint was a man towards women. Thus Charley had no inkling there was a certain something that Flint had never been able to do with a woman, no matter how much he tried. And he *had* tried.

So Flint stood on the threshold, afraid to advance, afraid to retreat. He dared not hold back for fear men would think him a eunuch, but he dared not go forward and be *proved* one. Long seconds passed. Neal stared in growing disbelief as Flint dithered and quivered. Joe Flint that had no fear of any man. Joe Flint that every man was in terror of.

But then . . . maybe . . . Looking into the room, Flint found that . . . just possibly . . . he wasn't quite so lost as he'd feared, for he felt that something might be stirring that had long been dormant.

Finally he summoned his courage, stepped forward, and slammed the door shut behind him.

The room was bright lit. Bentham was in shirt and breeches on a couch with two tarts from the top end of the Charlestown trade. Both were stark naked except for laced-up riding boots, tight black gloves and little feathered hats tied with ribbons under the chin. They were exceedingly well chosen by Bentham himself, who was hopelessly addicted to the flesh. That's where his money went, and he knew how to spend it.

One girl was white, the other black, and the white girl was laughing while the black girl rode on Bentham's back, one hand inside his shirt and the other cracking him with a riding whip.

"Take *that*, sir!" cried the black girl.

"Ow!" cried Bentham, and flinched at the blow.

Flint gulped. There was definitely something awake below, even if he was in a fury with Neal over Danny Bentham not being what "he" was supposed to be – as witnessed by the scene in front of him, with Bentham's open shirt revealing what it was that the black girl's hand was squeezing!

"Cap'n Flint?" cried Bentham, spotting his guest and shaking off his rider. "Is it you, Cap'n?" Throwing the whores aside, he – she? – stood up, hitched breeches, tucked in his breast, and stepped forward with a smile.

Bentham was big: taller than Flint, and handsome and friendly and on his uttermost best behaviour. Flint was taken aback, and allowed Bentham to shake his hand, and sit him down and offer him a glass and a girl.

"Which d'you fancy, Cap'n? All charged to me, of course."

"The black one," murmured Flint, his mind fevered.

"*Nancy*," said Bentham. "They're all called Nancy or Poll," he laughed, and the girls simpered and giggled, and Flint gasped as Nancy sat her silky-soft, dark, warm self in his lap and curled her smooth arms round his neck and stuck her tongue in his ear.

An hour later Flint and Bentham emerged, Bentham grinning, Flint smiling. And Flint was changed. In childhood, his father had made it painfully clear to young Joseph that certain acts – bodily acts – were so inexpressibly vile that God had forbidden men to perform them, except with whores. Hence Flint's problem, a problem made worse by unfortunate experiments, but recently and miraculously soothed by his feelings for Selena, feelings which he knew

146

were finer than lust, but which – tragically for him – he did not fully understand, and which in a normal man could have been his salvation.

But Flint was Flint, and saw things his own way. What he'd just enjoyed, he'd enjoyed with a whore. A black whore. Now . . . *Selena* was black, and *she'd* been bought from Charley Neal's liquor store, where all the girls were whores . . . *ipso facto* he could do with her what he'd just done here! Flint could hardly wait, and the very thought of it – even after his recent exertions – caused a vigorous stand of manhood to rise up between his thighs.

It was a fine start to business. Flint took to Bentham wonderfully, and accepted "him" as him with never another thought. They sat in the long room, where they were joined by Neal and O'Byrne, and talked.

"Danny," said Flint. "I may call you Danny, may I not?"

"Of course . . . *Joe*." Neal and O'Byrne nodded in approval.

"I need ships, Danny. Ships . . . with crews. *Crews accustomed to our profession.*"

"Joe, I have both! And I'm open to offers – offers in gold."

"Danny, I do have some gold . . . a little . . ."

"How much, Joe?"

"Enough to keep the lower deck happy . . ."

Flint smiled. He knew Bentham was facing mutiny if things didn't improve.

"Truth is, Danny," said Flint, "I need to convey men and stores . . ."

"But where, Joe? Where'd we be going? And what to do?"

"Danny! If only I could say!"

"Aye, I've heard you can't even tell Meshod Pimenta."

"And what might you know about that, Danny?"

147

"A little."

And there Joe Flint foundered. Like Pimenta, Bentham wanted to know what was on offer, where it was, and what had to be done to get it. But Flint wouldn't tell. He trusted nobody. Not even Neal, who had got him alongside Pimenta and Bentham in the first place.

Neal had his own plans, of course. He was over sixty and fed up with the squalor of Savannah. He'd made his pile and wanted a house in Dublin. But he knew all too well what Flint did with those who knew his secrets, once they ceased to be of use to him. So Charley was desperate to keep Flint happy, in the hope Flint might . . . just might . . . let Charley go. And with that in mind he resolved to take a risk, even though he knew there were things he wasn't supposed to mention.

"Gentlemen," he said, "if I might make a suggestion . . . ?"

"What suggestion?" said Flint.

"Let's hear it, Joe!" said Bentham. "Charley's a sharp 'un, and no mistake."

"Joe, Danny," said Neal, "there's another way to help one another."

"Oh?" they said.

"Yes," said Neal. "Now, gentlemen . . ." Neal's legs trembled under the table, but he pressed on: "There's gold in this . . . yes?"

"Yes," said Flint and Bentham. So far so good.

"There'll be fighting to get it," said Neal, "yes?"

Flint blinked, fast.

Holy Mary, Mother of God! thought Charley. *He's going to blow . . .*

"So what?" said Bentham. "How else would we get it?"

"Oh?" said Flint, surprised. "You know that?"

148

"Of course, or you'd not be talking to me, would you?"

"No," said Flint, and relaxed.

Thank God! thought Neal. "So," he said, "a lot more men will be needed."

"Charley!" said Flint, blinking again.

"Aye!" said Bentham, and nodded.

Charley summoned courage. Charley jumped.

"At least three hundred men . . ."

Flint shook with anger. His hands dived into his pockets. Neal knew he'd gone too far.

"God help me, God help me, God help me . . ." Flint fumed.

But Bentham laughed. "Hold hard, Joe," he said. "The poor swab's only trying to lend a hand."

"He should shut his trap!" snapped Flint, but he took his hands from his pockets.

"So we needs a lot more men," said Bentham. "And I knows where to find 'em."

Neal held his breath. That was exactly what he'd hoped Bentham would say. Neal could have told Flint himself, but that would have got him deeper into danger for knowing too much. Better it came from Bentham.

"Where?" said Flint, recovering on the instant.

"Ah," said Bentham, "*if only I could say!*" and he winked at Flint. "But I'll tell you this: they're some o' the finest fighting men you ever saw, and I can take you to 'em. So, how much gold is there, Joe? And where is it? And who's sitting on top of it?"

Ahhhh, thought Neal, basking in the warmth of a job well done. *There it is, Joe: you've got your ships and your army and all you've got to do is trust the bugger!* Neal smiled. He saw himself in one of the fine new houses in Drogheda Street, with a staff of servants and a cellar of wine.

But Flint wouldn't have it. He frowned. He wouldn't and couldn't tell.

His stubbornness had Neal despairing and Bentham sneering, when the flat, heavy detonation of artillery could suddenly be heard echoing round the town: threatening, steady and continuous. Everyone in the Golden Fish sat bolt upright and strained to listen.

1 p.m., 20th November 1752
21 Broad Street
Charlestown, South Carolina

There is no sight that stirs human emotions like that of a beautiful woman in a beautiful gown. Esther Pimenta and her friends gasped and clapped as Selena entered the salon dressed in a sack-back gown underpinned with stays and panniers, laced across the bust with ribbon, and with sleeves bearing cuffs trimmed with French lace.

The gown was the pride of Esther Pimenta's collection: fearfully expensive, superbly cut, and of the most lustrous yellow silk. It was a gown to enhance the beauty of any woman, but never had it shown to such advantage as when worn by Mrs Selena Garland. Only her darkness could set off the yellow quite so well. Only her daintiness, elegance and femininity could so perfectly compliment the complex trimming of the gown, which on lesser women was merely pretty, but on her was glorious.

Selena smiled at them and curtsied, and they rose and returned the compliment and applauded still louder. Esther Pimenta applauded with them, even though it was her gown, and even though she could never wear it again for fear of the comparisons that would be drawn. But in compensation she

150

glanced at Mrs Judith Harrow, whose rivalry had been definitively squashed by the delivery into Charlestown society of the exotic black nymph Esther was parading before them now. She didn't actually *own* the nymph, but Charlestown treated her as if she did.

Selena spotted the glance and smiled to herself. It was an enormous pleasure to be a woman, to dress as a woman, to be among women, and to recover all the elegance that had been hers when Miss Eugenie Delacroix had loved her. It was a joy to be among something softer and cleaner than dirty sailors with their constant violence, gluttonous drinking and filthy speech.

At the same time, she was aware that, while Meshod Pimenta was indulging her because he still had hopes of a bargain with Flint, Mrs Esther Pimenta was parading her round town in fine gowns for an entirely different reason. It was the same reason Eugenie Delacroix had taken Selena as a companion. She had become a doll again, a little black doll to be dressed and made pretty and shown off, displaying for society's entertainment the tricks she'd been taught: speaking properly, using a teacup and reading French. At least, that was how it seemed to Selena now, listening to the applause – supposedly for her, but actually aimed at Esther Pimenta.

Ah well! Selena shrugged. She'd learned to live for the day. There was little point in making plans. She was as trapped now as ever she'd been on the Delacroix plantation. So she played the role, sat down, took tea, chatted and gossiped and was persuaded to read once more from the *Mercure* and to suffer the pride and ownership in Esther Pimenta's eyes as she did so. Then . . .

Windows shook, tea-cups rattled to the thud-boom of

artillery. The ladies gasped, and a servant was sent to find out why the guns of the battery were firing – if it *was* the batteries and not the French! Or even the Spanish! There was real fear in the room. Charlestown's walls hadn't been built for nothing; her residents were all too aware that a war which started in Europe with proper warnings and diplomacy might announce itself out here by the arrival of an enemy fleet with guns run out and loaded.

Meanwhile, Selena had her own cause to be alarmed. What if Flint were taken? What if he were killed? Where could she go? What would Meshod Pimenta do? She'd seen how he looked at her.

"There ain't no cause to worry, ma'am," said Thomas the butler, hurrying into the salon. "It's an English squadron, salutin' off Fort Johnson as they comes into the bay. There's four ships, ma'am, and . . ."

But nobody was listening. The ladies were all transported into excitement, in anticipation of the wonderful calendar of social occasions that must follow the arrival of a naval squadron – a squadron packed with officers who would need to be entertained by the town.

"Ladies!" cried Esther Pimenta, before Judith Harrow should think of saying anything. "Up! Up!" she clapped her hands like a schoolteacher. "Why are we sitting here when a fine new squadron is coming in? Let's go up on the walls to see them!"

So Esther Pimenta led her own squadron through the streets of Charlestown, and since the weather was cool but comfortable, the squadron sailed without cloaks or topcoats, the better to demonstrate the fact that they were the elite of Charlestown, proclaimed by the rich colours and costly materials on display. Under full sail, they proceeded down

152

Broad Street towards the Half Moon Bastion and a fine view of the bay.

Meanwhile, the town shook to the multiple concussions of warships discharging their guns. The city walls and bridges were black with townspeople cheering, gaping, and pointing across the confluence of the Ashley and Cooper rivers to where a Royal Navy squadron was coming in – and doing so in style! Where merchantmen crept nervously under topsails, the squadron charged into the anchorage under full sail, as only men-o'-war could do with their massive, expert crews. And the four ships sailed in a line astern that could have been drawn with a ruler and measured with a chain.

They were led by HMS *Oraclaesus*, flying a commodore's broad pennant at the main and a red ensign astern. She was one of the finest ships in King George's navy: an eight-hundred-ton frigate, the first of her class, mounting twenty-eight twelve-pounder guns, with two hundred and fifty men aboard, including fifty marines. Behind her came *Bounder*, *Leaper* and *Jumper*: identical sloops of two hundred tons each, with ten six-pounders and a hundred and fifty men embarked. Like the flagship, they were brand new, with no expense spared in their fitting out, right down to the very latest advance in ship-building: actual copper sheathing on their hulls – a technical marvel that gave greater speed, and complete protection from ship-worm.

Any man could see that the bringing together of such splendid ships showed serious political interest was at work. Undoubtedly some heavy purpose was being served here.

Having saluted Fort Johnson at the mouth of the bay, the four ships forged onward in silence, coming closer and closer to the out-jutting piers of Charlestown, heeling to the wind under bulging sails: topmasts and topgallants curving to the strain, colours flying, white water under their bows. Not even a bosun's call was heard as the squadron drove deep into the anchorage. It was a magnificent sight, but the show had only just begun.

Boom! A gun spouted smoke from the bows of the flagship and – like parts of a machine – the four vessels came into the wind together. It was majestic to behold: like dancers performing a quadrille, they came about in perfect synchronisation, dropped anchor with a roar and a rumble, and simultaneously struck canvas.

When the powder smoke cleared, the four ships were as steady at anchor as if they'd been there a week.

There was a moment's silence then a band struck up on the flagship's quarterdeck and all hands in all four ships, sang with a will:

> *God save Great George our king!*
> *Long live our noble king!*
> *God save our king . . .*

Grown men wept at the beauty of it, and those who knew the words of this patriotic song joined in with choking voices: especially those who dreamed of the homeland; especially those afraid of the French; especially those who were seafarers – and that meant most of Charlestown.

Two who did not sing with choking voices were Joe Flint and Danny Bentham; both being infinitely far from King George's grace and his navy's favour. Also not singing were Charley Neal and Brendan O'Byrne who – as Irishmen – had no time for songs about English kings. These four stood silent on the Half Moon Bastion among the crowds of singing, cheering Charlestownians, but they still marvelled at the seamanship displayed.

"Look at 'em!" said Bentham. "You've got to credit the bastards!"

"Aye," said Flint, as the ghost of pride arose, "it takes the navy to do that!"

Flint and Bentham meant what they said. They honestly believed they'd never see a finer sight. But they were wrong.

"Joe?" said a familiar voice, right alongside.

Flint turned into a cloud of colour. He'd been so entranced, he'd never noticed. But there it was: a shoal of women in their gowns. He didn't know how many there were because he saw only one – Selena . . . Selena in the yellow silk gown. He'd seen her before a thousand times, but never like this.

His jaw dropped. A shudder ran up his body from ankles to neck. He shivered and marvelled as the thunderbolt struck. Never – not *ever*, in all his life – had he seen a creature so beautiful. Everything he'd ever thought about Selena came together like broken fragments magically reforming as a vase.

And of course, in the same instant, he realised that she was a goddess.

The filthy acts men performed upon whores could never be applied to her.

Tears sprang from his eyes.

She was a thousand miles from him.

Flint was true to his upbringing, and in Hell his father smiled.

"Selena . . ." said Flint.

"Joseph," she said, "may I introduce . . ." and she brought forward a gaggle of women, one of whom seemed to be Pimenta's wife, and they simpered and smiled, and all the while he gazed at Selena. A wooden block could have seen

155

the worship in his mind, and she certainly could . . . as could her companions; and she registered the tremendous envy in their eyes. For Flint was a dazzlingly handsome man and – in their innocence – they must have supposed that his character matched his beauty.

Selena sighed. What did they know? What could she say? So she faced front, raised her head, and fell back on good manners. She spoke, but Flint didn't hear at first. He was away in his dreams.

"Joseph?" she said. "*Joseph!*"

"What?" he said finally.

"Who are these gentlemen?" she was saying. Flint turned to look.

"Oh!" he said. "May I present Captain Daniel Bentham, and . . ."

Flint stopped, hit by a second bolt.

Danny Bentham was positively grovelling before Selena. Any lower and he'd have hit the ground. He had hold of the hand she'd offered, and was slobbering over it while gazing at Serena in naked, drooling adoration. Flint could all but *hear* the pulse that beat in his veins.

It wasn't only Joe Flint that had been pierced to the heart by a beautiful lady in a beautiful gown.

Chapter 19

12.30 p.m., 20th November 1752
Aboard Lucy May
Charlestown Bay, South Carolina

*T*he frigate's guns flashed and thundered as she led her consorts splendidly past Fort Johnson, and saluted the British flag. She stormed past the six ships of the Patanq fleet and comprehensively ignored them, for they were mean and shabby vessels compared with herself, and she was on the king's own duty besides.

Aboard *Lucy May* – the nearest equivalent within the Patanq fleet to a flagship – the passing of the squadron caused a tremendous stir, such that the vessel almost rolled gunwale under as three hundred members of the Patanq nation surged forward for a better view.

"Belay that!" cried Captain Noll Foster. "The buggers is only saluting the fucking fort!" But they paid him no attention; not the women and children, anyway. These terrified creatures simply yelled and pointed and climbed into the rigging ... and then when they saw that there was no risk to themselves, their mood spun on a sixpence and they laughed and joked and the children made faces at Foster and chattered at him.

"Get out o' them fuckin' shrouds, there!" cried Foster, yelling at the children. They jabbered and laughed all the more, so he turned to two Patanq men who stood apart from the rest. "I say!" he said. "I say there! Can't you get them little sods out o' the fuckin' rigging?"

The two Patanq so addressed were Dreamer and Dark Hand. Dreamer stared at Foster till the other blinked, then said a word to Dark Hand, who snapped his fingers, and the children fell silent, and stopped playing, and climbed back on deck and went softly to their mothers.

"Huh!" said Foster. "Fuckin' little sods!" And he stalked off to the stern, to be with his crew. He was more comfortable there. Among them he could convince himself he was still in command. The two Patanq watched him go. They spoke in their own language.

"Always these same words," said Dark Hand. "*Fucking . . . sod . . . bugger.*"

"Yes," said the other, "they cannot speak without them."

"Tell me, Dreamer, you are wise: do these words have any meaning?"

"Oh yes," said Dreamer, "but mainly they are used to strike blows."

"The French have similar words," said Dark Hand.

"And the Spanish," said Dreamer, "and the Germans. All of them do."

"And we have none!"

"Except those we have learned from these . . . *buggers,*" said Dreamer, and smiled. Dark Hand would have smiled too, but these days it was hard to smile in Dreamer's company for he looked so ill. The lifelong affliction – the curse that

158

he'd suffered since childhood – was striking so often now, and worse than ever, bringing pain and dark visions. Not all of these proved *true*, for Dreamer's visions never told the entire truth, but always they were disturbing and tormenting.

"What about them?" said Dark Hand, looking at the passing squadron. "They are a great force of arms. What do they mean to us?" He glanced at the Patanq warriors, on this ship and on the rest. All were gazing at the warships. "They will ask this question."

"Yes," said Dreamer, "and they should! It means the Charlestownians will feel stronger. Perhaps they will turn their guns on us. We are only here because we gave gold to their leaders . . ." He waved a hand towards the city. "And now we have been here forty-seven days, and they want us gone even more than we ourselves *wish* to be gone."

Dark Hand looked at the stern of the ship where Foster the shipmaster stood with his men. They too were staring at the new ships, pointing and talking, and looking through their telescopes.

"Forty-seven days!" said Dark Hand. "Are we being cheated, Dreamer? They find one reason after another. Always a good reason, but still we do not leave this place."

Dreamer thought hard. First it had been "unfavourable winds". This lasted two weeks. Foster said it was common for the winds to blow the wrong way, and the other sailors clearly agreed. But then, when the wind *was* good, even as the fleet was raising its anchors, one of the ships was found to be leaking badly. The ensuing repairs took two weeks and cost more gold. And then another ship was found to have foul water in the great casks down below, so *that* had to be replaced, for she couldn't sail without drinking water. And so it went on, always at great expense.

159

"Dreamer," said Dark Hand, "do they cheat us?"

"I think not," said Dreamer, and looked at the fleet. "But I fear these ships are bad ships. With so many shipmasters refusing even to speak to us, we had to take what we could get," he sighed. "And what do we know of ships?" He looked at Foster, and frowned. "Bring *him* here," he said. "We cannot judge ships, but we *can* judge men."

Soon Foster stood before Dark Hand and Dreamer. He cast frequent glances over his shoulder, peering through the fifty Patanq warriors who had gathered around him to the quarterdeck, where his crew looked on anxiously. They had pistols in their belts and a few were armed with swords or hangers, but it wouldn't do them a scrap of good if the savages turned nasty, not when they were so outnumbered by the murdering, blood drinking, heathen! He swallowed, his mouth dry. He was master of the ship in name only.

"Foster . . ." said Dreamer.

"Aye-aye, sir," said Foster instinctively, and touched his hat.

"Why does the fleet not sail?"

"Sprung foremast aboard of *Dungeness Rose*, Mr Dreamer, sir."

"Yes," said Dreamer. He already knew that. "And what is the cure?"

"Carpenters hammering home new wedges, sir."

"Foster," said Dreamer, "if this fleet does not sail within five days . . ."

"Sir! Sir!" said Foster. He looked at the tall, dark, tattooed men all around him. He looked at their snake-eyed faces. They were gargoyles and demons to him and he was very afraid. "Mr Dreamer, sir," he said, "I swears on me children's

160

lives, it ain't no more'n to be expected with a shoal of queer-arsed old hulks like these 'uns, and every fucking thing's been done – and is being done – to get the fuckers fit for sea, and I take my bible oath and God blind me if it ain't Gospel truth, sir!"

Dreamer nodded. The emotions of white men were shown on their faces for all the world to see. They could not withhold these signs as true men did. So he waved a hand and sent Foster back to his mates, wiping the sweat from his brow as he went.

"There is no deceit," he said to Dark Hand.

"I agree," said Dark Hand, and the warriors dispersed, contented.

When the warriors were gone, Dark Hand spoke.

"Dreamer, even if Foster speaks truth, he cannot make the wind."

"I know."

"So what if the good wind never comes?"

"It will come."

"If it does not come, we shall die here."

"Trust me. We shall not die here."

"We will spend all our gold, eat all the food, and see the children starve."

Dreamer sighed.

"Dark Hand, listen to me. The Patanq shall not starve aboard these ships, I promise you this. Because Satan is coming, and he brings another death entirely – I have seen it."

161

Chapter 20

Six men moved like cats. They crept on tiptoe. They did not breathe. They gripped their muskets with sweating hands and judged the distance.

"Nicely, lads!" said Long John, and smiled at the monkey squatting in the branch of a big tree. "Here, my pretty," he said, waving a piece of fruit at the beast, "come and get it." For once, Silver's parrot wasn't perched on his shoulder. She couldn't abide monkeys. She'd have squawked her head off and frightened it. That was why she'd had to be left back at Fort Silver, secured to her perch.

"Think I can hit the sod from here, Cap'n," said one who thought himself a marksman.

"You wait till you're bloody sure, Conky Carter," said Long John. "And all the rest of you draw a bead, and be ready in case the bugger jumps."

At first it had been easy shooting the almost-tame monkeys. But the creatures were clever and learned to run off when a man with a musket got close. Fortunately they weren't quite clever enough and there was a distance from which they could be hit with an ounce-charge of the goose-shot saved from *Lion*'s cargo.

That worked, provided the marksman moved slow and careful.

"Bang!" went Conky Carter's musket.

"Damn!" said Silver, as the little swine leapt at the flash of the lock, getting a split second's warning before the charge whistled past beneath its flying feet.

Bang-bang-bang! The others fired, knocking the monkey clear out of its tree and on to the ground, where it lay wriggling and shrieking with two limbs shattered and much of its tail blown off.

"Gotcher!" they cried in fierce delight. They hated monkeys now. Hated them with a passion, because they were afraid of them: deep, cruel afraid.

"Reload!" cried Silver. "Get it done, lads!" There was a scraping of ramrods, and powder and shot and wadding. Then a volley of shots ended the monkey's life and shut off its cries. There was no going near the little bastards while they were still alive. Trouble was, shooting them spread bits of monkey all over the ground.

"Spades and shovels, now," said Silver, and stood back as they got on with it. Drawing on what he'd read in the old Jesuit's journal, they had worked out a drill. For there was no leaving the monkeys be. They were too inquisitive, and every man was afraid of waking up one morning with one of them on his chest, pawing him with tiny pock-marked hands.

So Silver had teams out shooting them. Each team was accompanied by at least one of the half-dozen men who'd survived smallpox and had the scars on his face to show it.

These did the shovelling and scraping of remains, while the rest piled wood on top and lit a fire.

"To the windward, lads!" said Silver as the flames rose. "Let's not breathe the smoke."

They stood and watched the fire.

"Is this what the old Jesuit did, Cap'n?" said Conky Carter. "Burned 'em, like?"

"No," said Silver, "he buried 'em. Didn't shoot 'em, neither. He trapped 'em and drowned 'em. Took him years. But he got 'em all in the end. Drove him barmy though, 'cos they was all the company he had."

"Where'd he bury 'em?" said Carter.

"In the cemetery. Dug a big hole, chucked 'em in, and filled it up bit by bit."

"But burying ain't no good."

"He didn't know that."

"What about our monkeys? Why didn't he do for them?"

"Different tribe," said Silver, depressed by the whole business. "The old Jesuit left 'em alone, for they never had the smallpox. Not until Ben Gunn gave it to 'em!"

That evening Silver was even more depressed. As he approached Fort Silver, back from his monkey-shooting, he could hear angry voices from within the earthworks.

"Shiver me timbers!" he said, and stopped and listened. There were no sentries outside the walls, nor up on the lookout tower.

"Come on!" he said to the six men behind him, and plunged forward as fast as he could go. There was no challenge on the drawbridge across the moat, nor was there any discipline within the walls. Just bellowing and shouting and slurred voices . . . they'd been at the rum.

"Avast there!" cried Silver, and some two dozen men turned round and gaped at him and all began to speak at once. It was almost comical. The neat tents were knocked askew, faces were flushed, there were smashed bottles and broken noses. Billy Bones was stamping towards Silver, yelling louder than all the rest, and Israel Hands was slumped on the ground, propped up against a cask with blood streaming from a head wound.

Silver as nearly gave up in that moment as ever in all his life. All his careful work was wasted. If the men wouldn't pull together, they might as well blow out their brains right now, to save Flint the trouble.

"Billy Bones!" he said. "What's happening here?"

"It's all that bugger!" said Billy Bones, pointing at Israel Hands, and he thrust his red, sweating, boozy face at Silver. "I'll not take no more 'oss-shite, not from him, *nor you, John Silver!* I'm as good a man as any here, and what I say is this: why don't we give the captain a chance when he comes back? Cap'n Flint, that is! Why don't –"

But that was as far as he got, because Silver's temper snapped. He leapt forward, one-legged, caught the back of Billy's head with his left hand, and drove a big right fist – smack, smack, smack – three times into the middle of Billy Bone's face. Bones was half drunk, taken by surprise, and in any case he was afraid of Silver and already cringing. Down he went, with split lips and swollen eyes, leaving Silver wobbling and swaying but master of the field.

"Here, Cap'n!" said Conky Carter, snatching up Silver's discarded crutch.

"Now then," said Silver, getting the timber under his arm and taking a firm grasp of a pistol butt, "next man's a dead 'un what speaks Flint's name to me!" All the shouting died

165

then, and there was silence except for the eternal, dismal surf.

"Huh!" said Silver, and singled out three of the biggest men. "You there! Take up this swab –" he jerked a thumb at Billy Bones "– heave him outside the fort, and tie him fast to a tree. And you two –" he chose two that were passing sober "– look to Mr Hands, and get him shipshape."

Later, in Silver's tent, with a candle lit and Israel Hands's head bound up with strips torn from a shirt, and over some more rum – because Silver needed it after the day he'd had – Silver asked what had happened.

"Well," said Israel Hands, "we was arguing over Flint."

"Flint, eh? And Billy Bones arguing the loudest?"

"Aye."

"So who hit you, Israel?"

"Dunno, Cap'n. We was throwing bottles."

"You too?"

"Me too."

Silver sighed, and slumped into a chair. What chance was there, if all hands didn't pull together? And in the morning it was worse, for Billy Bones was gone, and nearly half the men in the fort had gone with him, taking arms and ammunition and supplies. Silver was plunged into guilt.

"Why didn't I set a proper watch? How did they do it? Why didn't I wake up?"

"John," said Israel Hands, "you've done the work of ten these last weeks and – beggin' your pardon, Cap'n – you're a one-legged man that's gone from end to end o' this island, where any whole man would be wore out! So it ain't no mystery that you sleep sound."

As ever when anguished, Silver reached up and stroked the parrot, which nuzzled and nipped his ear and muttered

166

words and bobbed her head. She was a great comfort to him, and he smiled.

"This old bird's got more sense than me!" he said. But then he set to and sent out men to find Billy Bones, and made sure the fort kept proper watch and proper duties, including the daily removal of a calendar peg as the ship's bell struck noon. There were forty pegs left after that day's peg was removed.

Finding Billy Bones wasn't hard. Knowing that he'd not be welcomed in any of the other forts Silver had built, Billy had gone to the one *Flint* had built, years ago: the log blockhouse, up in the trees above the southern anchorage. His sole plan was to wait for Flint's return, and fall on his mercy so that he might again bask in the grace of his hero. So there he sat with the ten men that had followed him, and who now spent their time sweeping and cleaning, and polishing everything made of brass or steel, all the better to win *the Cap'n*'s favour on his return. Thus for a little while Billy Bones was happy, since he'd been used all his life to chasing men to their duties, and was never happier than when doing so.

He was a simple soul at heart, and his simple pleasure lasted until noon on the second day of his rebellion, when – convinced that Silver had seen sense and left him alone, and dozing comfortably inside the blockhouse, confident that all decent men were doing much the same – Billy Bones's teeth rattled, and the heavy timbers of the blockhouse shook, to the thunder of a ship's gun fired close by. A great cloud of smoke followed, rolling, choking and stinking through the blockhouse fence, and in through its open door.

"Mr Bones!" cried John Silver from outside. "Can you hear me?"

Billy Bones jumped up, and ran round kicking men awake and thrusting weapons into their hands.

"Alllllll hands," he cried, "stand by to repel boarders!" Up they got and stumbled dozy-eyed to their stations, and slid their muskets out through the loopholes and clacked their locks, and stood in the dark, hot shadow, peering out over gleaming barrels into the blazing sun.

"Mr Bones," cried Silver, "I'm willing to speak to you if –"

"Go fuck yerself!" yelled Billy Bones. "Go fuck your one-leggity self!"

"I'm warning you, Billy . . ."

"Bollocks!"

"Give 'em another," said Silver.

The gun spoke again, deafening at close range, and the shot howled, screaming over the blockhouse roof. When the smoke and noise died, Silver spoke again:

"Last chance to all within the blockhouse," he cried. "Next round is fired for effect, and fired by Mr Hands who never misses, and is the first of as many after that as it takes to knock you mutinous swabs into splinters!"

"Bugger . . ." said Billy Bones, which he shouldn't have, for it gave the game away to all hands, and they pressed forward to the side of the house facing Silver, and looked out . . . and saw the tall figure, in his familiar long coat and hat, and the green bird on his shoulder, and a four-pounder gun, mounted on an improvised land carriage, with solid planked wheels that somehow – at enormous labour – had been built and dragged through the forest and brought to bear on the blockhouse at the very hour when Billy Bones and his men would least expect it. Bones groaned. That was Silver, that was. Only Silver could do a thing like that . . . and Flint, of course . . . so he thought.

"Stap me vitals!" said Billy Bones, as the men round the

gun aimed it square at the house, and Israel Hands swung a match-cord to make the tip burn bright. The gun wasn't six feet from the fence, and so close it couldn't miss.

"Last chance!" said Silver.

"Stand fast all hands!" cried Billy Bones.

"Fire!" said Silver.

Boom! said the gun and smoke billowed and a thundering blow struck home and every log in the blockhouse jumped and spouted dirt and muck, and the roof timbers cracked open and sunbeams stabbed the darkness, bearing oceans of swirling dust.

"Give 'em a volley!" snarled Billy Bones, and Bang! Bang! his own pistols spoke. Two men pulled triggers, but only two. They were half-hearted, and soon the four-pounder roared and the blockhouse trembled as Israel Hands put a second shot into the same spot as the first, knocking the jagged ends of a log into the dark inside, and killing a man stone dead with his teeth smashed out through the back of his head.

Which was the end of the rebellion. The men in the block-house threw down their arms and jammed the doorway to get outside. Once there, they fell to their knees, raised their arms, and begged for mercy, which Long John granted, as he had to. There couldn't be any hangings or shootings for he had too few men as it was.

Long John knew that from now on he would have to abandon all other plans and keep most of the men in one place, under his leadership, for his command of the island depended on it. To delegate would risk losing the lot of them in this endless fighting.

It was a dire prospect. Even Long John, in his heart, was beginning to give up.

Chapter 21

Evening, 22nd November 1752
Aboard Lucy May
Charlestown Bay, South Carolina

Seven men sat in a circle on *Lucy May*'s quarterdeck, all lesser persons having been removed: Dreamer, the medicine sachem, and Dark Hand, the war sachem, sat for the Patanq nation; Captain Flint, Mijnheer Van Oosterhout and Mr Charles Neal, sat for the men of the schooner *Walrus*; Captain Daniel Bentham and Mr Brendan O'Byrne sat for the men of the snow *Hercules;* and Captain Lewis Parry sat for the men of the sloop *Sweet Anne*. It was Danny Bentham who'd explained to the white men that, if they were to be taken seriously by the Patanq chiefs, they must be introduced as representing more than just themselves.

For Danny Bentham knew Indians, having grown up among them as a fighting tomboy, wearing breeches and running wild with the Mohawk boys from Cana-Joharie, the *Upper Castle*, and Tion-Onderoga, the *Lower Castle*: the Indian villages near Warrensburgh in the colony of New York. The whites called them "castles" because of their heavy palisades, which made them a damn sight more impressive than Warrensburgh itself. Danny even earned an Indian name: *One-who-understands*, for his fluency in the Mohawk tongue, and interest in all matters having to do with hunting, fighting and woodcraft.

Of course, that was before Danny got fed up with winters so cold that ink froze in the bottle even by the fireside. And it was before Danny got tired of fist-fighting and wrestling, and adopted the tomahawk, and became unwelcome among the Mohawks, who, like any civilised people, understood the difference between youthful high spirits and murderous violence. So One-who-understands was obliged to seek other amusements – and ran away to sea.

Nevertheless, it was Danny Bentham who'd arranged the great council of Charlestown harbour. He'd been the one who'd chosen presents that the Patanq sachems would appreciate: fine shirts with ruffles at neck and cuff, body-paint of Chinese vermillion and verdigris, Stroud blankets in rich colours, and good hand-mirrors in strong frames . . . *that* and the powder, shot and rum that any fool would have given.

And months earlier it had been Danny Bentham who had acted as intermediary in finding ships to take the Patanq nation on its wanderings. Naturally, he had taken a slice of the Patanq's money in the process, for it had been hard work; most shipmasters – especially good seamen with prime vessels – refused outright, unwilling even to consider taking Indians aboard ship. Of those that said *yes*, the majority were desperate or in command of worn-out vessels. So, even if he *had* dipped his hand in their purse, he'd not dipped too deep, and he'd acted fairly on their behalf . . . or at least as fairly as he was capable of.

For their part, the Patanq leaders were also desperate, though Dreamer and Dark Hand gave no indication of this when Captain Bentham came to them proposing a solution to their present problems. They were prepared to trust him . . . within limits . . . and to meet Captain Flint for a great council.

The bargaining had been long, and hard. It had lasted all day. For the white men it had been maddeningly slow, with eloquent speeches by the two Patanq sachems using formal and poetic words. But agreement was now close, and a tobacco pipe was passing from hand to hand, giving each man his chance to speak. The whites were shifting and fidgeting to ease limbs unused to sitting cross-legged on a hard wooden deck. But Dark Hand and Dreamer were impassive; they spoke in steady, deep voices seemingly devoid of emotion.

"So," said Dreamer, "we are agreed that *this cause* is not part of the coming war that the English will fight with the French." The whites nodded. "Because the English are sending messengers across the land to find allies for this war, and the Patanq will not be part of it." The whites nodded. "Good," said Dreamer, "then I ask the sachem Flint to tell us again what it is that we must do. And for what reward . . ."

The pipe was passed to Flint, who drew on it, and spoke.

"I shall lead the Patanq nation – the entire nation, in their ships – to an island where there is buried a great quantity of gold and silver. Only I know the location of the island, and only I know where the gold is buried. But the island has been stolen by others. There are about seventy of them. They are well armed, with powder and muskets, and maybe cannon. They are strong men who will fight hard, and who

172

know that we are coming." Flint looked at the two Patanq, and each nodded briefly. So far so good. There was no point in pretending it would be easy.

"I propose," said Flint, "that we fight these men, and kill them, and recover the gold . . ." He blinked. "And . . . and . . ." He paused, "I promise that I will share the gold equally with the Patanq nation." With this Flint stopped, as if exhausted by heavy labour. He looked down. He frowned.

Charley Neal held his breath. Every other white man present held his breath as Flint faced the last fence: the fence that had blocked all agreements so far.

"I believe," said Flint, "that the value of this treasure . . . in English money . . ." He took a breath. He made the effort: "I believe the value to be . . . over eight hundred thousand pounds."

There was a united gasp at this colossal figure. Only the two Patanq remained unmoved – at least externally.

Dreamer stretched out his hand, seeking the pipe.

"Here," said Flint, and handed it to him so he could speak. Dreamer took a long, slow time, thinking and smoking. Then:

"Good," he said. "It is my word that we should do this thing." He turned to his companion: "What is your word, my brother?"

Dark Hand took the pipe.

"I say *yes*." He looked at Flint. "The Patanq nation puts three hundred warriors into the field. They are yours for this cause."

Flint sighed. He closed his eyes and nodded. Charley Neal dared to breathe, Danny Bentham and Brendan O'Byrne grinned, and Van Oosterhout closed his eyes, the better to make the delightful calculation of what his own share might be, when converted into *Nederlanse Gulden*.

"There are other matters . . ." said Dreamer.

"Oh?" said the white men.

"Yes," said Dreamer, and pointed at Van Oosterhout: "Men say that you, *Red Beard*, are skilled at finding a way across the waters. You will take command of this ship and the Patanq fleet. You will bring the women and children safe to the island. And you – *Sun-Face* –" he turned to Flint "– you that have secrets to find this island: you will share them with Red Beard. For I tell you, Sun-Face –" he fixed Flint with his eye "– if Red Beard does not come to the island, then you and I shall not be friends."

Flint bade farewell to his plan to lose the Patanq women and children at sea, and nodded.

"And," said Dreamer, "we shall go tomorrow to all the ships of the fleet, taking Red Beard to the shipmasters that they shall know him as the leader who shall bring them to the island of gold, where they shall be kept from the fighting but shall be richly paid. For without this, why should they obey Red Beard?"

"So be it," said Flint, amazed that he'd ever thought Dreamer a savage.

"Good," said Dreamer. "Meanwhile, I and Dark Hand, and the three hundred warriors, will sail. Some in *your* ship –" he pointed at Flint. "And some in *your* ship –" he pointed at Bentham. "And some in your ship –" he pointed at Parry. "I have spoken!"

A great argument followed, for it had never occurred to Bentham, O'Byrne and Parry that they would be outnumbered aboard their own ships, so there was much shouting and pointing. But Dreamer sat impassive and the agreement was breaking apart when Flint spoke. In that dire moment, facing failure of all his plans, he thought of other days and imagined how someone else would have resolved this impasse: someone whom he'd greatly admired.

"What does it matter?" he said. "If we can't rely on one another, there's neither point nor prospect in this expedition. We're either jolly companions or we're not!" He reached across to Dreamer. "We've followed *your* customs all day, sir, so now here's one of *mine*. It is *my* word that we should sail as you ask, and I offer you my hand on it as a gentleman of fortune . . ."

The gesture was so splendid, and Flint's prestige so great, that Bentham, Parry and O'Byrne shut up, and held their breath to see what should happen next.

There was silence as Flint and Dreamer looked at each other across a poisoned wasteland – a sea of scars – ruined by the collision of two races that were opposite in culture, incompatible in spirit, and utterly mutually hostile. Physically the two men could not have been more different: the thin, sickly Patanq, hook-nosed, tattooed, dark and wrinkled, with his shaven skull, and his rings and his feathers and his dangling lock of hair . . . and Flint the smooth, menacing white man with his beautiful face, and his shining smile and immense charm.

Then Dreamer slowly reached out his hand and clasped Flint's, and the white men cheered. Agreement was reached.

So toasts were drunk, and Flint, Bentham, Neal and the others stood up and smiled, and stretched their legs, and nodded and told one another what jolly dogs they were and what a fine deal they'd made. Many more of the Patanq came up from below and then . . . a sudden and dreadful transformation took place. The immensely dignified Dreamer took up one of the rum bottles that had been given as a present, knocked off the neck with his hatchet, and up-ended

175

the bottle over his mouth. Dark Hand did the same. The other Patanq warriors yelled and squabbled for their share of the drink. They drank to be drunk. They drank to oblivion. They screeched and hollered and staggered and fought and fell. It was bedlam and chaos aboard *Lucy May*.

Soon the women and children came up too, and there was Dreamer, sat in the middle of a circle of them, propped up, grinning and guzzling and singing, while they howled with laughter and egged him on.

"It's always the same," said Danny Bentham, seeing the expression on Flint's face. "They can't help it, Joe. They just pour it down." Bentham searched for words to explain and excuse. He had to, because he'd been the one who'd sold these men to Flint as mighty warriors.

"They don't brew no drink of their own, d'you see? It's uncharted waters for 'em. They got no pilot nor guide. Where we might drink a bottle with a friend, or a good dinner, they drink the whole damn cellar all in one go, just so soon as they get hold of it. They don't know no better, d'you see? They'll fight. Never doubt that, Joe. But they just can't help it with the rum."

"Yes," said Flint, thoughtfully, "I'd heard that. Heard it, but never seen it." He drew Bentham aside, finding a quiet corner. "I'm glad you took my lead, Danny, over sailing with so many warriors aboard."

"I did wonder, Joe. But I supposed you had your reasons."

"Which I did, Danny."

"And which were . . . ?"

"Well, they'll outnumber us – *outward bound*."

"Yes?"

"But that don't matter, because we'll all be of one mind."

"To find the island?"

"Yes. But once *on* the island, it's *them* who'll fight John Silver's men."

"Ah!"

"And there won't be half so many of them . . . *homeward bound*."

"Suppose not."

"And beyond that, any time we need, we can splice the main brace."

"And see the lot of 'em three sheets to the wind!"

They stood a while, looking at the pitiful spectacle of the virile Patanq reduced to slobbering drunkards. Then Flint roused himself.

"Well," he said, "boats away, I think. We're done this day."

"Joe," said Bentham, "just one more thing . . ."

"What?"

"Our agreement – about the lady . . . that stands?"

"God bless your soul, yes!" said Flint. "I gave my word!"

As it was now dark, Danny Bentham couldn't quite see the expression on Flint's face.

Then Charley Neal and Van Oosterhout came up, followed by Captain Foster, who had just learned that he was no longer even nominally the master aboard his own ship. There was a considerable deal more shouting and arguing before Neal and Flint could go over the side and into *Walrus*'s launch, but their unique powers of persuasion triumphed in the end.

"Goodnight, Cap'n Flint!" cried Bentham, as his own boat pulled away.

"Goodnight, Cap'n Bentham!" cried Flint, waving his hat.

"You send my sea-chest tomorrow, yes?" cried Van Oosterhout, leaning over *Lucy May*'s rail. "And my instruments and my tables?"

177

"Of course, Mr Mate," said Flint, teeth gleaming in the darkness.

"Better I come back with you tonight!" said Van Oosterhout in surly mood.

"What's that?" said Flint, affecting deafness.

"Why do I stay here now? I do not agree!"

"Goodnight, Mr Mate!" cried Flint. It was better that Van Oosterhout stayed where he was. Had Dreamer not offered so excellent an excuse, Flint would have invented one.

"Give way!" said Flint. The oarsmen swayed, the oars splashed, darkness wrapped *Lucy May*, and the harbour spread out in sombre shadows all around, with distant lights from Charlestown, a dark forest of spars and rigging over the ships in the anchorage, and the water slick and gleaming in the moonlight.

On the ship, among his women and children, Dreamer bawled out a song and was so gracious as to give his wives a go at the bottle. He laughed aloud as the white man's fire ran through his body . . . and then he stopped. He stopped, and fell silent and sat up, and all his good drunkenness ran away like water from a smashed pot.

He thought of the white sachem: the one greater than all others. The one who struck fear with his eyes. Then he thought of the left-handed twin, who cut his way from his mother's body at the Beginning, and made everything that was bad. Dreamer now knew that this twin was indeed Satan, though he had many other names: Warty-Skin, Ugly-Face and Stone-Blade were common. But he was also named for the stone from which sharp blades were struck. That stone was called . . . *Flint*.

*   *   *

"Well, Cap'n," said Charley Neal, "that went very well!" He was still wheezing with the effort of clambering down the side of a ship in darkness. He was too fat and too old for ship's boats, what with them rocking and heaving and trying to put him over the side. But for the first time since Flint had dropped anchor in Savannah, Neal could see his way clear of his troubles. The day had indeed gone well.

"Aye," said Flint, then, "Watch your steering there!" he snapped at the man at the tiller. "Follow my orders, you swab!"

Hmm, thought Charley, Flint was in one of his moods. You could never tell with Flint, for it'd been an uncanny couple of days. First Flint had gone head over heels for Selena and turned into another man entirely, such that none of the old things mattered any more. Then there was the bizarre matter of Bentham being caught in the same trap, and coming to Flint, asking for her hand in marriage – *marriage,* for Christ's sake! – when the bastard knew she was supposed to be Flint's bloody wife! Or did he know she wasn't? Who could tell? Bentham was as mad as Flint. *Differently* mad, but bloody mad all the same.

None of that mattered though. All Flint's problems were over. He didn't need Pimenta now. He could bring Selena back aboard and roger her cross-eyed. Flint had secured three good ships to carry an army, he'd *got* his army, and if the Patanq fleet was to trail along behind him – why, Joe Flint would soon lose them! And then he'd get rid of all the rest of the poor bloody Indians who thought he was going to treat them fair! That's my boy. That's Joe Flint!

Best of all, thought Charley Neal, there's myself right at the centre of all these happy events. Wasn't it myself stopped Flint murdering Danny Bentham when he went goggle-eyed over Selena? Wasn't it myself explained that Bentham was the key to the Patanq? And wasn't it myself spent bloody hours talking Flint into making agreement with the Indians, and telling them – and nobody else – enough to bring them aboard of his blasted expedition to the blasted island?

Holy Mary Mother of God! Neal had guided him like a child. He'd shown him the true and righteous path. And now it was time for Charley Neal to dip his bread in the sauce. There'd never be a better time. No matter how many of Flint's secrets he knew, there were others who knew as much, and even Flint couldn't be planning to get rid of *everyone*, could he? Having done all that Flint asked, Charley felt sure he must be well on the way to Dublin now.

"Captain," he said, "I've been thinking. You know I've always planned to go back to Ireland one day . . ."

"Have you, Charley?"

"I have, Joe."

"And when might this be?"

"Well, Joe . . ." Neal frowned, he looked around. "Where are we going?"

"To the ship, Charley."

"But we're heading for the harbour mouth."

"Are we, Charley?"

The oarsmen pulled steadily towards deep water and the ebb tide sweeping out to sea. The boat was no more than a tiny smudge on twinkling waves under a black sky pricked with stars. When the moon went behind a cloud, the boat was invisible.

There was a small struggle and a soft splash.

Chapter 22

Late evening, 24th November 1752
The Corner Tavern
At the junction of Church Street and Broad Street
Charlestown, South Carolina

*T*he tavern's reception rooms were packed with the elite of Charlestown in their finest clothes: the governor and his lady – who were the host and hostess – the councillors and their ladies, the assemblymen, churchmen, lawyers, merchants, and all their ladies, along with every other man in the town who'd sold his soul for an invitation in the interest of advancement in colonial society, together with their ladies.

A fortune had been spent on candles, the town's bakers had lost their flour to powder hundreds of wigs, the finest musicians in the Carolinas were playing, corks popped in volleys, wine flowed as if without cost. Outside, the streets were packed with all those who couldn't get in but had come to ogle the rich and the mighty, and especially to cheer the arrival of Commodore Sir Richard Scott-Owen and the officers of his squadron, come to save Charlestown from rape and pillage by the French – for what other purpose could this naval presence have?

In the midst of all this, Selena was transported nearly

unto heaven, even though she knew it would be her last night in Charlestown, and that Allardyce – at Flint's orders – would be knocking at Meshod Pimenta's door in the morning to take her out to the ship. She knew all about Flint's business with the Indians, and what that meant, because Flint had told her. He'd told her earlier that evening, aboard the ship, and he'd gazed at her and opened his heart.

"You go to the ball, my dear," he'd said. "You enjoy yourself."

"The invitation says *Mr and Mrs Garland* . . . won't you come, Joe?"

"Can't be done. I've three hundred savages to embark aboard this ship and Danny Bentham's, and shiploads of stores to shift. I want that done neat and nimble! I've no time for dancing, but I'm happy for you to go."

And then he kissed her! He dared to kiss her cheek, then her chin . . . then her lips. He put his arms around her and held her close, and kissed her with something approaching a lover's passion . . . something approaching it, but not quite reaching it . . . which was a huge relief to Selena, who dared not reject him, but *would* not encourage him; not while she had strength of mind to be her own woman and make her own choices.

So she stared up at him as, finally, he released her with a smile. The workings of his mind were a mystery, but she'd known something like this was coming ever since he'd seen her in the yellow gown. At least he wasn't a full man towards her . . . not yet.

"Now," he said, "go to the ball!"

So he stayed aboard, and in the boat pulling for the shore, she wished Charley Neal hadn't gone: headed back to Ireland, according to Flint, seizing the sudden good luck of a ship on the tide for Dublin. It was a shame, because Charley was kind and wise, and she could have spoken to him.

Soon, however, she forgot the dangers all around her and began to enjoy herself in the company of Meshod and Esther Pimenta and their friends . . . and the delight of wearing the spectacular yellow gown . . . and knowing she was spectacularly beautiful, and that every man in the room was elbowing his way forward to ask her to dance! This was especially wonderful, because – while she'd grown up on such books as Tomlinson's *Art of Dancing* and Rameau's *Le Maître à Danser,* and while she'd learned the minuet with Miss Eugenie and the maids – she'd never danced with a gentleman. Plantation nigger-women didn't do that.

So she danced. And never noticed that one particular gentleman – a gentleman in green silk – was looking at her very curiously and very carefully, and taking great care that *she* should not see *him.*

She danced with shoals of others, though, including both the young gentlemen who seemed to be the centre of attention among Commodore Scott-Owen's officers: Lieutenant George Hastings, a tall, shy young man, with curly hair, and Mr Midshipman Povey, a relative youngster – he was just fifteen – but already settling into heavy muscle and lead-footedness. He was a poor dancer but an exceedingly jolly fellow who made her laugh.

He said a number of very silly things to her when he came up and begged a dance, and even contrived to whisper in her ear, so he could tickle it with the tip of his tongue. Some men were nervous around beautiful women, but not David Povey, for all his youth. She rapped him with a fan for that, but she still laughed.

"It's all his mother, you know!" he said, when he led her on to the floor away from a reluctant Hastings. "I'm nothing, don't you know! Unlike your good self – you're like an elf

183

from a story book!" And he gazed at her in wonderment – but then, all the gentlemen did. Selena was becoming used to it.

And all the while the gentleman in green stared harder at Selena.

"What about Mrs Hastings?" she said, as the band struck up and they executed the formal steps of the minuet, timing their conversation to the gentle rising and falling of the music, and the gliding choreography of the other dancers in their silks and brocades.

"*Lady* Hastings. Constance Manners as was."

"Yes?"

"Well, her sister – Lady *Catherine* Manners as was – is married to the Prime Minister, Mr Pelham."

"Oh!" said Selena.

"So she's got the most colossal interest, don't you know."

"What's *interest*?"

"It's what runs the navy, ma'am. It's *who you know*!" He grinned. "We was knocked about a bit, you see, me and George Hastings, so his ma, the lovely Lady Constance – who's so lovely, she's *almost* as lovely as you . . ."

Selena laughed, intoxicated.

". . . Lady Constance had a word in the right ear, and that's why we got such fine ships and Commodore Scott-Owen, who's the best there is!"

"But what for?"

"So's we can hunt him down. We're the only ones left who know him."

"Know who?"

"*Him*. We sailed with him, did Hastings and me. We were set adrift by him."

"Who?"

"What? Don't you know? I thought everyone knew."

"I don't."

"Flint. That villain Flint! We're here to catch him and hang him."

The gentleman in green saw Selena's hand go to her mouth.

"This is the poster," Mr Governor, said Commodore Scott-Owen, and the blue-and-gold, white-powdered, sea-service officer handed a rolled sheet of paper to the red-and-gold, white-powdered James Glen, the middle-aged, long-faced professional politician who'd been Royal Governor of South Carolina since 1743. "This is the reason for our presence in Charlestown, which soon will be common knowledge."

"Thank you, Commodore," said Glen, Scots accent still strong after all his years away. "But can't this wait?" He looked at the pleasures of the ball, from which he'd been drawn into a quiet corner, trailed by a clutch of councillors and assemblymen: climbers-of-the-greasy-pole who sniffed after him even tonight . . . just as Scott-Owen was likewise followed by a clutch of his officers.

"No time, sir!" said Scott-Owen, a serious and surprisingly young man – he was barely thirty – who was determined to make the most of the ships and command he'd been given. "We have so little time before the villain knows we're in the Americas. We must maintain the precious advantage of surprise!"

"Huh!" said Glen, unrolling the document and feeling the paper. "Who paid for this? Thirty inches by twenty-two, finest quality . . ."

"Don't worry, sir," Scott-Owen smiled a small smile, "the navy's paying." He looked down. "Handsome, don't you think? And we've enough of 'em to post in the high street of every British town in the colonies!"

Glen read:

WHEREAS
The former Lieutenant

˧OSEPH FLINT

of His Majeſty's Ship *Elizabeth*,
Now expelled in diſgrace from His Majeſty's Sea-Service,

Has committed diverſe and atrocious acts of

MUTINY PIRACY MURDER
& REBELLION

the sum of

ONE THOUSAND POUNDS IN
GOLD

Will be paid to any perſon delivering up the body of the said
Joſeph Flint, dead or alive, to Officers of the Crown, or providing
said Officers with information which shall lead to the capture and
succeſsful proſecution of the said Joſeph Flint.

Joſeph Flint being a man of middling height: slim-built,
dark-haired, dark-eyed, olive-skinned, with strongly handſome
features, fine teeth, athletic bearing, of perverſely cruel and violent
habits, and poſſeſſed in marked degree, with the power to inſpire
fright in other men.

Given this fifteenth day of September MDCCLII,
in His Majeſty's Name,
At The Admiralty, White Hall.

GOD SAVE THE KING

Selena fell back on the ancient excuse of a headache. Which worked. She danced no more, and Esther Pimenta fussed over her, and sat her down on one of the chairs that lined the room, and a cold drink was found, and a series of most solicitous gentlemen came to voice their sympathy. Mr Midshipman Povey was one of them, offering *my heart in a handkerchief* if she'd only fly off with him to Elysium. He was very young and very charming, but she wished him dead, because he was here to hang Flint, and Flint was her only way back to Silver . . .

So she wanted to be out and gone. She wanted to be back aboard *Walrus* and warning Flint. She didn't know what'd brought the navy down on him – bad luck? Betrayal? Cunning? But she had to warn him . . . *or did she?* Perhaps this was the way out? Perhaps she could be free? But she was supposed to be his wife. What did that mean? Would they hang her for it? Or would they pity her? Would they send her on her way with their blessing and a guinea from the poor box? And in any case, could there ever be another life for her . . . somewhere, anywhere . . . with John Silver? If *he* could get off the island or *she* could get back on it? Flint was the only man who knew how to find the island, and he wanted to kill Silver! Her head spun. She didn't know. She'd have run straight out of the door, but she was laced into a gown worth a fortune, and she'd surely be seen and followed.

So she sat where she was, and it helped her excuses that she really did look ill. She cowered in her chair, till even Esther Pimenta got fed up with her, and deserted her to make the most of the evening. It was very late when finally the Pimentas left with Mrs Garland: the two ladies riding the short distance to Pimenta's house in sedan chairs.

The gentleman in green watched all this, and came to a conclusion.

At Pimenta's house, the servants took over. Selena was extracted from her gown and put to bed in the pretty bedroom that was hers when she stayed with the Pimentas. Esther Pimenta wanted badly to talk over the evening, but found her little protégée to be wooden, distant and cold. So she gave up, and was in her dressing room in the middle of being extracted from her own gown when there was a heavy knocking at the front door.

She listened. The front door was opened by Thomas the butler. There were voices. Thomas came upstairs. He went into her husband's dressing room. More feet on the stairs. More voices. Raised voices! Then feet came upstairs fast, and Meshod himself burst into her dressing room with the fear of God on his face.

"Esther!" he said, then caught sight of her maid. "You! Get out!" he said, bundling the girl outside. "Esther, what's Mrs Garland's name?"

"Why?"

"Never mind *why* – what's her damn name?"

Esther Pimenta gaped. Meshod *never* used strong language.

"What's her bloody name? Her given name?"

"Selena."

"God help us! God help us all!"

Pimenta clapped a hand to his brow and walked up and down the little room while his wife looked on in horror. She'd never seen her clever, devious husband in fear. Then he breathed deep, opened his eyes and stopped pacing. He came close and spoke softly.

"Listen," he said, "there are things you don't know."

"What things?"

"Her husband's not Garland . . . he's Flint!"

"Flint?" she said, standing up and clutching at him. "The pirate?"

"Yes. The one the navy's chasing."

"And you let his wife into the house!"

"I didn't know the damned navy was coming!"

"You should have known!"

"Shut up! There's big money – Charley Neal said it's hundreds of thousands."

"What money?"

"Never mind. I'd hoped to get her out tomorrow, quietly . . ."

"Mr Pimenta!" a loud voice from downstairs. "You must bring the girl, sir! You must bring her now!"

Pimenta shrugged, a helpless gesture, and put a finger to his lips.

"Leave this to me," he said.

He went out on to the landing, to Selena's bedroom, and knocked. She opened the door. She'd heard the noise. She was dressed; dressed in the green gown that she'd worn when first she came to the house. It didn't fit. It didn't suit her. Not like the yellow silk. Pimenta couldn't help but notice.

"Mrs Garland," he said, "there are gentlemen downstairs . . ."

"Bring her down, sir!" came a loud voice. "Down this instant, I say!"

"*Say nothing of your husband!*" said Pimenta. "All our lives depend on it!"

She nodded and they went downstairs to the hall, where Thomas was standing with a lighted candelabrum, and two gentlemen were looking up at her. One was a commoner: a big, heavy man, with thick boots and a greatcoat and a staff of office. He was nothing, but the other was young and arrogant, obviously commanding wealth and power. He was powdered, and wore a swirling cloak. Beneath the cloak was embroidered silk: a coat, vest and breeches, en suite and all in green.

Selena, however, saw only his face. She recognised him and nearly fainted. She stumbled and Pimenta caught her and put an arm around her.

"Mrs Garland," he said, "these gentlemen are Constable Granger –" the big man nodded curtly "– and Mr Archibald Delacroix."

Selena flinched again, and Pimenta patted her hand and tried to make all normal.

"Never fear, my dear," he said. "Mr Delacroix is a good friend and a frequent visitor to this house." He looked at Delacroix. "Isn't that so, sir?" But Delacroix gave him only the briefest nod. He wasn't here to see Pimenta.

He pointed at Selena and stepped forward, grim-faced.

"You're the one!" he said. "I've been watching you all evening. I wasn't quite sure at first, for you've changed. But I'm sure now. You're Selena, the slave that murdered my father!"

Selena groaned. She shook her head. It wasn't true. She'd not murdered anyone. Her own mother had taken her to the master's "special house" where he raped the slave girls that took his fancy. She'd left her there, and told her to be good, for the sake of her family. And Selena had tried, but the master was a sweating oaf who'd had too much food and drink . . . and had choked on his own vomit on the floor at her feet. And so she'd run away. That was the truth, but who'd believe it? No white man, that was for sure! And never the master's son. Not when his face was flushed with revenge.

"Oh yes!" he said, staring at Selena, "you're the one."

Then he frowned mightily as the delight of capture faded and darker thoughts erupted.

"Have you any idea what disturbance you brought upon my estates?" he said. "That a slave should kill the master and escape? D'you realise what ideas that plants in the minds of the rest?" He licked his lips as wild pictures formed in his mind. "An example must be made of you. You shall be stripped naked before them all, and the hide flogged off you. The hangman shan't get a touch of you till I've done that."

"Sir!" said Granger. "Leave this to the law. If she's a runaway, she'll be returned to you as your property. But if she's done murder, then there must be due process of law."

"Don't tell me the law," said Delacroix nastily. "I can buy you, and the law, and all the lawyers in Charlestown. You just mind your tongue and don't get in the way of your betters!"

"Well," said Constable Granger, less certain now, "she's still got to be arrested."

"Pah!" said Delacroix. "Come here!" And he stretched out his hand for Selena. She dodged and he missed. He lunged again, caught her, and – stung to anger – *SMACK!* He struck her back-handed across the face.

Meshod Pimenta, who'd kept quiet thus far, jumped forward and seized Delacroix's hand. He was shaking with fright and all his instincts told him to keep out of this, but Selena was a woman, and Meshod Pimenta had a mother and sisters, as well as a wife.

"Don't!" he said. "Don't hit her!"

"Keep out of this . . . *Jew!*" said Delacroix.

Pimenta stood in agony. Delacroix was a member of the planter aristocracy, the most powerful class in the colonies.

The Jews were accepted in Charlestown, with a new synagogue on Union Street to prove it, and Pimenta did much business among the gentiles, including Delacroix himself . . . but . . . but . . . there were those who wanted no Jews – some of the Anglicans and Dutch Protestants, for instance – so he dared not make an enemy of Delacroix. Pimenta stood back.

"Good!" said Delacroix. "Now, Constable . . . take her in charge!"

Granger stepped forward, producing a set of manacles from his coat pockets.

Selena looked round, head ringing from the blow. There was no help. She had only herself. She wrenched free. She slipped her hands through the slits in gown and petticoat, to the pocket hoops beneath that shaped the gown: linen bags stiffened with cane and ideal for the little things ladies carried. But Selena was a lady who'd lived among Flint and his pirates, and her hands came out with a pair of pistols: short in the barrel, wide in the bore. She levelled them both at Delacroix.

"You'd never dare!" he said, and laughed. He might have been right, for Selena had no plan, her hands were trembling and the pistols were shaking madly. But Delacroix made a mistake. He grabbed her. "Come here, you nigger bitch!"

CRACK! CRACK! The pistols went off together. One – jammed against Delacroix's vest and its trigger deliberately pulled by Selena – seared the silk and dropped him to his knees, fumbling at the hole blown into his vitals, and gulping and choking as the living colour drained from his face, leaving a pallid expression of infinite disbelief.

"Uuuuuuuuh . . ." he said in his death-gasp and fell, face down, on the floor.

"God help us!" said Pimenta, seeing ruin for himself and all his kin.

192

"Oh . . ." said Granger, weakly, "oh, my liver and lights . . ." And with that he slumped beside Archibald Delacroix. The second pistol – discharged convulsively with the first – had picked its own target and sent a ball fairly into him.

Now there were two dead men in Meshod Pimenta's hall. Two dead men and a runaway slave who was making a habit of murder.

Chapter 23

*F*lint was called from sleep after a day of exhausting work. It was dark and *Walrus* was rolling gently at her moorings when a boat bumped alongside, the boatman shouting and yelling. Selena was brought aboard and fell into Flint's arms, tearful and frightened, which delighted Flint, who assumed she was appealing to him as her saviour and champion.

But the reality proved more complex, and even as he took her in his arms and closed his eyes in pleasure, she was in a turmoil. Certainly there *was* relief at being within his protection, but she was morally exhausted by her need to keep him alive, yet to control him – if she could – and somehow find some independent future for herself, if only she could escape the gallows, having – this time – just committed undoubted murder.

If that wasn't enough, she looked around and saw that the ship was full of Indians: fierce Patanq warriors, many of them sleeping on deck because there was no room below.

The ship stank of them, a sharp animal smell. They rose and stood like silent grey statues: bizarre, exotic, and wrapped in their blankets with guns enfolded in their arms.

She didn't know what to do for the best, so she calmed herself as best she could, and simply told Flint everything that had happened that evening. What else could she do? And he listened and smiled in pride.

"Two of them! *Two?* God bless my precious soul!" He kissed her. The crew stared. The Patanq looked on impassive. Flint laughed. "My little tigress!" he said. "My Amazon, my chickie!" He swung her off her feet and kissed her again. Then he frowned.

"The boatmen," he said. "They'll know!"

"Leave them," said Selena. "They're Pimenta's men."

But Flint trusted nobody. Not when he didn't have to.

"Allardyce!" he cried. "Get 'em aboard. *Now!*" But the boatmen had been listening. They shoved off and pulled for their lives.

"Shall we sink the buggers, Cap'n?" said Allardyce. "All guns is loaded."

"No," said Flint. "We'd wake the anchorage." He turned to Selena.

"What *about* Pimenta? What'll he do?"

"He'll hide the bodies, and his household's sworn to silence. They're all slaves, Joe, under fear of being sold away. They won't dare talk . . ." she paused. "And he said to tell you . . ."

"Tell me what?"

"He says he's got to tell the navy."

"Oh, has he now?"

"Yes. He has to think of his reputation. But he'll wait till tomorrow."

195

"How kind!"

"He said there's an ebb tide just before dawn."

"And?"

"He'll wait till it turns before he tells the navy. To give you a chance."

"Hmm . . ."

"And he said . . . he said . . . he still wants to do business with you, if . . ."

"God in heaven and all his angels!" said Flint.

He laughed. He laughed long and loud, with a hot, unholy laughter, and the crew looked on. Some laughed with their captain, but not the brighter sparks among them. They knew it wasn't healthy. Not when he laughed like this. Flint had been a new man since leaving the island, and better still since he took to gazing at Miss Selena. But it looked like the old Flint was coming back, and there wasn't a man present who didn't shudder at the prospect, not even when they outnumbered him so many times over, and every man of them was armed, 'cos with Flint, a blade or a pistol might be no more defence than empty hands.

Then Flint stopped laughing and wiped his eyes. He smiled and stood up straight and took command, and *Walrus* was made ready for sea at utmost speed. A boat was sent to Captain Bentham aboard *Hercules,* warning him to do the same, and to do it in silence. Another boat was sent to Van Oosterhout aboard *Lucy May*, ordering the Dutchman to take the Patanq fleet to sea so soon as Flint was cleared and gone.

So . . . topmasts and yards were sent up, anchors and cables got in, boats hoist aboard as they returned, log line, sandglass and lead made ready, and breast lines secured in the chains for the leadsman. And all this was done quietly. The very windlass pauls were muffled with rags, and there were no shanties, no bosuns' calls, no shouted orders – not even a boot up a seaman's behind to help him on his way.

Other ships in the anchorage – honest merchantmen – made all the noise they wished, ready to sail on the ebb tide, and welcome to it. They had no reason to avoid the attention of King George's four ships and seven hundred men, still quietly anchored and mostly asleep.

With dawn coming up on the Atlantic, the tide rolled out past Fort Johnson and the miserable little fleet bearing the women and children of the Patanq nation. These poor creatures waved and called to *Walrus*, *Hercules* and *Sweet Anne* as they thrashed past under an easterly with the Patanq warriors standing straight-backed, unmoving and seemingly unmoved. But in the privacy of their minds, they trembled at this alien, ocean adventure, having no experience to guide them in all the history of their people, and trusting only in the wisdom of their leader.

Through sheer necessity, Flint had given Bentham the island's latitude and sailing instructions, but he planned to sail in company, for neither Bentham nor Captain Parry of *Sweet Anne* was a navigator capable of finding a pin-prick on the empty ocean, and Flint needed all his three hundred fighting men. This worked well until mid afternoon, in bright sunshine and calm seas, when the weather turned flat and dull and calm, and the wind – which had been erratic from the start – died away completely.

They were less than twenty miles south of Charlestown with the American continent a black line on the horizon. The three ships rolled on a slow, heavy swell and such that even hardened seamen felt the motion, and the Patanq warriors hung groaning over the rail, heaving up their guts to King Neptune.

Selena, now in her boots, breeches and shirt, with pistols in her belt and a scarf round her hair, stood beside Flint, who was looking back towards Charlestown.

"Let's see," he said, "we've just struck two bells of the first dog watch. That's about twelve hours from the turn of the tide we came out on, and the *next* tide is on the ebb in Charlestown harbour. That means – if Mr Pimenta's kept his word – they should be bellowing like bulls aboard Scott-Owen's squadron, and the bosun's mates laying on with rope ends. Then, once they've cleared the harbour, they'll stop every ship they meet to enquire after our course."

"But we've escaped," she said. "They can't catch us now."

"D'you think so, my chickie? You don't know the navy."

Nothing happened for hours. The day passed. Dinner was served. The Patanq were too sick to eat but got drunk on the grog. The seamen waved and shouted from one ship to another. Night came. Men slept. And then the dawn came up with just the present Flint didn't want.

"There they are, Cap'n," said the lookout, a Cornishman named Penrose.

Flint, having made the climb to the maintop, braced himself on the swaying, heaving platform high above the deck, and let go with both hands for a good look through his telescope.

"Damnation," he said. There were two . . . three . . . no . . . *four* of them, under every stitch they could set, and the sails hanging slack and barely filling. But they had a bit of wind and were still moving. Scott-Owen's squadron was coming after Joe Flint.

"I'd say they're ten mile astern of us, Cap'n," said the lookout, "makin' a couple o' knots at most. If you ask me, Cap'n . . ."

"Penrose, would you prefer the deck or the sea?" said Flint, not taking the telescope from his eye.

"What?" said the lookout.

"Shall I throw you to the deck or into the sea?"

Penrose gulped. This was the old Flint, all right. Penrose took care to say nothing more and was exceedingly wise to do so. Flint ignored him, then went swiftly down the shrouds to give his orders. But he was intercepted.

"Flint," said Dreamer, coming on to the quarterdeck with Dark Hand at his side and many of his men behind him.

"Not now," said Flint.

"*Now*," said Dreamer. Flint looked at the tall, stern figures. Like Captain Foster of *Lucy May*, he was no longer master of his ship.

"What is it?" snapped Flint.

"What is happening?" said Dreamer. "You are afraid."

"Damned if I am!"

"Then why do you look back in fear?"

"It's the blasted Royal Navy, that never blasted gives up."

"So they follow us?"

"Yes."

"Will they catch us?"

Flint blinked and thought of pistolling the savage, or cutting him down.

"Dreamer," he said, barely in control of himself, "there are things I must do, ship's things. I have no time to talk. You must trust me."

Dreamer looked at him, considered the words, remembered where he was, and nodded and stood aside.

Flint instantly set to work. *Walrus*'s two boats were swung out to warn *Hercules* and *Sweet Anne* of what must be done. The ships would have to be taken in tow by their boats.

199

Thus, on their return, *Walrus*'s boats were packed with round-shot to give them weight, and double-manned. Then a towline was passed from the ship's bowsprit to the cutter, and another from the cutter to the launch. Then the launch pulled ahead of the cutter and the cutter pulled ahead of the launch . . . till boats and ship were nicely in line and the towlines tightened.

"Now, my boys, my jolly boys," said Allardyce in the cutter, "give way together – now! *Heave*, me buckos, heave away! *Heave*, me buckos, heave away!"

Hercules and *Sweet Anne* likewise rigged for towing. Soon there were dozens of men swaying under a hot sun in six boats, sweating rivers, cracking muscles and succeeding – on the uttermost limit of what human strength could achieve – in hauling a combined burden of three ships and nearly seven hundred tons, at a pitiful crawl across a flat sea. But at least they were moving.

"How long can they keep that up?" said Selena.

"Till they drop," said Flint. "Then I'll change the crews. All hands must take their part, and God help him that doesn't!"

It went on for hours. The boats' crews did indeed pull till they dropped. They had to, and they knew it. There was a hanging looming for every man aboard if the navy caught them, so they pulled to exhaustion. Then more crews took their places and *they* pulled until *they* dropped. And so on.

But it didn't stop the pursuit. The squadron still had a breath of wind and came up over the horizon: first white canvas, then as black hulls, and finally whole fighting ships in all their complexity of rigging and gear.

So it continued for hours, with the men-o-war steadily closing and all those not undergoing torture in the boats crowding the sterns of the fleeing ships, measuring distance, guessing times and calling on seaman's lore to send a wind. One tried a little too hard: Penrose the Cornishman, an expert on such matters.

"Don't worry lads," he said, "I've stuck me knife in the mainmast, which is sure to fetch a wind."

"Shouldn't we whistle for one?" said one of his mates.

"No!" said Penrose, with profound seriousness. "On'y the boys must whistle, not the men, and *never* a landman –" he looked uneasily at the Indians "– *like them buggers*" he whispered. "Don't want none o' them doin' it, or we'll get a soddin' hurricane!"

"What about throwin' a coin overboard?"

"Aye," said Penrose, "that's good!"

"Mr Penrose," said Flint, "will you be so good as to keep your thoughts private?"

He said it quietly. He didn't shout. But those that knew him should have taken heed, for Flint was under tremendous stress: the frigate alone could pulverise *Walrus* and her companions, never mind the sloops.

"Aye-aye, sir!" said Penrose, but his mates were around him and encouraging him, and Penrose had never been one of the sharpest hands aboard, so the talk continued in hissing whispers.

"What about an old broom? I've heard that if we throws one over . . ."

"No," said Penrose, "only the head, you lubber. You throws the head in the direction you wants the wind to come from. Only the head."

Flint punched through the crowd. He ran to the mainmast arms rack. He snatched a boarding axe. He ran back. He grabbed Penrose by the hair, kicked his legs away, threw him over, and swung the axe thumping down on his neck. The axe was blunt. It took many blows, and finally the bone wouldn't part except by Flint dropping the axe and twisting two-handed to a sharp, nauseous . . . *snap!* Then he stood up, blooded to the elbows. He raised the dripping horror for all to see, and hurled it over the side.

"Is there any other man," he cried, "that wishes to summon the wind?"

There was not. Indeed there was not. The crew, like Selena, were sickened and terrified, and none dared meet Flint's eyes. But the Patanq were tremendously impressed. They were even more impressed when the sacrifice, while not bringing wind upon Flint's ships, *took it away from the pursuers*, who had to launch boats and begin their own long tow.

Flint's men cheered at that, but the cheers died when, about an hour afterwards, it was seen that Scott-Owen was acting clever, and the boats of the squadron concentrated on towing *her*, abandoning the sloops and bringing the frigate's battery of twenty-eight twelve-pounder guns steadily closer.

So team after team of Flint's and Bentham's men took their places in the boats, and came back half-ruined. Even seamen's leathery hands had their limits, and skin and blood were shed, and a few men strained their backs and could pull no more, and – in time – others couldn't be roused, even with kicks and blows, when it came to their turn in the boats again. It was the same on all three ships. And the navy was steadily gaining.

Flint stared through his telescope at the big frigate, under tow from no less than eight boats, including a heavy longboat – ideal for the work – and all of them packed with men. Flint slammed a fist against the taffrail. What could he do?

"Cap'n," said Allardyce, daring to approach him. Daring to speak. "The hands is done in, Cap'n, and I wants to put them savages to work, but they won't go, Cap'n, and . . ."

"Oh!" said Flint. "Will they not indeed?" And he sought out Dreamer, among his followers in the waist. But Dark Hand saw him coming and saw the look on Flint's face. He gave an order and Flint was facing a dozen raised guns. Flint stopped, his face white, his lips black, and he wrenched a pair of pistols from his belt. Seeing their captain threatened, *Walrus*'s crew stood behind him.

"Wait," said Dreamer, and pushed Dark Hand aside. "What do you want?"

"Your men must take their turn in the boats."

"No. We are not black slaves that do the white man's work."

Flint nearly tore his hair.

"But every man must pull his weight!" he said.

"*You* have not," said Dreamer.

Flint was silenced. No, he hadn't pulled his weight, and he thought of John Silver who would have been the first in the boats to encourage the rest. Flint had been very close to John Silver once . . .

"Dreamer, listen: pulling is men's work. It is honourable. I will go into the boats myself . . . if you will sit beside me and show the way to your men."

So Flint sat beside Dreamer and none could tell who enjoyed it least. But they took their turn, and came away shaking and exhausted, and by their example, three hundred Patanq warriors added their strength to the task.

There was no rest when night came. All Flint could do was change course, hauling the three ships eastward in the hope of losing the pursuit in the dark. That's what he'd have done under sail, and it would have worked. But it was no good when towing at less than one knot. Not when one ship could spot another from the masthead at twenty miles. There just weren't enough hours of darkness.

At dawn, with the tow in its twenty-fourth hour, and all hands exhausted aboard *Walrus*, *Hercules* and *Sweet Anne*, the sloops were out of sight but the frigate was not. Flint's ruse had failed.

Chapter 24

*B*illy Bones was in irons. Not proper leg-irons, for there were none on the island. They were the best Israel Hands could forge out of iron barrel-hoops, with a flat rock as an anvil and old nails serving as rivets to close the links around Billy's left ankle.

Clang! Israel flattened the last nail, and stood up dusting the sand off his knees. He pointed his hammer at Bones, who sat scowling under a tree with his legs stretched out in front of him. Billy-boy couldn't stand. There were too few links for that, but at least he had a bit of shade.

"There!" said Israel Hands. "And serves you right if they chafe your precious skin, you no-seaman lubber. Me, I'd have slit you from ear to ear!"

"Belay that, Mr Hands," said Silver. "Just make sure the swab can't get free."

"Not him, Cap'n!" said Israel Hands. "It ain't a clean job, but it's a good 'un."

"Aye," said Silver, for it was. The crude chain ran from Billy Bones to the tree-trunk, where it was secured by an inch-thick copper bolt from *Lion*'s keelson, passed through a hole bored in the trunk and clinched over on the other side, so nothing short of a crowbar could shift it. Silver looked down at the prisoner. "Well, Billy-boy, here you are in the bilboes and only yourself to blame, for I shan't trust you again. Not this voyage nor never."

"Bollocks!" said Billy Bones. "Go fu—"

"Ah, *stow it*, Billy! Don't you never say nothing new? Don't you never learn? Flint'll gut you like a herring when he comes!" There were jeers from the hands, most of whom were idling on the beach nearby, waiting for the day's orders. "And you swabs can belay that too!" cried Silver, irritated beyond measure by Bones's stupidity, who'd otherwise have been a most useful officer.

"Pah!" said Silver, and left him cursing and spitting under his tree, still loyal to the master he worshipped. Israel Hands followed with Sam Hayden – the last of the ship's boys – carrying his bag of tools. Silver looked back at the boy.

"You're to see him victualled, Sammy lad," he said. "Food and water so the bugger don't die. God knows when we might need his blasted quadrant."

"Aye-aye, Cap'n."

The rest of Silver's officers were waiting in Fort Silver by the big tent. They doffed hats as Silver appeared: Black Dog the carpenter, who wasn't gifted with brains; Blind Pew the sailmaker, who *was*, despite being near as mad as Ben Gunn – now rated ship's looney and left to wander; and Mr Joe, gunner's mate – a bright candle in a dark night, and Silver wished for more like him! Time was growing short now, with just thirty-seven pegs left in the timber calendar.

As ever, Silver told them the truth. There was monstrous heavy work to be done. They'd have to re-build the forts to fit smaller garrisons, levelling one completely, for there were only enough of them to man three, and they must complete the battery up at the northern inlet that Sarney Sawyer's men never finished. That and some other ideas Silver had for making life hard for Flint. Considering the ugly mood of the men, the thought of such labours brought protests, especially from Blind Pew, whose sharp mind pounced on flaws.

"Forts? But you wants to keep all hands to-*ge*-ther!" said Pew in his Welsh lilt. "To-*ge*-ther, so's we don't go splitting and fighting, yes?"

"Aye," said Silver, "I wants 'em under my hand!"

"So where's the sense in three forts and a battery? Don't that divide us?"

Silver sighed. He put his head in his hands. Pew had hit the mark dead centre.

"Now listen to me," said Silver, "I've told you why we can't just sit behind ramparts, haven't I? And how we must take the fight to Flint or we're lost?"

"Aye," they said.

"And the best chance of doing that is with ourselves in more than one strong place so we can move round the island."

"But . . ." said Pew.

"Wait!" said Silver raising his hand. "I knows we might split among ourselves. I knows nothing's certain, and I'm just hoping to spot some chance when it comes, for if we sits in one place, then Flint'll trap us in it, and keep us in it, then leave us to die on this blasted island like that poor bloody Jesuit and his mates."

207

There was silence.

"So," said Silver, "let him speak up as has a better plan, say I!"

Nobody spoke. Not even Pew. There was no more argument. Silver nodded, and moved on to the new design for the forts.

"See here," he said, producing a drawing. "This is a star fort, what can be held by as few as a dozen men . . ."

They leaned forward. It was a plan for a four-pointed earthwork, surrounded by a ditch. Near the tip of each point was an emplacement for a four-pounder gun, shielded by gabions – musket-proof, earth-filled baskets improvised from saplings. This allowed each gun to be trained such that any attack must face at least two of them, while being held up by a palisade on the outside of the ditch, and pointed stakes sticking out of the bottom of it. It was a far more formidable design than Flint's old blockhouse – but that had never been intended as a serious fortification.

"What's this, Cap'n?" said Mr Joe, pointing to a circle drawn at the centre of the star.

"That's the *redoubt*," said Silver. "My orders to all hands – should a fort look like falling – is to run. Just kill as many of 'em as you can, and then cut your cable and make for our nearest fort. But should you be surrounded and they're coming over the wall – why, then you gets in here as your last chance. It's an earthwork circle, raised higher than the rest, with a firing step inside, and muskets ready, and these – Israel . . . ?"

Israel Hands reached into his bag of tools and brought out a rum bottle with a fuse sticking out of it.

"Grenado," he said. "It's packed with powder and pistol balls. You light the fuse, duck down and drop it over the wall. Don't have much range, but if the buggers is alongside of you, it'll blow right up the leg of their drawers!"

It was nearly noon by the time they were done, so there was no work until the mid-day heat had passed. But then Silver mustered all hands, gave them their orders, and marched the whole company northward, leaving only two men and a boy to guard Billy Bones. It was a long march with so many men and so much gear, and they didn't reach the northern inlet until the next day. But once there, Silver found great advantage in having the extra men. The battery, already marked out by Sarney Sawyer's men, was completed in four days, the men proving surprisingly cheerful and setting to with a will.

When they were done, six of the brass nine-pounders stood mounted on good carriages, on planked platforms, behind banked-up sand, revetted with timber, and ready with all necessary stores and tackles, and with powder and shot stored under weather-proof shelters. Six guns was a compromise, being as many as men could be spared for. The rest of the guns, Israel Hands ruined – to deprive Flint of their use – by laying each in turn on a pile of sand, close up before a mounted gun, and blowing off one of its trunions with a round-shot. It was dangerous work, with all hands kept clear and only Mr Hands or Mr Joe setting off the charges, Israel Hands insisting the latter do some of the work exclusively by himself, as part of his training, and which he did to Mr Hands's beaming satisfaction.

With the task complete, Silver stumped up and down the battery, parrot squawking on his shoulder, for a final inspection. Then he addressed the men. He praised them for their efforts, made them laugh at what the guns would do to Flint. Finally he surprised them.

"Now, listen to me, lads," he said, "for this here battery ain't meant to stop the enemy from landing."

"No?" they said.

"No, lads." He waved a hand at the inlet, which was four miles deep and a mile across at its widest. Standing on the sands between the waters and the trees, Silver and his men were just a speck on the beach. "There's too much room for boats to get round us," he said, "especially at night. So I've got other plans . . ."

They listened and they cheered him for it, and Silver smiled. The air was fresher up here, and the men were cheerful. Silver himself felt optimistic and threw off the depression that had sat on him since Billy Bones's rebellion. Things were looking better. Whenever he did return – and return he would, never doubt it – Flint would be met with round-shot, lead and steel.

Chapter 25

*I*t was a perfect, beautiful day, if somewhat cold and still:
the sky cloudless, the sea a perfect blue, and everything
sharp and clear, with only the creaking of ship's timbers to
be heard . . . that and the rhythmic splash of oars, and the
chanting of the coxswains.

Flint was sure now that he couldn't escape by towing. He
had too few seamen and the Patanq had suffered badly.
Totally unused to the work, their hands and backs couldn't
stand it. *Walrus* was barely moving. He looked across to
Hercules on the larboard beam, and *Sweet Anne* straggling
to starboard. It was the same for them. And he looked at
the big warship, now less than a mile away, her shoal of
boats packed with jolly tars who were making light of the
work because of the prize money that was almost theirs.

"Bring up a gun, Mr Allardyce," said Flint. "Best gun
we've got. And have the carpenter cut me a port here –" he

pointed at the taffrail. "And send me as good a gun-crew as we've got. Oh, to have Israel Hands aboard now!" He looked round. The stern was packed with idlers who couldn't resist watching the oncoming doom.

"Get forrard," said Flint, "every blasted one of you!" The hands moved at once. But Selena, Cowdray, Dreamer and Dark Hand hesitated.

"Joe," said Selena, "can you sink her – the big ship?"

Flint laughed.

"With a six-pounder? I doubt we can *hit* her at this range!"

"What about when it gets close?"

"Then she'll come broadside-on and turn *her* guns on *us* till we sink or strike."

"So why bother?"

"'Cos it's my life and my neck, and him that wants 'em will pay in blood!"

"Flint," Dreamer stepped forward.

"What do you want, damn you?"

"Here –" said Dreamer. He unfastened his belt and held it out.

"What's that?" said Flint, scowling.

"Tie this round the gun," said Dreamer.

"Why?"

"He never misses," said Dark Hand, "with gun or bow."

Flint looked at the belt. It was about three inches wide, made of coloured beads worked into a bizarre, zig-zag pattern. It had a cheap, English-made brass buckle.

"It is wampum," said Dark Hand. "It is a great honour."

"Your gun will shoot true," said Dreamer.

"Good heavens!" said Cowdray. "*Migraine!* May I see?"

"The belt it is not for you," said Dark Hand. "It is for Flint."

"But the patterns on the belt are those of a migraine attack."

Flint's heart thundered. The blood boiled in his veins. Insanity sparked in his eyes. Here he was, *facing death,* and these morons were discussing beads! One more word and he'd be stabbing and hacking till there wasn't a living creature stood within reach.

Cowdray adopted his most solicitous professional manner. He bowed to Dreamer and addressed him as if he were an alderman with the piles:

"Are you afflicted thus, my poor sir?"

Flint burst. He laughed hysterically. He laughed till he staggered. Then he wiped his eyes, turned nasty again and thrust everyone bodily from the stern, except those following his orders. And these orders were followed, at the double. The chance to do something had put life into the men.

A maindeck gun was heaved out of its carriage and hauled aft in lashings by a dozen men. The carriage followed and the gun was re-seated while the carpenter and his mates hacked a square hole in the taffrail and drove heavy ring-bolts into either side. Meanwhile Flint hailed *Hercules* and *Sweet Anne*, and set their carpenters thumping and cutting too.

Walrus spoke first, with a crash and a roar, her gun bounding back, checked by tackles rove through the ring-bolts.

"Take your time, now," said Flint. "This ain't a race. See if you can't sink me one o' them blasted boats!"

Soon the other two ships were firing: a deeper boom from *Hercules* – a pair of them – for she mounted two nine-pounder bow-chasers and Bentham brought both to bear on the enemy.

"Let's see, now . . ." said Flint, aiming his glass on the frigate's bow. There was a big, gaudy figurehead – some monstrous creature of ancient Greece – and beneath it her name in gold leaf: *Oraclaesus*. And . . . yes . . . there was a pair of bow-chasers mounted, one to each side of the bowsprit. *Come on, my boys,* thought Flint, *stand to, now!*

For half an hour *Walrus, Hercules* and *Sweet Anne* pounded away. Shot screamed through the air, smoke rolled, the thud of the guns bounced across the flat sea. A flew splashes were seen, but no hits. This was not surprising, for the range was great, especially for the smaller guns, and even a nine-pounder was reaching a long way.

"Cap'n," said Allardyce, "can't we try that savage's belt? Can't do no harm, can it?"

"If you must," said Flint, barely noticing, still studying the frigate.

"It's in your pocket, Cap'n, beggin'-yer-pardon. Where you put it."

"Bah!" said Flint. There was no limit to the nonsense seamen believed, nor to Flint's contempt of them for it. He pulled out the belt and threw it on the deck at Allardyce's feet.

"Thank'ee, Cap'n," said Allardyce, snatching it up and running forward to bind the belt round the smoking gun, just behind the swell of the muzzle. "Go on, lads," he said, "give her a try with that!"

The gunners swabbed, reloaded and ran out. The gun captain took aim. He stood aside and dipped his linstock . . .

Boom! said the gun. Boom-Boom, said the two long nines in the same instant . . .

And delighted cheers rang out as a shot ploughed fair and square down the length of *Oraclaesus*'s longboat, smashing

214

flesh and timbers and sending broken oars overboard in a shower of fragments. The big boat slewed sideways and lost way. Groans and cries came over the water, the towline parted at the longboat's stern and – she being next to the frigate – the entire chain of boats was rendered impotent.

"Got 'em!" cried Allardyce. "How's that for Indian magic?"

But there were cheers too aboard *Hercules* and men clambering up on her taffrail, to drop their breeches and show their buttocks to the navy, claiming credit for the hit.

"Good!" said Flint, and looked at the activity around the frigate's bow-chasers. "At last!" he said. And soon . . . white smoke, followed by: Thud-bang! Thud-bang! *VWOOOOOM* as shot flew overhead. But in the boats ahead of the frigate, men staggered under the concussion of the guns, fired so close over their heads that they were surrounded by the flattened ripples beaten into the sea by the shockwave.

Now pull, you swabs . . . if you can! thought Flint. He'd been hoping for this. An actual hit was a bonus, but Flint wanted mainly to sting the frigate into firing, confident that her boats couldn't tow half so well while she did. And he was right. The combined effect of the lucky hit – if luck it was – and the frigate's own fire so hindered her men that *Walrus*, *Hercules* and *Sweet Anne* pulled ahead another half mile before the frigate was properly under way again, with the towline re-rigged, and the ruined longboat cast adrift. And even then, the loss of their best boat and the hammering of *Oraclaesus*'s guns meant that the tars were badly shaken, while Flint's, Bentham's and Parry's crews were pulling their hearts out, encouraged by the rumour that Indian magic was on their side, and they were hitting the enemy with every shot.

Scott-Owen, meanwhile, had seen his boats' crews cringe and falter when his guns fired, and eventually gave the order to cease firing. The range was too great now anyway. With the guns silent, the tars picked up stroke, pulled for England, and within an hour the navy was closing the gap again.

And then . . . all matters of boats and stern-chasers became irrelevant. The surface of the sea shivered and the rigging whispered as the weather changed again. The sky darkened, the wind returned but sultry and gusting, with squalls striking sudden and hard, the masts bending to the strain, such that no wise man set too much sail for fear of losing it.

At least there was no more towing to do. As the sails filled, exhausted men were driven – on all sides – to a different drill. No time for hoisting in boats; roles were reversed as each ship took hers in tow, recovering her men, while sails were trimmed. Flint put *Walrus* to her best point of sailing, leaving Bentham and Parry to follow as best they could. He didn't care if they kept up or not, for his life was on it, and there'd be other chances for the treasure if *they* got lost.

But they didn't. Danny Bentham wanted his share far too much for that.

Well and good, thought Flint, but what *wasn't* well and good was the brand-new, copper-bottomed frigate coming on under full sail like the angel of death. She was a magnificent sight, a thing of majestic beauty, with acres of canvas spread. It was obvious from the start that she could outsail *Walrus*, *Hercules* and *Sweet Anne* all three.

Van Oosterhout took the first possible opportunity to show Captain Foster the error of his ways. It was a necessary precaution, because once the Patanq men were taken out of his ship, Foster became a different man, and so did his crew. They breathed easy, they forgot their fear of the tattooed warriors and swaggered round the ship, shouting in big manly voices at the women and children – especially the women.

Van Oosterhout had guessed what would happen sooner or later, and had the good fortune to come up on deck from his calculations in time to catch Foster licking his wet lips and running a hand up the skirts of an Indian girl he'd got backed into a corner, with his crew laughing merrily all around him.

Ah, thought Van Oosterhout, *all together. Good!* and he darted through the crowd, seized Foster by the scruff of his shirt, twisted the cloth under his chin, and swung him round and down so Foster's head hung, pop-eyed, across Van Oosterhout's knee, and the rest of him struggled so hard and fierce that he throttled himself without putting Van Oosterhout to the trouble. Foster's crew stood astonished at the ease with which it was done, and each looked round hoping some other would baste the bloody Dutchman.

Van Oosterhout kept an eye on them, and when he thought they'd had enough – them and Foster – he dropped Foster's head with a clunk on the deck, stood up and looked around. He was not a particularly big man, but he had great physical presence. He was bony and muscular and quick in his

217

movements, with fierce sandy moustaches that curled up on either side of his nose like the tusks of a boar.

"So!" said Van Oosterhout, and looked them all in the eye. He'd faced down Flint's men and didn't expect much trouble from *this* shipload of ruptured ducks. But you never knew with seamen. Cowards didn't go to sea. So he glared at them, waiting for a challenge. But none came. Foster's men muttered a lot, but they didn't do anything.

"Good!" said Van Oosterhout, and pulled Foster to his feet, where he stood red-faced and choking, weeping tears and rubbing his throat.

"Why'd yer do that?" he said, in deepest self-pity.

"To save you from skinning," said Van Oosterhout.

"What?"

"The Indians take the skin off any man who insults their women."

"The skin?"

"Yes. From here –" Van Oosterhout pinched the loose skin at Foster's neck.

"Agh!"

"– they slit all round. Then they grip the edge of skin and they pull. Like this –"

Van Oosterhout mimed the hideous act of wrenching the skin off Foster's chest and shoulders. Foster fell silent. So did his men. Van Oosterhout nodded. It was a grand tale. It might even be true, for all he knew. Undoubtedly it would help Foster's men behave. Like everything Van Oosterhout did, it was neat, precise and accurate.

"So," he said, "remember: we meet the Patanq at Flint's island. Yes?"

"Aye," they said.

"See, that girl?" he pointed in the direction she'd gone.

"Aye."

"Perhaps you are lucky. Perhaps she don't tell her father. Yes?"

Silence.

"So," said Van Oosterhout, "Flint is gone. The English Squadron is gone. I have my orders. We bring all the captains of all the Patanq ships here on board and I tell them what we do." He pointed at Foster. "You – bring them aboard. *At the double!*"

Instinctively, Foster touched his brow and stamped his foot. "Aye-aye, sir!" he said, and Van Oosterhout had jump-to-it discipline aboard ship from that day on.

Two days later, in accordance what was agreed at the great council with the Patanq, Van Oosterhout took the Patanq fleet to sea. They sailed on the morning tide and all the women sang for joy at the prospect of following their men.

Three bells of the first dog watch (c. 5.30 p.m. shore time)
27th November 1752
Aboard Walrus
The Atlantic

Flint was all but chewing his nails. *Walrus* was awake again under a roaring, heavily gusting wind that needed his constant attention. *Hercules* and *Sweet Anne* were keeping station, plunging and rolling under an increasingly lively sea. The red sun was reaching for the horizon and soon it would be dark. But *Oraclaesus* was gaining too fast; there was no time to hide in the night, and Scott-Owen obviously knew which ship had Flint aboard for the frigate's bow-chasers had opened up a steady fire on *Walrus*. Shot whooshed and hummed over-head and plunged heavily into the sea, throwing up spray.

Walrus, *Hercules* and *Sweet Anne* fired back, but without success.

Flint stamped round the ship, ever trimming his sails, ever sending up more canvas, till the topmasts bent, the yards groaned and the rigging sang: highly dangerous in the erratic wind, for a sudden blow could carry away masts. But the alternative was certain capture and certain death, and every man did his best, with even the Patanq hauling on lines with the rest, the better and faster to get speed out of the ship. Yet for all that, every time a seaman looked back, be it from deck, rigging or tops, the frigate was visibly closer. A great fear was on them now, for there'd be no mercy shown to any of Flint's people if they were caught.

Zoom! A round-shot tore through *Walrus*'s rigging. SPANG! A line parted and a sail flapped high above the deck. On instant initiative, without orders, the topmen leapt like acrobats, fearlessly splicing the line and making it good, and the ship drove on, barely faltering. Then voom! – another shot and POP-*RRRRRIP* the fore t'gallant was punctured, and by ill chance it tore from top to bottom. *Walrus* staggered and the crew groaned.

"Bring her about, Mr Allardyce!" Flint cried, rising to the occasion. "They're going to catch us anyway, so let's die like men! Bring her about and open fire with every gun in the ship!"

They cheered him for that. With the wind on her larboard quarter, a touch of the helm brought *Walrus* foaming round, and Flint hove to by backing the fore topsail. The ship now had no way on at all, and it was *Walrus*'s broadside of seven six-pounders against the frigate's two nines.

Seeing the change of artillery, Allardyce and Dark Hand raced to the stern-chaser in its hacked-out port. Without a word said between them, they tore the wampum belt from the gun, and ran to the rolling, heaving maindeck, now jammed with men scrambling to their guns.

"Which gun?" said Dark Hand.

"Buggered if I know," said Allardyce.

"That one!" cried Dreamer, running forward and pointing to number four.

"Why?" said Allardyce.

"It is the centre," said Dreamer. "It will inspire the rest."

"Get off my gundeck!" screamed Flint.

"Please, Cap'n, *please*," begged Allardyce. "It worked before!"

VOOOOM! ZOOOOM! More shot whizzed overhead. More lines parted. A spar shattered. Flint cringed and looked to larboard. The frigate was now just over a cable's length off. Every detail of her rig and gear could be seen, and the figures of the men manning her, all of whom seemed to be cheering and waving.

"God damn you!" said Flint, and looked at Allardyce and the two Indians: three faces, two red, one white, different as any creatures could be . . . but united in their stupidity and superstition. Mad laughter seized Flint again. "Go on, then!" he said. "Gunners – to your pieces. Steady-aimed fire!"

The men cheered again. Dark Hand and Allardyce tied the belt around number four gun, stepped back, and the gunners fired, each in his own time, the whole roaring broadside. Dense, rolling smoke hid the enemy for long seconds. And then . . . there she was again: whole and unharmed.

"Bugger!" said Allardyce, who'd expected every spar blown off the frigate's masts.

"Jump to it there!" cried Flint. "Reload! Fire at will! A thousand guineas to the man who hits her hardest!"

But nobody fired. They were leaping in the air and shrieking for joy. Yet another squall was blasting out of the darkening sea, bigger than any so far, and it struck the frigate a mighty blow, all the worse for her towering masts that reached high up into the full strength of it. She nearly went over as her bulging fore and main topsails blew out thunderously and shredded into streaming rags, while yards and topmasts snapped like gunshots as much of her top gear went over the side. In minutes the big ship had lost way and was wallowing helpless. The same blow fell upon *Walrus,* and she rolled as if to dip her yards, but she was nowhere near so lofty as the frigate and therefore missed the worst of it. In no time she recovered and drove onward, wounded as she was, and even picked up speed.

Allardyce cheered and threw his arms around Dark Hand and danced for joy, and even Dark Hand smiled, and thumped his hands against Allardyce's back.

"There, Cap'n!" said Allardyce. "What d'you say now to Indian magic?"

"Bah!" sneered Flint. "It wasn't your gunfire. It was a squall."

"What? Just in the instant we needed it?"

Flint turned away. It was no use arguing with ignorance. But then he smiled. What did it matter what Allardyce believed? Him and a herd of Indians? What mattered was that the sun was half under, the frigate well astern, and her squadron out of sight. Flint scanned the darkening horizon.

Ah-ha! There were *Hercules* and *Sweet Anne,* waiting like little lambs, half a mile ahead, with their topsails backed, ready to take up station on the flagship. Either the squall had missed them or they'd survived it as *Walrus* had. And now they were standing by, eager for their chance of a dip into the island's treasure!

Flint nodded in satisfaction. He would escape the navy now. The frigate must make good her damage and resume company with her sloops, and he'd lose her before she could do that, even without the cover of night. So he could risk showing lights for Bentham and Parry to follow . . . and so . . . and so . . . to the island.

Once there, he planned to see the colour of John Silver's insides, for it wasn't just gold Flint was after – not him, God bless his precious soul! Flint would never again make the mistake of leaving enemies behind.

This time – as Billy Bones would have said – *them as die'll be the lucky ones.*

Chapter 26

Two bells of the first watch
27th November 1752
Aboard HMS Oraclaesus
The Atlantic

C ommodore Richard Scott-Owen was such a splendid officer that he was a little too aware of his own splendidness.

He owed everything to talent, coming as he did from a modest family of Deptford ship builders; prosperous but plebeian craftsmen who'd sought gentility for their brightest son by getting him into the king's sea-service, where his progress had been gratifyingly rapid. Blessed with the good fortune to be a lieutenant on HMS *Baltimore* under "Black Dick" Howe – one of the best-connected officers in the service – he so distinguished himself as to become Black Dick's favourite protégé and an instant and popular choice to command the elite squadron sent after former-lieutenant Flint.

Scott-Owen had thereby acquired so much self-assurance, that he remained calm when the Charlestown thunderbolt struck:

Flint himself had actually been in harbour – anchored within sight of the squadron – while Scott-Owen was dancing at a ball, and now had taken fright and sailed!!

According to Governor Glen a patriotic merchant named Pimenta had, by chance, discovered Flint's activities and informed the authorities. On hearing the news, Scott-Owen calmly ordered the squadron to sea, and left the bawling and hauling to those beneath him. He had fine ships, fine officers, and could walk the quarterdeck, hands clasped behind him, while the squadron got under way at the speed of the Devil with his arse on fire.

He further remained calm while his sloops stopped every ship in Charlestown roads to enquire after Flint's where-abouts, and learned that he was travelling in the company of fellow villains Bentham and Parry. Having discovered where they'd gone, and set off in chase, Scott-Owen continued pacing his immaculate quarterdeck among glittering brass, shining steel, towering canvas and hundreds of subordinates who treated him with more respect than Catholics did the Pope.

He remained calm all the while, and serious too, because that's what he thought a sea officer should do. There was no place for vulgar displays of emotion in the king's service. Inwardly, though, Richard Scott-Owen was leaping up and down and turning cartwheels for such a perfect realisation of his chosen profession as few men could dream of.

He was only twenty-nine, after all, and was constantly attended by Lieutenant Hastings and Mr Midshipman Povey, who were even younger than he and buzzing with excite-ment at being close on Flint's tail. These two had once been Flint's shipmates. They'd been cast adrift by him in a long-boat, a torment they'd miraculously survived, having been

225

picked up by the Spaniards off Trinidad. As a result, they hated Flint something poisonous.

So Scott-Owen could hardly contain his excitement. Only the world and the oceans were his limits. Only God and the wind could stay his hand. There was no squadron equal to his, from Newfoundland down to Brazil. It was wonderful, wonderful, wonderful. But then . . . calamity. God and the wind *did* stay his hand. With Flint in sight from the maintop, the wind failed and it was boats-away and rig for towing. And when that wasn't enough, a word from Scott-Owen – still calm – set the entire squadron's boats towing *Oraclaesus* alone, to ensure an advantage in speed over the pirates. The sloops could always catch up later. Having spent endless hours exercising his gun-crews, Scott-Owen was keen to give them their first opportunity to fire in anger. And what could be more congenial than firing into a proper enemy, one deserving a pounding and yet too weak to be dangerous in return, with all the world praising you for doing it?

Wonderful indeed.

Alas, it was then that God really turned nasty. After a tow lasting a day and night, and the longboat smashed and men lost to a chance hit, the wind returned and *Oraclaesus* began overhauling the pirates hand over hand. As Scott-Owen gave the order for boarders to stand by, Flint had the impertinence to bring his ship broadside on, firing off his pop-gun battery without so much as a drop of harm, when suddenly the weather turned foul. In a matter of minutes the squall had carried away everything above the topsails on both fore and mainmasts. It snapped the forestay, unstepped the foremast and threw *Oraclaesus* into chaos . . . thus ruining Scott-Owen's entire wonderful world.

"Move your fucking bastard sodding selves!" shrieked

Scott-Owen, laying on with his speaking trumpet across the backs of the tars as they scrambled to clear the appalling wreckage of smashed spars, tangled rigging and heavy canvas that lay across the ship's lee side. "It's all your bloody fault," he screamed at the sailing master, "for carrying so much sodding sail, you sodding bastard. I'll bloody well break you for this, you bugger!" The ship rolled heavily as the sea hauled on the trailing wreckage. "Get out of my fucking way!" yelled Scott-Owen at Mr Midshipman Povey, who happened to crash into him as all aboard staggered and stumbled.

Scott-Owen stamped and screamed and swore. He dredged up every foul curse and dirty word from his memory. He ran around shoving men to their duties who were already doing their best. They needed no orders. They knew what to do. They cut away the remains of the royals and stun-sails. They fixed and spliced and mended. They made good. They jury-rigged. They brought up fresh spars. They worked all night, until men fell exhausted at their labours and had to be dragged clear of harm's way. They were an exceptionally fine crew. They were prime seamen to a man. They did their duty. They put their ship in order.

And Scott-Owen sulked horribly.

Morning came: grey, red-eyed and stubbled. The ship – temporarily – was at peace with herself and the elements. All had been done that could be done. She had sail aloft, she was answering the helm, and the Atlantic was no longer coming aboard over the rail.

Thus Scott-Owen stood on his battered quarterdeck, attended by his equally battered, equally tired officers, while the ship's people peered back nervously from the waist. Some two hundred and fifty men – mostly in their twenties, and all of them volunteers – awaited his judgement on the damage. Scott-Owen sighed. There might be no serious leaks in the hull, but the totality of reports from the ship's specialists – bosun, gunner, carpenter, sailmaker, blacksmith, and the rest (including the much-abused sailing master) – was that urgent repairs were needed *in port*. She was good for fair weather, but another blow like last night's would take the foremast out of her.

Scott-Owen, now himself once more, was ashamed. He'd been eighteen years afloat and knew that the sea was his worst enemy, far more dangerous than the Frogs or the Dons, and there was no point complaining. He sensibly made no reference to any harsh words he might . . . perhaps . . . possibly . . . *just* . . . have uttered, and the crew sensibly forgot them and forgave their captain for losing his temper. He was, after all, a very splendid young man and they were proud of him.

"Charlestown, gentlemen," said Scott-Owen. "We are fortunate to be so close to a major port. We shall refit there."

"Aye-aye, sir," they said, and touched their hats.

As word spread, a deep groan rose among the foremast hands, their happy thoughts of prize money fading away. They all believed that Flint's ships – being pirate ships – must be crammed with Spanish dollars, and it was bitter hard to lose them.

Three days later, *Oraclaesus* anchored in Charlestown harbour, accompanied by *Leaper, Bounder* and *Jumper*. It had been a slow passage, for the frigate had been forced to sail tenderly, taking care of her wounds, while the three sloops had been required to live up to their names and dash about the ocean to find Scott-Owen. Their entry into harbour was less showy with a damaged flagship, but still neatly done. And the commodore was relieved to see a sheer hulk in the anchorage, for this highly specialised vessel would be vital in lifting out and re-seating the foremast.

Scott-Owen went ashore at once to consult with the governor, anxious to ensure that every possible co-operation would be given to re-fit *Oraclaesus* and sequester all necessary stores and ship's fittings. Money at least was not a problem, since Scott-Owen had a substantial war chest aboard for precisely such emergencies.

It was at the governor's residence, with Mr Povey and two marines in attendance for dignity's sake, that Scott-Owen took the first step towards the tremendous surprise that was awaiting him in Charlestown.

Governor Glen wasn't in. Which left the governor's butler facing a dilemma.

"Sir," he said, "my master is gone out –" he looked around to check for eavesdroppers "– on most secret business."

"Oh?" said Scott-Owen. "Is it the king's business?"

"Yes, sir!" said the servant, not quite adding *Of course*.

"Then what is it?"

"I do not know, sir."

"Hmm," Scott-Owen looked at him. Servants usually knew everything.

"Then where's he gone? Can you not tell me that? My own business is also urgent."

The butler paused. The butler pondered. He reached a decision.

"My master is gone to the lock-up, sir."

"The what?"

"The cells where the constables secure felons, sir."

"And where might that be?"

The butler told him, and Scott-Owen dashed off through

the streets of Charlestown in full dress and silk stockings with his marines and midshipman scuttling astern.

The gaoler at the lock-up – a dingy stone building in the base of one of the town's many bastions – was awestruck at the arrival of so magnificent a person, and bowed low. In his suit of grubby clothes and leather apron, he looked like a tradesman as he stood in his dirty little vestibule with its entrance barred by a half-door and a small wooden counter. The place reeked of damp.

"Yes, Commodore. Yes, sir," he said. "The governor is already here, sir. Down in the cells, sir, with Constable Carleton and Constable Denny."

"What the hell is he doing here?" said Scott-Owen, and saw the same, shifty look on the gaoler's face as there'd been on the butler's. "Pah!" he said. "Where is he? This way, is it?" There was a short corridor, leading into the building. The gaoler nodded. Scott-Owen turned to the marines. "You wait here," he said.

With Mr Povey in his wake he plunged into the corridor, which led to a double row of six cells, three on each side, with heavy studded doors. One of the doors was open, and voices could be heard from within. Voices and the sound of blows.

"Last time, cocky!"

"I dunno. I dunno."

"Right!"

Thump! "Aaaah!" *Thump!* "Aaah!" *Thump!* "Aaah!"

Scott-Owen darted forward. One big fellow was holding a seaman – identifiable as such from his slops and striped shirt – while another laid into him with meaty fists. The man doing the beating had taken off his coat and rolled up his sleeves for the work, while Governor James Glen stood looking on. The victim had already taken a considerable battering and his eyes were mostly closed, and blood smothered his face.

"What in God's name is going on here!" roared Scott-Owen in his best mast-head bellow. "Marines – to me!" The clatter of hobnails on stone flags was soon followed by a pair of muskets with bayonets fixed, while Povey drew his dirk – a blade more ceremonial than functional, but it was all he had. "Release that man at once," cried the commodore, "in King George's name!" As a red-blooded Englishman his every sympathy was with the under-dog. Especially when he was a seaman.

The two bruisers jumped as if scalded. They let go of the seaman, who slumped to the floor. Then, mouths open in surprise, they turned to Governor Glen.

"Ah!" said Glen. "Dear me. Dear me." He frowned. He thought. He smiled ingratiatingly. "Commodore Scott-Owen," he said, "I'm delighted to see you. I should have sent after you had you not come by yourself!"

"What?" said Scott-Owen, who immediately launched into a rant on the iniquities of torture and the war that must soon be fought against France and Spain, the natural homes of such vile and detestable practices . . . et cetera, et cetera.

Glen let him finish. He was a far more complex creature than Scott-Owen. He waited patiently till the young officer ran out of words. Then he spoke:

"Commodore," he said, "this is one of Flint's men."

"Who is?" said Scott-Owen.

"Him –" said Glen, pointing at the seaman. "Tommy Farrell's his name."

"He's a pirate?"

231

"Indeed! One of *Flint's chickens*. He got drunk in a tavern and boasted of it."

"Did he?" said Scott-Owen. Glen nodded.

"He was arrested yesterday." Glen looked at the bruisers. "Wasn't he?"

"That's right," said one of them. "By me and Constable Denny, here."

"Aye," said the other. "Me and Constable Carleton." They nodded.

"We been looking for scum like him," said Carleton.

"Since Constable Granger disappeared," said Denny.

"But they found something bigger," said Glen.

"What do you mean?" said Scott-Owen.

Glen spoke quietly to Scott-Owen. He tried to whisper, but everyone heard every word.

"He knows something . . . about Flint's treasure. Can we speak privately?"

"Oh!" said Scott-Owen, who, for all his rapid promotion, had been unlucky in the matter of prize money – which is to say he'd never had any. "Oh!" he said again. "Perhaps we might step outside?"

They did. Governor Glen and Commodore Owen stepped out into the bright cool sunshine, and took a stroll up and down, and talked. It was mainly Glen that talked and Scott-Owen that listened. Mr Povey, the marines, the constables and the gaoler watched them. Their eyebrows shot up at one stage when Scott-Owen stopped in his tracks, grabbed Glen's arm, and said:

"HOW MUCH?"

"Shhh!" said Glen. They carried on talking. They talked for quite a while. Finally they shook hands like brothers, smiled like sunshine, and each dashed off in a different direction, bent on the common cause of getting *Oraclaesus* to sea in such a time as would amaze not only mankind but Almighty God Himself.

Later, aboard *Oraclaesus*, Scott-Owen summoned all officers to his stern cabin. Not only were all the lieutenants, midshipmen and senior warrant officers of the flagship present, but the commanders and first lieutenants of *Leaper, Bounder* and *Jumper* too. It was a sea of blue coats and gold lace, with every chair taken and men standing at the back and sides. The excitement was intense, because A GREAT SECRET was to be revealed – which, like all secrets, was already leaking furiously, to the point there was hardly a creature aboard the four ships that didn't have a good idea what was going on.

"Gentlemen," said Scott-Owen, "earlier today I met with the Honourable James Glen, Governor of the Royal Colony of South Carolina."

"Ah," they said.

"I also met one Thomas Farrell, lately a pirate on board Flint's ship *Walrus.*"

"Oh?"

"This miserable creature has been persuaded – we need not ask how – to reveal that Flint has amassed a great treasure and has buried it on a secret island." Everyone looked at Lieutenant Hastings and Midshipman Povey, now sitting like greyhounds in sight of a rabbit. "Aye, gentlemen," said Scott-Owen, "is it not a treat that we have on board the only two British officers who've been on Flint's island and know where it is?"

"Huzzah!" they cheered.

"And is it not a treat that *our very duty* is to chase Flint, when it's certain that it is to this secret island that he's bound . . . and . . . and . . . *It's a fortune in prize money to all hands once we lay hold of him!"*

"HUZZAH!"

"Mr Hastings, Mr Povey," said Scott-Owen, "will you give us the benefit of your knowledge? Show us where it lies – this secret island!" Scott-Owen indicated a number of large charts, unrolled and flattened out with weights on the cabin table, representing the Caribbean, the Americas, and the Atlantic.

"Aye-aye, sir!" said Hastings and Povey, and passed through the press to stand at the table, where they re-iterated the discussion they'd had so many times since being cast adrift by Flint three years ago. There were grins and nudges from most of those present, because Hastings and Povey had bored all hands with their constant discussion of the location of Flint's island, and nobody had paid attention, since there'd been no reason to go there: they were chasing Flint, whose natural home was the Caribbean or the Americas, where rich prizes could be taken. What would he want with a lonely island in an empty ocean?

So they'd thought! But now, everything was different, and Hastings and Povey were allowed their moment of theatre.

"Well," said Hastings, "Flint cut us loose a day's sail from the island."

"And we were in Trinidad on July the second."

"After thirty-two days at sea under sail."

"Which means we could have covered anything up to three thousand miles."

"Which we didn't, 'cos we were becalmed a lot of the time."

"And discoursing."

234

"You were saved by a Spanish frigate, were you not?" said Scott-Owen.

"Yes, sir, *San Dominico*, Captain de Oveira, on course for Port of Spain."

"And you'd been heading west?"

"Yes, sir. Hoping to make the Windward Isles."

"So where was your starting point?" said Scott-Owen. "Where's the island?"

Hastings and Povey looked at one another. Hastings was the elder. He was a lieutenant while Povey was a midshipman. But Povey was a first-class navigator and Hastings was not. Hastings glanced at the chart and nudged Povey.

"Ah-hm!" said Povey. "As best as I can guess, sir . . ." and he leaned forward, and stretched out his hand, and every man present ceased breathing. "It'd be about – *here!*" And he stuck his finger on the chart.

Scott-Owen picked up a pencil, moved the finger slightly, and marked the chart with a firm, bold cross.

Chapter 27

Three bells of the afternoon watch
24th January 1753
Aboard Walrus
The northern archipelago

*I*t was cold. The sea was lively. The wind was erratic, there was mist and fog, and Joe Flint was on the limit of his skills. He was attempting to lead three ships southwards through the vast horseshoe of dangers that guarded the island to the north, east and west. He did so because he had to, having guessed that Silver would discover the archipelago and pay less heed to danger from the north, offering Flint his only chance of a surprise landing, since the island's two anchorages were unsafe to enter at night, and the southern anchorage would certainly be watched.

So he was taking Flint's Passage: a death-trap of swirling waters, vicious rocks, mist and hungry sandbanks, some displaying the wooden bones of ships, barnacled, weed-draped and rotting. The route was made all the more dangerous because it was impossible to see much more than a ship's own length ahead, for there was always fog here, no matter what the weather all around.

Flint himself led the way, taking Danny Bentham's long-boat – the best in the flotilla – and the best of the men, the best compass, and his own chart. He had a lead-line going in the bow, and men probing with pikes besides, for the dangers were hidden, being constantly awash, and many ships had run unknowing to their ruin hereabouts, especially at night or in bad weather, with timbers smashed and cargoes lost, and men drowned and never heard of again.

Even to those who knew the dangers it was fearful work. Flint was dripping sweat as he concentrated on finding the way, with a dozen men at the oars and Allardyce at the tiller, steering to Flint's hand-signals, and doing his best to keep the boat on course against the fierce, ever-changing currents.

"Back larboard, back larboard . . . *Pull*togethernow!" cried Allardyce.

"By the deep four!" cried the leadsman.

"Back starboard, back starboard . . . *Pull*togethernow!"

"By the mark five!"

Close behind the longboat came *Walrus*, *Hercules* and *Sweet Anne* in line astern, under close-reefed topsails, creeping onward with lookouts posted, anxious faces peering over the rails, and each helmsman placing his ship exactly in the wake of the one ahead, knowing certain ship-wreck lay in wait on either side. Flint, meanwhile, looked back constantly to make sure the flotilla was following on the true course, and – seeing the lumbering hulls, and the extreme narrowness of the "safe" channel – even he wondered if he wasn't making a mistake.

Aboard *Walrus* the fo'c'sle was crowded. Men pointed

and muttered and argued the best course through the hazards – but they offered no advice to Flint. They knew better than that. Among them, Dark Hand and Dreamer stood talking in their own language. They watched these ship matters, but left them to the white men. They had other issues.

"Why do we follow him?" said Dark Hand, looking at Flint.

"Because he knows the way," said Dreamer.

"No! Not this path through the angry waters. *Why do we serve his purpose?*"

"Because he will pay us in gold."

"But he is the Devil. He is *our* Devil as well as the white man's."

"We have no Devil."

"But you dream of our Devil. And you say his name is Flint."

"His gold will save our people."

"But he is evil."

"It will buy us our new lands."

"But how can we build good upon evil?"

Dreamer said nothing, for he didn't know. But who could blame him? No philosopher born has ever solved that particular puzzle.

Next to Dreamer and Dark Hand, and in their own different world, Selena and Cowdray were also discussing Flint.

"Are you saying he hasn't come near you?" said Cowdray.

"Yes," she said.

"But he treats you like a princess. We all assumed –"

"Then don't assume!"

"But I thought you'd come to an . . . er . . ."

"To a what?"

"To an accommodation. To a friendship."

"Huh!" she said.

Cowdray moved closer and whispered, "Is it still Silver, for you?"

She said nothing.

"Ah!" he said, but she looked away.

"What choice have I got?" she replied at last, staring at Flint.

He was standing upright in the bows of the big longboat, chart in hand, making quick darting movements of his hands to guide the boat. He was leading the whole flotilla and the four hundred men embarked. He alone bore the responsibility. Whatever his flaws, he was unquestionably a remarkable man and Selena wondered where her future lay.

Late afternoon, 24th January 1753
Foremast Hill lookout station
The island

At the summit of Foremast Hill, George Merry and Whitey Lowery had a stock of victuals, a good tent and a fine view in all directions, especially to the north. And now they wrestled for their fine telescope.

"Gimme that!" said Whitey.

"Garn!" said Merry, and pulled away. But Whitey was the stronger. He snatched the big glass, set it to his eye, adjusted the focus . . . and tingled in excitement.

"Shag my tits!" he said. "It's *Walrus* herself, with Flint aboard and flogging the arse off all hands!"

Merry gaped in amazement. He wasn't the sharpest pin in the cushion.

"What?" said he. "Can you *see* the swab?"

"No, you blockhead, but it's *Walrus* all right. I'd know her anywhere. *Walrus* and two others: a snow an' a sloop." He shook his head. "Long John was right an' all! Flint's come back with a bleedin' army!"

"Stap me," said Merry. "Just six days after the timber calendar ran out. That's precious close, ain't it? Long John got that right, near enough!"

"Buggered if I know," said Whitey, and looked at the distant flotilla: white sails and grey smudges of hull in the disturbed waters some fifteen miles north. "We got to pass the word. They'll not make landfall this night, but'll need to drop anchor offshore. Here!" He passed the telescope to Merry and slung a canteen of water over his shoulder. "You got the watch, George Merry. I'm off!" And he took off down the hill.

Next morning at dawn, Whitey Lowery was one of thirty men lying in hiding behind the earthworks in the northern inlet. Long John, Israel Hands and Mr Joe were there too. While most of the hands – including Whitey – were snoring deeply after a forced night-march, they were awake. But at least all hands were present and correct, likewise the six nine-pounders, with charges rammed and waiting.

"D'you think they'll see us?" said Israel Hands.

"No," said Long John, "they won't be expecting us. Leastways, I hopes not!"

"We'll find out, soon won't we?"

"Shhhhh!" said Silver. "They'll hear us!"

So they sat quiet, these three that were too excited to sleep.

They had just over an hour to wait.

Then the steady chanting of a leadsman was heard, and

240

the clank of oars, and a longboat entered the mouth of the inlet at its northernmost corner.

"Beat to quarters, Mr Joe!" said Silver.

"Aye-aye, sir!" said Joe, standing and saluting formally. Then he ran from man to man: no fuss, no bother, no shouting. He roused them all, and the men stretched and ran to their stations, gun-captains priming touchholes from powder horns, then taking glowing matches from the match-tub to secure into the ends of their linstocks. Not a word was said. Every man knew his duty.

"Look!" said Israel Hands, telescope to his eye. "Damn my soul if that ain't *him*!"

Silver raised his own glass and nodded. It was Flint, all right, conning the boat.

"John," said Israel Hands, "we've loaded grape over the round-shot. We can smash the bastard as he passes!"

"No!" said Silver. "Wait!"

"Please, John."

"No! We must hit the ships, and them aboard. Not just a boat . . . look!"

First a bowsprit, then an entire ship came round the headland astern of the longboat, and entered the inlet.

"There's your target, Mr Gunner," said Long John.

"Ahhh!" said Israel Hands and nudged Mr Joe, for a great moment was coming.

They'd placed the battery very carefully. It was on the southern side of the inlet where the waters ran wide but shallow, and the *deep* channel – where ships must pass – was close to the rocky shore, such that the muzzles of the guns – hidden with palm leaves and driftwood – were less than fifty yards off, and placed to inflict murderous harm on any vessel coming in to anchor. Israel Hands of all people knew how vital it was to reserve the first fire, with carefully loaded guns, against an enemy that wasn't expecting it. You didn't waste that on a boat. But he was sorely tempted by the sight of Flint coming steadily into the arc of the guns' fire – for the guns were trained far round to the right, to enable as many salvoes as possible to be delivered before the target should pass beyond them to the left.

"Look'ee there," whispered Silver. "He's taking good care not to send *Walrus* in first!"

Three ships were coming to anchor in the tree-lined inlet with its white sands and circling gulls and lapping waves and bright cheerful light. The first was a medium-sized sloop, the next was *Walrus* herself, then a big snow. Shouts echoed across the water as the men aboard called out to each other and pointed out the sights. It was an idyllic scene . . . for the moment.

"Go to it, you sods," said one of Silver's men. "Ain't you just got it coming!"

"Silence between decks," hissed Silver. "I'll slit the next bugger as speaks!"

Now the longboat was right in front of the battery and still hadn't seen it. Silver watched Flint sweep his glass round the bay looking for just such a surprise as was waiting for him. But the front and sides of the battery were well hidden, and even Flint never spotted them.

"Please, Cap'n," whispered Israel Hands, "just a drop of grape . . ."

"No! We'd warn off the rest."

"Oh, bugger!"

"Shut up!"

Then the longboat was clanking past, and the sloop was coming into line. Men were at the rail and in her rigging, grinning and merry. But some were not grinning and merry. Some were tall and dark, and wore feathers and carried long guns.

"John!" said Israel Hands. "He's brought soddin' Indians!"

"So what? Who'd you think he'd bring – the bleedin' foot-guards?"

Israel Hands said nothing more. He pointed at the sloop. He looked at Silver. Silver nodded.

"See if you can't sink the bastard and block the channel."

Israel Hands beamed in delight.

Long Hatchet stood with his half-brother Fine Shirt, gazing in wonder at the shores of the island, which appeared to be sliding steadily past while the ship remained still. It was joyfully smooth after the constant motion of the past weeks and the hideous sickness as the wooden planks shifted beneath a man's feet.

"A happy day!" said Fine Shirt. "Soon we'll be done with ships."

"Let it be *very* soon," said Long Hatchet.

"What's that?" said Fine Shirt, and instantly whistled the bird-call that gave warning, such that every Patanq aboard *Sweet Anne* cocked his gun. "There!" he said. "See? *There are men moving!* On the shore, behind the green branches and that long mound."

"Men made that mound!" said Long Hatchet.

"And *he* didn't see it," said Fine Shirt. "*Sun-Face* didn't see it." He looked at Flint, in the long boat ahead of the ship. "Sun-Face Flint is supposed to be –"

Fine Shirt's words were lost in pulverising detonations as the shore-battery fired. It deafened and battered, and the muzzle-flash shrivelled men's hair. The smoke burst out in clouds and the shot pounded and crunched, not one single round missing its target, but smashing and tearing.

Fine Shirt was dismembered, Long Hatchet decapitated, and a dozen of their kindred instantly killed. A rain of sundered timber and wrecked gear came down, and the air was split with the screams of those so horribly wounded that not even Patanq stoicism could still their tongues.

Flint spun round, deafened and shocked. He saw the battery! He saw John Silver! And Danny Bentham, aboard *Hercules* saw the wounding of his precious second ship. The two stared in horror, but neither could do a thing to stop the gun teams from sponging and ramming and delivering their second salvo.

Aboard *Sweet Anne*, Captain Parry did what he could. Staggering through the smoke, clambering over mutilated men, he brought the gunwale swivels into action, he made the Patanq return cannon fire with musketry, he got together a crew for one of the maindeck six-pounders, and was giving the order to fire when a couple of grapeshot came aboard and struck him in the left hip, blowing the contents of his bowels and bladder spattering out through his right hip, and dropping him howling and unheard under the concussion of the busy guns that were beating his ship to pieces.

Only *Sweet Anne*'s motion saved her. Israel Hands's crews did their best, serving their guns like men-o'-warsmen, but the two-hundred-ton mass of the ship, still with way on – even with rigging broken and helm shot away and the hull slewed sideways to the channel – ran slowly past the battery, streaming blood and entrails. No matter how hard they tried, the gunners couldn't train their pieces to bear on the target. Meanwhile *Walrus* and *Hercules* backed topsails and came to rest clear of the battery, and immediately began hoisting out their boats, bosun's calls and chanting crews sounding out over the anchorage in competition with the Hell's choir of howling that rose up from *Sweet Anne*'s reeking, slippery deck.

"Where's Flint?" said Israel Hands, running from his guns to John Silver, who'd stood out from the battery for a good view.

"There!" said Silver, and pointed. The longboat with Flint aboard was pulling steadily into the anchorage, keeping well clear of the battery's arc of fire, and looking for a landing.

"Trust him to save his skin!" said Israel Hands.

"Aye," said Silver, turning to the ships, "but look at the way them swabs is getting their boats in the water." He shook his head. "The buggers knew what to do! That's Flint, that is, as laid plans against eventualities! And I'd hoped we might get a bit more use out of this..." He looked at the battery. "Ah well, there's a few of 'em out there as won't see their mothers again!" He laid a hand on Israel Hands's shoulder. "Well done, Israel my son. Let's see what happens next!"

The battery's guns kept the boats off till dusk. Then they crept forward, crammed with armed men. As soon as it was fully dark they'd get round the battery and land.

"Time to go!" said Silver. "Do your duty, Mr Hands."

"Aye-aye, Cap'n."

Israel Hands left the rest to Mr Joe, nudging Silver so he shouldn't fail to see how the lad was coming on.

Once again, with minimal commands because he'd made sure all hands knew what to do, Mr Joe had the six guns hauled inboard from their embrasures and turned in pairs, such that each gun was muzzle-to-muzzle with another, one

245

of each pair loaded with a double charge and two shot, then primed and a slow match laid to each touch-hole.

"All hands stand clear!" cried Mr Joe.

"Aye-aye, sir!" they cried, and Israel Hands nodded approval as the men doubled to his orders, streaming past himself and Silver as they made their way off the beach and into the cover of the trees. Silver couldn't run. He stumped along as best he could.

"I see you loaded only one of each pair," said Silver. "Why not both?"

"No point, Cap'n," said Israel Hands. "They'd never fire in the same instant."

"Ah! And I suppose it's no good just spiking the buggers?"

"No! They'll have gunners tools aboard and they'd just drill 'em out. Spiking's what you do only if you can't do nothing better."

Silver grinned.

"An' you can do better, can't you, matey!"

"Aye, Cap'n!"

They sheltered behind a tree. Mr Joe lit his fuses and ran towards them. The rattle and clunk of oars sounded over the darkening anchorage. Mr Joe arrived breathless and panting.

Then . . . *BANG-CLANG!* The first gun went off, shortly followed by the rest, and orange flame lit up the anchorage, revealing the creeping boats and their white-faced crews, dreading a blast of canister. They breathed again, but chunks of gun-metal, blown off the nine-pounders, rained down from on high, splashing into the waters, leaving six thoroughly ruined barrels, blown out of their carriages into the sand.

Soon Flint's men were in possession of the anchorage. Flint and Danny Bentham looked over the ruined battery while the Patanq searched the beach and attempted to track Silver's men in the dark.

"How many did we lose aboard *Sweet Anne*?" said Flint.

"Thirty at least," said Bentham, "killed and ruined." He shook his head. "That bastard Silver!"

"Huh!" said Flint. "Don't I just know it!"

A mile away, Silver was dividing his men into two teams. One would go to Fort Foremast under Mr Joe, the other would go back to Fort Silver with Silver himself. Night marches had been planned and practised. The men were used to it.

Silver was shaking Mr Joe's hand in farewell when a rumble came from the northern inlet.

"Ah!" said Israel Hands.

"Ah!" said Silver.

On the beach, two Patanq warriors ran towards the smoking, blackened body that had been blown into the air and landed thump on its back, having just attempted to pick up a sheath-knife, temptingly laid on top of a keg. The keg contained gunpowder and a pistol-lock, rigged by Israel Hands, which was connected to the knife by a thread.

The campaign had begun very well for Long John Silver.

Chapter 28

*A*s soon as it was light, Flint and Dreamer sent out the Patanq warriors. In a single day's swift running, they scouted the entire island and found all Silver's forts. It was childishly easy for them. They sighed and shook their heads at the paths, the hacked undergrowth, and the clumsy tramplings of men who seemed utterly ignorant of bushcraft – as indeed they were, being seamen; just as the Patanq didn't know a keelson from a kedge anchor.

They did, however, know about forts. And on the next day at dawn, Flint and Bentham stood beside Brendan O'Byrne, Tom Allardyce and some others of their crews within sight of the fort nearest the northern inlet. They stood well back, though, because it was time for the Patanq to earn their gold. So Flint and the rest hid behind the trees that filled most of the plain up in the northwest corner of the island, and they watched the Indians go forward.

There were three hundred Patanq on the move, led by Dark

Hand the war sachem, who took precedence over Dreamer in time of battle. They were highly organised – by clan and family – into small companies, as disciplined as a regiment of the line but without the polish and buttons, for they fought almost naked, wearing just leggings and loincloths as protection from the undergrowth, and going barefoot for silence.

And they were profoundly silent. They moved like smoke. They gave nothing away: their brown bodies – crossed and speckled with tattoos – merged among the shadows as they moved out from the cover of the trees and crept over the scrubland towards the fort that Silver's men had built by Foremast Hill, which had been selected for assault . . . and which seemed so utterly unaware of their coming.

They hid behind tussocks. They slid along folds in the ground. They signalled with gentle bird calls so each company could keep its place in the advance. They were almost invisible: the bright feathers and glittering adornments were gone, leaving only knives and hatchets, guns and ammunition. The guns were fusils and fowling pieces rather than heavy regimental muskets, which were too cumbersome for the Patanq mode of warfare.

Slowly, carefully, led by Dark Hand with Dreamer following, the Patanq moved out into the dawn . . . and disappeared. There was utter silence save for the birdsong – if it was birdsong – and the booming of the island's surf.

"Where are they?" whispered Bentham to Flint, after ten minutes. "Can you see them?"

"Over there," said Flint, pointing to the east of the fort. "I think they're trying to get the sun behind them as it comes up." He paused. "Leastways, I *think* it's them. I'd fixed one with my eye, trying to follow him. But it's hard . . ." He shook his head. "No," he admitted, "I don't know where they are." He smiled his gleaming smile. "So much the better. What a surprise for Silver's men!"

"Aye," said Bentham. "Damned if I'd like the Patanq creeping up on me!"

Ba-Ba-Ba-Bang-Bang-Bang! Smoke and flame as the Patanq rose together, right up against the fort's palisade, and gave a single thundering volley, and a demon's shrieking of war cries. Half dropped their guns and leapt at the wooden fencing, hatchets between teeth. Half plied rammer, powder and bullet-bag, and delivered a crackling fire on the ramparts. The noise was deafening. The excitement was intense. Flint and his companions leapt to their feet, cheering loudly.

"Go to it, me buckos!" cried Bentham.

"Kill 'em! Rip 'em!" cried Flint, round-eyed and staring.

"Chop their bastard bollocks off!" cried O'Byrne.

They danced in their glee. It was magnificent entertainment: a wonderful spectacle wonderfully executed. It was the classic Patanq dawn raid, polished in frontier warfare between France and England, with the Patanq on whichever side suited them, tomahawking whichever enemies. It was a perfect delivery of a perfect surprise attack, to negate the advantages of those in the fort, to minimise losses to the attackers, and to win the day in a single, rolling, over-the-wall assault.

Except that it didn't achieve surprise.

Mr Joe saw to that.

He had everything ready just as John Silver had insisted:

. . . guns primed, and loaded with canister

. . . matches burning in tubs

. . . crews at their guns

. . . muskets loaded

. . . grenadoes ready

. . . sentries alert.

250

And above all, no man showing his head over the ramparts, such that the Patanq attackers had nothing to aim at, and fired purely to terrify the defenders, whom they doubtless thought asleep. But they weren't asleep, just hiding, and the three guns that bore to the eastward fired together in a thundering detonation. Each was charged with over sixty musket balls. Each blasted directly down upon packed ranks of Patanq warriors as they scrambled over the palisade, clambered out of the moat, or stood shooting at the ramparts.

And when they'd fired, the gunners rammed home prepared charges, made up by Blind Pew into sail-cloth cartridges, with powder and shot together for speedy loading. Then a jab down the touch-hole with a priming wire to pierce the cartridge, a sprinkle of fine powder, and the gun trained into the reeling mass of bleeding bodies, a stab of the red match – and another bellowing roar and blast of dragon's breath, and still more Patanq drilled like colanders and blinded and burned and thrown down kicking and wriggling.

Dark Hand felt the blow of the lead ball. He staggered but took instant appraisal and raised a great shout, telling his men to retreat. To stay was to die. As the guns fired, he sped from man to man, turning them, shoving them, sending them running. Dreamer, and all who were heads of families, did likewise, even those who were broken and bleeding. By their leadership and example, no living man was abandoned. Even as they were scourged by gunfire, warriors died trying to carry away their wounded comrades rather than leave them behind.

No regiment of the Old World could have fallen back under fire with more selfless and magnificent courage. And these virtues the Patanq displayed not through imposed discipline but because every man knew every other. Each was a brother, a father, a son, or a cousin, or a little boy who'd played in the long house before ever he became a man.

Dark Hand was the last to come away, and only when he saw that all those who lived were safe did he retreat to the forest and fall and allow his wound to take him to the next world.

A total of forty-five men were killed in the failed attack, and of those who escaped, another three soon died and six were crippled. Since landing on the island the Patanq had lost ninety-nine men without inflicting a single casualty on their enemy. It was a cataclysmic disaster, for the men on the field that day were not just the flower of Patanq manhood, they were *all* of it. They were the entire strength of the Patanq nation. Every death was a tragedy. Losses on this scale were unthinkable.

Flint watched the bedraggled survivors go past him, deeper into the woods. He groaned, seeing the failure of all his plans, and beside him Danny Bentham cursed and spat and told O'Byrne to get ready to up anchor and set sail.

Dreamer alone was not dismayed. He walked back with his gun in his arms. He didn't flinch. He didn't weep. He found Dark Hand's brother, Cut Feather, and raised him to the rank of war sachem. He found a clearing in the forest, far away from the fort, and he brought together his men. There, as Flint and the other whites looked on in wonder, he dressed in his finest clothes, and his best robe, and his most sacred wampum, and he made a speech in memory of those who'd died.

He named the fallen: every one of them, beginning with Dark Hand. He spoke of Tears, Throat, Heart, the sacred ways of combating Grief: that dark power of the newly dead which causes the living to lie on the long-house floor with ash on their faces, waiting for death.

"It can happen, my brothers," he said. "I have seen it. And I have seen the future of our nation, which is *not* to perish here in battle. Trust me! I have seen it and I know . . ."

He spoke for a long time. He spoke with the poetry and rhythms of Patanq oratory. He reminded them that the only salvation for the People, was to move north. He reminded them that this could not be done without pain. He assured them that the People would survive, and that the present suffering was worthwhile.

He gave strength to those who were burdened.

He gave courage to those who were afraid.

He gave faith to those who doubted.

He was a very great speaker and a very great man.

With the speech made, and the warriors content – as often happened when Dreamer was at peace after great effort – the lights flickered black-yellow-violet. They flickered in his eyes just as they did in his wampum belt. The lights were followed by great pain, and by sickness and visions.

It was not until the next day that he was able to speak to the white men, explaining the *second* way to deal with forts.

Morning, 28th January 1753
Aboard Walrus
The northern inlet

Cowdray found Selena in Flint's cabin, dressed in her usual rig of shirt and breeches, boots and pistols. She was standing by the open stern windows, looking into a mirror as she wound a red scarf round her hair.

The surgeon stared. Her movements were extraordinarily feminine. He'd noticed that before. He thought it was something to do with the slenderness of her hands and wrists and the dainty grace of everything she did . . . that and the fact that raising her arms lifted her breasts tight up against her shirt and made them bounce.

Oh dear. Cowdray sighed. A sensible man knows his limits, and it was a pleasure to be accepted as her friend: a wise, older friend who wasn't supposed to be dreaming about kissing her tits and giving her a thundering good shafting.

"Cowdray!" said Selena, and she smiled. She was lovely when she smiled. It was beautiful to see: a real pleasure. Not pleasure enough, but it would have to do. Cowdray smiled in his turn . . . and locked other thoughts in the cellar.

"Selena," he said, and looked over his shoulder. There was nobody about, but he was careful. "I think I can get you ashore."

She lowered her hands, abandoning the kerchief-winding, and considered him carefully.

"Why should you do that? Flint says I'm to stay aboard. He's frightened I'll run."

"Do you want to run . . ." he lowered his voice to a whisper " . . . to Silver?"

"What's it to you?"

"I asked you before if you wanted him . . . and you didn't say no."

"And I didn't say *yes!*"

"Look . . . do you want to come ashore or don't you?"

"I don't know . . ."

"I think you should. At least then you'd have the chance."

"To run?"

"Yes."

"So how would you get me ashore? Against Flint's word."

"He's busy. He still thinks he can conquer this island."

"Don't you?"

Cowdray went quiet. "You saw *Sweet Anne* under fire as we came in."

"We both did!"

"And you heard the cannonading, yesterday?"

"Yes."

"That was a Patanq attack being thrown back with dreadful losses."

"Yes. I heard. Some of the men told me."

"I think John Silver has made most careful preparations."

"What preparations?"

"Forts, entrenchments, infernal engines . . . All very clever. I'm no soldier, but he seems to have achieved much success . . . and you might be safer with him than Flint."

"Hmm . . . So how would you get me ashore?"

"Ah! These matters are connected."

She shrugged her shoulders as if bored. "Which *matters*?"

"For God's sake, woman, show some interest and don't play cat and mouse!"

"I'm sorry." She reached out and touched his arm. She smiled and Cowdray tingled with delight. He was more smitten than he'd thought. It was such a joy when she smiled at him. "Ah-hem," he said, hoping he wasn't making a fool of himself.

"Well," he said, "I've set up a hospital ashore, where the wounded are being treated. There are about a dozen of them, all Patanq savages, and they need the attentions of a nurse . . ."

"A *what*?"

"A nurse."

"Me?"

"Well, yes. You *are* a woman, the only one here."

"That don't mean I'm dancing round with piss pots, wiping men's butt ends!"

"Dammit, Selena, all the world thinks that's women's work, even Flint and his crew! They'd accept it as natural, and it'd get you ashore!" He paused, and in his confusion, he took refuge in Latin: "*Non est ad astra mollis e terris via!*"

"What's that?"

"Seneca: There's no easy way from Earth to the stars."

Selena frowned. It was time to decide exactly what she *did* want.

28th January 1753
The northern inlet

The day after the attack on the fort, Flint set up camp close to where Silver's battery had been. Tents were raised, stores unloaded, and all hands sent ashore who hadn't duties aboard. And when the noonday heat passed, he took a stroll along the beach accompanied by Danny Bentham.

"This is the very spot where my career began," said Flint. "Those few timbers there . . ."

"Would be HMS *Elizabeth*," finished Bentham.

"Why, Danny," said Flint, "how well you know my story!"

"How well indeed, Joe!"

Flint smiled. Bentham smiled, and all the other leading men of the expedition clustered round, and they smiled, too, as they gazed upon the wreck of a fine ship. Like Bentham, these men – Allardyce, O'Byrne and the rest – were keeping constant company with Flint, for Flint knew where the gold was buried, and nobody else did. More than that, they'd heard about Flint . . . how he'd raised mutiny, killed his own captain, murdered most of his shipmates, and became a gentleman of fortune . . . before meeting John Silver and falling out as badly with him as he had with King George.

For Flint was the rollicking boy, and no mistake! You jumped when he said *jump*. You doffed your hat. You addressed him as "sir". You didn't dare cross him. And you didn't turn your back on him, not for a second – not ever! You wanted Flint in front of you, where at least you could keep an eye on him, for all the good it'd do you.

On the way back to the camp, Flint and his followers met Dreamer, Cut Feather and five others of the Patanq, who'd come from their own camp, which by mutual consent had been set up apart from Flint's.

The Patanq had their nose-rings and bracelets again, and their formal robes and moccasins.

"Joe," said Bentham, "they've come to talk. We'll have to sit down with them."

Flint sighed. He didn't like the long-windedness of Patanq negotiation. It was tedious . . . except that this time it wasn't. It was fascinating.

Dreamer led them to the treeline where the beach merged into forest, and they sat in a circle, the Patanq spreading elaborately decorated deerskin bags on the ground in front of them. After formal greetings on either side, Dreamer nodded and the Patanq unfastened the bags and took out long, slender guns with little brass trapdoors in the butts, and double triggers, and barrels that weren't round but octagonal in cross-section.

"These are not common guns," said Dreamer. "These are long-rifles. They are new. There are few in all the land and only seven in the Patanq nation." The white men nodded.

Dreamer continued. "Sun-Face," he said, "after the battle, I promised you a better way to take the forts."

"Yes," said Flint.

"This is the way," said Dreamer. "With these rifles."

"But rifles are for hunting," said Flint, "not for war."

"These rifles are for both," said Dreamer.

"But rifles can't stand against muskets," said Flint, frowning. "They shoot too slowly. I've seen it. You load an oversized ball, knock it down the barrel with a mallet and ramrod for the ball to grip the rifling. And a man with a musket fires *five* times while you do that!" He shook his head. "No – rifles are fine for hunting, where the beast don't shoot back, but they won't serve for fighting."

"Aye!" said most of the other white men, for it was the universal opinion of fighting men.

Dreamer, however, was unmoved.

"Do not the *German* white men use rifles in war?" said Dreamer. "In their homelands across the sea?"

"Perhaps," said Flint, uneasy at Dreamer's knowledge of the world. "But I don't know. I'm a sailor, not a soldier!"

"Wait a bit," said O'Byrne. "I was a soldier once, and I know Germans. I served under Frederick of Prussia. And he had men called *Jaegers,* which are huntsmen that are used as scouts. And they shoot rifles." He pointed at Dreamer's rifle: "But not like that. Theirs are short, with thick barrels."

"You speak truth," said Dreamer. "For many years I have spoken with the Germans of Pennsylvania. I know their ways. They are the best gun-makers in all the land, and their rifles are just as you have said . . . But I have caused new rifles to be made: differently and to my own wishes. See –"

And he explained, using his own rifle.

A musket took a ball of fourteen to the pound, and a Jaeger rifle some twenty. But Dreamer's rifle took balls of *fifty* to the pound, and the powder charge was proportionately smaller, enabling far more rounds to be carried – vital to a far-travelling woodsman. And the barrel was long for accuracy's sake, and to burn all the powder and waste none, and drive the ball fierce and hard. And there was no need for a mallet in loading; a measured charge went down the barrel from a powder horn, then a thin, greased leather patch – from the trapdoor in the butt – on the muzzle, and a ball on the patch, and both driven home with a steady pressure of the ramrod.

Priming was the same as for any gun, but then there were two triggers.

"How do *they* work?" said Flint.

"I will show you," said Dreamer. "Stand!"

Flint stood up, brushing the sand from his clothes. Dreamer stood. He loaded smooth and easy. Then he primed the rifle and set it to half-cock. He passed it to Flint.

"Sun-Face," said Dreamer, "do not touch the triggers!"

"At your command, sir!" said Flint, and bowed.

"Raise the gun," said Dreamer.

Flint levelled at the horizon. He frowned.

"The barrel's heavy," he said. "It's clumsy! It don't come up to the shoulder like a musket."

"No matter," said Dreamer. "Now, there are two triggers – yes?"

"Aye-aye, sir!"

"One trigger is broad and curved. One is thin and straight. Yes?"

"Aye-aye, sir!"

"Good. Now cock the rifle fully."

259

"Aye-aye, sir!"

"Now . . . carefully . . . pull the curved trigger."

Flint pulled. *Click* went the lock. But the rifle didn't fire. Not yet.

"Good," said Dreamer. "You have set it. All is ready. Now . . . take your aim. And when you are ready, touch the second trigger."

Flint aimed out to sea. He reached for the second trigger with his finger . . .

Whoof-BANG! said the rifle.

"Ah!" said Flint. "But I barely touched it!"

"No," said Dreamer. "It has a hair-trigger. It sets off the gun with a touch that does not disturb the aim." He nodded. "The German white man calls this *stechabzug*."

"Oh!" said O'Byrne, sitting up. "*Sie sprechen Deutsch?*"

"*Ja*," said Dreamer. "*Ich habe ein bißchen.*"

"Huh!" said Flint. "But how well does it shoot, this special gun?"

"I will show you," said Dreamer, and he began to reload.

Cut Feather and another Patanq stood up, and while Dreamer was loading Cut Feather found a piece of driftwood about a foot long and six inches wide and set off walking away from them. The other man brought a log and placed it at Dreamer's feet. Dreamer finished loading . . . he carefully touched the rifle against his wampum belt . . . he closed his eyes briefly . . . then stood waiting with the rifle butt on his foot, to save it from being scratched by the rough ground, and with his arms wrapped round the barrel. He looked steadily at Cut Feather, and an excited murmuring arose from the white men.

When Cut Feather had gone about a hundred paces, he turned and stood facing Dreamer. Dreamer laid down in the sand. He put the rifle to his shoulder and balanced the long barrel on the log.

"Sun-Face?" he said.

"Yes?" said Flint.

"See – the weight does not matter. I do not hold it."

"I see," said Flint.

There was complete silence. Cut Feather raised the piece of wood till it was next to his face. He nodded.

Dreamer took aim.

Click! said the hair trigger.

Whoof-BANG! said the rifle.

Smack! said the piece of driftwood and jumped from Cut Feather's hand.

Calmly he picked it up, walked back, and gave it to Flint. A sharp round hole ran through its centre.

"Sun-Face," said Dreamer, "this way we shall take the forts."

Chapter 29

*M*r Joe looked carefully out between the big, earth-filled gabions that protected the gun emplacement on the south-facing side of the fort.

"Where?" he said.

"There, Cap'n!" said Johnny Bowden, and pointed. Mr Joe straightened his back in pride. They called him "Captain" as if the fort were a ship and himself in command. And they were doing it of their own free will. Nobody had told them to.

Bowden was in charge of the gun. He and the five-man gun crew had hardly moved from it since they came in behind the walls. That was Silver's drill and it had saved their lives once already.

"Me don't see nothin'," said Mr Joe.

"Bah!" said Bowden, turning to his men. "You – Atty Atkins! You show the cap'n. It was you as saw it." Mr Joe frowned, straining to follow their conversation. It was always hard, no matter how long he'd known them. For he'd been raised in Jamaica, while they were from England's West Country. He had no ear for accent; to him, their speech sounded like dogs growling: "*Arrrrrr, arrrr, arrrrr,*" they said.

"It were a rag, Cap'n, a-wavin' on the end of a stick." Atty Atkins, who was a little taller than the rest, stretched up. He got his head clear over the gabion for a good look.

"Well, bugger me!" he said. "There it is ag—"

THACK! Something struck Atty Atkins's brow like a hard-swung cricket bat. He jerked back and a cupful of blood, brains, hair and bone-splinters burst out of the back of his head and all over his comrades.

At the forest edge, white smoke rolled in the breeze. Then all was silent and nothing moved.

"Fuck me!"

"Christ!"

"Get down!"

And five living men threw themselves flat beside the warm and twitching corpse of Atty Atkins.

Ten minutes later, Johnny Bowden was shot dead, looking out over the barrel of his gun. Then another man was killed as they tried to block up the gun-slit with timber. After that Mr Joe ordered them away from the guns and behind the ramparts. But then a man was shot going to the water butts, where he should have been safe.

"It came from up there, Cap'n," said one of his mates. "I saw the smoke! Them buggers is looking down on us from Foremast Hill, and they must be bloody magic, 'cos it's way out o' range."

Mr Joe went up on the ramparts. His heart was pounding. He had to look. But if he put his head over, he might get shot. But if he *didn't* look . . . He gathered his courage, started to stretch up . . . but his nerve failed. Then he saw the men looking at him in fear, and being their captain he tried again . . . and failed again. Then he sobbed and stretched, and rested his telescope on the packed earth of the thick, musket-proof wall. He focused on the hill, which should have been too far away for accurate fire – as indeed it was, for *musket* fire. That's why the fort had been built in this spot.

He blinked and swept the hill with the glass. There weren't so many trees up there. He could see bare ground, and bushes and . . . ah! He caught a flick of movement and saw a brown-skinned savage, crouched behind a rock, and he saw – actually saw – the puff of the lock and the muzzle-flash.

CRASH! The telescope shattered, a deflected ball whined past Mr Joe's ear, and needle shards of glass slashed his right eye to dripping, slimy pieces.

"Ahhhhh!" he cried, and fell back clutching the mess and the blood, screaming with the pain.

But he was a stubborn man. He didn't give up. He clapped a bandage on his face and got all hands into the central redoubt, and up on the firing step behind the walls, and made sure the muskets, pistols and grenadoes were ready. He expected an assault at any minute. But none came. The blasted savages just waited until some poor fool couldn't contain his impatience and put his head up, and looked round . . . and got a bullet through the bridge of his nose.

It was four men dead by nightfall.

Next day, despite every precaution, the Indians shot two more.

That made six out of the garrison of fifteen.

"We got to abandon ship, lads," said Mr Joe. "We don't got no edge here no more. Them buggers pick us off day by day! We go over the side tonight, and we go to Fort Spy-glass."

So they spiked the guns, and took what they could, and nine men crawled over the palisade in the dead of the night and crept like mice, southward towards the far end of the island, imagining be-feathered, staring-eyed savages behind every tree and blade of grass.

But they saw no Indians. Not at first.

Morning, 2nd February 1753
Fort Silver
The island

"Left a bit, left a bit..." said Israel Hands, and the four-pounder creaked and groaned as the men heaved and it shifted in its carriage. "Well!" said Israel Hands, and took a final sight. He looked back to check all hands were clear of the recoil, and touched off the gun with a flash and a roar... and a spurt of earth and stones jumped up two hundred yards off, where a savage was getting down on his belly for a shot at the fort.

"Huzzah!" cheered the gun-crew as the creature leapt up and ran back into the forest, fifty yards behind him. The ball didn't strike close enough to hurt him, but it told him there'd be no quiet target practice that day.

"How's that, then, Cap'n?" said Israel Hands.

"Well enough, Mr Gunner, but it don't change nothing," said Silver. "We're stuck behind these walls, just as I feared. They can't get in and we can't get out. We could be here for months!"

"T'ain't so bad, John!" said Israel Hands. "We're better

265

placed here than the other forts, and well provisioned besides."

"Hmm," said Silver. Warily he looked out past the crenulations they'd raised atop the ramparts, working at night when the Indians couldn't shoot. That'd been Israel Hands's idea. Now the fort looked like a story-book castle, but a man could take a bit of shelter when he looked out. They had timber shields mounted round the gun-barrels too, with a slot for sighting, to hide the gunners so the swabs outside couldn't shoot into the emplacements.

Yes, they'd learned some new tricks, and Fort Silver always had been the strongest. It was on rising ground, and they'd cleared the trees and bushes further out, for the work had been done early on when there was more time. The result was that the sharp-shooters with their long guns couldn't overlook the fort, and couldn't get close enough for their best marksmanship: not without a four-pound shot coming out to greet them!

Now there were twenty-seven men and a boy inside the fort, counting Billy Bones, still in leg irons and not to be trusted, but not Ben Gunn, who'd gone off on his own when they manned the fort, since he couldn't bear being locked in, and Silver couldn't bear being locked in with him.

"You're in command, Mr Gunner," said Silver.

"Aye-aye, sir," said Israel Hands, and raised a hand to his hat. Silver went down the ramp from the walls and found Mr Joe, sat quiet in the shade by himself.

"Hallo, lad," said Silver, and sat down with his one leg stretched out in front of him and the green parrot on his shoulder.

"Pretty thing!" said Mr Joe, and reached out to touch the bird.

"Wouldn't if I was you," said Silver.

"Awwwwwwwwwwk!" said the bird. "Bugger off!"

"Sorry, lad, but this old bird's contrary, and she don't like it here, do you, Cap'n?" He stroked her head and ruffled her feathers, and she rubbed herself against him and nibbled his fingers.

"*John Silver! John Silver!*" she said, and gently nipped his ear with a beak that could crack walnuts.

Silver looked at the bandage over Mr Joe's eye.

"How's it doing?"

"It hurt a bit."

"Is it hot? Swolled up?"

"No. It bad when I got here. Very bad. But Mr Hands, he cleaned it out with a spoon." He tried to be offhand, tried to be bold, but he shuddered at the memory.

"Had to be done, lad . . . But never mind, the girls'll like you with a patch!"

"Huh!"

"Them Indians . . ." said Silver.

"Cap'n?"

"You say they jumped on you in the woods outside Fort Foremast?"

"Aye, Cap'n. And they catch all the rest. Eight men. But not me."

"Why not?"

"Me run fast. Me run to Fort Spy-glass. Me call out loud. They let me in."

"So then what?"

"Me tell them in Fort Spy-glass. Me tell them we got to come here."

"To Fort Silver?"

"Aye, Cap'n."

Silver nodded. The garrison of Fort Spy-glass had been twelve men. Thirteen, including Mr Joe. Of that total, just seven had reached Fort Silver.

"Blasted Indians!" said Silver.

"Aye, Cap'n."

"So why'd you come here?"

Mr Joe blinked. It was obvious.

"For *you*, Cap'n! You the big man. The *best* man. You know what to do!"

Silver sighed.

Night, 28th January 1753
The forest by Foremast Hill
The island

Selena turned away. It was another council: long and protracted and herself forbidden to take part. She walked off. It was very dark. The few Patanq not already at the fireside looked sidelong at her as they edged past to get there: tall, dark figures, with gleaming skulls, black eyes, and the animal smell that hung over them. The smell was sometimes the first you knew of their presence, for they made no sound at all.

She made them uneasy. They didn't know how to treat her. Bentham said they'd walk straight into one of their own women if she didn't get out of the way. They'd knock her down and never look back. But they didn't know how to treat a woman who wore men's clothes and carried pistols, and who was ranked as an equal by Sun-Face, whom they treated with profoundest respect . . . and fear.

Bentham said Dreamer thought Flint was the Devil – Satan, Lucifer, the Evil One – walking the Earth in a man's body . . .

a nasty thought on a dark night! Selena shuddered and looked all around. Then she frowned. Bentham said too much! Bentham was always trying to talk to her, and it was Bentham that'd made it a joke that she'd come ashore to treat the wounded, and insisted that she should be part of the fighting instead. And Flint had laughed too, and Dreamer and the Patanq had looked on, blank-faced with their guns in their arms, and wondering what was a man and what was a woman among the white ones.

"Selena!"

She turned. Huh! It was Bentham himself . . . *herself* – whatever – following her. She stopped.

"What do you want?" She put her hands on her pistols. She wasn't what she'd been a year ago. She knew what was in Bentham's mind – whatever Bentham was – and once it would have frightened her, and disgusted her. But things were changed. Bentham might be nearly twice her weight and a foot taller, but she'd seen how men dropped when she shot them, and saw no reason why Bentham shouldn't do the same.

"Well?" she said.

"I wants to talk," said Bentham in his soft voice.

"That's close enough!" she said, half pulling a pistol.

It was hard to see Bentham's expression in the dark forest, but he raised his hands and bowed his head.

"Miss Selena," he said, "please listen. Please listen to what I'm offering. I wants you to know that my intentions –"

That was as far as Danny Bentham got.

"No!" said Selena. Flint was bad enough, but *Bentham?* "Now you listen to me," she said, "I don't know what you think you are, and I don't care. But I don't want any of it. Go away, Danny Bentham . . . *you're just a woman dressed up as a man!*"

Bentham stopped dead. Nobody said that! Nobody dared! And it hurt. Especially from her. Bentham tried to be angry but couldn't. Instead, Bentham was belittled and bereft. And when Selena turned and walked away, Bentham couldn't find the will to follow her but stood with the slow tears flowing.

Selena walked off and found a quiet place and stood with her hands over her face, burdened by all the old fears and hopes. Flint would kill Silver. She knew that now. Never doubt it. He'd been chuckling about the Patanq and their rifles, and said it was the end of Silver's forts, and he was already planning how he'd kill Silver when he got hold of him. So Silver was gone. But even if he wasn't, what would Silver, or Flint, or even Cowdray – who looked at her so moon-faced – what would they want with a black woman, even a lovely one, once they'd rolled her on her back? What did any white man want with a black woman? Even in Charlestown, they'd treated her as a doll, not an equal.

What could she do?

Chapter 30

*J*ust before noon Cornelius Van Oosterhout came up on deck, and the crew instantly doffed hats and moved respectfully to the lee side of the quarterdeck, for he was a man of great authority. He commanded aboard this ship – and throughout the Patanq fleet – by order of Dreamer the medicine sachem, by order of Flint the pirate, and by virtue of his skill as a navigator . . . not to mention his ability to put any man flat on his back who gave trouble.

He'd soon had quite enough of Mr Foster and *Lucy May,* and had moved to the best ship of the fleet: *The Lord Stanley* a Whitby-built collier-bark of three masts and four hundred tons. She was a stout, weatherly ship with deep holds, comfortable cabins, and a master, Mr James York, who was a muscular young man, thick-waisted, black-stubbled, and heavy-fisted, who ran so smart a crew that Van Oosterhout could concentrate on his calculations, leaving the ship entirely to him.

271

Van Oosterhout could also concentrate on the puzzle of why so honest a man as himself had become – *de facto* – a pirate, serving the cause of a villain? After all, the Indian warriors were gone, there was nobody holding a pistol to his head, and he could have taken his ship anywhere he wanted, telling the crew some suitable tale, and bidding goodbye for ever to Captain Flint.

Being an analytical man, he'd carefully considered all this and come to the conclusion that he was here, first and fore-most, because he wanted his share of Flint's treasure. And since he wasn't being asked to do anything actually wicked – not robbery or murder, for instance – he was happy to go along with Flint's plans. Besides that, he was well content with so large and fine a ship as *Lord Stanley* – vastly superior to the poor little *Christiaan Hugens*. And finally . . . finally . . . there were certain other possibilities of this present voyage, which he did not wish to spoil.

So he stood tall as he advanced to the quarterdeck rail, taking the quadrant his servant offered him, and acknowl-edging the salutes of Captain York and the rest. As ever, the Indian women and girls looked on from the fo'c'sle where they habitually gathered, and they chattered and pointed. They giggled and smiled at him, for he was the chief man aboard and they knew it.

It was a surprising pleasure to have women and children aboard ship. Van Oosterhout had never been to sea in a ship teeming with children. There were all ages on board, from babes in arms, to toddlers who must constantly be watched, to little boys who swarmed in the rigging and screamed in their incessant games. They were fine little fellows, bright eyed and brown-skinned, utterly unlike their hard-faced fathers, and they smiled and played and seemed endlessly happy.

And as for the young women . . .

Hmm, thought Van Oosterhout, and unconsciously glanced at Captain York, who looked pleased with himself – as well he might, for he'd got a favourite among the Indian girls. *Sally,* he called her, and he was taking her to bed every night, and making a great deal of noise in the doing of it . . . an intoxicating thought . . . But there was duty to be done, and Van Oosterhout completed his noon observation, then turned his telescope on the rest of the fleet.

They were a wallowing, lumpish collection of rigs and gear, lumbering along, anxiously keeping together for the miserable reason that they feared getting lost. This amazing fact he'd learned the first time he took his observations aboard *Lord Stanley* and York did the same. Van Oosterhout discovered that where *he* thought in terms of placing a precise cross on the chart, York had more modest aims.

"It's *lead, log and latitude* for me, Mr Van!" he said. "I was bred up to the coastal trade from Whitby to London, the which is in sight of land, or close by, and is sailed by learning from your dad, as I did! I can find me latitude at a pinch, but mainly I sails by finding them places *again* the which I has already been to, and has the knowledge of."

"Oh?" said Van Oosterhout. "Then how did you cross the Atlantic?"

"Why," said York, "I came out years ago, in company with other ships of the West India convoy for fear of war with the Dons. And there was plenty on board of the other ships as knew the deep waters and had sailed the West Indies afore." He shrugged. "So I followed them, mostly."

"I see," said Van Oosterhout, realising he'd been mistaken in his assumption that others knew what *he* knew. "What about the other shipmasters of our fleet? Are they *lead, log and latitude?*"

York grinned. "God bless you, sir! Some o' them buggers couldn't find St Paul's if they was anchored at the Tower!"

Van Oosterhout was brought back to the present by the sound of singing. It was coming from the fo'c'sle. He looked up. The Indian girls were playing some sort of game, in a ring, holding the little children in their arms so they could pass a ball around. They laughed and sang. They were a pretty sight, and the seamen looked on and smiled.

Just casually, and telling himself he'd no particular thought in mind, Van Oosterhout wandered down the deck, past the mainmast, past the belfry and the capstan, just idly wandering towards the singing, and the laughing. The women saw him coming and laughed all the louder. Then three young women broke away from the crowd and made a great business of chanting some sort of song, and clapping their hands and looking at him.

Van Oosterhout stared. Patanq women were tall and slender. Their clothes – by the standards of a Protestant Dutchman – were saucy in the extreme, with skirts that showed their fine legs and tunics that didn't hide the bounce of their breasts. They wore many bright beads, and had smooth skins and wonderful slanted eyes. Van Oosterhout gulped. He didn't wish to be a libertine like Captain Foster of *Lucy May* with his dirty hand up a skirt. But still . . .

The three girls advanced upon him, clapping and singing and stepping out some sort of dance. Those on the fo'c'sle joined in the song, and the girl in the middle smiled at Van Oosterhout, and looked him straight in the eye, and pressed something into his hands. Then the three of them ended the song with a stamp and a clap of the hands and ran off.

Van Oosterhout looked at what she'd given him. It was a little wooden doll, neatly carved, brightly painted, very much male and very much aroused.

"Oof!" said Van Oosterhout, and blushed bright red. But the girl smiled at him. And that night, he made as much noise as Mr York as she knelt upright on his loins in his narrow bed, pressing her buttocks on to his thighs to drive all well home, and digging her nails into his chest and biting his ears and laughing and laughing and laughing.

And as he gazed at the long black hair swirling over naked brown shoulders, in the lantern-light, and the lovely breasts . . . even intoxicated with pleasure as he was, the calculating part of Cornelius Van Oosterhout's mind congratulated itself for keeping faith with Flint, because that meant keeping faith with Dreamer – and Van Oosterhout knew he wouldn't now be enjoying the favours of this delectable girl if he hadn't. He even wondered whether she was giving herself to him for precisely that reason? Doubtless they had their own forms of marriage and chastity? But who cared . . .

"Ahhhhhhhhhhh!" said Van Oosterhout.

So . . . a fine merry voyage it was too, until late February of the new year, when Van Oosterhout's calculations told him that the fleet would soon be running on to the northern archipelago as shown in his copy of Flint's chart. His orders from Flint were that he must on no account approach the island from any other direction, and that he must sail with utmost care, and only in daylight, and with a careful lookout for the perils ahead.

"There, Mr York!" cried Van Oosterhout, pointing.

"Aye!" said York, shouting in his ear. "Damned easy to run on to it!"

Indeed," said Van Oosterhout, "but we have Flint's chart!"

The two were swaying in *Lord Stanley*'s fore-top with the lookouts beside them and the wind blowing so strong it was hard to speak. Behind them the whole fleet was hove to, for the deadly rocks and quicksands of the archipelago were but a few miles off, and *Lord Stanley* was ahead and seeking the entrance to Flint's Passage, the safe route southwards through the archipelago. Even such a navigator as Van Oosterhout couldn't pinpoint the entrance without going in to look for it.

It took two days of hard work before Van Oosterhout was satisfied that he'd found the entrance. Meanwhile he had the fleet come to anchor in the lee of a vast sandbank that broke the force of the prevailing winds. It was no harbour, but it was better than the open seas. Then he took *Lord Stanley*'s longboat, rigged for sail with a small crew, and with the chart on his knees, and with Captain York left in command of the fleet, Van Oosterhout entered Flint's Passage, and headed for the island.

It wasn't easy passing through rocks and shoals, but eventually it was done, and they cleared the shallows . . . and there was the island! Not just a smudge on the horizon, but a clear profile of land, trees and hills. Van Oosterhout looked at it. He knew that *he* could find it again. He knew Flint could. But . . . the fingers-and-thumbs persons who steered the ships of the Patanq fleet *couldn't*. Not without detailed sailing instructions.

So, he wondered, could there be advantage in this? Presumably Flint would dig up the treasure and share it out. But what if he didn't? What if something went wrong? Van Oosterhout didn't know, but it was fascinating to speculate, and the wheels turned and turned in his mind. Meanwhile, there was work to be done. Flint would have anchored in the northern inlet. Van Oosterhout steered towards it, keen to discover how things had gone for Flint and the Patanq warriors.

Chapter 31

Afternoon, 15th February 1753
The woods near Flint's Camp
The northern inlet

*F*lint was happy. Everything was going well. He'd shaken off Bentham, O'Byrne and the rest. Even *they* left him alone when he dropped his breeches and squatted behind a tree. And as soon as they'd gone, he'd darted off to spend some time alone, to develop some ideas in his mind. But first he had to make sure his *courtiers* were really gone ...

Ah, there they were! He peered between the leaves and saw the backs of his ever-present followers as they wandered back to camp to find their lord and master – himself – whom they loved so dearly because only *he* knew where the treasure lay. Flint smiled and corrected himself, because in fact he knew the *several different places* where various parts of it lay, accompanied in some cases by members of that happy band who'd been so delighted to come ashore with their commodore to do the hard work of burying. Flint thought of their innocent faces: so coarse, so open, and so ridiculously expectant. He laughed when he thought what he'd done with them.

Then he strolled along the beach towards the wreck of *Elizabeth*, keeping close under the shadow of the trees so he shouldn't be seen.

Every day now, the savages pressed him to raise some of the treasure. Enough to pay them. Every day he pointed out that the last fort had not fallen. Ridiculously, that was accepted by Dreamer as excuse enough. And so it went on, with Flint content. He hadn't yet quite worked out how he would raise the goods and ship them aboard *Walrus*, and sail off leaving the island – and all those on it – but he had several good ideas, including a most ingenious plan for a frontal assault on the fort, which would trim a few dozen more off the total of Patanq warriors, of whom there were more than he needed and more than enough to be dangerous.

That's why he had to be alone. So he could think. And he liked to come to the remains of the old *Elizabeth* for the memory of days past . . . which brought back thoughts of Silver. It was always Silver, before anything: Silver, Silver, Silver! The only man he feared. The only man he'd ever admired. The man who'd taken Selena, the island – even the damned parrot. Flint half raised a hand to his shoulder to stroke the bird that wasn't there.

"Bah!"

And then he smiled. He smiled with the enormous relief that all Silver's preparations had been in vain. All that planning and calculating and back-breaking labour – all of it futile! A few forts, that was all it amounted to, of which all but one had fallen. Was that really the best Silver could do? Perhaps he'd –

"Sun-Face!"

Flint jumped as if scalded. He'd not heard. He'd not seen. Damn! Damn! Damn! It was always the same.

Dreamer, Cut Feather and some others had come out of nowhere, from some path in the woods. And they had a prisoner.

"Well, bless my living soul!" said Flint, for trembling wretchedly between two of the tall warriors, his arms bound tight with leather thongs, was a man he knew.

"Good day to you, Ben Gunn!" said Flint.

"Cap'n! Cap'n!" cried Ben Gunn, desperate in terror. "God bless you, sir, for a Christian gentleman, and don't let these heathen take me!" He shuddered and shivered and looked around. "I knows Indians, Cap'n. I been in the Americas years ago, and I seen what they done to their prisoners!" Ben Gunn fell to his knees, with the tears rolling down his cheeks. "Don't let poor Ben Gunn come to that, Cap'n! Not him! Not you, Cap'n . . ." On and on he went.

Well, thought Flint, *here's Ben Gunn, got hold of the wrong end of the stick!* Unlike other Indians, the Patanq did *not* torture their prisoners. They killed and scalped them, certainly. But they didn't play with them. No need to tell Ben Gunn that, though, Flint decided.

"Shut him up!" said Flint. Dreamer nodded and one of the Patanq clouted Ben Gunn's head a heavy smack.

"Ugh!" said Ben Gunn, knocked half senseless.

"We found him in the forest," said Dreamer. "He has spied on us for many days. He treads softly and moves fast, but we caught him at last." Dreamer looked at Ben Gunn. "He is clever in the forest, but his mind is broken." He turned back to Flint. "And now he begs your protection, Sun-Face. He says he is your man."

"Mine?" said Flint, stepping forward and poking Ben Gunn with the toe of his shiny boot. "Are you mine,

Ben Gunn?" He smiled his smile. "I thought you went over to Silver."

"No! No! Not I!" said Ben Gunn, and out poured a tumbling torrent of words, which were the adventures of Ben Gunn as told by Ben Gunn. He was particularly eloquent on the subject of monkeys. Flint listened, and a possibility twinkled elusively at the back of his mind. But first he must get a firm hold on the very slippery Ben Gunn.

"You're no use to me, Mr Gunn," he said. "I shall give you to the Patanq."

Ben Gunn howled in terror. It was a hideous death for him: death by slow torture.

"Or perhaps not," said Flint, once he was sure Ben Gunn had taken sufficient fright. "Dreamer – he is my man. He is under my protection. Release him."

Ben Gunn grovelled and slobbered and kissed Flint's boots when they cut him free, and followed Flint when he walked off towards the ruined ship, and the Patanq disappeared into the forest.

Flint found a quiet corner where the trees sheltered them from view but they could see the moss-grown timbers, and there were some rocks to sit on.

And there Flint had a very long and most fascinating conversation with Ben Gunn and pumped him dry of every scrap of information held within his miserable memory. And in that dark and tangled place – among the disconnected jumble of facts, fears and misapprehensions – Joe Flint found some gemstones.

Or at least they were gemstones to Flint. They were rubies, sapphires and diamonds, and *this* because Joe Flint perceived certain unique opportunities. He then concentrated his mind on devising a means to exploit them. The result was a plan that decent men would have despised and rejected. But Flint was proud of it. He was proud, and amazed that Ben Gunn – damaged, wretched creature that he was – should be the source of so much power.

So Flint turned to practicalities, and began to give Ben Gunn his orders, and to make arrangements . . . arrangements which, to his annoyance, were interrupted by the arrival of that peerless navigator, that esteemed friend of Selena, that confidant of Cowdray, that practitioner of the Batavian art of silat: Cornelius damned Van Oosterhout. For the Dutchman had chosen that moment to land his longboat right opposite the northern inlet camp, and having disembarked he began strutting up and down, and sending men to find Captain Flint so that he might proclaim the safe delivery of the women and children of the Patanq nation.

At first, Flint was taken aback. He had long since realised that Van Oosterhout was by far the most talented and intelligent of all his followers, and therefore the most dangerous. The last thing Flint wanted was the Dutchman joining the politics Bentham was brewing behind his back, and in any case he couldn't abide Van Oosterhout's solemn, self-satisfied face and just wanted him out of the way. But how? He could order him back to his ship, but what would he get up to there, out of Flint's sight?

Fortunately, Flint was seized with inspiration. He greeted Van Oosterhout with smiles, and called for fruits and rum, and sent an Indian runner to bring the good news to Dreamer and Cut Feather. Then he had a private word with the master of silat.

"You're come not a moment too soon," said Flint.

"Why?" said Van Oosterhout.

"Because . . . the treasure is threatened!"

Van Oosterhout's eyes made circles.

"I can trust none but you!" said Flint.

"Me?"

"Yes! For there's mutiny and murder ahead, and we need new burial sites . . ."

They talked for nearly an hour before Van Oosterhout was convinced. Then he nodded firmly, shook Flint's hand and set off with map, notebook and compass, on a most privileged and trusted mission: to check that the treasure was still where it should be, and to survey new sites for its re-interment, in case of need. Flint even passed over some of his own notes for guidance, and when Van Oosterhout walked off, Flint congratulated himself on a job well done.

Van Oosterhout would be busy for weeks, especially once he'd dug up some of the treasure, and goggled over it – for Flint knew the key to Van Oosterhout. Otherwise what was he doing here? He'd had plenty of opportunity to run. With Van Oosterhout it was gold, gold, gold. And Spanish dollars, of course.

Fortunately, he'd be on his own, sworn to secrecy, and unable to take more than a handful or two for himself. Better still, during their intense conversation, Flint had taken a close look at Van Oosterhout's face beneath the sandy whiskers, and seen how easily the Dutchman's total silence could be assured.

And so back to Ben Gunn. Making haste, before Bentham and O'Byrne could close in, Flint found the mad creature and made completely sure that he knew what was expected of him.

"Tell me what sort of men you must find," said Flint.

Ben Gunn told him.

"And where must you take them?"

Ben Gunn told him.

"And what must they do?"

Ben Gunn told him.

"And finally," said Flint, "tell me what shall happen to you, should you play me false."

Ben Gunn shuddered. He lowered his eyes. A thin stream of terror ran from his bladder and down his skinny leg, and made a dark patch in the sand.

"You'll give me to the savages."

"And what if you try to run away?"

"They'll catch me anyway."

"And what will they do to you?"

In a tiny voice, with eyes tight shut, and hands over his face, Ben Gunn told him. Ben Gunn knew, because Flint had told *him*. Flint listened and nodded and looked to the future, and saw all things smoothed and his plans going forward like a ship in a steady blow – never suspecting that another threat, one he'd thought dead and gone, was even now reaching out to grab him.

Two bells of the forenoon watch
15th February 1753
Aboard HMS Oraclaesus
The Atlantic

The maintop of a frigate in a lively sea was lavishly provided with opportunities for a man to kill himself.

It was a timber platform some twenty feet long by fifteen wide; rounded forward and square-cut aft (where, it must be said, there *was* a flimsy rail that might stop a man from going over and dropping a hundred feet to the hard deck or the hungry sea). Likewise, to either beam, the main topmast shrouds with their ratlines closed the maintop under a narrowing pyramid of black-tarred rope, making it almost impossible to go over either way. But forward, the top was entirely innocent of restraint, and inboard, where the platform admitted the great shafts of the mainmast and topmast, there were great gaps – *lubbers' holes* – that lay in wait for some fool to put his foot in, and proceed downwards by that swift route.

Which was one of many reasons why, aboard His Majesty's ships nine men were killed as a result of mishap, shipwreck or disease, for every one so fortunate as to be killed by England's enemies.

None of which worried Lieutenant Hastings or Mr Midshipman Povey, who'd been bred up to the sea and imagined no other life, and today were at the pinnacle of professional joy, finding themselves at the epicentre of such a manoeuvre as only men-o'-war could perform at all, and which, in their opinion, only King George's ships could do well.

Each had a telescope and each had a ship under observation. The ships were *Leaper* and *Bounder*. Of these, *Leaper* – observed by Hastings – lay to larboard, and *Bounder* – observed by Povey – lay to starboard, each being some twenty miles off: the furthest distance from which signals were visible by the aid of a glass. Then to larboard of *Leaper* was *Jumper,* another twenty miles off. So, with four ships deployed in line abeam, and the outermost ships looking their twenty miles further out on each side . . . that meant a total width of one hundred miles was under observation as the ships proceeded on course.

"Signal coming up, sir!" said Povey as a hoist of flags ran up the halyard and broke into the wind. The signal read

"Inquiry" – a challenge to ensure all ships were alert and smart.

Hastings and Povey studied *Leaper* and *Bounder*.

"Acknowledge!" said Hastings, as Leaper responded with signal flags. "Aye-aye *Leaper*!" he roared, for the benefit of the officer of the watch, below.

"Aye-aye *Bounder*!" cried Povey.

"Aye-aye *Jumper*!" cried Hastings, as *Leaper* hoisted the "Repeat Acknowledge", indicating *Jumper* too was awake and alert.

Thus ship spoke to ship in seconds across a hundred miles. A remarkable feat of seamanship, but routine to those involved. Which was just as well, because they had to keep it up day after weary day to find Flint's island, for the ocean is mighty and laughs at so small a distance as a hundred miles. Also, for all Mr Povey's natural talent for navigation, he'd not put his finger on quite the right spot. Nobody could have done better, but it was only a guess, and nothing less than the skilled teamwork of a naval squadron could have found the island based on that guess.

In the event, all was merriment and anticipation aboard Commodore Scott-Owen's ships, for they came within sight of the island's southern anchorage after only ten days of searching. It could have taken much, much longer, and every man of them knew it, and there wasn't one who didn't believe they were blessed with especially good luck.

The future could only be bright.

Chapter 32

*F*lint put away his notebook. It had served its purpose: this was a site that did not appear in the notes given to Van Oosterhout. Looking around him, the forest glade began to seem familiar now that he was actually *in* it, but even he couldn't have found it without the notes. He sighed in contentment, took out his pocket compass, opened it, and set his back to one of the giant pines that rose over the island like a cathedral spire. He let the needle steady itself . . . took a bearing . . . and paced out the correct number of steps.

"Here, my jolly boys!" he said. "Bring your spades and your strong arms, and dig here!"

"Huzzah!" they cried.

"Shhhh!" said Flint. "Hush lads! We don't want the savages upon us, do we now? Helping themselves with their greedy fingers!"

They grinned, and dropped their spars and tackles, laid aside pistols and cutlasses, and took up their spades and began to dig furiously, while Flint sat on a rock watching them.

He fanned himself with his hat, for it was hot and dark in the glade, with legions of buzzing insects, and a stifling scent of pine and wild garlic. He spread his fine coattails neatly on the rock so that they shouldn't be creased. He fingered the linen of his shirt, and the plume in his hat, and tried to put on a serious face . . . and failed totally. For he couldn't help chuckling at their bright eagerness, and the vigour with which they threw up the earth, and drove in their spades, already imagining themselves home in England, rogering tarts, gorging themselves on rum-duff, and riding in gilded carriages.

Look at them! he thought. *Those bright eyes . . . those smooth cheeks!* But that was too much. It was just too much. He doubled up laughing, for Ben Gunn was – even at this very moment – off about his duties, choosing men of quite a different kind, and Flint laughed at the thought of it.

The six men doing the digging grinned and nudged one another as they worked. It was a fine thing to see the captain so merry, for Christ help a poor sailorman when he *wasn't!* But they didn't stop digging. They'd been told most explicitly that this wasn't the great share-out they all dreamed of. Still . . . a man couldn't help but *hope* that just a *little* might – entirely accidentally and by chance – drop into his own pockets when nobody was looking. Or perhaps into the tops of his hungry boots . . . for no one would notice *that*, now, would they?

Thunk! Scrape! Thunk! went the spades. Then: *CLUNK!*

"Ah!" said Flint, up like a cat and among the diggers on the instant. He grinned. He looked into the sandy, earthy hole . . . *There they were!* Three fine chests of iron-bound wood. In fact, only *one* was visible, but Flint knew that two more were there. "Careful now, my boys – my jolly boys!" he said. "There's over five thousand Spanish dollars in these boxes, and I want them out of the ground, and not spoilt!"

"Oh?" said one of the diggers. "Is that *all?* We thought there was hundreds of thousands . . ."

"Aye!" said his mates, miserable as children denied a feast, and surly besides.

"No, my lovely boys!" said Flint. "Not *here*. But there's plenty elsewhere!"

And he said it so nicely, and tapped a finger against his nose with such an air of secrets shared among shipmates, that they nodded and smiled and beamed.

"*AAAAH!*" they said, and were well content. They remained content as their captain explained what was to be done, and why, and where the dollars were to be taken. And they marvelled at his foresight in bringing spars and ropes so a pair of men could easily manage one of the heavy chests by slinging it from a spar laid over their shoulders. And above all they thrilled at the knowledge that they knew where the treasure lay – some of it, anyway – *and nobody else did!*

And neither did *they* know that what they'd raised was worth considerably more than five thousand dollars, since one of the chests – the smallest but the heaviest – didn't contain silver dollars, but gold doubloons. Flint thought it best not to tempt their naughtiness with such knowledge as that. Especially as there were some stones in there as well . . . precious stones.

Fifteen men on the dead man's chest! he sang as he led the way. It was the good old song he always sang when happy. But he sang only to himself. He sang silently. He didn't want these poor souls bellowing out the chorus and drawing attention to the three chests swaying along to their new home. Aside from Van Oosterhout, six men now knew the whereabouts of at least *some* of the goods, and six was enough, because God alone knew how many Patanq savages were hiding in the woods, a-creeping and a-spying.

So Flint was merry as he walked, occasionally looking back to make sure that they were following. Indeed, he was so merry that it soon became very hard for him to deny himself the fun of ensuring *personally* and *with his own hand* that the shared secret went no further. But he managed to hold these urges in check. For one thing he wasn't about to carry three hundredweight of treasure by himself. And for another . . . there was a totally new and totally wonderful game to be played: a game he'd never played before, and he didn't want to spoil it.

When the work was done, Flint sent his spadesmen to get drunk at a quiet place he'd shown them, and where he would join them later. As soon as they were out of sight, he settled down to enjoy a little interlude by himself before returning to the camp and the enfolding arms of Bentham and the rest. He smiled. Things were shaping up nicely. Not everything had gone to plan, but there'd been compensating surprises. For the time being, a little of the raised coinage would keep the savages happy, and the promise of more should spur them on to greater efforts against John Silver. Alas, it would involve sitting down with the savages for yet another of their appalling formal councils – a dull task, but unavoidable. And then he must deal with Bentham, who was too nosy; and Cowdray and Van Oosterhout, who were too clever; and even Mr O'Byrne, who was too ugly! A lesser man would have trembled at the tasks ahead, but not Joe Flint.

Finally there was Selena . . . and the thought of her stopped Flint dead in his tracks. His mouth dropped open in horror. And this time he trembled like any lesser man. For he'd been on the point of making a most appalling mistake. He realised in that instant that it would be necessary to tell Selena everything. In particular it would be necessary to tell her what he was going to do with those who were surplus to requirements. Otherwise his wonderful scheme for killing *almost* everyone would end up with Selena among the dead.

And Flint could not bear the thought of anything harming Selena. Not a hair of her head. Not a fingernail. Not an inch of her lovely body.

Sunset, 25th February 1753
Outside Flint's Camp
The northern inlet

As was her habit, Selena walked away from the camp, and into the darkness, as ever keeping the edge of the trees on one side and the waters of the inlet on the other. That way, even in darkness she kept her sense of direction. She had nothing to fear. There were no wild beasts in the woods and the only wild *men* were Flint's or Silver's or Dreamer's – none of whom would harm her. She was immensely privileged, and she knew it. The only trouble was that she had no idea which of these various parties she wanted to be part of.

Bentham was following her. She knew that too. He . . . she . . . *still* wouldn't let her alone. Whatever it was that burned inside Danny Bentham was stronger even than the lust that drove *men* to make fools of themselves. But Selena wasn't afraid of men *or* Danny Bentham any more, just tired of all of them, and their greed and their violence and the hideous things they did to one another. That, and the equally hideous knowledge that she could think of no better or finer place to run to . . . even if she could run.

"Selena!" said Bentham.

"Oh, go away."

"I got to talk to you."

She nearly killed him there and then, overwhelmed by the surge of anger, the thought blazing in her mind: *Draw! Fire!*

But she didn't. She'd killed in self defence, but wasn't quite ready for cold-blooded murder. So she thought a bit . . . and tried something new. She turned to face him.

"Flint don't like you talking to me," she said, and saw at once that she'd hit the mark. Bentham scowled, but for a moment she saw the fright in his big, smooth face.

"Damn Flint!" said Bentham. "He's nothing to me!"

"Really?" she said. "Let's see you tell *him* that!"

Bentham wasn't done, though. He stepped forward, then stopped about ten feet off, and raised his hands.

"Selena," he said, "we're near the end o' this voyage."

"What voyage?"

"The raising of Flint's treasure."

"Oh . . . that."

"There was another council earlier, with Dreamer."

"I know."

"Flint had a plan. A plan to take Silver's fort."

"Yes."

"It's clever."

"It would be, since it came from him. But don't trust your life on it."

"I won't – it's the Patanq who'll take the risks!"

"So?"

292

"Well . . . once it's done, and we're done with Silver, then my share'll make me rich, and I'm fixed on givin' up the sea life, and going ashore and –"

"Selena!"

Flint's voice. Distant. Coming from the direction of the camp.

"Better not let him find you with me," said Selena.

"Bollocks to that! I'll skin and gut the swab!"

"Really?"

Bentham turned and stared at the distinctive figure coming towards them along the beach.

"He knows I come along here," said Selena, "but he hasn't seen you yet. You've still time to make up your mind . . . So," she sneered, "just what are you going to do now, *Mister* Bentham?"

Bentham thought. Flint was the only creature who knew where the treasure was buried. Flint couldn't be killed. Not even harmed.

"I want you, Selena," he said. "I'll find a way!" And with that Bentham ran and hid in the dark woods. He hid so well that when Flint marched up there wasn't even a sniff of him, and Selena was quite alone.

Flint stepped up to her, took her hands and kissed them.

"Selena!" he said.

"What d'you want?"

"I have good news."

"What?"

"Things are going well. We're going to be rich."

"We are?"

He smiled, but only God knew what was behind the smile. Certainly Selena had no idea. Not when Flint could smile one instant and kill the next.

"Ah!" he said. "I see you are unsure. No matter, I've been unsure myself. Unsure for months."

"Have you?" she said, and prickled in fright because she guessed where this was leading.

"I thought I wasn't fit," he said. "Would you believe that? Not fit for you." And he smiled again, and spoke such words as drew Selena clean out of her depth, and into very deep waters indeed.

For Flint was arguing a case. Where a normal man – a man in love – would have pleaded and begged, Flint was beating the drum that marshalled the facts, that destroyed the opposition. He did it with great skill, magnified by his undoubted charm, and founded on the rock-bottom truth that he was master of one of the greatest treasures ever assembled in one place.

Selena was still young. She had no experience of life beyond the Fitzroy plantation, Charley Neal's liquor store, or sailing with gentlemen of fortune. By comparison, life with Flint was the best she could hope for – that was how Flint told it. That was what he was offering. And Selena wondered. She really wondered. Perhaps this *was* the best she could get in a vicious, cruel world, because it *could* be, it *might* be, a very comfortable best . . . and perhaps Flint himself had changed?

A second later she was convinced of it, for Flint was so persuasive that he succeeded in persuading even himself and took the final step, as a rush of genuine feeling overcame him.

"Marry me!" he said. "Be my wife!"

There was utter silence as each reacted to these extra-ordinary words. Selena could not believe that he'd actually spoken them, while Flint was astounded that something so powerful could exist within himself without him knowing, until it burst forth, passionate, spontaneous and sincere. And in that uncanny moment they stood together on the brink of the fathomless, uncharted unknown.

"Joe," she said, "where do we go from here?"

"I'll tell you," he said, "we've come to a parting, Selena!"

"What do you mean?"

"You don't think we're going to *share* the goods, do you? With the rest?"

"Well, yes!"

Flint laughed aloud. "God bless you, no! There's you and me, and there's *those we do not want*. Now listen, my little flower, for this is what I shall do with *them* and this is what *you* must do to be safe . . ."

And so he explained. He explained in detail, and a great shame fell upon Selena that she'd considered – even for an instant – the possibility of giving herself to Flint while John Silver still lived. Even if Long John were a thousand miles away and she might never see him again.

"Stop it!" she cried, breaking into Flint's hideous lecture. "D'you think I could be part of *that*? D'you think the whole world is like you? D'you think I don't know a better man? Get away from me! *I despise you!*"

Flint blinked. His face went white. He shook with rage. He had reached out. He'd reached for something he wanted badly, never dreaming it wasn't his for the taking, and he'd been scorched, sizzled and seared, right down to the bone.

Danny Bentham was watching from the trees, teeth grinding in rage. It was all the worse because Selena had forced Bentham to face the loathsome truth that *her* lusting after other women was cause for derision so far as the rest of the world was concerned.

So when Selena cried out and pulled away from Flint, and when he seized her and began to slap her face with the full swing of his arm, Danny Bentham was already running forward with drawn steel and lunging at Flint with all the strength of her seventy-seven inches and fifteen stone.

"Bastard!" she cried, but should have kept quiet. Either that or move a lot faster, for the same rapier-thrust – delivered a split-second earlier – would have sliced into Flint's spine and out through his sternum. Instead, Flint heard, and saw, and a cutlass flashed, and the rapier was parried, and Bentham stumbled and nearly went over.

"Ugh!" cried Flint, "Bang!" cried one of his pistols, and missed, and then whizzed as he threw it, spinning and empty, at Bentham's head. *Clash!* It was cut from the air by Bentham's blade as she stamped and came on again, stabbing at Flint's legs, and Flint jumping clear, and hacking shallow into Bentham's sword arm.

"Aaaaah!" screamed Bentham.

Bang! Flint's second pistol – pulled left-handed – shot flame, smoke and a ball that tore through Bentham's scalp, scoring blood and flesh. Then Bentham was coming forward and thrusting left and right and dripping blood, and Flint was staggering back under such an onslaught as he'd never faced before, from a huge opponent with a vastly greater reach than his own, and Bentham shrieking and roaring and cursing and damning, who'd fought men face-to-face all her life and had never been beaten, and was the full, raging, blinding equal of Flint in lunatic, animal ferocity.

But Flint recovered like lightning. Dropping his cutlass, he ducked under her swinging arm and shoulder-charged with all his strength, knocking Bentham over. The two went down struggling, pummelling, kicking, biting and gouging, and

Flint pulled a razor-edged knife from his sleeve and tried repeatedly to get the point under Bentham's ribs, and was repeatedly fended off, and so searched elsewhere, and sliced sharp and accurate into Bentham's left thigh, opening the great artery that ran alongside her femur.

"Ow!" said Bentham, more in anger than pain, for the wound didn't hurt all that much. But she soon slackened her grip and Flint shoved clear, and jumped up, and leapt back, and staggered away, safe from all harm.

And there he stood, panting and gasping with the sweat dripping off his nose, as Danny Bentham's heart did all the hard work of killing her by pumping her life's blood straight out through the side of her leg with enough force to spatter the sand for a good three fathoms all around.

It didn't take long. A couple of minutes and the twitching, wriggling body gave up twitching and wriggling . . . and stopped groaning and damning . . . and breathing . . . and lay quiet.

"Huh!" said Flint, when he'd got his breath back, and he walked over and savagely kicked the late Captain Bentham. *Damnation!* he thought. This would mean trouble with Bentham's crew, especially O'Byrne. He turned to Selena, suddenly penetrated with guilt for what he'd done to her, and fumbled for words to explain, to beg forgiveness, to win back something – anything – other than rejection. But it was too late. Selena was gone.

Chapter 33

25th February 1753
Aboard Oraclaesus
The southern anchorage

*O*raclaesus crept warily towards a fine natural harbour enclosed in a curving sweep of white sand fringed with trees, with Hastings and Povey in the maintop hysterically yelling down to their superiors that this was indeed Flint's island, the very one and only – bugger them blind – and *this* was the southern anchorage, and another anchorage – not so good – was to the north where the wreck of the *Elizabeth* must be lying – God damn the pair of them if it weren't – and there was the bloody damn stupid blockhouse they'd been made to build by Flint, and where he'd caned their precious arses for pointing out it was a waste of sodding time, and . . .

"Hallo!" said Povey. "What's that?"

"Where?" said Hastings.

"There! It's a bloody fort. Earthworks, guns an' all!"

"God bugger and beach me, so it is!"

"*That* weren't there before!"

"Well, it bloody well is now!"

"I'll go below and tell the captain, shall I?" said Povey.

"Aye-aye, sir," said Hastings who was the senior, but in his excitement revealed a deeper truth.

On the quarterdeck, Commodore Scott-Owen noted the presence of such matters as forts and blockhouses, but without immediate interest. He had a vastly complex task to complete: the getting of four vessels into an unknown harbour without beaching or stranding any of them.

Being his calm self again – outwardly – he left the execution of these practical matters exclusively to his subordinates. But all *responsibility* sat exclusively upon himself, for it was himself first and foremost whom their lordships would break, should any of this expensive and beautiful squadron be lost without good reason. So, while Scott-Owen knew he had good officers and good crews, and while he sensibly kept out of their way, he wrenched his guts into agonised knots, worrying and worrying and worrying as the work was done.

Boats were launched and sent ahead, sounding the way. *Leaper* led the squadron, with *Oraclaesus, Bounder* and *Jumper* following in her wake. Guns were run out and matches lit in case of eventualities. Marines were mustered with sixty rounds, canteens filled and three days' rations packed into their knapsacks, and every tradesman from purser to carpenter prepared his list of stores, for no opportunity should ever be lost to make these good on landfall.

The most pressing need was for fresh water, with heavy work to be done in bringing up the water butts from the ground tiers down below, and filling them ashore in the streams Mr Hastings and Mr Povey said were easily found, then hoisting their ponderous weight back aboard. The urgency of this latter task was particularly acute for the sloops, which were thereby prevented from cruising the island at once to search for Flint's ships as Scott-Owen would have wished. So this too had to be allowed for and planned for, to be undertaken the very moment the squadron had anchored.

Thus there followed the most wonderful display of disciplined chaos as the hundreds of men aboard the four ships darted this way and that, busy in their labours, doing a dozen things at once . . . and never ever getting in each other's way. With the exception of Scott-Owen, every creature aboard had some vital task to perform; even the ships' cats were on duty against vermin stowaways.

"Commodore, sir?" said Captain Baggot of *Oraclaesus*, passing through the press, and touching his hat in salute.

"Captain!" said Scott-Owen, delighted to have some role, but instantly adopting his pose of calm. "Ah-hem!" he said, and folded his hands behind his back.

"Here's the list, sir," said Baggot. "The landing party, sir."

"Ah! Show me!"

"Here, sir . . . One hundred seamen and all fifty marines from this ship . . ."

"Good, good!"

"With seventy-five men each from the sloops."

"Good!"

"Making a total of three hundred and seventy-five men, sir."

"Excellent! And a *brace* of pistols to each seaman? Not just one each?"

"Indeed, sir. And muskets, too, for as many as possible."

"And cutlasses sharpened?"

"Indeed, sir!"

"And shining?"

"Indeed, sir!"

"Excellent! Never neglect *that*, Captain Baggot!"

"Indeed not, sir! The *moral effect*, sir! Gleaming blades, sir!"

The commodore nodded, the captain saluted . . . and went about his busy business, leaving Scott-Owen to go back to his pacing of the deck, and his worrying, and his looking at the island and worrying some more.

Later, once all preparations had been made that could be made, the furious activity aboard the four vessels reduced to one, dull, heavy task, for the wind had failed and the squadron had to be brought in by kedging. This was a tremendous labour of many hours duration, with each ship sending a boat ahead with a kedge anchor, and dropping the anchor, and then hauling in the cable by the capstan . . . and then raising the anchor and sending it forward again . . . and then the same thing over again . . . and then again . . . and again . . . such that the sun was sinking by the time the job was finally done, and the squadron neatly moored within cannon shot of the beach.

At that stage, the hands were sent to their supper, for there could be no landing in the dark. Not on an unknown island.

So the entire squadron, from commodore to cooper, from captain to carpenter, sat down to a merry meal and made enough noise to be heard from end to end of the anchorage as they bawled out shanties and toasted every jolly thing they could think of. They particularly toasted that most wonderful, beloved and splendid system whereby ships and treasure captured in His Majesty's service are condemned by a Court of Admiralty and the value – some of it, anyway – distributed among the officers and men concerned, as prize money.

They drank a toast to "Prize!" because two mighty assumptions were held by every man of the squadron. First, that

Captain Flint and his ships and men were somewhere on or about this island – an assumption for which there was very little evidence. Second, that Captain Flint, being a famous pirate, was in possession of a vast fortune – an assumption for which there was no evidence whatsoever, but which was a beloved and unchallengeable item of faith.

Thus it was incredible good fortune for the squadron that both assumptions were absolutely correct, and that – even without taking into account the men left aboard the squadron's ships – their landing force alone, being three hundred and seventy-five men, was more numerous than the entire force ashore, including Flint's men, Silver's men and Dreamer's men combined.

All they had to do now was find Flint, persuade him to divulge the location of his treasure, and they'd every man jack of them be rich. What could go wrong with so simple an expectation as that? How could Flint prevail over so many?

Night, 25th February 1753
Flint's camp
The northern inlet

Flint crept through the camp. He stepped over and around the snoring bodies. He circled the smouldering campfires and the dark tents. He wasn't as silent as a Patanq, but silent enough to leave these hogs in their snorting slumber. And as for the sentries, they saw him and saluted and turned back to their duties. After all, he was their captain and their leader. Why shouldn't they let him pass? Why shouldn't they remain silent and not call out a challenge when he cheerfully smiled and put a finger to his lips. There were men asleep, after all.

He found O'Byrne's tent. He slid inside. He smelt the foul

breath and the fug, and dropped on his knees beside the neat camp-bed that *Hercules*'s people had built for their first mate, who was now on his back with his mouth open, and Flint thankful that the kindly darkness hid the display of revolting bad teeth and bad gums, and a thick-furred tongue.

He put a hand over O'Byrne's mouth and gripped O'Byrne's right hand, where it cuddled O'Byrne's constant and faithful bed-fellow: a long, sharp dagger. Flint gripped hard enough to keep the hand still, but not so hard as to be a threat.

"Urrr!" said O'Byrne, and two pale eyes opened over the bulbous, rum-swollen nose.

"Shhh!" said Flint, "Captain Bentham needs you!" And he withdrew his hand, and hesitated, and thought of Billy Bones, upon whose shirt he'd have wiped the snot and slobber from his palm . . . but not Mr O'Byrne's shirt. No! There was a need for care with him.

"What d'ye fuckin' mean, in the middle of the fuckin' night?" growled O'Byrne. But he didn't use the knife and he didn't shout.

"Mr O'Byrne," said Flint, and looked around as if in fear of eavesdroppers, "we're going to need some help, Danny Bentham and I! And we thought first of you. We thought of you before anyone!" But O'Byrne wasn't so easily led.

"Where's the cap'n?" he said, brimming with suspicion, and he sat up and pulled on breeches and boots. "What's afoot?"

"Ah . . ." said Flint, with a sly grin, and O'Byrne stopped dead, and glared at him. *Careful, careful, careful,* thought Flint. "Truth is, Mr O'Byrne, Danny and I were raising a little of . . . *the goods.*"

"Oh?" said O'Byrne, his eyes widening at the introduction of this wonderful thought: the thought of thoughts compared with which there is no other thought. "The goods, you say?" he licked his lips, but frowned. "And why wasn't I told?"

"Shhh!" said Flint, and dropped his voice to a whisper. "Because the agreement was between Danny and myself, privately. If he'd told *you*, then I'd have had to tell *Allardyce*, and then everyone would've known!"

"Oh, would they now?" said O'Byrne. "So where's the cap'n?"

"Fallen in the blasted hole, and I can't get him out, great hulking fellow that he is!" Flint grinned. He winked. He worked every last ounce of his charm. "But he sent you *this* as a little something for yourself!" Flint reached into his pocket and drew out a leather purse, which he tipped out on to O'Byrne's grimy bed.

O'Byrne goggled and gaped ... and became heart, soul, mind and strength committed to the enterprise in hand, for there lay a dozen gold doubloons – each one worth fifteen to twenty dollars – together with a string of pearls and three big rubies!

Instinctively, he grabbed them and fondled them, and loved them, and kissed them, and bit one of the coins ... and grinned, and stuffed everything back in the purse, and put the purse in his own pocket, and finished his dressing and stuck his knife in his boot, and took up his usual pistols and cutlass, and smiled his gap-toothed, rotting smile ... and got up as Flint beckoned, and followed him like a dog.

And so, out of the camp past a sentry that Flint knew was asleep, and into the forest, along a path beaten by many feet that led southward towards Silver's forts, and finally to a dark, quiet place where a hole had been dug.

"Cap'n, sir!" cried O'Byrne, and ran eagerly forward ...

*   *   *

304

Later Flint returned alone, with a handkerchief bound round his left hand, where he'd been *just* a little careless. He was carrying a spade and was cheerful. Bentham's crew would follow him now. They already stood in awe of the famous Captain Flint. He'd have to speak to them, of course, and he rehearsed the tale of the tragic falling out between Bentham and O'Byrne, and how they'd grappled and gone into a stream and been washed away . . . or perhaps fallen off a cliff . . . or flown to fairyland in the arms of Queen Titania? What did it matter? A glimpse of gold would bring them round, and the selfsame purse that had persuaded Mr O'Byrne was already back in Flint's pocket, standing by for further duties.

And so it was. And Joe Flint replaced Danny Bentham and Brendan O'Byrne as if they'd never been, and – the actual words occurred to Flint – Bentham's crew became *jolly companions* one and all with Flint's own crew, and lived in happy expectation of riches for two whole days.

Night, 25th February 1753
A lonely place
The island

Van Oosterhout sat by his campfire with his arms round his knees and his head bowed. It was black dark beyond the firelight with no friendly creatures within miles; but he was too deep in thought to worry about any hostile ones that might be creeping, now that the sun had gone to bed.

"*Kalf!*" he said, and "*Oetlul!*" and repeated it in the English that had now become so familiar: "Idiot!" he said. "Bloody idiot!" For he was sure that Flint had made a fool of him. It only remained to work out why.

Van Oosterhout stirred the fire with a stick, and put on

305

more wood for a better light. He reached into his knapsack and took out Flint's notes, as if yet another look at the neat writing would reveal why Flint had sent him wandering round the island to check on burial sites so artfully chosen, so utterly secure and so completely unvisited by anyone other than Van Oosterhout.

And they were the true sites. Oh yes! Van Oosterhout had tested that with his spade. He'd even – purely in the cause of philosophical satisfaction – opened some of the chests to take a modest sample . . . one that now weighed heavy in the bottom of the knapsack. And then he'd re-buried and made everything smooth, and had re-planted the stringy grass, and had scattered twigs and branches overall, as if by nature not artifice.

In fact, growing suspicious as to the true reason for his quest, Van Oosterhout hadn't even bothered to dig after the first two sites. It seemed pointless; besides it was heavy work and he couldn't carry away more than he'd already got. So he'd just stood and looked at the secret places, and worried. And that was days ago. Since then he'd been wasting time on the other half of Flint's orders: seeking out new burial sites, of which he'd found plenty . . . but why?

"*Stront!*" he said. "Shit!" He fiddled with his boar's-tusk moustaches and stroked his beard. Why was he sent on this fool's errand? It couldn't be that Flint just wanted him out of the way, could it? More important, why would Flint give him such knowledge? And was it wise – *was it safe* – to share Flint's secrets? Van Oosterhout remembered standing on the plank with the ocean below and a pike at his breast, and Flint's excited, delighted eyes as he made ready to push.

A spasm of real fear shook Van Oosterhout and he looked out into the night, and resolved to give up these dangerous, solitary wanderings and get back to the main camp as soon as it was light. Then at least there'd be other eyes to see what Flint might do, and he'd not be alone and vulnerable as he slept.

Finally, as on each night of his life, he closed his eyes and asked the Good Lord to forgive him his sins, and so found a moment of peace before falling asleep.

Chapter 34

Sunset, 25th February 1753
Fort Silver
The southern anchorage

Silver looked out over the ramparts on the southward, sea-facing side. There wasn't such need to watch out for Indian marksmen here, since the ground was completely cleared to give a view of the anchorage and any ships that might come in – as now they had. There were four of them: a fine plump squadron with a big frigate, and three sloops identically rigged and fitted. An array of smartness that John Silver had never seen the like of, not in all his years! He shook his head at the thought of the cost.

"This'll be on account of Flint," he said.

"Why's that, Cap'n?" said Israel Hands.

"It's 'cos of him and his bloody mutiny!" Silver looked at the activity in the bay: six boats in the water, fussing round the ships, bosun's mates yelling, capstans clanking, guns run out, and lordly officers in blue and gold peering every way at once with their telescopes. "You don't think all this is for you and me, do you?" he said.

"Don't rightly know, Cap'n."

"No! We're just gentlemen o' fortune, Israel: worth a *guarda costa* or a revenue cutter. But not this. Look at 'em! They's even got copper sheathing!"

"Stap me!" said Israel Hands. "You're right – all four of 'em!"

"Aye, you mark my words: Flint's gone and stirred up someone powerful. Someone with seats in Parliament and ten thousand acres."

"Who'd that be?"

"Buggered if I know. Buggered if I care ... but we're finished here, matey."

"Aye," said Israel Hands, "it's the navy we've to beware of now. And they'll not just pop away with muskets. They'll haul up guns and blow this fort to pieces." He looked at Silver. He swallowed. He fiddled with his collar. He bit his lip. "John ..." he said.

"What?"

"What we goin' to do?" He nodded at the ships in the darkening anchorage where long shadows stretched from tall masts. "*Them* sods'll hang us. Them *other* sods –" he jerked a thumb towards the forest trees "– they'll do bugger-knows-what to us. So what we goin' to do?"

"Huh!" said Silver, and laughed. He clapped a hand on Israel Hands's shoulder. "First we count our blessings, 'cos a hanging ain't such a big thing, and a sight better than hoping you'd have time to blow out your brains before the savages could play with you!"

Israel Hands grinned feebly, wondering if Long John were joking or not – as indeed Long John was wondering himself. But after thinking for a bit, and stroking the parrot that sat on his shoulder, Silver spoke softly to her:

309

"Ah, my old bird," he said, "shall I leave you without Long John . . . and himself washed by three tides at execution dock?"

"No!" said the bird. "No! No! No!"

"Hear that?" said Silver. "Marvellous creature. Understands every word!"

"John?" said Israel Hands. "What we goin' to do?"

"Get the men together, Mr Gunner," said Silver. "There might be something we can do – if we're quick about it. It all depends on what them blasted Indians do, now King George's men are here!"

That night when it was properly dark, and the men of the naval squadron were noisily at dinner, Silver led the twenty-eight survivors of his crew – the last of the Lions – over the southward walls of the fort. But he did something else first. He led the men to where Billy Bones was made fast in his barrel-hoop leg irons, to a post driven deep into the ground inside the fort's central redoubt.

Clunk! Israel Hands struck off the irons, while Billy Bones looked on in fear and wonderment, not daring to face Silver and shaking with fright.

"Now then, Billy-boy," said Silver, "on your feet!" Billy Bones rubbed his ankles, and struggled up, swaying and wobbling on unsteady legs, for he'd been anchored in his present berth a long time. He looked around, and saw that all hands were gathered in the darkness behind John Silver, and in that moment he knew his time was come. Billy Bones heaved a sigh and tried to be brave. He was no coward. He'd led boarding parties across blood-soaked decks and faced the wrath of the sea.

But he'd been too long sitting on his backside waiting for

this moment. And he didn't share Long John's views on hanging, for he'd spent many an hour imagining what it was like to have a noose under your chin, and what it might feel like when they hoist you up and you began to choke. He'd wondered what was best: should you take a deep breath . . . or should you breathe out hard, just before the rope crushed your windpipe? Which one would end it quickest? For he'd seen men kick when they was hanged, and some of them had lasted a hard, long time.

So his knees shook and his voice quavered as he spoke, which had never happened before. Not to Billy Bones. Not in all his life.

"Cap'n Silver," he said, "I akses a favour."

"What favour?" said Silver, who'd not yet said a word.

"Shoot me! Do it quick. Don't let it be the rope."

"Stow it, Billy!" said Silver. "There's no hanging for you tonight."

"No?"

"No!"

Billy Bones trembled all the more. He snivelled and slobbered and shook. The relief was almost worse than the fright.

"Brace up, Mr Bones," said Silver, "I'm come to give you your orders . . ." But Bones just gazed at the ground, not knowing what to say or to do. So Silver continued. "Listen!" he said, "I can't trust you, Mr Bones, for we've tried that and it failed."

"Aye!" said the men.

"I'm off on my travels, Mr Bones. I'll be gone directly and I shan't tell you where I'm going, except to say that these lads here – the which are my jolly companions – why, *they're* coming with me . . . *and you ain't!*"

Again, Billy Bones jumped in fright.

"But I'll not leave you for the savages," said Silver, "nor for the king's men neither. I'll grant you that for good times past and kind old memories. So, you'll find your sea-chest in the big tent there –" he pointed. "And some arms, and powder and shot. D'you understand me, Mr Bones?"

"Aye," said Billy Bones feebly.

"Good," said Silver. "'Cos I have a thing to give you, Mr Bones. And here it is –"

Silver stretched out his left hand, and took Billy Bones's right hand and brought it up, and dropped something into the palm, from his own right hand.

Billy Bones gasped.

"The black spot!" he said.

"That it is," said Silver. "Read it, Mr Bones, for you're a scholar."

Billy Bones looked at the small paper disc. He raised it up for what little light there was from the moon and stars. He turned the blackened side over and read the single word written on the other side.

"Expelled," he said.

"Aye," said Silver. "For myself, I don't never want to see you again, Mr Bones, but I puts it to all hands –" he turned to them "– I puts it, according to articles, that Brother Bones be expelled from our company on pain of death. What say you, brothers?"

"All show for *expelling* Brother Bones!" said Israel Hands.

"Aye!" they said in a single growl, and every hand was raised.

"All show for *keepin'* Brother Bones!" said Israel Hands. Silence. No man moved.

"Then Mr William Bones is no longer a brother," said

312

Israel Hands. "He is cast out, and shall suffer death at our hands, if ever our paths shall cross, from this day onward!"

"Aye!" they said.

And Billy Bones hung his head and wept.

With that, Long John led his men out of the fort. It was very dark. There was still plenty of noise from the squadron, but they were moored at the westward end of the anchorage, and Fort Silver was to the east, and it was further eastward still that Silver went, and all hands as silent as could be, moving together in a bunch for protection against the Indians, should they strike.

It was fearful work at first, with every man expecting an attack, or a shot from out of the dark, or the bird calls that they'd learned weren't bird calls at all but the savages talking to one another. There was none of that.

"Where are the bastards?" hissed Israel Hands.

"Not here – that's all I care!" said Long John. "And shut up!"

Silver wanted no talking. He wanted silence, as the dark block of men shuffled down on to the beach and struck out towards the long spit of land surrounded by sandbanks that closed the eastern end of the anchorage to ships. To ships but not to boats, and *Lion*'s two boats – the launch and the jolly-boat – had long since been hidden at this end of the bay, as far as possible away from Flint, should he have chosen to come into the southern anchorage. Well, it weren't Flint they were afraid of tonight, but the same facts applied: the squadron was at one end of the anchorage, and the boats nicely at the other!

There was only the Indians to worry about, and it was Silver's guess that there never had been very many of them around the fort: just enough to keep them under fire should they get the chance, and enough to summon reinforcements, should anyone try to break out in force – like now. It was an unpleasant thought. Silver hopped and swayed along, conscious at every step that he stood head and shoulders above any man present and would likely be the first target for the blasted Indians if they *were* making ready to fire.

So they scuttled across the sands, splashed through the shallows on occasions, and headed for the looming dark of the land spit. The hands cheered up wonderfully as bushes and trees reared up out of the dark, offering cover and a place to hide, and nearly all of them were into the safe darkness and off the beach when finally the Indians struck.

Four dark figures came tall and leaping out of the undergrowth where they'd been waiting, and fell on the three hindmost of Silver's men. They made no sound. They moved fast. They struck from the side.

Thunk! Thunk! Two seamen went down, stone dead with hatchets in their skulls. The third man – the hindmost – was Mr Joe, who'd been ordered to follow up the formation to chase stragglers. He never saw where the Patanq came from, but he saw his comrades go down and his cane-cutter was out in a flash, and swinging at the demon coming in from his right.

Chunk! The heavy blade curved up and through the down-swinging tomahawk, sliced an arm off just above the elbow and Mr Joe spun like a top, carrying round his stroke and found himself facing another Patanq charging with knife and hatchet, whom he killed with instant un-thinking speed and a tremendous down-slash that landed just to the right of the Indian's neck and buried the blade a hand's breadth into the chest, slicing lungs, pipes and blood vessels and dropping his man beside the two tomahawked seamen.

And then they were gone. He didn't even hear them run. He didn't even see where they went. They just fled into the bushes. If it weren't for three dead men and half an arm laid out on the ground, he'd never have known they'd been there. But Silver was hopping back with a pistol in his fist and the rest behind him.

"Where are they? What happened?"

Shhhhk! Mr Joe hauled his cutlass, two-handed, out of the dead Patanq's chest. He was sweating, his heart was pounding and his head was thick.

"Don't know, Cap'n," he said. "They's gone, that's all."

"God damn and blast 'em," said Silver, looking at his two dead.

"It was a sneak attack," said Israel Hands. "They ain't minded to face us all."

"Aye," said Silver, "which means they ain't out in strength, and the sooner we're gone from here the better. Come on, all of you! And some of you take the firelocks off them poor brothers what's dead. No use letting the savages have 'em!"

Quickly they found the boats, they dragged them to the eastward of the landspit, they launched them, muffled the rowlocks with rags, and pulled away into the darkness: Long John Silver and twenty-five men, on the cool black sea. And the parrot, too, this time. She squawked and flapped, until Long John spoke to her.

"None o' that you silly sea-cow! There ain't no way but this way. Will you not be quiet and sit still?" He made a bit of a fuss of her, and put down his hat as a nest for her to curl up in, and finally she accepted her fate.

"See?" he said. "Clever bird, that!"

Meanwhile they pulled steadily out into deep water, clear of the rocks and sandbanks that fringed the island. Once safely out, and heaving on the big waves, with the island on their larboard beam, they rigged sail on the launch and took the jolly-boat in tow. It was slow progress, but better than rowing. That would have left all hands tired at the end of a long, hard pull . . . and they were going to need their strength.

Twenty-five men and a boy was a heavy load for the launch and the jolly-boat, and they were bailing non-stop, from start to finish of a journey which was a fearful risk, in so small a craft in the dead of night, on a perilous coastline – a voyage which had been risked *only* because the alternative was certain death of every man aboard.

But with Long John at the tiller of the launch, they came safe and sound past the shoals and the rocks and the sandbanks, and the powerful currents that swept the eastern side of the island. And finally, just before sunrise, Silver gave the order to strike the sails and mast, and the two boats lay side by side, heaving and rolling in the heavy swell. For the massive, southerly headland of the northern inlet was visible now, even in darkness, and it was time to take to the oars for the final, careful pull that would take them into the inlet. Though nearly a mile wide at its mouth, the many rocks and shallows made the inlet so treacherous that even small boats dared not risk entering until daylight.

"Now then, Sammy lad," said Silver to Sam Hayden, ship's boy, who was in charge of their store of victuals. "A fair tot of rum to all hands, to warm their bones, and a bite of food, while we've time."

"Sending the hands to breakfast, Cap'n?" said Israel Hands.

"Aye, Mr Gunner, they'll fight all the better for that!"

Sammy Hayden filled the men's mugs to be passed from

316

hand to hand, and from boat to boat, in the clammy wet darkness, followed by some cold ship's biscuit that'd been softened, days before, by a good, long immersion in the fat and juices of their last hot meal. The biscuit was still tough, and it was coated in gobs of cold grease, but nobody complained and there was none left when they'd finished chewing. Like all seamen, they were never short of appetite and they scraped their plates of whatever was offered.

Long John looked at the dark, huddled figures. There were men here that he'd trust with his life: old shipmates like Israel Hands, Black Dog and even Blind Pew – mad sod that he was. And there were newer hands like Mr Joe, who was a likely lad too. As for the rest, there were some good lads among 'em, and there were some who'd slit their granny for the price of her drawers. But there wasn't one who wouldn't fight. And that was good.

"Drop more rum for all hands, Cap'n?" said Sammy Hayden, dim in the darkness, with a pannikin in his hand. Silver couldn't see the boy's face; he was just a smaller figure than the rest, greys and blacks and shadows, nothing more. Silver thought of Ratty Richards and hovered on the edge of misery, which wouldn't do at such a time as this.

"No, lad," said Silver, "just enough to warm 'em up – and they've already had that!" He patted the boy on the shoulder. "You put that back in the cask. We'll have it later, once we've done."

"Aye-aye, Cap'n!" he said, and Silver saw his teeth gleam in the dark . . . which wasn't so dark. The sun was coming up.

"Now then, lads," said Silver. "Just once more, so all hands shall know, tell me your duties, one by one as I asks." He turned first to Israel Hands: "Mr Gunner?" And Israel Hands rattled off his duties as did the other chosen ones.

"Well and good!" said Silver. "Stand by oars, and not another word to be spoken now. And the jolly-boat to take station in line astern of the admiral, which is myself!"

They laughed at the small joke.

"Give way!" said Long John, and they pulled slowly as the dawn glow came up on their starboard beam . . . to reveal a rolling white bank of fog inside the inlet.

"Belay oars!" said Long John, and peered into the mist. He'd planned a dawn attack, but he'd not thought there'd be fog.

"What do we do, John?" said Israel Hands. "We can't be caught out here!"

"No," said Silver. "We goes in slow and careful, that's what we do. Give way, but handsomely now."

It was a long, slow pull, which meant that there was enough work to keep the blood pumping, but not so much as to make the men tired. It was nearly an hour before Silver could see anything more than the looming headlands, and the high, fjord-like sides of the inlet, but that was enough – by guess and by God – to keep the launch and jolly-boat in the safe channel down the middle until such time as the masts of ships could be seen, standing out of the fog.

And . . . Ah! That one was *Walrus*. There was at least one other ship moored in the inlet, but *Walrus* was the one they wanted. Most of them knew *Walrus,* and that would help.

In uttermost silence they pulled just hard enough for steerage way. Now was the most dangerous time. They were utterly vulnerable to a blast of grape, or even to shot heaved over a ship's high sides to plunge through the bottom of the boats and drown them in the cold, misty waters, or simply to bash their brains out with a torrent of plunging iron. And if even *that* didn't work, then twenty-six hands – including a one-legged man and Blind Pew – would have to clamber aboard a ship fully alerted, with hands standing by to repel boarders by the simple expedient of pushing pike-heads into them as they came over the rail.

Silver peered into the mist. Twenty-six fit men wasn't nowhere near enough for the job, not if there was a watch kept aboard *Walrus*, and not with the sun coming up and driving off the mist . . . which even that very instant began to clear most wonderfully in the anchorage, with the shore lines appearing, and tents and beached boats, and a man aiming his morning piss into the little waves of the shore, and idly staring . . . *and spotting the intruders* . . . and shouting with his dick in his hand.

"Give way, you buggers!" cried Long John. "It's hot shot and cold steel now, my boys!"

Chapter 35

*F*lint roused himself, sick from the rum he'd drunk last night. He hated being drunk and seldom ever was, but the Patanq had insisted, and they were in so ugly a mood that he couldn't say no. As usual, they had ended up rolling, roaring drunk and would probably be unconscious for hours yet.

He stood up, dusted and tidied himself as best he could, swilled his mouth with water from his canteen, and spat on the ground. He looked round the Indian encampment: no tents, just canvas thrown over bent saplings to make little round huts, all neat and tidy. He looked further . . . Ah, yes! Their sentries were out on the high ground, with their guns cuddled in their arms and their blankets over their shoulders against the cold morning. Presumably they'd been denied their go at the rum last night. Cut Feather was sharp enough for that.

Flint's men – and he'd wisely brought plenty of them, bristling with firelocks – were asleep on the ground under

320

their own blankets, and Flint shivered inside his long, full-skirted coat, that most times was too hot to . . .

"Sun-Face," said Dreamer, and again Flint jumped at the shock of being taken unawares. He spun round. Ah! There he was, the wrinkled little troll! There he was, with his blanket and his black eyes and his stone face, and his tattoos and nose ring. He was close enough to touch. Flint shook his head . . . how did they do it? Where had he come from? Was it the bare feet? Probably. Hmm . . . Dreamer was alone . . .

"Dreamer!" said Flint. "Where are Cut Feather and the rest?"

"Where are your own men?" said Dreamer.

Flint's eyes darted round the camp. Other than the sentries, everyone else was asleep, tucked up tight by the rum. And just as well. It'd been close last night. Another interminable council, sat cross legged on hard ground with a ceremonial fire in the middle and the Patanq in ceremonial face-paint, and ceremonial feathers . . . and ceremonial farts, for all Flint cared.

Sometimes, rum caused fights, but last night it was only the rum, and the quantities sunk by the Patanq, that had prevented one.

"We must talk, you and I," said Dreamer.

"Must we?"

"The matter is not settled. This war has gone badly. Men will die today."

Flint sighed. Here it came again. The blasted savages whinging, and moaning their losses, and not getting on with the job.

"Dreamer," he said.

"No. That is not my name."

321

"What?"

"Listen to me, Sun-Face-Flint. You, who are the evil twin."

"What are you talking about?"

"We, the People, are not of the Iroquois, for that is a foolish and mistaken name invented by the French . . ."

Flint clenched his hands. He groaned. Another dose of Patanq oratory was about to be shovelled down his throat. He would have preferred castor oil.

"We are of the *Haudenosaunee*," said the fierce little man, "the People of the Long House. And we are not Patanq, which is another foolish name invented by white men. We are the *Pah-Tah-Tana-Quay*, which means 'those who dig to live'. For we were first to grow the maize, the squashes and the beans, and which we name the Three Sisters."

Flint groaned. The Indian continued:

"Joseph Flint," he said, "a man never gives his true name."

"No?"

"No. Unless there is some great reason."

"So you say."

"But I tell you that I am not *Dreamer*. I am . . . *Laoslahta*."

"Are you indeed? How splendid for you!"

"Laoslahta means *seer*. It means *teller of the future*. And so . . ."

"Look here," said Flint, "where is this leading? What quarrel lies between us? Last night I promised you a thousand silver dollars . . ." Flint knew this was insulting by Indian standards. He knew he shouldn't interrupt. He knew he should let the blasted brown dwarf complete what he was saying, but he just couldn't bear to hear any more. "A thousand dollars," he insisted. "Didn't that show good faith?"

Laoslahta's face did not move. No emotion showed. Not a flicker. He continued as if Flint had never spoken.

"Sun-Face! It is my word that you shall know my name. So that you may understand."

Flint sighed.

"Understand what?"

"That I *see*, as I did last night." Flint sneered. Laoslahta continued: "Last night I was smitten with lights, and pain. And afterwards I saw."

"And what did you see."

"You raised *ten* thousand dollars, not *one*."

Flint frowned. He grew angry. *Little swine!* he thought. *He's had men watching while we dug!*

"The silver you have promised me is only a fraction of what you raised."

"Nonsense! It's all of it! I told you last night that the rest – *the main bulk of the treasure* – is in Silver's fort, *which is why you must take it!*"

"No. You raised ten thousand dollars. Joseph Flint!" said Laoslahta. "I have dreamed of you for years. I feared you greatly. But now things are changing – so listen . . ."

"Listen to what?" said Flint, and looked round the silent camp.

"Be patient!" said Laoslahta. "Listen!"

Flint listened. But aside from a stick cracking in the smouldering fire, the wind in the trees, and of course the booming surf that you didn't even hear any more . . . there was no sound. He stared at Dreamer – Laoslahta, if that's who he really was – but could read nothing in the dark, emotionless face. So Flint waited, and nothing happened.

"Bah!" said Flint. "Enough of this nonsense!"

"Wait!"

"Huh!"

Flint sneered. But then: Whoof-boom! Whoof-boom! Whoof-boom! Explosions beat flat and echoing across the island. They came from the north, followed by the rattle of small-arms fire. Pure dread struck Flint. It might be the ships!

"That is *your* ship, Joseph Flint," said Dreamer. "One-Leg is taking your ship from you. And there is more. There are four ships in the southern anchorage. They are King George's. They will put many men ashore this day. But One-Leg has escaped them and abandoned his fort. Tell me, Joseph Flint, has One-Leg given up the treasure under his fort . . . or is there no treasure there?"

Flint gaped. He gasped. He'd never been so utterly taken aback in all his life.

Then much happened very fast.

Laoslahta threw off his blanket and swung at Flint with a tomahawk.

Cut Feather – watching and waiting – leapt up and screamed a war-cry.

Flint's bosun staggered to his feet and bawled for all hands on deck.

And the whole camp awoke and reached for its arms.

Flint very nearly died. He very, *very* nearly died. His mind was in such turmoil that only his speed saved him.

He blocked the hatchet with his forearm: catching it below the blade and against the wood. He seized Laoslahta with his free arm – one hundred pounds of writhing, demonic fury – and over they went and down in a bitter conflict, which was pulled apart as a dozen men of each side rushed forward to save their leaders in a wild, brawling, tumbling melee of

324

thick-headed, stumbling seaman against thick-headed stumbling Patanq, and musket against pistol, knife against tomahawk, and all the anger and hatred bursting out that had been so barely contained last night.

Flint ran. He drew cutlass and struck down all in his path. But he ran. He ran away and left twenty of his men to fight the ninety Patanq that were in the camp. He ran with all his might, keeping clear of the swampy ground, across the open scrubland, and into the cover of some trees. Once safely out of sight, he sat down. He couldn't just run. The Patanq would track him as soon as they'd finished the fight – which was still raging. He could make out screams, yells, gunfire, but the din grew less and less by the second . . . then triumphant whoops from the Patanq . . . the solitary shrieking of a man being scalped who wasn't quite dead . . . then silence.

Flint sat with his head in his hands.

Think! Think, think think . . . Was *Walrus* lost? What was Silver doing? Where was Selena? Had the navy landed in strength? How could that be? How would they know? How could they find the island? How many men were left? Who was alive and who was dead? Was Dreamer – Laoslahta – dead? And how the blasted Hell did Dreamer know so much? Could his dreams be *more* than dreams?

Flint had little time in which to make some dreadful decisions. He was alone. He had nobody to advise him and wouldn't have listened if he had. *But* crooked in spirit, and warped in humanity as he was, he still had all the talent, courage and skill – *and* the invincible determination – to make a most splendid sea-service officer, if only it weren't for all the rest.

So Flint thought fast and made decisions.

He abandoned the island.
He abandoned the treasure – for the moment.
He fell back on pure self-preservation . . .
And made entirely new plans.

Chapter 36

Just before dawn, 26th February 1753
Alongside Walrus
The mouth of the northern inlet

*A*bandoning all pretence, the oarsmen heaved and the boats shot forward, while Israel Hands took a long match-cord from the tub where it had been smouldering, and blew on it to make the tip glow, and Silver steered for *Walrus*, as voices cried out from ashore, and faces appeared over her rail.

"Who goes there?" cried some fool who should've gone straight to the swivels.

"Stand by, boarders!" cried Silver. "Stand by, Mr Hands!"

"Aye-aye, sir!" they cried.

"Give a cheer now, lads!"

"HUZZAH! HUZZAH!"

And Whoof-boom! went the first of Israel Hands's grenadoes, lobbed on to *Walrus*'s decks.

"Ahhhhh!" cried someone caught in the blast.

"Huzzah! John Silver! John Silver!" cried the boarders.

Whoof-boom! Whoof-boom! Whoof-boom!

Bump, grind, rumble! The launch and jolly-boat were along-side the main-chains, and lines and grapnels were curving up and over to make fast, and all hands were swarming aboard, and Sammy Hayden and Blind Pew among them, for even they had belts full of pistols and were ordered to get aboard, and fire them into the air, and join in the racket. As for Long John himself, he slung his crutch by a lanyard and was up and out of the boat like a monkey and into the chains and aboard, and stamping his one good leg aboard a good pine deck, which felt like heaven after months of sand and earth, and getting his back to the rail and his crutch under his arm, and clicking back the lock of a blunderbuss, and blasting two ounces of goose shot into the front ranks of the men – *Walrus*'s anchor watch, a good two dozen of them – that swarmed out of the fo'c'sle hatchway in their shirts and bare legs, but armed with every weapon they could lay hands on, and *Walrus*'s decks rolling and stinking in white powder smoke, and laid out with the dead from Israel Hands's grenadoes, and echoing to the popping crackle of pistols and the clash of steel and . . .

"Ah, would you, you rogue?" cried Long John as one of *Walrus*'s people managed to wrench a pike out of the stand round the mainmast, and burst bellowing out of the tumbling, clashing fight, and aimed for the tall figure of Long John Silver, and charged screaming damnation and buggery and fixed on shoving steel through Long John's breastbone and out through his spine . . . only to jerk and falter as Long John drew and shot him straight through the heart, dropping him dead on the deck, with the pike clattering and rattling down beside him with its triangular steel point no more than an inch from Long John's shoe, and right next to its late owner's head, which lay with its mouth open, and the spit still wet and slippery on its tongue.

"Ah, is that you down there, Johnny Saunders?" said Long John, recognising an old shipmate. "Johnny Saunders as chose to stay with Flint at the parting of the ways? For it's a bad choice you made, my cocker, and no mistake!"

And that was the end of the short, brutal fight for *Walrus,* with most of the anchor watch dead or dying, and the rest throwing down their arms, and some of them – recognising old shipmates as Long John had done – begging aloud for mercy.

"Chop 'em like pig-meat, boys!" cried one of Silver's men.

"No!" cried Mr Joe. "We sign bloody articles!" And he smacked the flat of his cane-cutlass against the man's chest.

"Aye!" cried Silver, hopping forward, the men parting before him. Towering over the few, bloodied remnants of *Walrus*'s crew, he looked them over. "Bah!" he said. "I knows most of you, and you knows me!"

"Long John!" they cried. "Don't let them buggers slit us!"

"Over the side with 'em, John!" said Israel Hands. "Let the sods sink or swim or take one of our boats."

Silver looked around. The smoke was clearing. The beach was ringing with shouting. Boats were launching. There were two more ships in the anchorage that'd be clearing for action even this precious instant, with drums rolling and trumpets sounding. He studied the anchorage again. Deeper than *Walrus* was the sloop they'd pounded from Israel Hand's battery: *Sweet Anne* was the name on her stern. She'd taken a real hiding, and looked barely fit for the sea. Well done, Israel Hands!

But between *Walrus* and the sea, fit and ready for action, stood a big two-masted snow, a heavy ship with thicker timbers than *Walrus,* and they'd have to pass her on the way out to sea – assuming there was room in the channel for two ships, and assuming there was enough wind to get *Walrus* under way. He sniffed the air, he wetted a finger . . . yes . . . possibly.

And now everyone was looking at John Silver. They'd known from the start that taking *Walrus* was the easy part. It only got worse after that. Silver felt the load sitting on his shoulders, and laughed, as the thought made him wonder where the parrot had gone. Well, she'd have to take her chances like all the rest.

"John," said Israel Hands, "what do we do?"

"We best be under way!" said Mr Joe.

"What do we do with these here prisoners?" said Sarney Sawyer.

And . . .

"Good heavens!" said a voice. "John Silver, as I live and breathe! And Flint's own ship taken! *Sic transit gloria mundi!*"

"Dr Cowdray!" said Silver.

"*Mister* Cowdray," said the surgeon. "I was below." He looked at the wounds and the blood. "Can I offer help?" Cowdray was trying not to be afraid. He was trying to be calm. He was stunned at the turn of events. His world was overturned and he had no idea how Silver – or Silver's men – would receive him.

"Huh!" said Silver, and took off his hat and wiped his brow, and looked at the bookish, modest figure of the surgeon in his neat clothes and his tidy hair. It was just one more problem when he already had too many.

"John . . . ?" said Israel Hands, and shook the sleeve of Silver's coat. The men looked at him in alarm. He was plainly dithering.

Pop! Pop! Crack! Muskets went off ashore and a lead ball thumped into *Walrus*'s mainmast.

"Allll hands!" roared Silver.

"Aye-aye!" they cried.

"Mr Gunner, take five men and open fire on that ship!" He pointed at the snow.

"Aye-aye, sir!"

"And set another to the swivels to ward off boats!"

"Aye-aye, sir!"

"Mr Bosun, take the rest, cut the cables, and get this ship under way!"

"Aye-aye, sir!"

"Steer for the open sea, and as close to the snow as you can get!"

"Aye-aye, sir!"

"And now, you other buggers!" said Silver, and thumped over the planks towards the remnants of *Walrus*'s crew. They were sat by the rail, with Mr Joe standing over them, cutlass drawn. There were six men fit and unwounded, and three more dripping blood and looking green. They cringed and looked up at Long John's huge figure, expecting a cut throat and a plunge over the side. "Ah, you swabs," he said, recognising still more faces from days past, and the nasty memories that went with them. "You no-seamen, bilge-rats!" he said. "You sods as voted against Long John and took Flint's part!"

They shook with fright, they trembled and quivered. They knew it was all up, and just hoped it might be quick.

"Now then, you useless turds of dogshite, listen hard, for I take my Bible oath that here's the way of things!" He drew a pistol and clapped it to the head of the nearest man. "I could pop you one and all – you knows that, don't you?"

Silence.

"Well?" said Silver. "Speak up! Is it *aye* or *nay*?"

"Aye," they mumbled.

"Aye, indeed!" he said, and put away the pistol. "But I'm gathering a new crew for this ship, and it'll be 'good times afore, and old sins aft'. Such arse-licking lubbers as you are, you'll do to haul on lines and pump the bilge." They blinked, they gaped, they hoped. "So . . . who'll sail with Long John, and sign articles, and be jolly companions with fair shares for all?"

"Me!" they said with one voice.

"Good, but you knows what you'll get if you're false!"

"Aye-aye, Cap'n," said one. "Never did like Flint, anyway."

Silver sneered. "Don't give me that shite!" he said. "I ain't simple! Just do your duty."

He turned to his officers.

"Mr Gunner! Mr Bosun! Mr Carpenter!"

"Aye-aye, Cap'n!"

"New hands come aboard. Take your pick of 'em and set 'em to work!"

"Aye-aye, Cap'n!"

He turned to Cowdray.

"And you, *Doctor* – for doctor you'll be on my ship – see to the dead and wounded, for I welcomes you into this crew by the limb that I ain't got – being as you're the one as saved my life by cutting it off!"

With three of his own men lost in the fight, and nine more gained, Silver now had a total of thirty-two seamen to man, fight and work the ship, which was a sight better than he'd hoped.

The bosun's men set to work, taking axes to the cables,

and *Walrus* slewed in the current, then heeled to the press of the wind as the topmen loosed the topsails with a roar and a rumble, and yells of rage came from the boats pulling out from the shore, and men aboard them took long aim with muskets and opened fire. But Israel Hands himself, waiting his moment, set off the four gunwale swivels, steadily, carefully, one after another, and sprayed the boats with grape, thrashing the water white all round them, hitting a few men and warning the rest to stay clear.

"Get 'em reloaded!" he cried to Mr Joe.

"Aye-aye, Mr Gunner!"

"Quick, now!" said Israel Hands as a pair of bow-chasers opened fire from the big snow, sending shot roaring through *Walrus*'s rigging and all hands ducked. But the quartermaster sang out merrily:

"She's answering the helm, Cap'n. She's under way!"

"Steer for the sea!" said Silver. "Set every inch of sail, Mr Bosun. Mr Gunner, why ain't our deck guns in action?"

"Savin' 'em for going alongside the enemy, Cap'n. Do more harm that way!"

With *Walrus* gathering way, Silver took station on the quarterdeck, by the helm, and sent more men to the guns, which according to Flint's preference were always kept loaded and run out, and needed only priming from the powder horns kept in lockers by each gun. That was another reason why Silver had chosen *Walrus*. Trimming the sails was now the bosun's work, just as the guns could be left to Israel Hands, while Silver himself had little to do other than urge the helmsman to run as close past the snow as was possible, to avoid the risk of grounding.

And it was a tight squeeze, with sandy, swirling, yellow water to larboard as *Walrus* slid past the snow at less than six-feet range with pistols and muskets blasting from the snow. But none of Silver's people were hit, for the snow's crew were mainly occupied in trying to open port lids, cast loose and run out guns – which, unlike Flint, Danny Bentham kept secured and snugged down; a seamanly preference, but one which meant a slow start when action came uninvited.

Within minutes the creaking and groaning of wooden trucks on wooden decks was clearly audible, and the black snouts of the snow's guns began to emerge. But their progress was soon halted when three of *Walrus*'s guns threw shot, flame and smoke into the snow, blowing out ear-drums, searing flesh, blinding with smoke, ripping timbers and over-turning guns. Swiftly the other four deck guns fired as Israel Hands ran down the line, setting off the guns at a range so close that the entire possibility of missing was annihilated and men aboard the snow were thrown down by the con-cussion alone, with never a scratch on their bodies, but them shaking and kicking and useless, and others of their mates hideously wounded and fires started aboard by the flash of the guns and the ship thrown into utter chaos and confusion as *Walrus* slid past, with her topmen cheering and her gun-crews furiously re-loading, and the snow's spritsail-yard, fouled by *Walrus*'s bow, torn away with a rending crunch and a tear.

Walrus ploughed on over the jumble of rigging, leaving it swirling in her wake as she broke free and sailed on with nothing between herself and the open sea, and all her enemies confounded.

They'd done it! They'd done it, done it, *done it!* They'd escaped! They were seamen again! Seamen aboard a ship: free as air, free as birds, free as the plunging dolphin and the sounding whale. Oh the joy! Oh the blessed, sweet relief!

They'd been wretched miserable maroons, and pitiful landsmen, and now to be bold dogs and roaring boys again, and the whole precious world wide open to them! It was wonderful almost beyond bearing, and the men cheered and cheered and cheered.

"Shiver me timbers!" said Silver. "That's the way, my jolly boys!" And he hauled his telescope from his pocket and swept the beach in search of Flint. Where was he, the rogue? Was he there? Was he watching and gnashing his teeth? No. He weren't to be seen. But never mind. He'd clench his grinders and no mistake, once he learned his precious *Walrus* was took by John Silver.

It was a glorious moment, and even more so when Cap'n Flint the parrot swooped down from the maintop where she'd been hiding, and planted her claws on Long John's shoulder.

"Ah," he said, "my old matey! I've missed you."

"Long John!" she said, and squawked, and rubbed her head against his cheek, and Long John clapped Israel Hands on the shoulder as he ran up beaming from the gun-deck and turned and called out to all aboard:

"Three cheers! Three cheers for Cap'n Silver . . ."

Perhaps they cheered. Silver didn't notice. For he'd noticed something else. A flicker of movement on the beach. A smaller figure than the rest. And once he'd put his glass on the figure . . . he stopped breathing, and forgot all else in the entire universe.

"Selena!" he said.

Chapter 37

"*H*uh!" thought the two hundred and forty tars already landed from the three sloops. These unfortunates stood bleary-eyed and exhausted in their neat ranks, for Commodore Scott-Owen was so determined to dazzle the world with the efficiency of his squadron that the crews of *Bounder, Leaper* and *Jumper* had been obliged to work through the night filling their water butts. Thus they were able – immediately, promptly and at dawn – to be off about their special duty of sailing around the island to complete the search for Flint and his ships.

Taking advantage of the heavy traffic of boats, the sloops had landed half their crews, as ordered, while the profoundly miserable other halves must remain aboard, where they consoled themselves with the thought that Flint's treasure would be *in his ship* and not ashore, and that they would therefore be first to find it! All of which was a nonsense, because not a man among them would get their hands on treasure, which would be immediately bound up in the rigmarole of a Court of Admiralty. So the prospect of *finders*

336

keepers, losers weepers was miserably minimal. But young men don't think like that. They think they're immortal and in control of their fate.

All this withstanding, Scott-Owen had indeed worked wonders in landing three hundred and ten officers and men, fully armed and in all respects ready for service ashore, in so short a time, while his three sloops were working out of the anchorage under a breath of wind, and completing the pincer movement with which he hoped to seize the villain Flint . . . and of course Flint's treasure – of which, as commodore, he would get a walloping fat share.

A merry thought, but he banished it from his mind – most of the time anyway – and harried his officers to further triumphs in the bringing ashore of stores and the establishing of a proper base camp. Which work proceeded in a spirit of great cheerfulness until about an hour after dawn, when faintly but unmistakably there came the thud and rumble of explosions from within the island. Men looked at each other wide-eyed and wondering, and the excitement grew intense.

Scott-Owen turned to his officers.

"Mr Hastings," he said, "I had not intended to march so soon, but hearing that –" he nodded towards the sounds "– I shall throw a flying column inland. You will take half the marines and an equal number of seamen, and bring me a report on what is occurring inland."

"Aye-aye, sir!" said Hastings, brimming with delight at an independent command, convinced that treasure lay under every rock, and quite unable to prevent himself looking at his rival – the lieutenant of the starboard watch – with a pitying grin.

* * *

337

Nine-Fingers watched the column of Englishmen, and easily kept pace with them. These English had been spotted by the young men guarding One-Leg's fort. The newcomers were King George's men, as could plainly be seen from their flags. The young men had sent a runner for Nine-Fingers, who was chief – under Cut Feather – for the south of the island, and Nine-Fingers had come with two dozen good men, only to find that the young men had suffered heavily in their attempt to stop One-Leg escaping, and a grave dilemma must be faced.

Nine-Fingers was now falling back from the trees at the edge of the beach, with a total of thirty men around him, mostly men of the Deer Clan, all cousins and brothers, bred up in the same long house. They were good men. They moved through the woods as their fathers' fathers had done. They slipped like smoke. They passed like thoughts. They were gone like a dream.

These men, and Nine-Fingers, followed the clumsy, lumping, stamping Englishmen as they marched into the woods and away from the beach where they had landed There were red-coats and blue-coats: at least two dozen soldiers, followed by two dozen men from the ships, and they made enough noise to frighten every beast in the woods. They trampled and slashed, and beat down paths where a sensible man could have passed without disturbing a leaf. Nine-Fingers knew without looking that they'd be leaving a trail that a blind man could follow.

And they stank! They smelt of rum and meat, and the hot, sweat of the white man who – for his own unknowable reasons – must wear thick clothes in a hot forest when doing heavy work. And their leaders shouted and called out, and gave orders to the men. They made such noise! Always noise.

338

Nine-Fingers shook his head. Why did they do this? Why were they such fools in the woods? There *were* white men who'd learned the proper ways. They weren't *all* like this. But these thoughts were useless. Nine-Fingers had to make a decision. He was an old man of forty-five years, and acknowledged to be wise. He thought deeper . . .

It was Dreamer's word – known to all the People – that there should be no war against the white kings. Not King George of England, King Louis of France nor King Ferdinand of Spain. It was Dreamer's word that a great war was coming between them, and that they should be encouraged to kill one another to their heart's content, with the People standing aside. But if Nine-Fingers allowed this amazing column of noise-makers to go unhindered, they would be standing at Dreamer's side within the day. And Dreamer might not be ready. So Nine-Fingers made his plans. He sent word to Dreamer and made the best of a thoroughly bad job.

The column was halted. It was halted because Lieutenant Hastings and Mr Midshipman Povey were arguing. They did it very discreetly but it was an argument nonetheless, and the marine sergeant and the other mids stood aside and pretended not to notice, and told the seamen to sit down and rest while the marines stood guard.

"We've been going an hour at least," said Hastings, "and all's well!"

"That's 'cos we've been lucky!" said Povey. "*Lucky,* that's all!"

"Dammit, Povey, I'm in command here!"

"Oh, shut up, George – I'm talking sense. We should throw out scouts!"

"Don't you damn well talk to me like that! I'm your bloody superior!"

"George, listen! I've read about frontier warfare . . ."

"This ain't the bloody frontier!"

"Yes, it is. It's the bloody forest. It's the bloody same."

"No, it bloody ain't. This ain't bloody America and we ain't fighting Ind—"

He never said the word.

BA-BA-BA-BANG-BANG!

Thirty muskets fired point-blank from so close among the trees that anyone other than hopeless, useless, utterly incompetent woodsmen must have seen the fierce brown bodies hiding there.

Smoke, flame, screams and a dozen men went down bleeding and smashed, or bowled over, dead where they sat at ease.

More shrieks, fearsome and wild, and blood-chilling, as Nine-Fingers and his men closed in hand-to-hand to finish the job their gunfire had started.

It was a perfect ambush against wretchedly unprepared men. By all the conventions of frontier warfare it should have ended in the disintegration and flight of those ambushed, for the conventions of frontier warfare were *always* to run when ambushed, thus preserving arms and men, and falling back to a rendezvous point to re-form and carry on the fight another day.

But British seamen and marines didn't do that. There was nowhere to run in a ship-to-ship fight, and they were trained to grip like bulldogs and never let go.

George Hastings knew no tradition other than that, and he drew on it.

"Away borders!" he roared. "*Oraclaesus!*"

340

"*Oraclaesus!*" cried Povey, and the other mids – those that were left – and the sergeant of marines would've said the same, but he was down on his back with a musket ball in his belly and a Patanq warrior smashing in his face.

"*Oraclaesus!*" screamed the marines, and charged with musket and bayonet, the long barrels more encumbrance than use in forest fighting – which was why the Patanq had *dropped* their muskets to go in with knife and hatchet, screaming like fiends – and the marines went down, hacked and stabbed and dying.

"*Oraclaesus!*" screamed the seamen, and leapt up and drew pistols and cutlasses and charged as they'd have done when boarding the wreckage-strewn ruin of a battered ship, and this time the advantage in arms was with them.

Bang! Bang! Two shots per man from the neat, handy pistols, and Patanq warriors went over, struck by heavy service charges, and a hail of pistols was thrown at heads when empty, and the tars charged roaring and bellowing and laying on with twenty-seven-inch blades fresh from the grindstone, which outclassed and out-reached the puny knives and hatchets of their enemies.

The combination of thundering fire and razor steel hurled the Patanq back into the woods, and those of them that could fled silently away, leaving their muskets behind.

It was over in seconds.

Twelve seamen and marines were killed.

Another twenty were wounded, of whom five soon died.

Sixteen Patanq were laid out dead.

Eight Patanq, badly wounded, were trying to crawl away.

Shuddering from the fight, wondering if he were still whole and alive and not quite believing it, feeling his body to make sure, and finally rousing himself, Lieutenant Hastings ran round pulling his men off the wounded enemy, saving five from vengeful slaughter. He was joined by Mr Povey: they had both survived unharmed, if horribly shocked.

Nevertheless, they did their duty. They ordered firelocks reloaded. They put out scouts. They tended the wounded. They secured their prisoners, tending their wounds also. They fell back slowly, to the beach and the squadron, judging – rightly – that it was unsafe to penetrate the island interior except in full force.

And all the while they wondered why they were fighting American Indians on a tropical island, but could think of no reason.

Thus Nine-Fingers secured his objective of throwing back the noise-makers and giving time for Dreamer to prepare. This was doubtless a comfort to Nine-Fingers in the Spirit World, to which he was sent by three pistol balls and a tremendous cut to his shaven skull.

But Dreamer was warned and could act.

Chapter 38

Morning (there being no watches kept nor bells struck)
26th February 1753
Aboard Walrus
Under way and outbound in the northern inlet

"*J*ohn, what is it?" said Israel Hands.

"It's her, matey, it's *her!*"

Israel Hands didn't have to ask who he meant. There weren't no women but one on the island, and even if there'd been a thousand there'd have been only one for John Silver.

Oh, bugger me blind! thought Israel Hands, for *Walrus* was sailing bold and sharp and the hands were leaning over the rail yelling piss and derision on all those in her wake – even the nine hands that had been Flint's – and all the world looked sweet as ninepence for a bold new cruise and nobody hanged by the king or scalped by the savages. *Oh no,* he thought, for he knew what was coming. He'd known Long John too long. He knew what he'd do next.

Silver trembled with emotion. He stumped to the rail, he clung to the mizzen shrouds. He stared at the tiny figure on the beach. It was her, it was her, it was her . . .

And the first wave that hit him wasn't fear of cold steel and hot lead from those ashore, nor even fear that the crew wouldn't obey should he order the topsail backed and the ship hove to. For who should blame them as wouldn't risk their lives for another man's doxy, nor pull an oar in a boat that set out to fetch her? It was too much to ask, but even *that* wasn't Silver's first concern.

What really frightened him was the fear that now he'd found her . . . would she want him? Flint was a cracking fine man when all was said and done. Handsome as the devil, with all the air and manners of a gentleman, and well bred besides: a vastly finer man than a rough-handed, rough-speaking, cripple.

He looked again, the spy-glass trembling in his hand. She was standing, with her hands by her sides. It wasn't as if she was jumping up and down and waving. Not as if she was calling out to him, even if she knew he was there. He hadn't the slightest idea what was in her mind, and he was afraid. What in God's name would she think of him?

He sobbed. He actually sobbed as he reached up to pet the beloved bird with its fond gentleness towards himself, and its soft feathers and bright eyes . . . but which made so grotesque a figure of himself, together with his hideous disfigurement. What sort of a creature was he, that went on a wooden stick and had a parrot on his shoulder? Mr Joe with his eye-patch looked a rakish devil that the girls really would admire. But not John Silver. Not him. He was in despair. He didn't know what to do.

The gunfire woke Selena. Having fallen asleep curled up under a bush, with her pistols in her hands, she'd slept badly. As she got to her feet she was cold and damp, hungry and thirsty. She'd run into the forest the previous evening leaving Flint and Bentham fighting. She'd run even though she knew it couldn't be for long. Flint would send the Patanq after her and nobody could hide from them . . . But they didn't come. And she began to wonder: maybe Flint had other ideas?

Selena sighed, stuck the pistols in her belt and pushed through the trees and undergrowth towards the beach, following the direction of the noise. She was acting on sheer curiosity. And where else could she go, in any case? She couldn't hide, she'd got no food or drink. She was as much trapped in the forest as if chained to Flint.

She gasped as she saw what was happening. Two boats were alongside *Walrus*. Distant figures were climbing aboard, and the ship was full of gunfire and smoke. But that wasn't why she gasped. Even at such distance there was one figure – seen in a flash as he went up the ship's side – that was different from all the rest. He moved differently. He was a one-legged man. He was Long John Silver.

Selena stepped out of the bushes not caring who saw her; not that anyone was looking – Flint's camp was in uproar, yelling and hollering and launching boats. And Flint wasn't there. Where was he? No matter. She stepped out and stared. She stared as *Walrus* cut her cable and swung in the current. She stared as Flint's men were blasted with swivel-fire that beat off their boats. She stared as *Walrus* got under way and battered *Hercules* and headed for the open sea, with cheers sounding from Silver's men.

She stared and stood with her hands by her sides and all the dark thoughts that she'd suffered during seven months with Flint rising to a crescendo. What did she want? *Who* did she want? And had she a ha'porth of choice in the matter? And clamouring loudest of all was the thought that white men didn't keep faith with black women. Not when pretty black girls could be bought for fun and sold for fieldwork as soon as they stopped being pretty. They were good for whores or mistresses, but what else? What could Selena expect from John Silver . . . when he was white and she was black?

"Mr Bosun," cried Israel Hands, "back topsail, and heave to! And I'll have a boat's crew mustered this minute to go ashore, loaded and primed for action!"

"What?" said Silver.

"What?" said the crew, and they scowled and growled.

"Belay that!" said Israel Hands, and jabbed a thumb at the big man that stood beside him. "This here's Long John Silver. Him what saved us when *Lion* was lost. Him what kept us together on this blasted island. Him what never lies, and what leads from the front, and what brung us safe from death, and here aboard a fine ship!" He glared at them all, and Mr Joe instantly came up and stood beside him.

"Ah, you buggers!" said Israel Hands. "Stand forward now, says I! Stand forward any one of you as won't pay what you owe when Long John needs a favour! For I'm going with him wheresoever he leads, and I'll have a boat's crew mustered and ready, and I'll pistol the first man as hangs back!"

The launch was manned and pulling for shore in seconds, being already in the water and dragged alongside of *Walrus* by the lines and grapnels used for boarding. Silver was at the helm, Israel Hands was coxswain, and six good men, well armed, were at the oars, while Mr Joe – to his intense disappointment – was left aboard ship, together with Black Dog, just to make sure that the thought of abandoning the launch never occurred to any of those embarked, God bless their darling souls!

Besides that, Mr Joe was told to open up a steady, aimed fire at Flint's camp and boats, to keep them busy and out of Silver's way. Thud-boom! Thud-boom! *Walrus*'s maindeck, sent six-pound shot whizzing through the camp, ripping canvas, ploughing sand, and even scoring a lucky hit on one of the grounded boats, which sent the remnants of Flint's men running for cover – such as they were, for there weren't very many of them now. With twenty-four massacred by the Patanq, plus the losses they'd taken from Israel Hand's battery when they sailed in, and those killed in the battle for *Walrus* . . . there were now just two men aboard *Sweet Anne*, ten aboard *Hercules* and nine men and three boys running in terror.

Them . . . and another four on special duties with Flint . . . elsewhere.

So John Silver could look over the heads and shoulders of his chanting, heaving oarsmen and see a safe, cleared beach and no threat from the shore at all. Not until the boat's prow was seconds from the shore, and the hands already pulling shallow to avoid fouling the bottom, and Selena standing like a statue, giving no sign of any feelings at all – but at least not running away – only then did ferocious war-cries shriek from the trees a few hundred yards up the beach, followed by a dense mass of Patanq warriors charging towards Selena and the oncoming boat.

There were more than a hundred of them.

Chapter 39

Afternoon, 26th February 1753
Flint's Cove

*F*lint looked through the thick, green undergrowth which was entirely different from the undergrowth anywhere else in this strange place. Little lizards like salamanders – perhaps actual salamanders – were crawling across fat, glossy leaves, feeding on the tiny black ants that swarmed there. And the ground was firm beneath the trees, not damp and soft.

Flint looked and nodded quietly. There they were: four of them, the men picked out by Ben Gunn, according to orders. But there was no Ben Gunn anywhere in sight. Doubtless gone a-wandering. Still, the mad creature had done his duty all right. The four men were exactly what Flint wanted, that much was clear even from this distance.

Well done, Mr Gunn, thought Flint, while the four sat anxious and afraid and constantly looking over their shoulders. They'd obviously heard the sounds of fighting, for they'd got themselves into a nice tight corner, with a cluster of huge rocks behind, so they couldn't be crept up on. *A-ha!* thought Flint, taking in the boat: a fine big launch, hauled well clear of the tide. And *Good!* as he cast an eye over the timber slides laid out in front of the launch and greased, in accordance with his orders. The heavy boat would go smoothly down to the water, hauled by the few hands available. *What fine lads they've been, and no mistake!* thought Flint. *Everything so tight and seamanlike.*

Better still, staring hard at the boat, Flint could make out one of the chests that made up a fine fat half of its cargo, the same chests that had been left in the cove three days ago by his six spadesmen – a body of men who had now rejoined their comrades, but upon whose absolute discretion he could rely. He could rely on them because he'd extracted the most fearful oaths, given by moonlight, with round eyes shining, and right hands raised, and Flint blessing their smooth cheeks and knowing that in no time at all they'd be beyond all possibility of betraying anybody.

And so back to the present . . .

Flint deliberately rustled the undergrowth and the four men jumped up and levelled muskets.

"Who-zat?" they cried. Flint stepped forward.

"*Who goes there!*" he chided. "You must say *that*, lads. For it's proper."

"Who goes there?" they said, and "Cap'n!" for they were immensely relieved.

"We heard shooting, Cap'n!" said one.

"And gunfire from the ships!" said another.

"Aye!" they all said.

"Lads," said Flint, "there's nothing to worry about!"

"No?" they said.

"No! So let's sit down, and I'll explain."

So they sat down, and Flint smiled, and insisted they take a pull of the rum.

Then he explained as only he could explain, with his wonderful charm: the smooth, easy companionship that kept his audience enthralled, and more than that *privileged* to be part of so wonderful a scheme, and fully understanding why – temporarily – they alone must go forward to the Patanq Squadron, through the archipelago, taking two chests of silver and one of gold – happy smiles all round at this – together with that *other* half of their cargo, which lay square in the centre of the launch, covered in a tarpaulin.

Morning, 26th February 1753
The Patanq Camp

Of the twenty white men that had sat down to council the previous evening, only four were left alive after the fight. They were swiftly killed and plundered, and their bodies burned.

"So," said Laoslahta, "we have two dozen good scalps, and now we turn to greater matters. Come close, my children!"

They gathered round him, standing shoulder to shoulder, feathered and painted, with guns, knives and hatchets. They formed the dense half-circle that was the proper way to stand when a great man spoke. There were over a hundred and fifty of them now, the scouts and separated forces having been drawn in, save only a few keeping watch on the red-coats.

Now all stood listening: Cut Feather and the other sachems in the front rank, and the others behind, in strict order of precedence.

"Listen to my words!" said Laoslahta.

"We listen, O father!" came the rumbling response.

"We are in hard times, my children."

"We listen, O father!"

"Many have died," said Laoslahta, "but worse may come, for it is bad enough for warriors to die – and my cheeks run with tears for those we have lost – but now death falls upon our women and our children!"

It was formal. It was poetic. It was paced by Laoslahta's pauses and the deep-voiced chanting of the listeners. But it was sharp as a razor, telling every man his duty and his task, and as soon as Laoslahta finished speaking, the warriors split into three groups.

The first, some hundred strong and led by Laoslahta himself, set off for the northern inlet to secure the ships. The second, thirty strong and led by Cut Feather, ran southward to harass and slow the advance of the red-coats, with strict orders to fall back before them and not press home an attack.

The third, a group of just five men, the best trackers in the nation, was tasked with finding Flint. Laoslahta took them aside and greeted each one by name. He gave them their orders: special and solemn orders. Then he embraced them and blessed them and thanked them. Finally he knelt before them, with tears in his eyes, and begged their forgiveness, which they freely gave, being brave men.

He did not expect to see any of them again. Not this side of the grave.

Then all three groups ran off about their duties. They moved with utmost speed, for time was short and the peril was great.

Late afternoon, 26th February 1753
Flint's Cove

The launch ran smoothly over the slipway: two dozen six-foot logs, greased and laid across the boat's path to keep her clear of the sand that would cling, and drag, and stop her moving. Flint didn't even have to lend a hand. He stood back smiling as his four men heaved with a will, and got her under way. And once they were on the sloping run to the water's edge, the boat's own weight sent her down with a rumble and a roar, splashing into her natural weightlessness as the salt water took her.

"All stores aboard!" said Flint. "Leave nothing behind." There was no such a thing as a small boat over-provisioned for a voyage. Every cask of water, every tub of biscuit, might be needed.

"Aye-aye, sir!" they said, and three leapt to it, while one stayed with the boat, even without orders, so she shouldn't float off on her own.

Such good lads, thought Flint, and he tried to laugh at them and be merry . . . but couldn't quite manage it. Something was troubling him now that they were leaving. He wondered what.

So he stood back and let the four of them get aboard with what they'd recovered, and he let them take up their oars, and sit up like good boys, and face astern while he clambered aboard and sat in the sternsheets and took the tiller.

"Give way!" said Flint, and the boat pulled out of the small cove, and was soon in the fresh air and heaving rollers of the open sea. "Rig for sail!" said Flint, and he looked back at the island – and felt a surge of pain. He frowned. He worried . . . which wasn't like Joe Flint at all. He'd made his decision. He knew what had to be done. He was confident that – as before – he would leave the treasure safe and cosy, and come back in strength another day. He'd got his copy of the map, and his notebook, and enough coin aboard to pay for a new expedition, and – once he'd dealt with all those persons who were surplus to requirements – he'd have at least one good ship, and a crew to man her, to take him wherever he needed to go. So what *was* it that he was missing?

Flint had a most wonderful mind. It was inventive and organised. It was full of tight compartments with strong doors, guarding the places where thoughts were stored, letting them out on command. It was what made him so single-minded and formidable a man. But one door had burst open all on its own. He couldn't keep it shut, because he knew what was inside it. He'd known all the time what it was that he was missing. And it wasn't *it*. It was her . . . of course.

"*AAAAAAAAAAAH!*" he roared in anger and pain. The hands gaped in fright at their captain beating his fists against the thwart, like a child in a tantrum, crying, "No! No! No!" to the four winds and the open sea and the calling gulls.

"Cap'n?" said the man nearest to Flint. "What is it?"

He should've kept quiet. He got a kick that smashed front teeth and bloodied his nose, and a torrent of filthy abuse such as no man had ever heard before from Joe Flint, who never used a cuss-word nor an oath, and despised those who did.

But Flint recovered. He wiped his face. He tidied himself. He leered at the hands and went round pulling their noses – except him with the blood on his face; Flint patted his cheeks instead – and laughed.

"Well, my boys!" he said. "We're situated *as we are,* and that's a fact. As we are and not as we'd wish to be!"

"Aye-aye, Cap'n," they said warily.

"So here's to *some other day.*"

"Aye-aye, Cap'n."

"And meanwhile there's work to do."

"Aye-aye, Cap'n."

Flint looked at the tarpaulin and what it covered. Then he got out his map and looked at the boat's compass, and made sure they were on course for Flint's Passage through the archipelago. Hmm. The wind was fair, the boat was charging along merrily. Flint smiled. It should be interesting. It would certainly be something new.

Late morning, 26th February 1753
The northern inlet

Silver threw himself upright in the speeding boat. Selena looked back. The Indians were racing along the beach with sand flying from their heels. But they were a good two hundred yards off, while there was less than thirty yards between herself and Silver's boat. She looked at Silver. He looked at her.

It is a fact of human nature that, on sudden meetings, first reactions are true reactions, for truth comes quick and instinctive. And it comes all the faster with a tribe of savages bearing down with knives, hatchets and muskets.

"John!" she said, and ran towards the boat.

"Selena!" he said, and leapt clumsily out, and hopped forward and – wonder of joyful wonders – Silver was staggering back as the small, dark figure threw herself at him and clung to him, and him to her, and with only three legs between them, they wobbled and swayed . . . while certain death came on, a hundred and fifty strong, and a nasty death besides. But all doubts were blown away and all fears made nothing, and eyes clenched in absolute happiness, and each only aware that in all the world there was none other, and never would be, never could be, never should be, not for ever and ever amen.

"John! John! Get aboard!" cried Israel Hands. "Swing the boat, lads!"

They nearly did it. They threw Selena aboard. They heaved the boat round, all hands together. They pointed the prow at safety. They seized oars and pulled for their lives. A man can't run in water over his thighs, and he certainly can't fight another man in a boat. That's all it would take. A few strokes, good strokes, and they'd be free. Silver, meanwhile, was hauling his pistols and aiming and shooting at the savages: Click. Click. Soaked priming! Nothing! So he and Selena – the only ones not rowing – commenced picking up every firelock in the boat, and pulling them out of men's belts, and blazing back at the dense, on-rushing hordes and dropping two, but not stopping the rest. Then they were battering pistol-butts into the heads and arms of the brown devils that came plunging and whooping forward, and the boat rocking from the impact, and slippery wet bodies climbing aboard, and cutlasses and knives out, and the men dropping the useless oars and fighting for their lives, and roaring and yelling and crying. It went on, and on, and on . . .

And then it stopped. It stopped when Silver and his men grew tired. For the Patanq weren't fighting. They were defending and hanging on. They were taking wounds, and some even dying, but they weren't striking back. Silver was held down by three of them. Every man in the boat, and Selena too, was held helpless by overwhelming weight of numbers. A great mass of humanity filled and pressed down on the launch and gasped and panted and sweated and slowly got back its breath.

Utter despair filled Silver. It was over. All over.

Chapter 40

Late morning, 26th February 1753
The northern inlet

"Where is One-Leg?" cried a voice.

"Here!" cried the three men hanging on to Long John.

They spoke in their own language, so Silver didn't understand. He only knew that he was wrenched up and out of the wallowing launch – which was nearly sunk with the weight of bodies aboard – and thrown face down into the water to gasp and splutter, and attempt to struggle upright, which is so difficult a thing for a one-legged man to do that he'd have drowned if hands hadn't seized him and pulled him upright and dragged him to the shore, hopping and scraping his one foot and trying to keep up, and still coughing up so much salt water that he hadn't the strength to fight.

"John Silver!" said a voice in English. Silver wiped his streaming eyes, and swayed to keep upright, as the same voice said, "Find his staff. Give it to him!" And Silver steadied as his familiar crutch was shoved under his arm. When his eyes cleared, he saw a small, red-brown man with a stone-hard, cruel, face: tattooed, painted, and bald with a single topknot of hair that was stuck with a feather. Though he looked ill and shrivelled, he seemed totally in command. The other savages pressed round, half-naked, fiercely armed, and glaring at Silver, while two more hung on to his arms. But they kept a respectful distance from the little man, and treated him with profound respect.

"I'm Silver," said Long John, "I'm him!"

"I see that," said the Indian, as anyone would have. Silver was by far the biggest man present. "And I am Dreamer."

"Well then, Mr Dreamer," said Silver, "I knows what you're a-gonna do to me and the rest. But there's a woman among them there –" he jabbed his thumb at the boat "– and she ain't nothing to us." He shrugged his shoulders. "Why! She ain't even one of us. So just you leave her alone, d'you hear? Don't . . . don't . . ." Silver faltered. He stumbled over his words. He fell silent and looked at the ground. And when he looked up again and spoke . . . it wasn't very clever, and it wasn't very good, but it was all he could think of: "So don't you kill her. Don't waste such a fine woman. Take her for yourself!"

Dreamer looked at Silver, impassive and unreadable. To Silver, he was the embodiment of pitiless cruelty.

"I cannot take the woman," said Dreamer.

"And why not?"

"Because she is *yours*."

"What? No she ain't."

"Bring the woman!" said Dreamer, and Selena was pulled out of the boat and put beside Long John. He wanted to put an arm around her. His arm moved but he forced it down. That wouldn't fit the tale he was telling.

Dreamer looked at the two of them.

"You – woman! Selena, the black one who Sun-Face Flint

desires." Selena looked at Long John. "Speak your mind!" said Dreamer.

"She ain't mine, she's Flint's!" cried Silver, desperately trying anything to keep Selena safe. He looked at Dreamer. "Flint's a friend to you, ain't he? She's Flint's!"

"No, I'm not," she said. "Dreamer knows that."

Dreamer nodded.

"But Flint wants you," he said. "Him and many others. And so does *he* –" Dreamer looked at Long John.

"I told you," said Long John, "she ain't nothing to me!"

"So," Dreamer looked at Selena, "are you John Silver's woman? Would you be his wife?"

Selena looked at Long John. She considered the question Dreamer had just asked, and – as with her feelings on finding Silver again – her response was swift and true.

"Yes!" she said, and threw her arms around his neck, and pulled down his head and kissed him.

"Ah!" said Dreamer. He nodded. He stepped forward. He took Selena's left hand and placed it in Silver's right. "Then it is done," he said, and smiled. "Marriage is made by the woman's consent. So be together and be true!" The smile vanished. He looked up at Silver. "There is much to do, One-Leg. I need you and your men!"

Two bells of the forenoon watch, 26th February 1753
Aboard HMS Leaper
The ocean to the west of the island

Lieutenant Gordon Heffer, aged twenty-three years, was intoxicated with his triumph over his enemies: Lieutenant Simon Clark, aged twenty-two, in command of *Bounder*, and Lieutenant Arnold Comstock, aged twenty, in command of

Jumper, both being junior to himself and now under his orders.

To be precise, they were his *rivals* not his enemies, but Heffer couldn't help seeing them as that, for they – like himself – were junior, and inexperienced, officers in temporary command of their ships, while the true lords and masters were ashore with the commodore, digging up gold and diamonds, chasing pirates up trees and shoving bayonets up their arses. That meant that Heffer was actually in command of an actual squadron with orders to cruise the coast in search of any pirates that might be lurking thereabouts, and to inflict the most fearful possible violence upon them. Thus could Lieutenant Heffer expect to cover himself in glory and secure the promotion he craved – unless that glorious ambition was scuppered by one of his peers letting down the squadron with slackness or incompetence – or, worse, achieving some stroke of spectacular efficiency that would put Lieutenant Heffer's own efforts into the shade!

God forbid! thought Heffer.

"Make to the squadron!" he bawled to the signal midshipman.

"Aye-aye, sir!" cried the mid, and Heffer's chest swelled magnificently.

"Keep proper station!"

The flags were bent to the halliard. Willing hands heaved. Whizz-whirr went the blocks. And up went the totally unnecessary signal, to stream totally unnecessarily in the wind. *Bounder* and *Jumper* were already in excellent formation, in line abeam of the flagship, extended such that *Leaper* – sailing just offshore – got the best sight of anything anchored there, while *Bounder* and *Jumper* kept watch on whatever might be in the offing, with *Bounder* the furthest out.

"Pah!" said Lieutenant Clark, aboard *Bounder*. "Silly bugger!"

"Pah!" said Lieutenant Comstock, aboard *Jumper*. "Stupid sod!"

But they muttered these observations under their breath, and then set about blasting their crews as idle, no-seaman lubbers who couldn't keep proper station on the flagship, nor probably a proper watch neither! For all aboard the three ships were young men wound up with excitement. Maybe it *would* be them that found Flint? Maybe they'd be the ones, the lucky ones, God bless them one and all!

So they bowled along, with the miserable island to starboard, the merry breeze a-blowing, and their slick, copper-plated hulls gleaming and plunging, and their bowsprits dipping, and their banners flying. And they poked into every inlet, and they looked at every cove, and they searched every beach, and in all three ships there were men in the tops and men along the rails with telescopes and peering eyes, never neglecting to keep a watch on the larboard beam besides, for you never knew, did you? And wouldn't it be a tragedy on the face of the waters for a ship to slip past on the seaward side and get away full of wicked miscreants and treasure?

By mid morning they'd passed the shoals that lay off the northern coast, where a great hill rose up, the second biggest of the three that lay in a line, north to south of the island, and round they came, navigating the northernmost, out-jutting peninsula at the top of the island, and were working southward towards a great mile-wide inlet that opened up some four or five miles ahead. Heffer stared and a prickling excitement arose. Ah! That was better. That was a *real* anchorage. Best they'd seen yet. *That's* where they'd be if they were anywhere! Then from *Bounder*'s bow a gun threw white smoke and a flat boom, warning of an urgent signal.

"Damn!" said Heffer, as *Bounder*'s flags went up. He put his glass on them. "Bugger!"

The flags spelled "Enemy in sight. Larboard bow."

"Bugger, bugger, bugger!" said Heffer, knowing he'd have to report that *Bounder* spotted them first. *Let's hope it's a mistake,* he thought, searching with his glass. But one of his mids was quicker.

"It's a boat, sir. A launch. Heading north out of the eastward side of the island. It can't be Flint, sir. Not in a boat, sir . . . it's all right, sir!"

"Good lad!" said Heffer. The boy had his heart in the right place.

He trained his glass where the mid indicated and caught the boat in the bobbing, spherical field. There it was . . . a big launch under sail . . . three . . . no, four . . . no, *six* men aboard. *Enemy in sight* indeed! Rubbish! *That* weren't no pirate ship, now, was it? And there couldn't be no treasure aboard neither. Not the amount Flint was s'posed to have, anyway! Just six men . . . and something under a tarpaulin . . . hmm . . . Heffer wavered . . . *perhaps* . . .

"Make to *Bounder*," cried Heffer.

"Aye-aye, sir!"

"Pursue the enemy."

"Ah-ha!" cried Lieutenant Simon Clark, and snapped his fingers and danced for joy as he read the flags. He was independent! Detached from the squadron! Oh joy! Oh bloody rapture! Please God Almighty that the launch should fly like the wind, and have to be chased over the horizon, 'cos then *Bounder* would be *out of sight* of the commodore and Gordon bloody Heffer! Them and all the rest of the squadron, and he wouldn't have to share a penny piece with any of them! And Simon Clark, acting captain, would surely get his full two-eighths, as laid down in the Cruizers and Convoys Act of 1708, God bless it, God bless it, God bless it! *It* and the splendid men who'd shoved it through Parliament for the benefit of honest sailormen. Lieutenant Clark was fairly licking his lips at the thought of all the wealth that was going to be his . . .

Assuming, of course, that the launch had anything of value aboard.

Oh . . .

Clark calmed himself. He cleared his throat. He stopped jumping and grinning. He adopted the gravitas of a sea-service officer.

"Helmsman!" he cried. "Put me alongside of that launch. Mr Bosun, make all possible sail!"

So *Bounder* parted company with *Leaper* and *Jumper* . . . or would have done, had not the three sloops – now crossing the mouth of the northern inlet – realised at that moment what was coming out to join them.

Chapter 41

*A*gain the Patanq attacked the Royal Navy. As before, the volley of musket fire came sudden, and terrifying from close at hand. It came out of the trees with no warning, no drum roll, no hoisting of colours: no chance whatsoever for a man to stiffen the sinew and summon up the blood. It was all the worse for the fact that every man was strained to the utmost, trying – and failing – to keep a good watch on the wall of greenery through which the invisible enemy passed like the breeze: unseen, unknown and unheard.

Men fell, men trembled, men stood dismayed, and all of them looked over their shoulders, which was the first thing anyone did who was thinking of running. But not Commodore Scott-Owen. He went where the danger was worst, to where the column had been hardest hit. He drew his sword and raised it high.

"STAND FAAAAAAST!" he cried. "Marines rally to . . ."

Crack-Bang! Two muskets fired from the trees, and

363

Scott-Owen went down with a ball in the chest and another in the brain. He was dead before his sword left his fingers.

Which was very nearly the end of it. The men groaned dismally as their much-loved leader fell. It was too much. They were out of their element, being hit repeatedly by an enemy they couldn't even see, and who – having once made that mistake – never again attempted to fight hand-to-hand. One second more and the whole two hundred and one of them – which was all that remained of the two hundred and fifty who'd started out that morning – would have been streaming back through the woods, heading for the safety of their ships. As it was, they stood dithering, staring into the suffocating forest and clutching their firelocks as if they'd strangle them.

Bang! Another shot from the woods. Another man fell.

"Ahhhh!" cried the seamen and marines, and started to run.

"No!" cried Mr Midshipman Povey. "Down! Everyone down! Get low!"

And he ran up and down the column, pushing men down on their haunches. Lieutenant Hastings, ever in his wake, caught the idea at once and did the same, then so did the rest of the mids and lieutenants, till the whole force was crouched down among the undergrowth.

Then Mr Povey did something extremely brave. He stood up and yelled at the top of his voice. It was brave because – as he was soon to explain – he was taking a terrible risk.

"Officers to me!" he cried. "Officers, mids and sergeants . . . and corporals, too!" There were others present who outranked him, some considerably, but in face of danger, they responded to pure leadership, even coming from a lad of fifteen who wasn't a lad but a *man* because he'd been bred up in a manly service.

So they scrambled and ran and plonked down beside Povey and looked at him: a ring of blue-coats and red-coats, who gaped at the first thing he said:

"Take your bloody coats off!"

Povey was busy wriggling out of his own blue coat with its white-lined collar, marking him out as a midshipman, and its gleaming brass buttons.

"What?" said the senior lieutenant, aghast. "Never!"

"We've got to . . . *sir!*" said Povey, remembering rank just in time.

"Why, in God's name? You'll have us strike colours next!"

"Aye!" growled the rest, and Povey nearly lost them.

"Sir," he said, "don't you see – the bastards are shooting our officers!"

"What?"

"Yes! The sods aim at the officers. Look round, sir. We set out with five lieutenants, a dozen mids, and two sergeants and corporals of marines – and nearly every bloody man they shot was one of them!"

"Despicable!" said the senior lieutenant.

"And now they've shot the commodore himself!"

"Filthy swine!"

"Mind you," said Povey, "it's exactly what *we* do in close action, with sharpshooters in the tops aiming at the enemy's quarterdeck."

"That's entirely different!" said the senior lieutenant.

"Aye!" they all said, and nodded furiously.

"It's *this* that's different, sir," said Povey, pointing at the jungle all around. "*Land* ways ain't no good afloat, and maybe *sea* ways ain't no good ashore!"

"Hmmm," they said, considering this fearful heresy.

"So, off with your coats, gentlemen – let's not give the buggers something to shoot at. And off with the marines' coats, too, lest they should stand out."

"What do we do with 'em?" said a voice. "The coats?"

"Drop 'em in the sodding jungle!" said Povey. "Who cares? It's our sodding lives we've to worry about, not our sodding coats!"

"Oh," said the voice.

"And another thing," said Povey, "no saluting! No 'Aye-aye, sir'! No stamping feet! Nothing that tells the swabs who to shoot at. Are we agreed . . . sir?"

"Yes," said the senior lieutenant, not overly delighted at this display of sparkling talent in a midshipman. "Anything else? Do say if there is, Mr Povey."

"Yes, sir!" said Povey instantly. "Next time the sods shoot at us, everyone falls flat like this –" He jerked a thumb at the crouching seamen and marines. "And we don't just blaze into the forest, we mark our targets – if any presents – and shoot 'em . . ." Povey concentrated furiously. "And . . . and . . . scouts ahead, and a chosen team of our quickest and most active men standing by ready to charge into the enemy's smoke to drive him back when he attacks, but without pursuing too far and getting lost!"

Povey was inventing – *re-inventing* – forest warfare. He was improvising as he went. It was a remarkable achievement. Without him, the landing force would have given up its attempt to penetrate the island. But now they pressed onward, and with significantly fewer losses when the Indians attacked again.

"Where are they?" whispered the senior lieutenant, for now the two of them were out in front of the column with the scouts. They were flat on their bellies, looking over a slight rise in the ground where the forest opened into a clearing. This, they knew from experience, to be a deadly dangerous place. Just the sort of spot where the Indians lay in wait.

"I think they've retreated, sir," whispered Mr Povey, who persisted in acting as second in command, and was so good at it that the senior lieutenant had given up trying to stop him. The senior lieutenant sighed. Povey was a precocious little sod, but his ideas were saving men's lives.

"Why would they do that?" said the senior lieutenant. "Retreat?"

"Perhaps they were ordered to, sir."

"Ordered? They're bloody savages!"

"Don't fight like savages, do they, sir? More like men under discipline."

"Hmm. Yes. So we'll press forward . . ."

The senior lieutenant didn't actually say "*Shall we?*" For the sake of his rank and dignity, he suppressed the words. But his expression spoke volumes, and Mr Povey smoothly added diplomacy to his growing repertoire.

"Aye-aye, sir. I'm sure you're right, sir," he replied, with all the modesty and respect he could muster. He said it as if it wasn't the blindingly obvious thing to do, and just what he was about to say himself.

So they crept forward with the six men of the vanguard, as they'd dubbed them – picked because they were the nimblest – making remarkably little noise for sailors, though still enough to alert every Patanq on the island, had any been listening. And every few minutes they paused in their creeping for runners to go back and fetch the main column. In this manner they made good ground, in perfect safety, until . . .

367

Thud! A ship's gun fired some miles ahead.

"What's that?" said the senior lieutenant.

"It's a gun, sir!" said Povey.

"I know that, you impertinent little swab. But what *is* it?"
Povey couldn't resist it. The words leapt out:

"I'll go forward at the run, sir! I'll take the vanguard and
explore. There's something afoot, sir. I think the Indians have
gone, sir, so we'll be all right – I mean, if that's all right with
you, sir?"

"Go and be bloody damned!" said the senior lieutenant.
He was a big man, heavy and strong, and if he *had* to be a
soldier – which he didn't want to be – he'd rather be a
grenadier and stand fast, than a blasted light infantryman
mincing all over the field. "Oh, get on with it, you pushy
little bastard!"

But Povey missed the last part for he was already gone.
Off with the vanguard, running towards the sound of the
gun. It was hellish exciting, dashing through the trees: a
bit like fox hunting, only better, 'cos foxes weren't full of
doubloons, and it was wonderful to run and not crawl,
and Povey was convinced the Indians were gone and not
hiding.

And he was right. Ten minutes later, he and the other
runners burst out of the forest and on to a beach, and gaped
at the sight of three ships: one getting under way and two
more anchored, and an old wreck besides. Further up the
beach, there were tents and boats and men clambering aboard,
and on the water there were more boats being cast off and
others abandoned, and the decks of one ship were swarming
with Indians, and there . . .

There! There! There! Painted clear and bold on the stern
of the big schooner that was heading for the sea was the

name *Walrus* – that very same *Walrus* they'd so closely missed in Charlestown!

"God bli' me!" cried Povey. "It's Flint! We've found him!"

Chapter 42

*T*here was no doubt who held the power. It was Dreamer. He held the power but he wasn't in command. That was Long John Silver. It was as obvious as the fact that he stood head and shoulders taller than any other man there.

Dreamer had the strength, for his men swarmed all over the beach and throughout Flint's ruined camp, catching Flint's men where they tried to hide and hauling them out. Still more Patanq stood in arms around Silver – dozens and dozens of them – while Silver had just nine men ashore and another twenty-two aboard *Walrus*. But Dreamer was desperate to get off the island, and was gabbling nonsense about the dangers it held, which meant getting his entire force off the beach, and into *Walrus* – now the only undamaged ship in the anchorage.

And *that* was seaman's work, so everyone looked to Silver, and stood round him yelling and shouting for his attention, and pointing this way and that, and pulling at his cuffs, and even *Walrus* was suddenly demanding attention by firing a signal gun, and her crew jumping up and down and pointing out to sea.

"John!" said Israel Hands. "They've seen something!"

"*Mijnheer*!" said a bearded man. "I was forced into this. I am no pirate!"

"Demons, One-Leg!" said Dreamer. "We must escape them!"

"What demons?" said Silver. "And who's the bloody Dutchman?"

"He is Red Beard," said Dreamer, "the Wayfinder!"

"Who?"

"He came to us out of Flint's camp. He came of his own free will."

"Did he now?"

"John!" said Israel Hands. "It's the navy!"

"Red Beard shall find our new lands," said Dreamer. "If we escape the demons."

And all the time, Selena clung to John as if she'd never let go, and he clung to her, and stroked her hair and kissed her hands . . . for it was pure, shuddering relief that Dreamer wanted him safe and sound, and her too, and every seaman he could find. For Dreamer's one concern was to get his men back to their womenfolk, who it seemed were even now aboard a fleet of six ships anchored beyond Flint's archipelago. And then – this was the nonsensical part – once the Indians were off the island, they'd be safe from *demons*. That's what Dreamer was saying.

Silver looked at the fierce little man, jabbering and stamping, and his men beside themselves with excitement, their eyes rolling and teeth gnashing. The warriors were groaning and swaying, and wildly dangerous: one false word would set them off, butchering every man that wasn't one of them. It was uncanny. It made Silver's flesh creep.

And it was too much, too fast, for Silver to make sense of. And in particular he was struggling to make sense of Dreamer, who clearly knew *something* – but for the life of him Silver couldn't get a grasp on it, for he'd never met such a creature before.

"What bloody demons?" said Silver. "What the blasted hell are you talking about?"

"John!" said Israel Hands. "For Christ's sake, look – it's the bloody navy!"

"Navy?" said Long John. "Where?"

"There!" said Israel Hands.

"Shiver me timbers!"

Just visible, out to sea, about a mile from the mouth of the inlet was a big sloop. It was flying British colours.

"ALLLLLLL HANDS!" roared Silver. He shouted to rattle the t'gallant masthead, and even the birds in the trees fell silent. "Now then," he said, "we've to get aboard and under way this instant – and God help him as dawdles!" He turned to Dreamer. "How many men have you got?"

"One hundred, and half a hundred, and a little more."

"Well and good – *Mr Hands!*"

"Aye-aye, sir?"

"Take command of the beach. Man every boat you can, and get these buggers aboard – all of 'em – and tell Mr Joe to see 'em stowed wheresoever makes best sense. *At the double*, mind!" Silver looked at those few of Flint's men now standing under guard. "We need seamen, so I'll take *them* too. And as for the rest –" he looked at the faces peering from *Sweet Anne* and *Hercules* "– them buggers must take their chance along of Billy Bones and Ben Gunn, for we ain't got time to take all."

The job was done quickly, with five boats passing to and

fro, and Dreamer sending out his swiftest runners to call in Cut Feather and his men. Finally there were just two boats ashore, one pulling away, loaded with Patanq and seamen, and one with Silver and Dreamer climbing aboard, and Selena and Israel Hands waiting with four men at the oars.

"Is that all your people, Dreamer?" said Silver.

"It is all of them."

"So let's be gone!"

"Wait!" cried Dreamer. "Look!"

Five Patanq warriors were sprinting along the beach towards the boat. Dreamer stared at them, and said something in his own tongue. He said it sharp and amazed.

"What's that?" said Silver. "Who's them?"

"My trackers!" said Dreamer. "Sent to find Flint –"

"Flint? Where is he? Where *is* the bastard?"

But the five men were gasping and panting and throwing themselves at Dreamer's feet and pointing back towards the woods, and Dreamer was listening and nodding . . . and then he threw back his head and let out a cry that chilled the bones.

"What is it?" said Silver. "Shiver me timbers, what is it?"

"In! In!" said Dreamer, and the five Patanq leapt into the boat. "One-Leg," he said, eyes round in horror, "he had a boat! He has escaped! My dreams were true! I thought I had won, but I have lost . . . *he goes to the women and children!*"

Silver said nothing but grabbed Dreamer where he stood shaking and spouting, and hauled him into the boat.

"Get us aboard ship, Mr Hands," said Silver. "Buggered if I knows what's up his Indian arse, but it ain't nothing good, now, is it?"

"Dunno, Cap'n," said Israel Hands, "but never mind *him* – lookee there!"

"Oh, shite and corruption!" said Silver. It wasn't just *one* navy sloop. There were three of them. "Give way!" he cried. "Break your backs and sod him as slacks!"

And the seamen heaved and the boat shot forward, even as the Patanq huddled round Dreamer, wailing and gabbling in their own language, and totally ignoring the white men. And so they continued, even as *Walrus* was got under way, and out to sea to face her enemies. It took all Long John's talents to bring them under orders for what he planned to do next.

Three bells of the forenoon watch
(had bells been struck, which they were not: the ship
having beat to quarters)
26th February 1753
Aboard HMS Leaper
Northeast of the island

Lieutenant Heffer's head pounded as if it would burst. Here it was! This was it! Exactly what they'd been looking for! A big New England topsail schooner, just like Flint's. And it weren't showing no courtesy to a man-o'-war. *Leaper, Bounder* and *Jumper* were all flying King George's colours, and any honest merchantman coming upon them sudden, like this, would dip her colours and let fly her topsails. But this schooner flew no flags. She was pierced for fourteen guns, and she was coming on furiously, without the least intention of giving honours or heaving to.

"Flint!" cried Heffer. "We got the bastard, lads! Give a cheer and stand by to go alongside. We'll have his tripes for tow-ropes, lads!"

"Huzzah!" cried the *Leaper's* crew, all seventy-five of them, and the master at arms ran round issuing pistols and cutlasses to all those who hadn't already got them.

374

They were crackling with excitement. They'd got Flint! Three ships to his one! They'd board him, baste him and boil him! And he wasn't even trying to avoid them. He was coming on, bold as brass, and there wasn't a gob's chance on a griddle of him getting away.

Heffer leapt up into the main shrouds for a better look. With skill born of practice, he hooked a leg into the ratlines to cling on and leave his hands free for the glass.

Ah, he thought, as he scanned the decks of the schooner, *there's hardly a bugger aboard!* Instinctively he felt the pistols in his belt and the blade at his side. *I'll do it!* he thought. *I'll board the sod, and clap Flint in irons.* And all this, God willing, before *Bounder* and *Jumper* could join in and spoil the splendid completeness of his victory. And if *that* didn't end up with himself promoted, then God rot his soul!

The two vessels closed at speed, both on a good wind, on converging courses, and they slid diagonalwise, slanting together, with all hands cheering aboard *Leaper* and not a soul in sight aboard the schooner, other than a tall man with one leg standing beside his helmsman, and a few others in the rigging.

Leaper's maindeck fired, guns trained hard round on the bow, set to bear as soon as they might, and her shot howled and zoomed and some struck crunching into the schooner.

"Huzzah! Huzzah!" cried *Leaper*'s people.

"Damnation and buggery!" cried Lieutenant Clark of *Bounder* and Lieutenant Comstock of *Jumper*, and they screamed at their bosuns to make better speed. Neither wanted to miss out. All that remained to be decided was the matter of who got most credit. Flint was done for. The noose was as good as encircling his neck.

Then the schooner's topmen spilled wind from her sails. She slowed.

"Uh?" thought Heffer.

She slowed, at the precise moment necessary to line her up square alongside of *Leaper,* before Heffer could order grapnels away, at a range of twenty feet . . . and then she gave her entire broadside in a thundering cascade of flame and smoke, with guns aimed high to send a scything blast of chain shot into *Leaper*'s rigging: ripping spars, chopping lines and leaving the mainsail shredded and flapping like rags on a line.

In the same instant, shrieks and war-whoops rose from *Walrus*'s decks as over a hundred and fifty half-naked savages leapt up from where they'd been hiding, and gave such a volley of musketry as put the maindeck guns to shame, dropping men dead, ruined and wounded all over *Leaper*'s decks, and her helm unmanned, and her sail trimmers fallen, and herself falling off the wind, and left trailing and tattered in the wake of the speeding schooner.

Lieutenant Heffer had made a serious error. Something a more experienced man wouldn't have done. He should have waited until his full force of three ships could act together. As it was, his ship was thrashed, while the enemy, unharmed, was proceeding northward at great speed.

Heffer however was past caring, having been hit by a three-foot length of chain that flew somewhat low. As *Leaper* drifted in disarray, he lay like a fish on a slab: stone dead and gutted, with his entrails around him.

Israel Hands's gun-captains fired as the sloop came under their guns. They all knew their master gunner. They knew his ways and they knew not to waste shot – even those who, until half an hour ago, had thought themselves Flint's men. But Israel Hands couldn't help bellowing out the words of command:

"Let 'em come, boys! Wait your target! Fire as the guns bear!"

Walrus shuddered as the guns bounded back, jerked to a stop by their tackles, and Silver, standing by the helmsman, jabbed the end of his crutch against a brown figure laid flat on the deck.

"Now!" he said, and Cut Feather jumped up, screamed a war-cry, and all around Patanq warriors came pouring out of the hatchways, and out from behind every scrap of cover where they could hide. Soon Patanq were blazing away with their muskets into the sloop that had been decoyed into trying to board, and was now falling astern in ruins.

The Patanq by this time were crowded into the gundeck, grinning and chattering and pointing at the sloop, and getting in the way of the gun-teams as these experts fell on their pieces with swabs and rammers and wads to re-load.

"Get 'em clear!" cried Silver from the quarter deck. "Cut Feather – if you're a bloody officer, then act like one! Clear your men from the guns! Get them into the fo'c'sle and the rigging with their muskets!"

Considering he'd never been aboard a ship in action, Cut Feather learned most wonderfully fast. In a matter of moments he'd got his men where Silver wanted, leaving the gun crews to re-load and run out.

Meanwhile Silver found Van Oosterhout at his elbow, full of self-importance and tugging at his sleeve.

"What d'you want, damn you?" said Silver, who had two more ships to fight and wanted to be left alone to do it. They were trying to cut across his bow even this precious second, and would do it, too, if he didn't look sharp.

"You must take Flint's Passage!" said Van Oosterhout.

"What's that?"

"We go to the Patanq fleet, yes?"

"Yes. That's what *he* wants." Silver looked round for Dreamer, and saw him slumped with his back to the taffrail and his head in his hands. "Huh! What's wrong with *him*? Is he hit?"

"No," said Selena, "he's ill. He's ill all the time."

"What are you doing on deck? I told you to go below!"

"John," said Selena, "listen to him! To Van Oosterhout!"

"Why?"

"He's special. He's a better seaman than Flint."

"He's *what*?"

"He does a thing Flint can't do."

"What thing?"

But her answer was lost, for at that moment ships' guns roared, and shot screamed. Lieutenant Comstock of *Jumper* had calculated, correctly, that he couldn't get across *Walrus*'s bows – she was just too fast. So he brought his ship around and gave his broadside, slow and steady, five guns, carefully aimed, in the hope of doing some damage that would slow her down.

ZOOOOOM! VOOOOOM! said the two closest misses, which were close enough to make *Walrus*'s people duck, and the Patanq cry out in fright. But *Jumper* scored no hits.

"Hold your course!" cried Silver to the helmsman. "Steady as she goes!"

"Aye-aye, sir!"

"What thing?" cried Silver to Selena. Even in the heat of action he was intrigued, for Flint was a masterly seaman, and Long John knew of none better. "What can he do that Flint can't?"

"I find longitude. I find it at sea!" said Van Oosterhout.

"Bollocks!" said Silver. "Can't be done . . . can it?"

"Yes!" said Selena.

"Yes!" said Van Oosterhout.

"Well, stap my liver!"

"Cap'n!" said Israel Hands. "Belay this jawing – that bugger's got the wind of us!" He pointed at the third sloop, the one best placed to intercept *Walrus*.

"I know," said Silver, "and I'll do my best, Mr Gunner, if you do yours. Now then, madam –" he looked at Selena "– get below and out of the reach of shot. And you, *Mijnheer*: get a pair of barkers and stand by to fight with all the rest. But first, tell me this: is our present course good enough for Flint's Passage?"

"Yes, Captain. But you will need my guidance to pass through. Without that, the ship will be lost."

"Well and good. Come to me later, then. For now I must hold this course and not delay, or we'll have the two of them to fight all at once."

So Silver pushed *Walrus* as hard as she'd go, trimming her sails to utmost advantage, even heaving her two fore-most guns over the side and shifting stores below, so she'd sit more by the stern in the water, and which he felt would give her more speed . . . which didn't quite work.

Bounder was the furthest out to sea. She was best placed to cut across *Walrus*'s bow – and cut across she did.

But she wasted her chance. With Long John steering as best

he could to avoid her, she still managed to run slantwise across *Walrus*'s bow, firing off her guns as she went. It would have been a classic piece of seamanship – had she not been so eager. She should have hung back a little, and waited until she was all but snapping *Walrus*'s bowsprit . . . Instead, most of her shot went nowhere, just two thundering hits on *Walrus*'s bow, with heavy crashes but negligible damage.

And then *Bounder* was left behind, *Walrus*'s guns firing long-range in an attempt to do some damage in return, while the sloop tacked frantically in an effort to get back into the fight.

As *Walrus* surged onward, heeled to the wind, foam under her bows and all aboard cheering – except the Patanq, who were whooping and dancing like madmen – Silver looked back at the sloop.

We done it! thought Silver. He could scarcely believe it, but it was true. They weren't maroons no more. They weren't meat for the savages to roast. They weren't pirates to be turned off and hanged. There was clear water ahead, and the navy astern, and Van Oosterhout the only one what knew the way through the archipelago, and all those as tried to follow liable to run on to the rocks! And Selena was beside him and throwing her arms around him, who'd not gone below, not for a second, and Long John Silver had a good ship, jolly companions and the woman he loved and all the world was his. He'd even got a quadrant-monger to replace Billy Bones!

There can't be nothing to spoil this, he thought.

Chapter 43

*I*t was getting cooler. The closer the launch got to the archipelago the cooler it got . . . cooler and safer, for as ever there was a mist over the archipelago. Once in Flint's Passage, the launch would be invisible and safe. Safe from pursuit, though not from the passage itself where the sea rolled and heaved and broke over some of the bigger rocks, leaving the rest hidden. They lay a fathom or two below the waves, waiting patiently, knowing that in time their patience would be rewarded.

In fact there was a great need for patience all around. Flint had to be patient, knowing that the only cure for his ills was a slow one; it might take months or even years to re-unite him with what was his. And the four hands whom Flint had brought along as crew must be patient too: they were anxious to get out of sight, but had to sail easy because of the rocks Flint had warned them of.

Then came the sound of gunfire from the sloops that were

381

engaging *Walrus*. Poisonous rage boiled out of Flint's very liver at the sight of his darling in another man's hands – and was promptly suppressed. Flint smiled to calm the hands, who were gaping at the distant ships and the rolling smoke. The Royal Navy was their bogey man, and they were unsettled.

"Never fear, lads," said Flint. "That'll be the saving of us. Let them fight. Let them smash one another. And whatever's left can beach and wreck itself trying to follow us through Flint's Passage, that only myself knows the running of!"

They nodded at that, the oafs. God's bowels, but they were stupid! To them, Flint's Passage was as insurmountable an obstacle as the walls of Troy. Well, maybe it was, to anyone without Flint's chart . . . or a copy of it. There was a thought! Could Van Oosterhout be aboard one of those ships? Flint thought not. He'd be no friend to the navy or to Silver. Or would he? Who could tell? Best assume that he was with them. Best make good time through the passage and get the Patanq fleet under way – after he'd attended to them, of course. That might prove difficult; he would have to be very careful how he went about it . . .

Thus thought Joe Flint as he ordered his men to strike the sail and take up their oars, and occupied himself with the little matter of getting through the archipelago without ripping the bottom out of the launch or running her aground. He'd done it before, of course, and had even added notes to his chart to make it easier. But still it would require all his attention, even with so small a boat as this.

Spreading the chart on a thwart, Flint took bearings of the island with quadrant and compass, noting the lie of the hills and the shape of its black profile rising out of the sea. Yes, they were on course for the archipelago and Flint's Passage.

"Give way!" said Flint, and took the tiller. He looked along the boat. He looked at the swaying oarsmen, the neat-furled sails and the masts laid along the thwarts, and he looked at the chests and the big tarpaulin.

Ahhhh, he thought, and nodded to himself.

Ten thousand dollars' worth of silver, gold and stones in the chests – enough to get him the men and ships he would need. He couldn't go back to Charlestown, but there were other ports. The colonies were full of them. He might even go to England. To Bristol perhaps, or Plymouth . . . ?

But for now the gems and doubloons were as nothing compared with what he'd got under the tarpaulin. There, in the dark, was something even more vital to his plans. It was a pity it needed such constant attention.

"Stroke oar!" said Flint.

"Aye-aye, Cap'n."

"Heave off that tarpaulin – it's not so hot now. And change the water!"

Stroke oar leaned forward. He filled a pot with fresh water. He lifted the tarpaulin, he opened a little trapdoor, he replaced an empty pot with the filled one, which had to be lashed in place to prevent spillage.

Chk-chk-chk!

A hand reached out – a furry little hand – and took the man's index finger as a child might: with perfect gentleness and innocence. Stroke oar's pock-marked cheeks crinkled in a smile, for he liked the little buggers. His mates – equally scarred – grinned too.

Nearly noon, 26th February 1753
Aboard Walrus
Two miles south of Flint's Passage

Dreamer got up. He staggered. He'd just vomited into a bowl held out for him by Dr Cowdray.

"Fetch water!" said Cowdray. "And a cloth to clean him."

Cut Feather cradled Dreamer in his arms. The other sachems were gathered round, looking anxiously into Dreamer's eyes, and the one who ran for water and a cloth thought it an honour to do so.

"He should lie in a darkened room," said Cowdray.

"Father," said Cut Feather, "come – we will find you a bed."

"No . . ." said Dreamer, closing his eyes to the intolerable pain that burned in the side of his head. Usually when the lights and the pain struck, Dreamer would try to sleep. But this time he had to speak. It was difficult, for half his face was numb and tingling, and his tongue would not obey. "Bring One-Leg," he said. "One-Leg Silver." He had to say it several times before they understood.

"What is it?" said Silver, when Cut Feather ran to the helm to fetch him.

"One-Leg!" said Cut Feather, beckoning urgently. "Come! Come!" Silver cursed, for he had work to do. But with the ship full of armed men who thought Dreamer the next thing to God, he thought it best to obey.

"Dutchman," he said, "take the watch. See this ship into Flint's Passage."

"Yes, Captain," said Van Oosterhout. "But a boat must go ahead to sound the way."

"Well and good," said Silver, for that made sense. He looked to Israel Hands, Mr Joe and the others who'd gathered at the helm to pore over the Dutchman's chart of the archipelago, then jerked a thumb at Van Oosterhout: "This here's a good seaman," he said. "Do as he tells you!"

"Aye-aye, Cap'n!"

"One-Leg," said Cut Feather, "*now!*" And he dragged Silver down into the waist, where Dreamer was surrounded by a crowd of murmuring, frightened Indians.

"What's wrong with him?" said Silver, coming close to the swaying, drooling figure hanging in the arms of his followers, eyes screwed shut, head rolling from side to side.

"He has the migraine," said Cowdray. "The worst case I've ever seen."

"He suffers," said Cut Feather. "And he sees!"

"Sees what?" said Silver.

"He sees the future."

"Does he now?" said Silver. "And what does he see?"

"We do not know. But he calls for you!"

"Dreamer," said Silver, "it's me. What is it?"

Dreamer tried to speak. His mouth opened. Patanq words came out, slow and laboured.

"What's he saying?" said Silver, but Cut Feather shook his head.

"He speaks bad words, One-Leg. His tongue is not his to command."

"Facial paralysis," said Cowdray. "It comes with migraine."

"Flint!" cried Dreamer, making a huge effort.

"*Flint?*" said Silver.

And in that instant the foremast lookout hailed.

"Boat ahead!" he cried. "Fine on the larboard beam!"

"Yes!" cried Dreamer, briefly conquering the affliction that put false words in his mouth. "*Flint!*" he said, pointing ahead. "*There!*" He opened his eyes and stared straight into Long

John's face . . . and Silver flinched as hideous terror leapt out of Dreamer's mind and into his. It was terror of Flint and what Flint was going to do. It was occult and uncanny, and Silver staggered back, and crossed himself as he'd not done since a child.

But was it real? Was Flint really there? How could this blasted savage know where Flint was? Silver hopped to the rail, and aimed his glass where Dreamer had pointed. But he couldn't see anything. He was looking straight into a bank of mist and heat-haze on the surface of the sea. No doubt they could see more from the tops. He turned to Dreamer again.

"Is it Flint? What's the swab doing?"

But Dreamer had no more words, nor even strength to stand. They laid him gently down while everyone looked to John Silver.

"Flint!" said Silver, and looked past the masts and sails and out over the bow into the fog. Then he grabbed Cut Feather's arm and shook him, for Cut Feather – war sachem of the Patanq nation – was groaning in fright. "What's Flint doing?" said Silver.

"Sun-Face goes to the fleet," said Cut Feather. "We thought we had left him on land. But he has a boat! He goes to our women, taking his demons!" He looked at Dreamer. "Our father saw this! He foretold the demons! He said Flint would take demons to kill our women and children."

"What bloody demons?"

"Small demons. Demons with tails."

"And horns and cloven hoofs? *Pah!*"

"John!" Selena was pulling at his arm. "Listen! I know something – it might be important. He said a terrible thing to me. And we argued and he hit me."

"Flint?"

386

"Yes! He spoke to me on the beach. He said he wouldn't share the goods, except with me . . ." She saw the jealousy on Long John's face. "Don't blame me, John! That's what he said! He said he'd not share it with anyone but me. He said he'd kill the rest: the seamen and the Indians, and their women and children too. And I was to hide on the island till it was done, so I'd be safe. When I asked him how he'd do it, he laughed and he said 'with smallpox'."

And there it was. Silver jumped the gap. He understood. He thought of Sarney Sawyer and his men, and the old Jesuit and *his* men . . . and Ratty Richards's face, staring up dead and disfigured in the moonlight.

Silver was sickened.

"It's the monkeys!" he said. "There's some left. Flint's got 'em!"

"Monkeys?" said Cowdray. "What've monkeys to do with smallpox?" Silver told him. Cowdray gaped.

"I knew he was not a *good* man, but –"

"What'll it do to them?" said Selena. "The Indians?"

"Smallpox?" said Cowdray. "It is most dreadful for them. They have no resistance and few survive." He shook his head. "But that would be ordinary smallpox – this is worse! If it kills nine in ten *white* men . . ." he paused, pushed beyond knowledge. "If Indians catch it, perhaps none may survive." He turned to Van Oosterhout. "How many are embarked in the Patanq fleet?"

"About twelve hundred," said Van Oosterhout. "Mostly women and children, and a few old ones. Them and about two hundred seamen." He looked at Cut Feather. "Are they *all* of your women? Are there no more?"

"They are all," said Cut Feather. "They are everything. If they die, the nation dies."

387

26th February 1753
Aboard HMS Bounder
As she is left in Walrus's *wake*

Lieutenant Clark gasped. He clenched his fists. He ground his teeth. The tears sprang from his eyes at the shame of it. He'd shot so fast across *Walrus*'s bow that he'd failed to rake her with his broadside and he'd run on beyond her. So he'd attempted to resume pursuit by tacking through the wind, but bodged the manoeuvre such that *Bounder* fell all aback with her mainsail thundering against the mast, her blocks rattling and her people not daring to look him in the eye while the speeding schooner forged onward with her sails bulging and those damned bloody pirates openly laughing at the navy and making lewd signs with their fingers over the stern.

Clark looked at his men. A great guilt was on his head. He knew that it was his fault; had an admiral been looking on, his career would be at an end now, and his name would live on as a figure of fun and contempt: the man who let Flint get away by pitiful, lubberly no-seamanship.

But then fortune smiled. One of his rivals was in an even worse state.

"Cap'n! Cap'n!" cried one of his mids. "Look – the flagship's on fire!"

"What?"

Clark leapt to the rail, clapped a glass to his eye . . .

"Bugger!" there was smoke pouring off the tangled wreckage of *Leaper*'s deck, where her ruined mainsail hung in rags. No flame yet. Could be anything – a smouldering wad from the enemy's guns, a firelock discharged by accident – it was all too easy for a ship that had been battered and left rolling like a barrel to catch light. And then . . . and then

. . . *Ah!* thought Clark, and the sun came out in glory as he realised who was now in command, what with Lieutenant blasted Heffer's ship being disabled.

"Make to the squadron!" he cried. "*Jumper* to assist *Leaper!*"

"Aye-aye, sir!" said the signals midshipman.

"And the rest of you, get this ship under way and after them!"

He stabbed a finger towards *Walrus*, and wondered how much she had aboard in treasure, and how much might now be his, given the complexities of shifting precedence.

After that, things slid smooth as silk. *Bounder*'s crew excelled themselves in the speed with which they made good their previous mistakes. She was got before the wind, and once under way began to demonstrate just what a rake-masted, copper-bottomed vessel was capable of in the way of speed, to the extent that her young captain and his young crew were soon united in the thrill of the chase, the hopes of prize money, and yelling out to one another that they *really were* overhauling the pirate schooner, which unaccountably was slowing and lowering a boat as it crept into the mist bank ahead under close-reefed topsails. Soon, it would be in gun range, and Clark was contemplating bringing one of his maindeck guns into the fo'c'sle, just to show what he could do, when . . .

CRRRRUNCH!

Bounder ran full on to a sandbank going twelve knots. The lookouts hadn't being paying attention. They'd not seen the swirling waters. Or perhaps they just weren't visible.

Bounder had reached the archipelago. She'd reached it, found it, and sat on it. There was no possibility of her going anywhere else that day.

Flint was in the bow, paying careful attention to his chart and his compass . . . and the job was getting done. They were running the passage, hidden from view, and it was Flint's happy impression that any pursuit would be a slow one, because there was less water in the passage now than when he'd led through *Walrus, Sweet Anne,* and *Hercules.*

Ah! he thought. *Poor Danny Bentham. Where is he now – him and Mr Bulldog O'Byrne?*

Then the mist cleared ahead.

Huh! thought Flint. The climate was strange here, unique. It was like a door opening. And so he got his first sight of the Patanq fleet.

"Ah-hah!" he said, and snapped his fingers in delight, and his four hands grinned as they saw their captain so happy, for they knew how much their own happiness depended on his.

Flint looked at the thicket of masts and yards and the angular geometry of rigging lines . . . and he sighed with relief. For he saw at once that a certain problem was solved, one that had been causing him some concern.

"Chk-chk-chk!" he said to the monkeys. There were four of them.

"Chk-chk-chk!" they said, and looked at him with their intelligent eyes.

"Stand by, my pretties!" he said. "You shall have some new friends soon."

Chapter 44

26th February 1753
Aboard Walrus as Bounder goes aground
Just south of Flint's Passage

The seamen cheered and even the Patanq stopped their shivering at the cold that came with the mists at the mouth of Flint's Passage. For the moment, there was only delight at the confusion of the three Royal Navy sloops.

"That's *them* beached and buggered!" said Silver. "That 'un's caught fire and her mate's alongside, a-taking off her people, and that 'un's aground with her topsails hanging! The worst they can do now is send boats, and *Walrus*'s guns can load grape and canister for them!"

All eyes now turned to Silver.

"Captain," said Van Oosterhout, "will you come into the boat with me, or stay aboard? I've a crew going over the side, ready to sound ahead of the ship."

"John," said Selena, "don't leave me! I'm coming with you."

"But what about them navy swabs, Cap'n?" said Israel Hands. "They'll never give up. Not them! We'd best go back and sink the third bugger while we may!"

"No!" said Cut Feather. "Flint is ahead! We must hurry!"

There was a roar of argument: the seamen for finishing off the sloop and the Patanq for going after Flint.

"Silence!" cried Silver. "All hands pay heed, for here's the way of it. You, *Mijnheer*, shall lead *Walrus* into the passage – enough so's we're hid from view and there's rocks between us and what might follow! Then you, Mr Hands, shall take command, and drop anchor while I goes with *Mijnheer* to catch Flint."

"No!" said Cut Feather. "We go at once, after Flint!"

"No!" said Cowdray. "You mustn't touch him. Not him or any man of his crew."

"Belay that! Silence, I say!" Silver stumped across to Cut Feather. "Clap a hitch there, for I'll not be told what to do!"

"We go for Flint! Now!" cried Cut Feather.

"Now!" roared the Patanq, and Cut Feather levelled a musket at Silver.

"*We go now!*" he screamed.

"Now see here, my cocker," cried Silver, "we must come to cases, you and I, for there can only be one captain!" And he seized Cut Feather's musket by the muzzle and clapped it to the centre of his own chest. "Fire away, you sod! Fire – an' be damned. And *then* what'll you do aboard ship at sea?"

Silver's life hung by a spider's thread. Cut Feather's eyes showed white all round the black. His teeth glared. He jabbed hard forward with the musket and squeezed on the trigger . . . then groaned and looked away.

"Do what you must, One-Leg. But be quick!"

"Well and good!" said Silver, and looked for Selena. "And you, madam, will stay aboard where you're safe. As for you, Doctor – what d'you mean, *I mustn't touch him*? Are you talking about Flint?"

"Yes – he's been with the monkeys," said Cowdray, "Him and his crew. They must all have the smallpox. It's death to be near them."

Silver sighed.

"So what're we to do? We must stop him . . ." Then a thought struck. "No, Doctor, you're wrong! He must have 'em shut up safe. For Flint ain't had the smallpox. His face is clear! And he'd not risk his own sweet life."

"Aye!" said the seamen. They knew Flint. His cheeks were smooth and handsome.

"So who's had the smallpox?" said Silver. "Step forward only men what's had it and lived, for they can't take it again."

Four men stepped forward. All had scarred faces.

"Well and good!" said Silver. "That's you four, and me and *Mijnheer*." He looked at Van Oosterhout's smooth face. "That's if you're with me?"

"I am," said Van Oosterhout.

"And so am I," said Selena.

"Which you *ain't!*" said Silver. "Now I'm calling for two more hands – good lads in a fight!"

"Me!" said Mr Joe. And then there was silence. A bullet or a blade was one thing, but smallpox was something else.

"One more," said Silver.

"I will go," said Cut Feather.

"No!" said another voice, and the Patanq opened to let Dreamer through. He was weak. He was unsteady on his feet. But he was upright, determined, and ready with his fire-lock in his arms. "The nation has lost too many young men," he said. "I am old. I will go."

Uproar: the Patanq begging Dreamer to stay, Cut Feather insisting on his duty, Selena hanging on Silver's arm saying she'd take her chances, Israel Hands still shouting for an attack on the sloops, Van Oosterhout calling Silver to be quick, and Dr Cowdray, shouting un-heeded advice to all who'd listen – which was nobody – about not touching anything in Flint's boat, not on their very lives.

In the end, Silver had his way. *Walrus* passed between the misty walls of the passage, her anchor rumbling over the side into four fathoms, and Israel Hands and the rest cheering and waving from the fo'c'sle – except the Patanq, who never waved or cheered. They raised their right hands and stood silent.

Van Oosterhout conned the boat through Flint's Passage. Mist swirled astern, ahead and on either beam. The oars clanked, the boat pressed onward.

"I have thought a good thought, Captain," said Van Oosterhout.

"What?" said Silver.

"The ships of the Patanq fleet . . ."

"What about them?"

"Each is separate, yes?"

"Aye."

"Then he cannot put his monkeys on them *all*. Yes?"

"Ah! I see."

"So he cannot infect more than one or two. Most of the ships will *not* be infected . . . and the Patanq nation is saved."

"God bless my soul!" said Silver in delight, "Good man, *Mijnheer!* You're right! Damn me, but you're right!" Silver turned to Dreamer, who was staring out over the bow. "D'you hear that, Mr Dreamer? Things ain't so bad as what we'd feared."

"No," said Dreamer, "they are worse. I have seen."

Pah! thought Silver. *Bloody savage!*

But soon after that, they broke out of the mist and saw

clear ahead for three hundred yards. Flint's boat was alongside one of the ships of the Patanq fleet. A block and tackle was rigged and goods were being heaved aboard. Flint had beaten them. He was already there.

And the entire Patanq fleet was lashed together, side by side, bow to stern, into one huge floating platform.

Four bells of the afternoon watch, 26th February 1753
Aboard Lord Stanley
With the Patanq fleet
North of the archipelago

Captain York faced a dilemma. Should he let Captain Flint aboard or should he not? Him and his monkeys.

"I'm Flint!" said the splendidly dressed man in the boat below, coming alongside. And it was Flint all right. York had seen him in Charlestown harbour, and with Joe Flint it was once seen never forgotten.

"Captain Flint! I'm York, sir, Captain of the *Lord Stanley* . . ." York very nearly added, *Come aboard, sir!* but stopped himself. He knew exactly what Flint was, and Flint had four men with him: men like himself, all bristling with firelocks and staring up with hard faces. York was a merchant skipper: a tough man and a rough one. But his crew weren't killers like these, and he had every right to be cautious. "Where's Cap'n Van?" he said.

"Mr Van Oosterhout? He's ashore, sir!" said Flint, and smiled so open and friendly that York was almost reassured. Almost but not quite. "He's ashore, and I've brought out the first tranche of treasure for sharing among you and your crews, sir!"

"Oh?" said York. That was better! "You men there!" he

cried to some of his crew. "Rig a tackle and bring them goods aboard!"

"Aye-aye, sir!"

And it was done; the first chest was swaying aboard, and Flint was pouring out a smooth explanation of all the good things that had passed ashore, and York not quite ready to invite him aboard, still wondering where Cap'n Van was.

Meanwhile, the Patanq women were in no doubt at all. They were all around York, squealing and laughing, and their children too, for they liked the look of Captain Flint. They liked his fine face and his bright eyes. And they *loved* the little brown creature he pulled out of a cage in the boat, and cuddled like a baby. The women shouted and called out delight. They summoned kinfolk, and *Lord Stanley* swayed as more women and children came over the side from the ships moored alongside until the ship was rolling with them, hundreds of them, and hundreds more pressing forward from the other ships until it was one enormous crowd of Patanq women and children, dense-packed, shoulder to shoulder.

After all, that's why York had lashed the ships together. It made it that much easier to share stores, and for the women to go from ship to ship, in their eternal visiting and talking. For they didn't like going aboard boats at sea, not one little bit! In the absence of a proper harbour, and being on the open sea, it was the next best thing.

"*Ayorka!*" said the women. They couldn't say *York*, but they tried because they liked him. "Look! Look!"

"Hmm," thought York, and rubbed his black stubble and looked at them as they danced around him, and pointed at the monkeys. They liked *him* and he liked *them*. They were such pretty little things, and had smiled so friendly that he'd not been able to resist, and now there wasn't only "Sally"

– which was the closest he could get to *her* real name – but also "Molly" and "Jenny", her sisters.

"Little people!" they screeched. "Like beaver, like baby!" Obviously they'd never seen monkeys before, and were bewitched by them. York grinned and looked at the monkey in Flint's arms. It was a jolly little fellow and no mistake.

"Monkeys, sir!" said Flint, seeing his expression. "Found them on the island. Delightful and quite tame. Will you not take this one aboard? Just lower a line and he'll cling to it and you can haul him up."

"Yes!" cried the women. "Ayorka, bring him up!"

"Hmmm," said York. "Not so sure about that . . ."

"Go on, Ayorka!" said Sally and her sisters, coming alongside of him, and they wound themselves round him and tickled him, and all the other women laughed, knowing what was going on between them, and York laughed too.

"Get off!" he said. "Bring a line," he said to one of his men. "Let the monkey up!" Flint might be a bloody-handed pirate, but there was no harm in a monkey, now, was there?

The line dropped over the side. Flint reached out for it. He missed. He tried again, and York's first mate spoke.

"Cap'n! Boat pulling out of the passage, sir!"

"Where?"

"There, Cap'n."

York put his glass on the boat. There were four oarsmen, pulling like maniacs. There were two men in the bow, one an Indian. There were two men in hats and long coats – officers, obviously – in the sternsheets . . . and one of them looked like Mr Van . . . Indeed, it *was* Mr Van!

"What's this, Mr Flint?" said York.

"What?" said Flint, reaching again for the swinging line.

"That boat! That's Mr Van on board of her!"

"Ah!" said Flint, catching the line at last. "Good! I'm pleased to hear that!"

"Why?"

"Because . . ." said Flint, and pulled at the monkey's arms where they clung to his neck. But the monkey wouldn't budge. It cried out.

"Because of what?" said York. "What's a-going on, Mr Flint?"

"Just a moment," said Flint, and wrenched the monkey's arms free. The creature howled in pain and all the women cried out in pity. "Get *on*, damn you!" said Flint, and shoved the line into the monkey's hands.

Clank! Clank! Clank! The sound of the boat's oars could be heard.

"Flint!" said York. "What's going forward?"

"Nothing, dear sir."

Flint whacked the monkey. It shrieked. It jumped three feet up the rope and sat there hanging on, and chattering.

"Pull him up, dear sir!" said Flint, managing a lovely smile.

"Pull him up, Ayorka!" said the women.

Clank! Clank! Clank! The boat was two hundred yards off, the oarsmen hauling themselves off their benches with clenched teeth and muscles straining, and driving the boat onward at a tremendous rate of knots. York frowned. Something was wrong. Mr Van was waving. The Indian was lying in the bow.

"Flint," said York, "what's Cap'n Van doing in that boat?"

"I'll tell you as soon as I'm aboard, sir."

"Pull him up! Pull him up!" cried the women.

The seaman with the line shrugged and hauled it in hand over hand. He couldn't see no harm in no monkey, neither. So up it came.

Chapter 45

"Yes!" said Flint as the monkey clung to the line and the line was hauled in. "Go on, my little fellow!" he said, even as his neck ached from looking up and the boat swayed under his feet, bumping against the massive hull of the collier.

Flint could hear muttering from the four men behind him, nervously fingering their muskets and eyeing the progress of Silver's boat, which was coming on fast. It was still two hundred yards off, though; already they were too late. His plan was secure. The Indian women – hordes of them – were hanging over the side, chattering and giggling. By some quirk of good fortune, they'd all been brought together in one great mass, instead of different ships, as he'd been expecting – for that would have posed a problem even Flint had no solution for, though he'd been wrestling with it for days now.

He watched the monkey on its way. Up, up, up it went.

"A present for you, my ladies," said Flint. And they laughed and he laughed, and they stretched out their hands, each trying to be the first to snatch the pretty little creature from off the rope. To snatch it and stroke it and comfort the poor thing from its dreadful fright, from hanging over the fearful wet sea.

Chk-chk-chk! said the monkey, which was, in all truth, terrified. And everyone was reaching out for it, with Sally leaning out the furthest and Captain York grinning and hanging on to her behind, and she stretching . . . and stretching . . .

"Yes . . ." said Flint.

And her fingertips were closing towards the fur . . .

"Go on!" said Flint.

Smack-crack! The ball arrived before the sound of the shot, thumping into the small, furry body, knocking it clean off the rope, and spattering blood all over Flint. But whether by pure blind chance or the grace of a beneficent God, no blood, no fur, no tissue, no nothing came aboard *Lord Stanley*, nor did any of it touch those aboard.

The dead monkey plummeted into the mighty ocean which, forever and uncomplaining, swallows the filth of the land.

The women screamed. York cursed. Flint stood speechless with the blood spatter unwiped from his face . . .

A hundred yards away, with oars backed and the boat stopped and steady, Dreamer was rising to his knees, his long-rifle in his hands, and the white smoke clearing from the bow. Then the boat was rocking as all aboard cheered and reached out to clap him on the back.

But Flint wasn't done. Never one to give up, he fought on, even if what he was now doing was driven purely by spite – for there was no chance now of his ever getting aboard *Lord Stanley*. Not with York bellowing at him, and Van Oosterhout, Dreamer and John Silver yelling too, and their boat under way again, and Flint's four men grabbing at him

400

and demanding to be off, so that Flint had to flatten one of them to show the others . . . And when that was accomplished he got back to battering open the monkey-cage with the butt of his pistol, so that he might let out the other three, and throw, hurl, cast – whatever it took to get them aboard that ship and exact his revenge on the Patanq.

Silver's boat charged forward, backed oars, and within moments five muskets and six brace of pistols crackled and roared, and men went down all around Flint, but not before they'd fired too, each man with two brace, and a musket each, and two blunderbusses in the boat besides. Sparks and smoke and wadding flew in every direction in the ferocious fire-fight that ensued, at a range so close that it was all but impossible to miss, and not one man in either boat escaped unharmed.

Aboard *Lord Stanley* the women screamed and screamed, while York and his crew gaped at the battle – and took cover. When the firing stopped, they got up and looked, and saw two boats wallowing in their own powder smoke, and men sprawled out and bleeding and twitching.

Flint's crew were finished: all of them dead or rattling out their last breaths. Flint himself was pierced through the arm and leg, but not seriously. Aboard Silver's boat, Dreamer was hit low in the body, Van Oosterhout in the chest and hand, Silver had two deep shot-furrows gouged across his belly, and Mr Joe – who'd been burned by powder flash – was in the water, where he'd jumped to put out his burning clothes. Of the other four men, only one was still conscious.

Still Flint wouldn't give up. He stood. He raised his pistol butt, and smashed open the monkey cage.

"Kill him!" cried Van Oosterhout to York. "Cold shot – drop cold shot on him!"

Obediently York ran to the shot rack beside one of his ship's few guns.

Flint seized a shrieking, wriggling monkey. He threw it at the ship, but it fell back into his boat. He chased it.

"Stop him!" cried Silver, and Van Oosterhout seized a boat hook and tried, one-handed and dizzy with pain, to hook on to Flint's boat.

"No! No!" said Silver. "We can't touch him! Not him or them monkeys. It's death to all hands!"

Van Oosterhout dropped the hook and fell back, too sick to do more.

York's men began to heave six-pounder shot at Flint, but missed with every one. As projectiles rained into the sea around him, Flint grabbed another monkey and tried to throw it into the ship. The frightened creature bit him viciously, causing him to fumble and drop it, and as he staggered the boat slid under him, out away from the ship, and away from Silver's boat.

"Reload!" said Silver, snatching up a musket even though he was light-headed from loss of blood. "You there!" he croaked to York. "Never mind cold shot – get a bloody gun into action!"

Dreamer clutched the wound in his side and said nothing. The injury was painful but he knew it would not kill him. And he saw that Flint would escape. Silver was feebly trying to load. Van Oosterhout was barely moving. The men on the great ship were fumbling with a cannon. And Flint's boat was drifting clear. Flint, the left handed twin, the Devil in flesh, was escaping with his demons. And if he escaped, he could return another day.

Dreamer leapt out of the boat. He came down with a splash and swam the few strokes to Flint's boat. He tried to board. Flint struck at Dreamer with an empty pistol, but he wasn't quite himself. Hysterical with rage, he missed his stroke; Dreamer seized his hand, pulled Flint into the water and scrambled aboard. He chased the monkeys and struck them down with his hatchet, covering himself with their blood, guts and spittle. It was slow work because the monkeys were swift and agile and had to be caught.

Flint's knife took Dreamer by surprise. He hadn't seen Flint climb back aboard – but even if he had, he'd not have stopped what he was doing. As Flint seized him, he brought down the tomahawk one final time, before Flint's knife stabbed into him, and kept on stabbing and stabbing and stabbing until finally Flint heaved him out of the boat.

When he saw the dead monkeys, Flint let out a cry of rage and pain as if in the utmost desperation of his entire life, and damned all the world and those within it. Then he took two oars in his hands and began pulling with all his might.

The single shot that Silver managed with his musket achieved nothing. Neither did *Lord Stanley*'s hastily loaded gun, which York and his men were firing for the first time in years. Flint pulled for the open sea. Then he got the launch's sail up and ran westward into the mist-shrouded archipelago.

York and his men launched their own boat. They came alongside Silver's and found Long John and Mr Joe holding one end of an oar, with Dreamer – still alive in the blood-clouded water – clinging to the other. The two pirates were faint and weak, but they were hanging on.

"Leave go, shipmates," said York, clambering into the boat beside them and putting a hand on the oar. "We've got him now. We'll bring him aboard and look after him!"

"No!" said Silver.

"No!" said Dreamer.

"Why not?"

"He can't come aboard," said Silver.

"No," said Dreamer.

"Why not?"

"Smallpox."

York had many questions, but Silver just shook his head.

"So why are you hanging on to him?" said York finally.

"Dunno," said Silver, but he did know. And so did Dreamer, and they looked at one another as long as they could, and Silver hung on, and Dreamer hung on . . . until Dreamer could hang on no more. Finally, when his time was come, Dreamer slipped loose, and drifted off and quietly sank. Silver watched him go. Silver took off his hat.

"And so we commend his body to the deep," he said. Then he turned to a sorely puzzled York. "It's what we say, lad," said Silver quietly, "us gentlemen o' fortune." He looked at the spot where the waves had closed over Dreamer. "You don't let a man like him die all alone."

Chapter 46

Two bells of the forenoon watch
28th February 1753
Aboard Lord Stanley *with the Patanq fleet*
North of the archipelago

*T*he council held on the quarterdeck was a long one, even though some of the chief participants sat heavily bandaged in their chairs in the front rank, while the rest – and a great crowd of them it was, too, made up of warriors, seamen and gentlemen of fortune – sat or stood behind them, with those who'd signed articles shouting their comments whenever they wanted, as was their right, while the Patanq were shocked at such chaotic informality and spoke only when the ceremonial pipe was in their hands.

All of which was a considerable trial to the wounded.

Van Oosterhout had been lucky. Lucky in the man who treated him and who undoubtedly saved his life. Summoned from *Walrus,* Cowdray probed the Dutchman's chest wound, found the lung untouched, and removed a pistol ball, the shank of a brass button, and a bit of Van Oosterhout's coat. Thanks to Cowdray's obsession with boiling instruments before surgery, and with total cleanliness thereafter, a very dangerous wound was cleaned and drained, and healed well. Van Oosterhout was up and about the next day. He was even able to help Israel Hands bring *Walrus* safe through Flint's Passage, and out to join the Patanq fleet.

Mr Joe was lucky, too. His burns were superficial, and Cowdray laid on goose-fat and clean bandages, and healed him without scars.

Silver was lucky to be alive at all, but less lucky in his wounds. Cowdray cleaned the broad gashes across his body, but couldn't close them with stitching, because they were too wide. Despite Cowdray's best efforts, the wounds swelled and grew hot and painful. They would take weeks to recover fully.

With Silver quieter than usual, the discussion was led by Israel Hands and Cut Feather, and agreement was slow despite the profound gratitude of the Patanq nation, and a procession of sachems who came forward, one by one, to kneel before Silver and Van Oosterhout, and pronounce their thanks. The problem, as ever in this wicked world, was not high principle, but low money, for Flint's five chests had been opened and found to contain an astonishing amount of silver and gold – plenty enough and more for the Patanq nation to buy its new lands in the North.

There were many and different ingenious plans to split this wealth and ensure equal shares. But they were all too clever by half, for no man trusts a scheme he can't understand. Not where gold and silver is concerned. And so it rolled on, until John Silver, fed up and ill, and with Selena at his side pouring him drinks, called for silence.

"See here!" he said, sweating with the effort. "There's five chests of Flint's what's been brought aboard this ship. Ain't that a fact?"

"Aye!" they said.

"And four of 'em's dollars, and one's doubloons, and a few choice gemstones, too. Am I right?"

"Aye."

"So how's this – I'll take one chest of dollars, and a good handful of stones, and that's my whack. Me and my crew."

"Hmmm," they said.

"And all the rest – *all* of it – why, that goes to the Patanq nation, with Mr Van to be paid such sum as the nation thinks proper on safe arrival of the nation in its new home!"

There was much more argument, especially from Van Oosterhout, who'd have preferred a chest of his very own, right now. But Silver's plan was followed. It might not have been philosophically perfect, but it was simple, and everybody understood it.

Next day at dawn *Lord Stanley* and the Patanq fleet weighed and sailed on a fair wind, and with a great number of new lives already aboard, what with the joyful and vigorous reuniting of so many husbands and wives after long parting, such that the fleet had rocked at its moorings the night before. And if, in due course, some of the women – like Sally – were delivered of children a little paler than their husbands . . . well, nobody minded.

Walrus sailed at the same time, bound for Williamstown, Upper Barbados, possibly the last port in the Caribbean where she could drop anchor without fear of King George. For this purpose she had aboard two of the Patanq fleet's best navigators, men who'd been to Upper Barbados enough times to be sure of finding it again, especially with the help of the charts and detailed sailing instructions given them by Van Oosterhout.

"What do we do when we get there?" said Selena that night, as she lay in Silver's arms.

"Dunno, my girl, but I'll do it with you, whatever. And I'll not be parted from you again."

"No more the gentleman of fortune?"

"No."

"Really?"

"Aye."

"Pieces of eight!" said the parrot from her perch. Perhaps she knew Silver was lying, for he certainly was . . . he who'd never lied before.

John Silver was becoming a different man.

Chapter 47

Dusk, 4th March 1753
The southern anchorage
The island

It was Mr Povey who saw the launch come round the great eastern headland and into the anchorage.

Captain Baggot, who'd taken command on the commodore's death, had lookouts everywhere, for he was keen to demonstrate his own efficiency – and secretly delighted at the opportunity to do so. But the greatest incentive of all was his utter conviction that Flint's treasure could yet be found on the island.

With such a tremendous prize in his sights, Baggot had worked wonders. *Leaper* had been saved from the flames, but condemned and gutted, and her crew embarked aboard other ships. *Bounder* was salvaged and repaired, and got off her sandbank. The dead were buried, promotions made to fill dead men's shoes, and all made tight and shipshape. Even now, the wounded were busy either recovering or dying, as best pleased them, such that the tented hospital on the beach was emptying day by day.

Meanwhile, Baggot had two good longboats sounding and charting the fog-bound north of the island where *Walrus* had last been seen, and it was his personal guess that there was some safe passage to be found there, else why would Flint have gone so boldly in?

Above all, Baggot would not be downhearted. Total losses were less than a hundred men out of six hundred. Them and one sloop. Why, on his circumnavigation of '40 to '44 the famous Anson lost his whole damn fleet but one ship, and he'd still come home laden with gold and earned a peerage.

So men were on watch everywhere. This was Baggot's favourite ploy. He had small scouting parties out all over the island, and the two sloops were constantly on patrol off the coast. At least it was clear now that the savages, wherever they'd come from, were gone with Flint; they would be dealt with just so soon as the mysterious, foggy north was properly charted.

Thus it happened that Mr Midshipman Povey was in command of the beach when the launch came in under sail. It was pure chance that he was on duty at that hour, with his glass and his lookout station and his five marines and five seamen, as it came round the headland.

Who's this, then? he thought, focusing on the boat. But he couldn't see who was aboard. In fact, there didn't seem to be anybody aboard, except that it couldn't sail itself – obviously – so there must be *someone* in the stern, only . . . the sail was in the way. He was almost sure it wasn't one of the squadron's boats.

And then the sail shifted.

And Povey could see who was at the tiller.

And Povey was leaping and screaming and had men running in every direction at once, and drums beating and pipes calling and a great roar of voices rising over the beach, and officers running and Lieutenant Hastings sprinting across the sand, and every living creature converging on the launch, and fifty muskets at least levelled and dozens upon dozens of pistols . . . as Joseph Flint the pirate, with a thousand pounds on his head, grounded his launch, and got out and raised high his hands and walked towards the muskets and bayonets and swords and pistols and cutlasses!

It was almost funny. Flint couldn't tell which was rounder: the muzzles of the guns, or the eyes and the mouths of those who held them.

"Flint!" cried Povey.

"Mr Povey!" said Flint. "Stap me, if it ain't yourself!" And he drew his cutlass.

"AAAARGH!" they roared and cocked their locks in a furious clatter.

"Will you take my surrender, sir?" said Flint, and reversed the blade, presenting it hilt-first to Povey.

"Oh," said Povey, and took it.

After that the press was tremendous as men crowded round for a sight of the famous Flint. Even the officers came down to see him, once he was below decks aboard *Oraclaesus,* where they clapped him in irons. They all came.

And a few days later they came to see Billy Bones, a mutineer second in infamy only to Flint himself, who gave himself up as Flint had done, having nowhere to go and no food to eat, and believing hanging to be better than starving. There were others too, likewise in irons: the remnants of Flint's men, captured on the island or aboard his ships. But nobody paid attention to them, and they were kept apart from the prize exhibits: Captain Joe Flint and Mr Billy Bones.

When they first met, so blissful was the re-union of this master and slave – at least to the slave – and so grovelling was Billy Bones's behaviour down in the dim light below decks, sat chained to the floor, that Flint trusted Billy Bones with a little confidence.

When he was done, Billy Bones gulped and swallowed.

"Strong meat, Cap'n! Strong meat!"

"Yes, Mr Bones, but how else shall we avoid hanging?"

"Avoid hanging, Cap'n?"

"Yes, Mr Bones. It will be hard, but I think it can be done, for there will be but *one in nine* of them left."

"Them and us two, Cap'n?"

"Yes, Mr Bones."

And here Billy Bones grew puzzled. He felt his own pock-marked cheeks and looked at his immaculate master.

"But you ain't had it, Cap'n."

"No, Mr Bones, but never fear. I shall survive."

Flint remembered his father taking him to the Smallpox Hospital, where a visiting Turkish doctor made a tiny cut in his arm, inserted matter from the sick, and applied a bandage. A bandage which was seen by his mother, triggering a hideous quarrel and a kitchen knife brought out in rage, which his father struck from her hand . . . for the hysterical boy to thrust into his father's back, sinking him to the floor, where his mother took up the knife and butchered a man who was already dead.

Flint shuddered. Some memories were too much even for him.

But the Turk's technique was sound. Flint was immune to the smallpox.

Meanwhile, Billy Bones, who hadn't ceased his puzzling, came up against another stumper:

"But, Cap'n. All the monkeys is gone, ain't they?"

Now Flint smiled. For knowing British tars as he did, he guessed that they'd have searched the launch, and they'd have found the one that Dreamer didn't quite finish off. They'd have found it and made a pet of it, and healed it and cherished it, such that it would be scampering all over them . . .

Even now this very minute . . .

And he was right . . .

Chk-chk-chk!

Afterword

DREAMER'S RIFLE: LOADING, SHOOTING AND ORIGINS

This is near to my heart. My hobby is black-powder shooting and I own an American long rifle, which – in the hands of a skilled man – would do everything I have described in this book, including shooting a lead ball at supersonic speed.

I have, however, simplified the loading drill. Yes, you load with powder, and a patch and a ball, but if you use the ramrod, the ball won't go down, and you'll break the ramrod trying. I know – I did it, and with people looking on! Oh dear. What you need is a *starter:* a short stick with a fat end. You put the stick on the ball and smack the fat end with your hand. The stick drives the ball the first few inches down the bore . . . and *then* you use the ramrod to shove it all the way down.

That's what your dad would have told you in days gone by. I learned by trial and error, and I offer it to you young shooters with apologies for not putting it in the book, because nobody wants a lecture on shooting in the middle of a story.

Final thoughts on the long rifle, alias the *Pennsylvania* or *Kentucky rifle*: some modern scholarship[1] indicates that it

[1] Alexander, Peter A, *The Gunsmiths of Grenville County – Building the American Long Rifle*, Scurlock Publishing Company, 2002

may have been developed for – and originally used by – Native American hunters, so there really may have been someone like Laoslahta the Dreamer, who told the Pennsylvania German gunsmiths how to improve their European rifles. But I hesitate to enter so controversial a field, and one so close to the American heart.

THE HAUDENOSAUNEE: PEOPLE OF THE LONG HOUSE

Think *Iroquois* . . . then forget it, because it's a mistaken naming of the Haudenosaunee: the confederation of the Mohawk, Oneida, Onondaga, Cayuga, Seneca and Tuscurora nations – believed to have been founded in about 1500, though possibly much earlier – and which was extinguished by 1800 as the dominant civilisation of northeast America.[2]

Now think of the familiar Plains Indians (as in *Cowboys and Indians*), who were hunter-gatherers, with horses and ever-moving camps . . . then forget them, too, because the Haudenosaunee were entirely different. They were settled, agricultural people who lived in forest clearings, in fortified villages defended by heavy palisades of timber, which the early white settlers termed "castles", such was their strength. Their society was complex and formal, with decisions made by prolonged discussion, and women holding considerable status as matriarchal family heads.

They lived in long houses of very great size: perhaps a hundred yards long by twenty wide, with many families sharing one house. Fearless warriors, they were prized as

[2] Elmore Reaman, G, *The Trail of the Iroquois Indians,* Frederick Muller, 1967; Englebrecht, William, *Iroquois,* Syracuse University Press, 2003; Fenton, William N., Ed., *Parker on the Iroquois*, Syracuse University Press, 1968

allies by the English, Dutch and French. They took scalps, being encouraged to do so by white men who saw this as a way to kill enemies without personal risk, offering bounties of £100 per scalp – a tasty sum by eighteenth-century standards (equivalent to £100,000 in modern money).[3] And tax-free at that.

They were indeed hopelessly affected by alcohol, but considering the numbers of people in our own society who make idiots of themselves with booze and drugs, we have no cause to feel superior.

There was no Patanq nation. They are pure invention, but the descendants of the real Haudenosaunee still live in North America and cherish their ancient traditions.

FLINT AND THE HAUDENOSAUNEE CREATION MYTH

The story of the Left-Hand Twin and the Right-Hand Twin, born of Sky Woman's daughter, is a genuine part of Haudenosaunee mythology. Likewise, the Left-Hand Twin, responsible for all that is crooked and nasty, has many names, of which one really is . . . *Flint* – which made the hair stand up on the back of my neck when first I read it.

MIGRAINE, AND DREAMER'S WAMPUM BELT

Dreamer was a great man: a Haudenosaunee Winston Churchill. He suffered severe migraine attacks throughout life, and I've described his symptoms from personal experience, because it afflicts me too, though far less, and I don't foretell the future afterwards.

[3] A proclamation for encouragement of volunteers to prosecute war against the Saint John's and Cape Sable Indians. http://jerrygerrior.tripod.com/id11.html

416

Some migraine sufferers – including me – see a pattern of lights, called *aura*, or *fortifications* for the odd reason that, to seventeenth- and eighteenth-century people, they looked just like the zig-zag lines of earthworks displayed in plans of contemporary forts. These appear as a blob in the middle of the visual field, then grow and spread out to the edge of vision. They shimmer and twinkle and are coloured black, yellow and violet. These days, having grown out of the worst of migraine, I see only the lights and nothing follows, but for others the lights precede nausea and vomiting, and then a vicious headache.

So that's the zig-zag pattern Dr Cowdray recognised on Dreamer's wampum belt.

DANNY BENTHAM'S WEDDINGS

I have shamelessly stolen the marital history of Edward Teach – the legendary Blackbeard – and devolved it upon Captain Danny Bentham, whose taste for repeated marriage is described in Chapter 2. Blackbeard (c.1680–1718), probably the most famous pirate who ever lived, would get drunk ashore and marry . . . *any trollop that takes his fancy, and whom he might have had for sixpence . . .*

He took something in the region of fourteen "wives".[4] The only difference from Danny Bentham is that Blackbeard presumably consummated his unions in conventional style.

WALKING THE PLANK

In Chapter 4, Flint devises the cruel torture of *walking the plank*: that spectacular, piratical, and constantly depicted

[4] Perry, Dan, *Blackbeard: The Real Pirate of the Caribbean*, Thunder's Mouth Press, 2006

means of dealing with prisoners deemed surplus to requirements. When I started writing *Pieces of Eight,* it was my belief that walking the plank was a piece of fiction, but further research indicates that it really happened, with the earliest reported incident occurring in 1769.[5] I therefore presented it as a *novelty* aboard *Walrus* in October 1752, when Flint surprised his men with this special entertainment.

LONGITUDE

Also in Chapter 4, Cornelius Van Oosterhout gets himself *off* the plank by promising to show Flint how to find longitude at sea, which he duly does – and it is impossible to overemphasise how important that was by eighteenth-century seafaring standards. It must be remembered that, in those days, most sea-borne navigators knew *only very roughly* where they were. Thus in Chapter 30, Captain York confesses that he worked by "lead, log and latitude" – educated guesswork, in other words. As a result, it was common for ships to be wrecked and lost simply by running on to hazards that were supposed to have been elsewhere.

The classic example occurred on the night of 23rd October 1707, when the navigating officers of Admiral Sir Cloudesley Shovell's fleet, returning to England from Gibraltar in foul weather, thought themselves to be in open sea off Ushant. In fact, they were a hundred and twenty miles to the northwest, bearing down under full sail on the rocks of the Scilly Isles. Four ships were lost and two thousand men drowned in the disaster – the worst British shipwreck of all time.

Such dreadful mistakes were made because seamen could

[5] Botting, Douglas, *The Pirates*, TimeLife Books, 1978

easily find latitude by measuring the angle over the horizon of the sun at noon. But longitude, the other half of the equation, and the key to precise navigation, could not be determined at sea by most mariners until almost the end of the eighteenth century. See Dava Sobel's superb book *Longitude*[6] for the full and fascinating details, but, briefly, the solution involved either a chronometer (a highly accurate clock) and relatively simple calculations, or lunar observations and hideously complex calculations.

The lunar method came first, developed by Tobias Meyer, among others, and was tried at sea from 1757.[7] It involved neither conceptual leaps nor special equipment, springing directly from routine astronomical theory. But it demanded books of special tables, plus formidable mathematical skill, and in practice was too complex for mariners to handle.

It's not beyond the realms of possibility that a mathematician like Van Oosterhout, backed by Utrecht University, might have anticipated Tobias Meyer by a few years...In any event, it makes a damn good story.

SILAT: THE INDONESIAN MARTIAL ART

Van Oosterhout wasn't just a mathematician. He knew how to poke a man in the eye and kick him where it hurts. And he knew how to trip, duck, strike and chop. He was proficient in silat, a martial art practised for centuries in Indonesia – or Batavia, as it was known in his time, when it was a Dutch colony.[8]

[6] Sobel, Dava, *Longitude,* Fourth Estate, 1996
[7] Roger, N.A.M., *The Wooden World*, Fontana, 1988
[8] http://en.wikipedia.org/wiki/silat

There's nothing special or unusual in Indonesia having its own brand of martial art, since it's hard to find any civilised Asian country that hasn't got one: jiujitsu in Japan, taekwondo in Korea, kung fu in China, and so on.

What all these *arts* have in common is that – unlike a loaded pistol, for example – they cannot instantly be picked up and used. Proficiency is bought at the high price of years of practice and muscular development. We must presume, therefore, that Cornelius Van Oosterhout put in the hours and kept himself fit.

SMALLPOX: A VICTORY

Smallpox is horrible. The World Health Organisation estimates that the disease killed hundreds of millions of people in the twentieth century alone. In Europe, where the disease was endemic, it killed up to 30 per cent of affected adults and 80 per cent of children,[9] and those it didn't kill it mutilated. Among the native populations of the Americas – lacking genetically acquired resistance – it was far worse.

In 1798, Edward Jenner demonstrated that vaccination – exposure to cow-pox virus – gave immunity to smallpox. But inoculation – exposure to weakened smallpox virus – was much older. The practice was established in Africa and Turkey from ancient times. In 1717 Lady Mary Wortley Montague described the Turkish technique[10] – the very same that was applied to the young Joe Flint – but her efforts to popularise it in England were thwarted by strong medical opposition. During smallpox epidemics in eighteenth-century Boston, Benjamin Franklin

[9] http://www.who.int/mediacentre/factsheets/smallpox/en/
[10] Jack, Malcolm, Ed., *Lady Mary Wortley Montague: Turkish Embassy Letters*, University of Georgia Press, 1993

noted that some slaves were immune to the disease, having been inoculated in their native lands; again the technique was ridiculed by the medical profession.[11]

Eventually the doctors learned, and smallpox vaccine was mass-produced and deployed worldwide. So all those who believe that Nature is good and Science is bad should contemplate the eradication of this vile disease: a triumph that stands beside Beethoven's symphonies, Gothic cathedrals and the US Constitution as a great and noble work of mankind.

SMALLPOX: PERSISTENCE, AND TRANSMISSION BY MONKEYS

In Chapter 13, Ben Gunn opens a fifty-year-old grave, releasing smallpox which infects the island's monkeys, who pass the disease to Silver's men. This story is based upon half-truth. It is fact that a thirty-year-old grave, accidentally opened in Somerset in 1759, released a foul stench, and many onlookers later contracted smallpox, though it was a weak form of the disease and all survived.[12] But the idea of monkeys harbouring smallpox and then transmitting it to humans is entirely my invention.

On the other hand . . . transmission of diseases from animals to humans was once common. Such infections are termed zoonotic diseases. Tuberculosis, for instance, can pass from cows to humans, while other diseases originating in animals include plague and rabies. Finally, much debate has been generated within the scientific community over the possibility that the AIDS pandemic arose from a pre-existing

[11] Isaacson, Walter, *Benjamin Franklin: An American Life*, Simon & Schuster, 2003
[12] Razzell, P., "Smallpox Extinction – a Note of Caution", *New Scientist*, 1976: 71: 31

illness in monkeys, and it is known that simian retroviruses can pass from monkeys to humans.[13]

The smallpox virus is different, but it *is* a virus and my fiction is at least reasonable fiction.

So mind how you go when you meet a monkey.

[13] Wolf, Nathan D., et al, *The Lancet*, 368: 9413, 20 March 2004

ALSO AVAILABLE

Skulls and Bones

John Drake

High seas. High adventure. Low treachery.

Enjoy an excerpt now

Chapter 1

Three bells of the first dog watch
20th July 1735 (Old Style)
Aboard Isabelle Bligh
The Atlantic

The six-pound shot came aboard with a scream and a hiss, smashing one of the mainmast deadeyes, punching holes through the longboat secured over the waist, taking off the arm and shoulder of a seaman, as neat as a surgeon's knife . . . and throwing the limb shivering at his feet, as if still alive. The man screamed, and sat down flat with his back to the windward bulwark.

In the horror of the moment, Olivia Rose, sixteen years old and at sea for the first time in her life, turned from her father and clung to the heavy bulk of the lad who'd been doing his best to stand between her and the flying shot.

"Get below!" cried Josiah Burstein, her father. "And get away from *him!*" He snatched her away, blinking nervously at the boy, for Burstein was a small man while

425

the boy, also only sixteen, was broad and heavy with thick limbs, big fists and a dark, ugly face. But the boy stood back, nodding.

"Get below, Livvy," he said. "Your pa's right."

Seizing the moment, Burstein hustled his daughter down a hatchway, out of the way of shot. He cursed the day he'd set out from Philadelphia to make his fortune in London with his skills as a mathematical instrument maker, for nothing good had come thus far: only Livvy Rose keeping company with that lumpish oaf of a ship's boy.

Boom! A distant gun fired, and on deck, the crew ducked as another shot came howling down and smashed into the hull. The boy looked astern as his captain yelled from the quarterdeck.

"There, sir!" cried Captain Nehemia Higgs, seizing hold of the man beside him, the ship's owner Mr Samuel Banbury, and shaking him angrily. "Now where's your *peaceful way*?"

Banbury said nothing, but pulled free and, wrenching off his coat and shirt, ran forward to jam the crumpled linen deep into the fallen seaman's hideous injury in an effort to stem the flow of blood.

"Aaaaaaaah!" screeched the wounded man.

"And may I now – in God's name – turn to my guns?" yelled Captain Higgs.

"Aye!" roared the crew, nearly two dozen of them, angrily waiting for the order. Their captain might be a Quaker, but at least he was one of the *right* sort – unlike Mr Banbury, who was clearly one of the *wrong* sort. The crew, on the other hand, weren't no sort of Quakers at all

– not them, by God and the Devil! And they weren't about to give up their wages at the mere sight of a black flag!

Ignoring them, Banbury tugged off his belt and managed to strap it round the wounded seaman's chest to hold the dripping red bundle in place. Looking around him for help, he spotted the boy.

"You!" cried Banbury. "Give me your shirt!"

So two shirts were clapped on the wound, with the boy close enough to be sprayed by the victim's spittle and drenched in his blood. But he could see it weren't no use. Soon the screaming stopped and the man's eyes closed. Tommy Trimstone was his name; from Ilfracombe in Devon, and now dead.

The boy stood up from the corpse, wiping his hands on his breeches. He'd never seen death and didn't know what to make of it. He looked to his captain again, cussing and blinding as no Quaker should, and then finally raising a telescope to check on their pursuers, before calling to the boy.

"Come here, you young sod!" he cried. "Take this bastard glass and get into the bastard top, and keep watch on *that* bugger –" he pointed to the oncoming ship – "and be quick about it, or I'll skin the bleeding arse off you!" With all hands on deck, standing by to man his guns, Higgs needed a lookout.

The boy went up the shrouds at the run, and got himself nice and tight into the maintop. He levelled the glass . . .

"What d'you see?" yelled Captain Higgs.

The boy saw a sharp-keeled, rake-masted brig of some two hundred tons: deeply sparred, and with ports for

427

twenty guns. The wind was weak so she was under all sail, and coming on only slowly, but her decks were black with armed men, which was not surprising for a vessel that flew the skull and bones.

Boom! Up went another cloud of white from the enemy's bow, followed swiftly by the deadly howl of shot heading their way. It shrieked high over the masts as the boy called down to the quarterdeck, telling what he'd seen.

"You heard that," said Higgs to Banbury. "We must defend ourselves!"

"Can we not outrun them?" said Banbury. "You have *three* masts to their *two*!"

Higgs sneered from the depth of his seaman's soul at this ludicrous dollop of landlubber's shite. *Isabelle Bligh* was a Bristol-built West Indiaman: well found, and fit in all respects for sea. But she was designed for *cargo*, not swiftness. In her favour, however, was the fact that she bore sixteen guns and was heavily timbered, so if it came to cannonading, she might well drive off a lighter vessel that was built purely for speed. Higgs yelled this thought at Banbury, but dared not act without his word.

Up in the top, the boy looked down, puzzled. Banbury and Higgs were Quakers that weren't supposed to fight. But the ship had guns, like other Quaker ships, so why not use them? The boy shook his head. He didn't know. He only knew that Banbury was a very special Quaker, come out from England to staunch the slave trade among the Pennsylvania Quakers, and now going home. Clearly Cap'n Higgs was afraid of Banbury. Perhaps it was like the Catholics with their pope?

Boom! Another shot from the pirate's bow-chaser. They were close enough now that the boy could see the men working the gun. Again the shot went wide, and he watched them haul in, sponge out and re-load. And then he had a nasty thought. For the first time it occurred to him – in his youth and innocence – that the pirates . . . *might actually capture the ship!* He groaned in fear of what they would do to Olivia Rose.

Plump and luscious with shining skin and titian hair, Livvy was the only female aboard. He blushed for the things the hands said about her, behind her back. What chance would she stand if such men as them – but worse – got hold of her?

Then another flag went up on the pirate brig: a plain, red flag. The boy didn't know what it meant, but his mates did, down below.

"Bugger me," said one, "it's the Jolly Roger!"

"Gawd 'elp us," said another.

"Higgs," demanded Banbury, "what's that red flag?"

"The *Jolie Rouge*," said Higgs. "The 'Pretty Red One' of the French Buccaneers."

"What does it mean?"

"It means no quarter to those that fight," he said. "It's death to all aboard."

"But only if we fight?"

"Aye." Higgs scowled, for he knew this gave the game to Banbury.

Banbury heaved a sigh of relief as if a tremendous burden had just fallen away, relieving him of the agonising balancing act between principle and expediency. For he was a merchant as well as a Quaker, and wasn't quite so firm against fighting as he'd said. The truth was that he had his reputation to consider, having risen high within the Society of Friends, for he was clerk to The Meeting for Sufferings of the London Quakers, which was as near to a governing body as their prayerful egalitarianism permitted, and thus his actions would be closely examined upon his return by rivals ever-eager to take his place.

"Strike your colours, Captain," he said, "and pray for deliverance!"

The boy saw everything. *Isabelle Bligh* lowered her ensign and backed her topsail in surrender. The pirates cheered and came alongside in a squealing of blocks and a rumble of canvas, taking in sail and heaving grapnels over the side to bind the ships together. Then they were swarming aboard, fifty strong and heavily armed, as the two vessels rolled under the rumble of boots on timber.

The boy didn't understand their speech, which seemed to be French. But they yelled merrily and a man with a feathered hat and a bandolier of many pistols embraced Captain Higgs and kissed him on both cheeks for a good fellow, while his men herded the crew for'ard. Then the boy gulped as Sam Collis, biggest man aboard, took exception and started shouting . . . *and they shot him dead!* It was ruthless, merciless and hideous. Bang! Bang! Two puffs of smoke, and a decent seaman went down and was kicked aside like a piece of rubbish.

Isabelle Bligh's people groaned in horror, but they were pushed to the fo'c'sle with the pirate captain – he of the feathered hat – yelling at them in English: "Your lives are yours, messieurs! Be good and make no fight,

430

and you shall have your ship when we are done with her!"

"Aye!" cried Mr 'Meeting for Sufferings' Banbury. "It is loot they seek, not blood!" And he joined in, shoving Captain Higgs and the rest for'ard as if he were one of the pirate's own band, and agreeing with every word the villain spoke. The boy frowned heavily.

"Bleedin' traitor!" he muttered.

And then the pirates got down to the serious business of smashing open everything that was locked, and breaking into the cargo, and up-ending every bottle in the ship with the most tremendous noise, but all in good temper. Most of them vanished below for this vital work, leaving a dozen men, well armed with firelocks, to guard the crew.

And none of them took the trouble to look up into the maintop where the boy was hiding. And since nobody saw him, he watched as the smashing and cheering went on and on, and men staggered about the decks in the captain's best clothes and Mr Banbury's hat, gorging on pork and pickles and wine and brandy.

Later still, the boy shuddered in horror as a girl's shriek came from below, and men emerged through the quarterdeck hatchway, grinning and leering, with Olivia Rose and her father dragged behind them. The father was bloodied and staggering, and was kicked into a semi-conscious heap by the mizzenmast. But there was a roar from the pirates on sight of the girl, and greedy hands reached out to paw and grab and grope. Her long hair was loose, her gown was ripped, pale flesh gleamed and she screamed and screamed.

But the pirate leader – he of the feathered hat – kicked his way through the press, seized Olivia Rose by the arm, and merrily fired a pistol in the air for attention.

"*Après moi, mes enfants!*" he cried, grinning at his men. "*Je serai le premier!*" And they cheered and laughed, and fired off a thundering fusillade in salute.

Up in the maintop the boy shook with rage.

Rage doesn't just conquer fear. Rage annihilates it. Rage brings boiling fury such that no grain of self-preservation remains, nor any consideration of danger, nor threat of weapons. Hence the Viking berserker transported into blood-spattering frenzy . . . and the ship's boy that leapt bare-chested into open air from the maintop to slide down one of the backstays and launch himself – twenty feet from the deck – as a human projectile, landing feet first on the feathered head of the pirate captain – who went down with his neck snapped on a jutting boot, and his face burst open like rotten fruit as the impetus of the boy's fall drove him smashing into the pine of the quarterdeck planking.

Then . . . uproar and confusion. The pirates bellowed and roared, surprised for an instant, shocked and disbelieving, then snapping pistols at the boy, forgetting they were empty. Taking their example, he snatched the pistols from the dead pirate's bandolier – there were seven of them, ready loaded – and let fly, left and right. Men shrieked and fell as the bullets struck, and the rest hung back while the pistols lasted, then charged, and the boy was blocking slashing blades with the heavy barrel of a hot, smoking pistol, which soon got lost. Bodies heaved and bundled and swayed, and more men piled in, and the fight rolled and staggered, with the boy in the middle, armed only with his own two fists and his unhinged, manic fury. And then he got hold of a cutlass, which he couldn't swing in the dense press, so he used it two-handed as a spear, shoving it into an open mouth and out the back of a head, then wrenching it free and punching out another man's teeth with the iron hand-guard, and on and on . . .

But with nearly twenty pirates on the quarterdeck and more coming up from below, there could be only one end to the fight . . . except that the pirates were remarkably clumsy and got in each other's way, and they'd fired off their pistols and muskets . . . and on the fo'c'sle, seeing their guards with backs turned, gaping at the fight on the quarterdeck, Captain Higgs had his own moment of rage.

"Sod *you*, you bugger!" he said to the hand-wringing Banbury. "Come on, lads!" he cried, pulling a belaying pin from the pinrail, swinging it down with a *crunch* on to the blue-kerchiefed head of a mulatto pirate and snatching up the carbine that he dropped. The guards hadn't fired off their arms, so Higgs blasted lead and flame at three-feet range into the chest of another pirate even as he turned back to face the sudden danger.

After that, it was hellfire and damnation aboard the good ship *Isabelle Bligh* and Quakerism went over the side with the dead. For *Isabelle Bligh*'s crew were seething that they'd not manned their guns in the first place, and were out for vengeance for their murdered shipmate. So even though they were outnumbered more than two-to-one, they recaptured their ship, fighting at first with belaying pins and sailor's knives, and then taking up the weapons of their foes ... and with the considerable advantage that many of the pirates were blind staggering drunk.

When Captain Higgs finally called an end to the slaughter, less than a quarter of those who'd come aboard as bold dogs and roaring boys were left alive to be clapped like slaves under hatches, and the pirate ship was sailing under a prize crew, behind the triumphant *Isabelle Bligh*, such that even Samuel Banbury's conscience was eased by the money he'd make in selling her.

As for the boy who'd saved the day: he was ship's hero! Without his plunge from the maintop there would have been no fight, and no triumph. So there were glorious weeks of a merry voyage when even Olivia Rose's father did not try to keep her and the boy apart, and the two fell as deeply in love as ever it is possible for a pair of sixteen-year-olds to do: he loving her for her beauty and sweet kindness, and she loving him for those things that she saw that others did not, especially his limitless capacity to love. She saw that he would never be happy without a cause to follow and a loved one to serve. In her eyes this transformed Caliban the ugly into Ariel the shining one.

It was a wonderful, golden, glorious romance that approached ... reached ... and *transcended* Heaven on Earth, for the two young lovers.

"You are my *beau chevalier sans peur et sans reproche*," she said to him once.

"What's that?" he said.

"It means ... my fair knight, fearless and pure."

He blushed.

And so they sat together, and talked together, she telling him stories and playing that ancient game with seashells – at which she was adept – whereby swift movement of the shells deceives the onlooker who cannot tell which hides the pea. He loved the game, and the curious West Indian shells she played it with, and of which she had a collection. And he loved the country love songs that she sang to him of an evening, with the crew sitting quietly and joining in the chorus.

But voyages end. This one ended in London, and there the two were parted by duty: hers to her father, and his to his trade. There were bitter tears and mighty promises of faithfulness when finally, in the Thames below London Bridge, she was about to go into the boat that would take her and her father ashore to their new life. In that tragic moment, he gave her the traditional seaman's love-token of a staybusk that he'd carved from whalebone with his own hand. In return, she gave him a lock of her hair, and half a dozen of the West Indian shells that he loved.

"I'll be back for you, Livvy Rose," he said, "when I've made me pile!"

"Be a good boy," she said. "And remember me."

And indeed he did. He remembered her to the dying second of his dying day, and he really did try to come back to claim her. But he never quite made *his pile*, and day by day other duties intervened, until finally it was too late, because – in the meanwhile – he had become something very other than a *good boy*.

For he was led astray. He was led bad astray was Billy Bones.

ALSO AVAILABLE

The first in the rip-roaring adventure series of
Treasure Island prequels

Flint and Silver

When all your friends are dead, there's no choice but to join the enemy . . .

After pirates storm a merchant's ship, they find one opponent who won't go down – John Silver. With six men already dead at his hand, they make Silver an offer: join them or die.

On the other side of the world, the legendary Captain Flint is the most dangerous bandit on the high seas. He fears no man – until he meets fellow freebooter 'Gentleman' John Silver. Together, they forge a formidable partnership, chasing after rum, women and gold . . . hundreds and thousands of pieces of it.

But the arrival of Selena, a beautiful runaway slave, triggers a violent jealousy that turns the best of friends into sworn enemies. And as Flint schemes to secure the vast loot for himself, the legend of Treasure Island begins . . .

ISBN: 978-0-00-726894-8

What's next?

Tell us the name of an author you love

John Drake   Go ▶

and we'll find your next great book.